Romantic Suspense

Danger. Passion. Drama.

Witness Protection Ambush
Jenna Night

A Lethal Truth
Alexis Morgan

MILLS & BOON

WITNESS PROTECTION AMBUSH
© 2024 by Virginia Niten
Philippine Copyright 2024
Australian Copyright 2024
New Zealand Copyright 2024

First Published 2024
First Australian Paperback Edition 2024
ISBN 978 1 038 93531 1

A LETHAL TRUTH
© 2024 by Patricia L Pritchard
Philippine Copyright 2024
Australian Copyright 2024
New Zealand Copyright 2024

First Published 2024
First Australian Paperback Edition 2024
ISBN 978 1 038 93531 1

MIX
Paper | Supporting
responsible forestry
FSC® C001695
www.fsc.org

Published by
Harlequin Mills & Boon
An imprint of Harlequin Enterprises (Australia) Pty Limited
(ABN 47 001 180 918), a subsidiary of HarperCollins
Publishers Australia Pty Limited
(ABN 36 009 913 517)
Level 19, 201 Elizabeth Street
SYDNEY NSW 2000 AUSTRALIA

Cover art used by arrangement with Harlequin Books S.A.. All rights reserved.

Printed and bound in Australia by McPherson's Printing Group

Witness Protection Ambush
Jenna Night

MILLS & BOON

Jenna Night comes from a family of Southern-born natural storytellers. Her parents were avid readers and the house was always filled with books. No wonder she grew up wanting to tell her own stories. She's lived on both coasts but currently resides in the Inland Northwest, where she's astonished by the occasional glimpse of a moose, a herd of elk or a soaring eagle.

Books by Jenna Night

Big Sky First Responders

Deadly Ranch Hideout
Witness Protection Ambush

Range River Bounty Hunters

Abduction in the Dark
Fugitive Ambush
Mistaken Twin Target
Fugitive in Hiding

Rock Solid Bounty Hunters

Fugitive Chase
Hostage Pursuit
Cold Case Manhunt

Visit the Author Profile page at millsandboon.com.au for more titles.

Therefore if any man be in Christ,
he is a new creature: old things are passed away;
behold, all things are become new.
—*2 Corinthians* 5:17

For my mom, Esther. Always an encourager.

Chapter One

"Single vehicle crash. Sedan struck a tree. I'll check with the occupants and see if there are any injuries."

Part-time EMT Emma Hayes was actually off duty as an emergency responder for the small mountain town of Cedar Lodge, Montana. She was on the way to her second job as a librarian when she came across the accident scene along a narrow road skirting the edge of Bear Lake. But she always kept her emergency radio with her in case she came across situations like this when someone needed her help. She gave the dispatcher the specifics on her location.

"Copy EMT-26" came the staticky reply over the radio. The town was in a narrow valley surrounded by jagged mountain peaks and radio reception wasn't always the best. "Standing by for your update."

There was more radio traffic after that, but Emma tuned it out for the moment as she pulled up closer and parked. Lakeside Drive was curvy as it edged along the waterfront on one side and a grassy, forested hill on the other. Emma had caught a glimpse of the dark green four-door a few moments earlier, but she'd had the impression that it was parked alongside the shoreline. At the very least, it hadn't had the front bumper pushed up against a big pine tree like it did now.

She grabbed the basic first aid bag that she kept in the car—she didn't carry the advanced equipment the paramedics had, but it was definitely better than nothing—and got out. She approached the car and yelled, "Hello! You okay in the car? Anybody hurt?"

The car made some ticking, settling noises as a result of the crash.

Lord, please let the person or persons in this car be okay. And if they need my help, please guide my actions.

The driver's-side door was open, likely knocked that way in the collision. Emma approached it, concerned when she didn't see the driver's head, and she prepared herself to see them slumped over the steering wheel, possibly unconscious. But when she looked into the vehicle, she didn't see a driver. She didn't see anybody.

The accident had happened just moments ago. She put a hand to the dented hood. It was still warm.

The crunch of a footstep on gravel pulled Emma's attention toward two men walking in her direction. Like her, they were on the lake side of the road and they'd apparently been hidden from view by the trees. The occupants of the crashed car, she assumed. They must have gone searching for help. This stretch of road didn't get much traffic in the late morning.

It seemed strange, though, that they'd gone in the direction they had. Because the main section of town—where they could have found people and businesses—was in the opposite direction.

But they had just been in a crash. Could be that they'd bumped their heads and they were addled.

With her determination to help undiminished, Emma sped up to close the gap between them. "Hey, what happened?" she called out. "Are you guys okay?"

"We're fine," one of them—a bald man with a beard—called out. "Must have been a problem with the brakes."

His companion, a tall and slender guy with a ponytail, said nothing.

Both of them fixed their gaze on her in a way that caused her to slow her pace without consciously deciding to. And then she realized her mind had registered something. In the dappled light shining down through the branches of the trees alongside the road she saw sunlight glint off of an object. It was metallic and located just below Bald Man's right hand. The same kind of glimmer showed itself beneath Ponytail Man's right hand, too.

Guns.

Emma stopped. Her breath caught in her chest and her body tensed.

Eight years after her family was whisked out of Los Angeles and dropped into northern Montana, she'd believed they were safe. She'd imagined the threat was over.

Maybe this was unconnected to all of that. Maybe it was just some random robbery.

No, she knew better than that.

She thought of the car crashed into the tree. No occupants. *A staged accident.* Their witness protection handlers had told them stories of people who'd been captured and tricked by pursuers in the past. But those witnesses hadn't been securely hidden with solid cover stories and new identities. They'd all been people trying to evade the bad guys on their own. The point of the stories was to convince Emma's family to go into the protection plan.

"Emma Burke," Bald Man called out her old name. Well, same first name, old last name. Either way he confirmed what she'd just thought. He knew her true identity.

So what had happened? How had they found her? And what about the rest of her family? Fear twisted her heart. Had they already captured her parents and her younger brother?

Her thoughts froze as Ponytail Man raised his gun and pointed it at her. "You're going to have to come with us."

Her heart thudded so hard that for a moment it was all she could hear. Her body began to shake. She was on the sharp edge of panic with no idea of what to do. Emergency responders should be on their way, but waiting and hoping they'd get here in time was not a great plan.

A loud growling sound caught her attention. Someone riding a personal watercraft on the lake jammed by with the throttle fully opened.

Emma realized the gunmen were also distracted by the loud noise.

Run! Now!

She let the bulky first aid kit drop to the ground and darted across the road and up into the forested grassy hill. Her emergency radio slipped through her fingers. The crack of a gunshot kept her from stopping to retrieve it.

She still didn't have a coherent plan, just a panicked impulse to survive and get to her family to warn them—if they hadn't already been discovered and snatched up by Royce Walker's criminal gang members.

She raced up the grass-and-tree-covered hill, immediately feeling short of breath, as if her lungs were locking up. Some of it was triggered by panic and exertion, but there was no mistaking the tight, wheezing sensation of an asthma attack. And of course her inhaler was in her purse back in the car.

She forced herself to continue on. Trying not to leave a trail was hardly an option when it took all of her focus to keep moving and breathe. Finally, she slid behind a group of towering pines with thick trunks and a deep bed of dropped, dried needles at the base. Maybe she could bury herself underneath it. But first, she had to catch her breath.

Listening carefully, she dared hope that the pursuers were straight out of Los Angeles where the gang was centered and that they were helpless and unable to track anybody in the woods.

The sound of male voices along with footfalls in the wild grass and atop fallen pine cones confirmed that her hope was misplaced.

Where was everybody? Where was the cop who should have been on scene by now? Why were they taking so long? Even though she hadn't given the dispatcher an update, some kind of official response should have been activated.

With the next labored breath she realized that it hadn't been so long since she'd called in the crash. Just a few minutes. Of course all the emergency responders knew minutes could be critical, but you could only do so much. There were immutable laws of physics. There were other vehicles on the road and sometimes trains at railroad crossings. Even when you were responding to a call and desperately wished those things were not in your way, they were.

The tightness in her lungs eased a little. She didn't want to go farther up the hill because of the added exertion triggering her asthma, but heading that way made the most sense. It might not feel like it right now, but this was a relatively small hill. On the other side it dropped down into the edge of town where there were small farms and then farther on some streets with houses and shops. There had to be somebody in the vicinity who would help her. And maybe if she got to a populated area, that would be enough of a deterrent to make the gunmen back off.

Her body tensed with fear as the sounds of the pursuers grew louder. She pushed herself to her feet and continued up the hill.

She was gasping loudly now. She couldn't help it. Each step felt like her foot was chained to a block of cement. Sweat ran down to her brow and into her eyes. She told herself that she could rest when she was safe. Right now she had to keep moving.

She avoided the open areas on the hillside and kept to the shadows beneath the trees until she finally reached the top. She didn't hear anyone following her and she *had* to rest for a moment. Pressing her hand against a tree trunk to help her keep her balance, she took a moment to just breathe.

Bang!

A bullet tore through the tree trunk beside her hand.

Fresh waves of icy terror sent her diving to the ground and frantically trying to roll out of the way of gunfire. She tucked her body into a ball, desperately shrinking her profile so she wouldn't get hit as one of the thugs fired another shot.

After a few moments of quiet, she got back to her feet and continued down the hill on the other side to put some distance between herself and the attackers. But it was clear that continuing along in the same direction was no longer a good option.

New plan. Forging a different path, she'd head back the way she'd come. If she moved quietly enough, maybe the gunmen wouldn't realize she was doubling back to the road.

She'd just have to breathe the best she could while moving quickly enough to get to her car. Then she could drive away before the creeps noticed. She'd go directly to her parents' house to make sure they and her brother Austin were okay. Even better, she could grab her phone from the purse she'd left in the car and maybe even retrieve her emergency radio if she came across it and alert everyone in the county about the dangerous situation that was happening.

Doing her best to ignore the fear that nearly overwhelmed her and focus on a good outcome instead, Emma pushed herself to hike back downhill and toward the road.

Halfway there it was painfully obvious that her body was not receiving the benefits of optimal amounts of oxygen. Her head was pounding and her gait was stumbling and clumsy. But she kept going, telling herself that she was almost to the street and soon she would be safe.

She pushed through the edge of the forest where it met the

road, grateful to see that she was very close to her car. It was only a few steps away. But she *had* to take a moment and at least partially catch her breath before she fell over. She was lightheaded and her vision was getting blurry. Her fight to save herself would all be for nothing if she passed out here.

She didn't hear the bad guys behind her, so she figured she could just take a couple of good breaths and then move on. Well, as good as they would be in the middle of an asthma attack.

Exhausted nearly to the point of collapse, she bent forward and braced her hands on her knees as she took first one breath and then another. Then it was time to get moving again.

But before she could straighten, she felt the tip of a gun barrel press against the back of her neck followed by the voice of Bald Man. "It was a mistake to stop. You should have kept running."

Paramedic Cole Webb knew something was *off* as soon as he arrived on-scene.

It had been years since he'd served in a combat zone as a Navy corpsman routinely heading out on patrol with a squad of Marines, but the old instincts and habitual vigilance had never completely left him. Not even back home in Cedar Lodge.

He brought his pickup truck to a stop on the side of the road and began cataloging what was in front of him while considering what could have triggered his unease. Emma Hayes's SUV was parked by the side of the road but there was no Emma in sight. That was concerning. Initially he'd thought she might be working with patients on the ground and she was hidden from view by her car, but now that he could take a closer look, it was obvious that wasn't the case. In fact, he didn't see anybody at all.

"Dispatch, this is Webb. I'm on-scene at the single car crash. No sign of EMT-26 or the driver of the other vehicle. I'm going to look around."

"Copy," the dispatcher replied. "I've been waiting to hear back from EMT-26. Update as soon as possible."

Cole had just completed a fifteen-hour shift as a paramedic with the Cedar Lodge Fire Department. He'd been scheduled to work twelve hours, but a multi-vehicle crash with major injuries on the highway west of town this morning meant he was working for as long as emergency services needed him.

He'd heard Emma's initial transmission regarding the single vehicle accident. With resources already stretched thin and no report of the immediate need for emergency medical response or police assistance, her call dropped to a lower priority. Not an ideal situation, but an emergency system could only do what they could do.

When his shift finally concluded, he'd let dispatch know he would check on Emma. This was his usual route around the eastern edge of the lake and over to the ranch where he lived with his grandfather, his cousin and her husband. Emma, he knew, would have been on her way to the tiny Meadowlark branch of the public library where she worked a half day on Mondays.

"Emma, I'm here at the accident scene," he said into the handheld emergency radio all the first responders carried even when off shift. Cedar Lodge was a beautiful town, but it was also fairly remote. People needed to look out for each other as much as possible.

He'd already reached Emma's car and as he glanced inside he heard a sound to his left, seeming to come from the side of the road. It sounded like a radio transmission. He looked over and spotted an emergency radio on the ground. The transmission he'd heard was his own voice. That had to be Emma's radio.

His initial concern shifted to a chill racing up his spine. Something was *very* wrong. He quickly turned his attention back to the inside of Emma's car, searching for signs of foul play. There was no visible blood, but her purse and phone were on the front seat. His pulse quickened as his heart kicked into overdrive. Emma would not have intentionally, willfully, left all these items behind.

He checked the other vehicle. Looked like minor damage at first, but enough of a dent on the front left fender to make the car not drivable. No skid marks on the road, which indicated the driver hadn't hit the brakes in an attempt to regain control of the car. Was this an intentional collision?

If there was some kind of criminal activity going on, why hadn't the driver of the crashed car taken Emma's vehicle to leave the scene? Was the driver aware that Emma worked for emergency services and that most of the cops in town would recognize her SUV? Anyone who took it would be quickly apprehended.

Cole keyed his radio and requested that dispatch roll a law enforcement unit to the crash site.

A familiar voice popped onto the radio almost immediately. "Dispatch, show Volker en route to Webb's location." It was Officer Kris Volker, a friend of Cole's since their school days and an excellent cop.

Cole took a breath and focused his thoughts. He glanced at the dirt and grass beside the crashed car and also beside Emma's SUV, looking for an extra set of tire tracks. If assailants had grabbed Emma for some reason and left their own car as well as Emma's SUV behind, wouldn't that imply that they had accomplices with another vehicle for the getaway?

But why would somebody grab Emma?

They'd worked a few shifts per month together for two years. She'd started as a volunteer with the fire department when she was twenty. At the time Cole had thought of her as a kid. Not only was she eight years younger than Cole, but she'd lived a quiet, predictable life in Cedar Lodge while Cole had been in combat and had spent time in places around the world far different from northern Montana.

But then he couldn't say he knew her life story. Of course

they talked when they worked together, but they kept things professional. He knew she hoped to be a full-time librarian someday, but she could only get a part-time gig doing that for now. She'd told him she had to wait for someone with more seniority than her to quit or retire before she could get a full-time librarian job. Not exactly the kind of job that Cole could personally imagine sacrificing a lot of time waiting for an opportunity, but he had to admire Emma's determination.

A shadowy thought flickered across his mind. Maybe Emma had some other interest he knew nothing about and that interest had drawn her into a dangerous situation. Plenty of people had some aspect of their life they liked to keep hidden. Cole had seen evidence of that many times. Why should he be surprised if Emma turned out to be no different?

Cole's own father was not the man he'd pretended to be. He looked clean cut and fooled lots of people while he was actually a criminal lacking ethics or a conscience. His father's deception, revealed after his parents were married, might not have literally killed Cole's mom, but he was certain the stress of it had contributed to her poor health. She died when Cole was still in high school.

Enough.

Emma's personal life was not his business. Didn't matter if she was living some kind of secret life. Right now he needed to figure out what kind of trouble she was in and help her out of it.

Growing up on a ranch on the edge of the forest with his grandpa, Cole had obtained wilderness and survival skills long before he went into the military. Tracking was something he could do. If Emma was not taken from the scene by a vehicle, but by attackers who were on foot for some reason, then he had a pretty good chance of finding her.

Cole spotted trampled wild grass on the opposite side of the road a few yards away and took off in that direction. He had no idea what kind of situation he would be walking into and he had no weapon other than the short blade on the multi-use tool he carried on his belt. But he would find a way to improvise if he had to, because he couldn't just stand there and wait for Kris Volker to arrive in his squad car. He needed to see what kind of danger Emma was in right now.

Moving as quickly and quietly as possible while staying alert to his surroundings, Cole walked through the grass and up the hill into the forest. At least the path was unmistakable, with the grass just recently bruised. He guessed that he was following Emma plus one other person, possibly two. They were obviously heading up the hill and back toward town.

As an emergency responder he knew the streets and alleys and dirt roads of town and much of the countryside very well. He knew there was a small farm at the bottom of the hill on the other side. When he crested the hill he saw Emma walking with a man on each side of her. One guy with a long ponytail held her arm and kept yanking her forward as she stumbled. The other guy, a bald man, was yelling into a phone, but it wasn't clear what he was saying. Each man was carrying a gun in his free hand. They seemed to be headed for a dilapidated storage shed at the edge of the woods.

Cole didn't want to think about why they were headed there. To kill Emma and conceal her body? To hide themselves for a while because they knew someone was obviously going to be checking out the crashed car and Emma's SUV beside the road? The possibilities popping into his head were terrible, and he could not let any of them happen. Armed suspects with a hostage in a building was not a situation anyone wanted to deal with.

The small farm at the base of the hill looked quiet. If Cole could get someone to come outside, maybe that would redirect the thugs away from any of the outbuildings and back into the forest. Then Cole would have a better chance of keeping Emma from harm.

Skirting the edge of the woods and grateful the bad guys weren't bothering to look behind them, Cole picked up a rock and threw it at a farmhouse window. Glass shattered. Dogs inside the house started barking. As Cole had hoped, the attackers immediately changed direction and dragged Emma back into the cover of the woods.

Cole's phone buzzed. It was his cop friend, Kris Volker. "I'm on-scene, where are you?"

Cole gave a quick description of where he was, the direction he was going and what he'd seen.

"On my way," Volker said before disconnecting.

Cole couldn't let up in his chase. Volker was fast in an emergency, but in this instance he might not be fast enough. Fortunately, the assailants still weren't bothering to look behind them. They appeared to be on a panicked run to get deeper into the forest. Cole would use that to his advantage. He followed them into the shadowy woods and moved up closer on them.

Emma kept stumbling and the thugs were getting impatient. The one who had hold of her jerked hard on her arm and Cole was afraid the man would lose his cool and shoot her. When Emma finally tripped and fell, Cole grabbed the opportunity to jump on the back of the man with the ponytail who'd been hanging on to her. Yanking on the startled gunman's arm, he wrested the weapon away from him.

On the forest floor where she'd fallen, Emma turned to Cole, an expression of shock on her face.

Ponytail man scrambled into position to take a swing at Cole, but then the criminal saw Cole pointing his own gun at him and he froze.

The bald guy had already vanished into the forest. Cole hated to see the thug get away, but Cole wasn't a cop. He was a medic. And there was no missing the fact that Emma was having trouble breathing. He could hear her wheezing. She hadn't even said anything yet. Probably because she couldn't catch her breath. Cole knew she had asthma and he was concerned for her.

Ponytail guy, now without his gun, put his hands up. Then

he slowly backed away. "See you later, Emma Burke," he said before disappearing into the dark forest.

"Cole." Emma sounded breathless when she said his name.

Mindful to keep an eye on their surroundings in case the criminals snuck back, Cole radioed Volker with the specifics on where they were and the current situation.

"Almost there," Volker replied.

Having done all he could, Cole squatted down beside Emma. "Take a minute to rest and try to catch your breath." Without even thinking about it he was already counting her respirations, which were too fast. He reached for her wrist to take her pulse and she burst into tears, moving her hand so that she was gripping him so tightly his hand went numb.

"I thought they were going to kill me," she said, gasping and crying as she tried to speak.

Against his better judgment, violating his own rule to keep things completely professional with all of his coworkers, Cole moved closer and wrapped his arms around her until she was clinging to him, her tears soaking his shirt. He could feel her heart racing as she was pressed against him. The paramedic side of him couldn't help confirming that it was beating way too fast. But the compassionate human side of him felt the stirrings of a protective tenderness that wasn't exactly part of his job description. Though normally a decisive man, for a second he wasn't certain what to do about that.

Finally, she released her grip on him and drew back. She was breathing a little easier but still wheezing. Tear tracks ran through the dust on her face.

"What happened?" Cole asked. "Who were those men? Where were they taking you? And why?"

She closed her eyes for a long moment, apparently steadying herself. And when she opened them again, she focused her gaze on his shoulder instead of his face before saying, "I don't know who they were or what they wanted."

She was lying. And he wanted to know why. In fact, there

was a lot about Emma Hayes he wanted to know right now. He couldn't help being curious about the woman he'd thought he knew after working with her for two years. Whatever the situation was that she'd gotten herself into, he felt responsible for her safety. Maybe she'd made some bad decision somewhere along the line. Lots of people did. His own mother had made a bad decision in choosing his father. That hadn't made her a bad person.

Officer Kris Volker pushed his way through the pine trees and stepped up with his gun drawn and his gaze shifting as he surveyed the scene.

"I'm a little concerned they'll try to jump us as we make our way out of here," Cole said.

"I've got four more cops just a little bit behind me," Volker said.

Of course. Cops and medics oftentimes used cell phones because anyone could listen in on a radio transmission. Just because Cole hadn't heard Volker call for backup didn't mean he hadn't done it.

When the other officers arrived to make sure everybody got out of the forest without any further trouble, Cole helped Emma to her feet. "I'm assuming your asthma inhaler is in your purse back in your car rather than in your pocket."

She nodded.

"Are there any officers still at the crash scene who could bring Emma's asthma inhaler?" Cole asked.

Volker shook his head. "I brought them all with me. I thought the perps might still be lurking nearby and we could catch them and bring them in." He glanced around. "Doesn't look like it."

Breaking another one of his rules regarding coworker professionalism, because apparently this was the day for it, Cole swept Emma up in his arms intending to carry her back to her car. It would be faster than having an officer go fetch her inhaler.

"Are you all right with my doing this?" he asked. "I don't think a hike would be good for you right now."

Wide-eyed, Emma nodded, her cheeks red with exertion or embarrassment, Cole wasn't sure which. "Yes, I'm okay with it. Thank you."

Relieved that she was alive and safe for now, Cole started walking back toward the road with Volker and the other cops accompanying them.

Emma *Burke*, the thug had called her.

It was Emma's choice how she lived her life, and maybe there were some details she kept hidden. Didn't matter what Cole thought about that. His immediate concern was for the safety of a coworker who was capable, diligent and kind. He worked as a first responder because he cared about the safety of the people in his town. He had some added skills thanks to his military service that could keep Emma safe until the cops got the bad guys. Cole would stay by her side as much as possible until this dangerous situation was stabilized.

Whatever her real name, whatever her true story, Cole had no doubt Emma was in serious danger. Whoever wanted her kidnapped no doubt *still* wanted her kidnapped. They would try again.

Chapter Two

"Thanks," Emma said to Cole as he set her on her feet on the edge of the road after they exited the forest. She nodded her appreciation to a cop who'd already gotten her purse out of her car and brought it to her. She took a dose of the medicine that quickly eased her breathing.

She took a couple of deep breaths, wincing slightly at the sharp pain at her collarbone where she must have injured it when she fell. Then she turned to Cole with an awkward smile. "Now that I'm feeling better, let me properly thank you for checking on me and for dealing with those thugs."

His appearance from out of nowhere and attack on the man who'd been clutching and controlling Emma had been especially impressive. She'd known Cole was a military veteran with combat experience, but still, seeing a calm man she'd worked with on a regular basis leap into life-or-death action like that was something else.

"And thank you for carrying me while I was having trouble breathing," she added awkwardly. Suddenly she couldn't act normal around Cole.

She avoided eye contact with him because it was overwhelming having her work buddy rescue her so dramatically and then hold her so closely.

Okay, yeah, *she* was the one to grab him and hold him close for a moment or two right after he rescued her. And in the midst of that she'd felt something that she hadn't expected. Appreciation, but also something else. Something that had significantly changed her reaction to him. An unexpected attraction, actually.

"Happy to help," Cole said in that confident, easygoing manner that he always had. "Glad you're okay."

No doubt her cheeks were red with embarrassment when she finally glanced at him. He looked cool and collected as ever.

"Can you walk to your car?"

Emma nodded. "Sure. I'm perfectly fine now."

They walked side by side. Emma noted that the much taller Cole shortened his stride to match hers. Something he normally didn't do when they were working together.

The cop who'd brought her inhaler had left to rejoin the other officers. Volker had law enforcement on scene doing a quick search of the nearby streets looking for the kidnappers and conducting an interview with the residents of the farmhouse to see if they had any useful information.

A rookie officer Emma had seen on calls a couple of times stayed nearby and was checking out the crashed car as Emma and Cole approached.

"Have you gotten any information that could help identify the assailants from the vehicle registration?" Cole called out to the rookie.

The young cop shook his head. "The vehicle is on the stolen car hot sheet. Reported missing last night at the end of the owner's workday down in Baylor."

"Any chance the kidnappers' prints could be lifted?"

The cop shrugged. "Chief's sending a wrecker to tow it to the police garage so Tammy and her team can go over it."

These criminals are pros, Emma thought grimly. *Tammy won't find anything helpful.*

"What do you know about those men?" Cole turned to Emma. "Why'd they grab you? Where were they taking you?" It was the second time he'd asked her.

"I don't know."

"But the one guy knew your name."

Emma hated lying to Cole. He'd been a good work friend for years and just now he'd gone way beyond anything she could have imagined or expected in helping her. He could have gotten *killed* jumping on the gunman. But in a way, she'd been lying to him from the moment she'd first met him. She'd withheld the full truth of who she was because, for the sake of her family's safety, she had to.

Drawing on the determination and focus she'd had to use so many times after her life had taken the strange turns that had brought her and her family to Cedar Lodge, she lifted her chin to look directly into the blue eyes of the medic. "That guy had me confused with someone else. Didn't you notice that he used the wrong last name?"

The expression in Cole's eyes sharpened. Not like he was angry, but as if he didn't believe what she'd told him and he wasn't going to just let this go.

At the moment Emma was less concerned with his drive for the truth and more concerned about her mom and dad and Austin. She took a deep breath, felt that sharp pain at her collarbone again and reached up to it. Touching it only made it hurt worse and she sucked in her breath.

"Get in my truck and I'll take you to get that x-rayed," Cole said.

"Later. Right now I'm tired and I need time to rest."

He didn't look happy, but he gave her a curt nod of acknowledgment.

She turned away from him and sat down in the driver's seat of her car where she could grab her phone. She tapped the listing for her mom's number and the call rolled to voicemail. She took a deep breath and tried not to panic over the unanswered phone call. Maybe Mom had just gone to the store for something. Her mother didn't like to talk on the phone when she was driving, not even with a hands-free device.

Even as Emma told herself that semi-comforting story, she was pretty sure it wasn't true. Dread and fear settled heavy in her gut as she tried her dad's number and got his voicemail, too. And then she tried her younger brother, Austin. He didn't answer, either.

All the while, Cole lingered by her open car door.

"Did you actually see those men crash into the tree?" he asked her. "Did you see what caused them to swerve?"

"I didn't see the crash." Emma wasn't paying much attention to him. What if the bad guys had gotten to her parents and Austin? Fear for her family clawed its way up into her throat, feeling as if it might choke her. *Please, Lord, protect them.* She coughed and cleared her throat and began trying to call the numbers again, wishing for at least the thousandth time in her life that she had a *normal* family. If they didn't have this huge secret that must be kept she could call 9-1-1 and request that a cop make the drive to their house and conduct a welfare check. But doing that would lead to too many questions. And obviously, if they were a *normal* family, they wouldn't be in this situation.

While tapping her phone and then listening to her mother's voicemail response, Emma was vaguely aware of Officer Volker's voice coming through on Cole's radio. She was fairly sure one of the responders on scene would have found her own dropped radio by now and would get it back to her. Right now that was the least of her worries.

"I'm on my way back," Volker said through the radio. "Let Emma know I want to talk to her."

I'll talk to you for as long as you want after I know my family's safe.

Emma's hands shook with fear and adrenaline spiked in her system again as she imagined her parents and brother not answering her calls because the worst had happened.

Volker stepped out from the forest a few yards down the road and Cole walked in his direction.

Growing frantic with fear, Emma pulled her car door shut and turned on the engine. The cops didn't need her to stay on-scene. There was nothing here for her to do. Perhaps her mom and dad and Austin weren't answering their phones for some totally innocuous reason. Maybe they were all outside doing yardwork or washing their cars, completely unaware of the danger.

Maybe they weren't answering because they were gravely injured. But if she got to them in time they could be saved. For a split second she thought of asking Cole to come with her, but he was a by-the-book kind of guy and she didn't have time to argue. If she got to the house and her family needed help, Cole would be the first person she would call.

Already, he and Volker were looking in her direction, a questioning expression on both of their faces.

Emma lifted her fingertips to give a slight wave of acknowledgment before turning the steering wheel and hitting the gas so that she was headed back toward town and her parents' house.

She didn't have far to go. After skirting the edge of the lake for a couple of miles she hit town and made the turn into a hilly residential neighborhood with moderate-sized homes on acre-sized lots. She braked at a stop sign and noticed a cop car in the distance behind her. Possibly Officer Volker and Cole alongside him. The whole secret life her family lived was about to get blown apart. There was no getting around it now. Even a town cop and a paramedic knowing their true identities would compromise everything.

She threw aside that worry. The fact that the thugs had been able to find her proved that her family wasn't secure anymore, anyway. She should have already thought of that.

She pulled up the curving driveway to her parents' house, slammed the car into Park and leaped out.

The front door was partially open and there was a footprint on it, like maybe someone had kicked it open.

Emma knew she should be careful, but she couldn't make herself slow down as she pushed the door the rest of the way open and stepped across the threshold.

"Mom!"

No one answered.

A few steps farther and a turn to the right took her to the kitchen. The coffeepot was half full and still warm to the touch. There were a couple of dishes and some utensils in the sink ready for someone to rinse them and put them in the dishwasher. Her mom was a bit of a neat freak, and it wasn't like her to leave things that way if she was going out somewhere.

"Dad!" Again, no response.

Sick with fear, Emma opened the door to the garage. Both of her parents' cars were in there.

"Austin!" Now that her brother was eighteen and out of high school, he'd started to build somewhat of an independent life for himself. Officially, he lived at the house with his parents. In reality, he stayed with a couple of buddies from school who'd gotten an apartment together. Austin might not have even been in the house today.

Walking into the living room, Emma looked through the window at her dad's prized garden in the backyard. It was a beautiful combination of ordered flowers and rustic wilderness, with the back of the property opening up to forest. She strode toward the slider window. When it was nice out, her parents loved to sit on the patio and sip coffee and talk or get some work done on their laptops. Both of her parents worked from home.

Her heart sank when she saw the empty chairs at the table beneath a cheerful, floral umbrella.

Something moved at the edge of the yard.

The flash of motion and color wasn't a bird or an animal. It was too big. What she saw was less a clear image and more scraps of color that she put together in her mind to try and make sense of it.

Was it a man, maybe? In a red and black jersey?

Neither of the men who'd kidnapped her had been dressed that way.

She threw open the slider door—noting that it was un-locked—and started to step outside and yell at whoever it was. But at the last moment, she realized that probably wasn't a good idea. The person might be armed, like the thugs who'd grabbed her had been.

She stepped back into the living room, closing the door, and grimly told herself that she had to search the rest of the house even if she was afraid of what she might find.

"Hey, Emma. What's going on?"

Emma turned at the sound of Cole's voice. Volker was be-side him, and both men looked very concerned.

"My parents—" She got only those two words out before she choked up and started to cry. "We need to search the rest of the house for them and my brother," she eventually added. It took a huge amount of effort to force out the words between rack-ing sobs. The wave of emotion she'd fought to keep in check since today's horrible ordeals had begun was now crashing over her and there was nothing she could do about it.

To their credit, neither man questioned her. Instead, they walked down the hallway toward the bedrooms and family room while Emma waited and prayed and wiped the tears from her eyes.

"Nobody back here," Cole called out a few moments later.

He reappeared in the living room with Volker who said, "Let's check the garage."

"Their cars are here," Emma told them.

Volker nodded. "We'll go have a closer look."

They weren't gone long. "Nobody out there," Volker reported when they came back.

Cole walked over and stood in front of Emma. "Tell us what's going on."

What should she say? How much information might help her family if they were in danger? And how much would make things much worse?

"We need to find my family," Emma said after a significant pause. "That's what's important."

Cole gazed at the sable-haired woman who looked defiantly at him through coffee-colored eyes. "If we're going to look for them we need an idea of where to start."

She shifted her attention to Volker. "You can put out an alert for them, right? A be-on-the-lookout or something?"

"I can. But the search would be most efficient if you gave me all the pertinent information you have. Context for whatever is happening right now would be helpful."

Emma looked around the room, crossing and uncrossing her arms, then brushing her bangs back from her eyes.

Cole had seen her work under pressure during medical emergencies she'd responded to as an EMT. He'd been impressed by how calm and collected she was in the midst of chaos and people yelling or screaming. She'd been cool when he'd needed her to assist with life-or-death emergency procedures. He realized having her own family in danger made the situation different, but her angsty gestures still seemed out of character.

Then again, driving away from a crime scene before getting cleared by the cop in charge was out of character, too, even if it wasn't illegal. She knew the routine. Cole had been with her treating injured people at crime scenes on numerous occasions. Generally everyone hung around until they'd given a report of what they'd experienced or witnessed.

A transmission came through Volker's radio reporting that the wrecker had arrived to tow away the kidnappers' car and the scene was now officially cleared.

"Copy," Volker replied at the end of the update.

By now Emma had walked to the slider window where she stood rubbing her hands up and down her arms as if she were cold. While it was warm and sunny right now, Cole could see rainclouds closing in on the jagged mountain peaks in the distance.

"Someone was in the backyard when I first got here," Emma said as she turned around.

"Who?" Cole asked. He wasn't the official investigator here—clearly Kris Volker was—but Cole couldn't help butting in. As a military medic in a combat zone, he'd gotten dragged into situations that involved kidnapping and stalking and ambushes and all sorts of other crimes. He'd learned things beyond medical treatments that he could use here. In this case with Emma, he was determined to get more information.

He admittedly felt protective toward her, too. She was a smart, competent woman, but she was no street brawler. And since those thugs were willing to attack her once, it seemed a reasonable possibility that they'd do it again. Cole wasn't about to step out of the way and make it easier for them.

"I don't know who I saw at the edge of the garden," she said, glancing at Cole to answer his question and then averting her gaze.

What was she hiding? "Okay, who would you *guess* it was?" he asked.

She shook her head. "I don't have a specific idea. But I'd say it was an adult man. He moved fast so I'd say he must have been youngish. And he was wearing a red and black jersey." She shrugged. "That's all I can tell you."

Volker had been listening and he walked over to open the

slider door and stepped outside. Cole went with him, while Emma stood at the doorway but remained inside the house. A wise choice, since someone could be out there waiting to take a shot at her. They took a quick look around, but didn't see anything significant. Nobody hiding. No sign anyone had spent a significant time hunkered down out there watching the house.

Emma had tears in her eyes when they walked back inside. "My family and I have been in a witness protection program for eight years," she said so quietly Cole barely heard her. It seemed like a struggle for her to say the words. "We were living under false identities. We kept the same first names but were given a new last name." She fixed her gaze on Cole. "That kidnapper in the woods who said he'd see me again before he ran away, he knew my real last name."

Witness protection? Living under a false identity? Cole felt like he'd had the wind knocked out of him. What else did he think he knew about her that wasn't true? And what else might she be keeping hidden?

"Apparently the people we've been hiding from have finally found us," she added, her voice breaking.

"Do you have a case handler you can contact?" Volker asked.

Emma startled. "Yes, I do. I don't know why I didn't think of calling him."

Because you were just abducted and nearly killed, Cole thought. She had to be traumatized and not thinking clearly, whether she was aware of it or not.

She stared at her phone for a minute. "I can't think of the name it's stored under," she said with a strained, nervous laugh. But after a moment she appeared to remember and tapped the screen, turning the phone on Speaker so that Cole and Volker could hear.

"Baker and Company," a female voice answered pleasantly.

Cole was surprised at first, but then realized it would hardly make sense for a secretive agency to answer a phone call by clearly identifying themselves.

"I need to talk to Cliff Martel," Emma said. "It's an emergency."

"I'll have him return your call." The woman spoke in the same, unemotional tone.

"I can't wait," Emma said, her voice growing louder. "My family could be in danger."

"I'm relaying the message right now," the woman answered. And then she disconnected.

For a moment Emma just stared at her phone, looking stunned.

"Did you have a safe place planned for your family to meet up in case your security is breached?" Volker asked.

Emma shook her head. "No. I was fifteen and my brother was ten when this started. My parents planned on us being together nearly all the time and assumed we'd be together if there was trouble. Since Austin and I are now both adults, security is focused mainly on our parents, not us." She shrugged. "Guess we're kind of on our own."

"Why would somebody come after you now?" Cole asked. "You said it's been eight years."

"I don't know." She shook her head. Then she took a deep breath and slowly blew it out, her eyes tearing up again. "Why did they want to drag me into the forest? Why didn't they kill me when they had the chance?" A tear rolled down her cheek and she wiped it away. "I thought they were going to," she added in a near-whisper.

"They might have grabbed you so they could use you as bait to draw out your parents," Cole said. Emma turned to him with a horrified expression and he winced inwardly. Volker was already nodding in agreement that it was a logical consideration.

"But it looks as if the bad guys already showed up here," Emma gestured toward the front of the house. "It looks like somebody kicked open the front door. If they'd already found my parents, why come after me?"

"By threatening to harm you, they could get your parents to do or say just about anything they wanted them to."

Even after learning the truth about Emma and her family being in witness protection, Cole still had no real idea what was going on. That was just one part of the story, and he was still trying to help Emma piece things together. "I'd guess having to chase after you in the woods wasn't in their plans," he said. "They probably somehow learned your work schedule, waited to stage the crash and knew as an EMT you would stop to help and then they could grab you. I imagine they thought you would be an easy target." Cole couldn't help smiling slightly at the reminder of what a *not*-so-easy target she had turned out to be.

She'd managed to evade the attackers until she could get help. Even with an asthma attack making things so much worse. She'd done everything she could and hadn't given up hope.

"The fender on their own car was dented too badly for them to drive away. In a small town like this, EMTs and cops obviously cross paths a lot and know each other. They probably figured if they'd taken your car for a getaway, they would have been found immediately."

Emma nodded, took a deep breath, and then tried to place calls to each of her parents and her brother again.

The sorrow on her face as each of the calls rolled to voicemail made Cole's heart ache in sympathy. Actively responding to an emergency medical call required a certain amount of emotional detachment. He could turn off his feelings while fighting to save a life, but trying to deny his emotions for very long led to some bad repercussions. He'd learned that lesson after his mom died when he was a teenager and he'd tried to avoid grieving her passing, and again after he left the Navy and initially tried to fit back into civilian life by living as if his traumatic memories could be ignored. At some point he'd accepted that dealing with his emotions and even being a little bit tenderhearted wasn't the worst thing in the world. Not that he went out of his way to let anybody know about the tenderhearted part.

"I need both of you to go to the station with me so I can get your official statements," Volker said.

"First I'll need you to give us a ride back to my truck," Cole said. Then he turned to Emma. "We should stop by the ER and get your collarbone x-rayed before we go to the police station."

"A walk-in urgent care place will be fine. It doesn't hurt that bad."

She'd need to wear a sling for a few days or weeks if her collarbone was indeed fractured. That would mean she wouldn't be able to work any of her EMT shifts for a while, but that would likely be the least of her concerns right now. Finding her family and keeping herself from getting attacked again were obviously more urgent priorities.

"After we're finished at the police station, I'll go with you to your apartment to make sure everything's okay." Cole had never been to her home, but he remembered her mentioning an apartment.

"Someone could be waiting for me there," Emma said slowly, an expression of fear appearing in her eyes. "I hadn't even thought of that."

"I'm sure everything there will be fine," Cole quickly added, which was a polite lie. He wouldn't actually be sure until he saw for himself that no one was lurking inside her apartment or nearby.

Emma glanced around the living room. "Hopefully I'll hear back from my parents and my brother or the witness protection handler soon. If not, I think instead of going to my apartment I'd rather come back here. Maybe their situation isn't as dire as I think. Maybe they'll come back home."

Wishful thinking. He hated to take that away from her, but he felt like he had to. "I think staying here would be a very bad idea."

"Agreed," Volker added. He'd been standing near a window

looking out at the street in front of the house. Now he took a step closer to the glass and pushed aside the edge of a sheer curtain. "Who's this?"

Emma took a look out the window.

A maroon sedan was coming up the driveway at a pretty good clip.

"I don't know who it is," Emma said. "I've never seen that car before."

Chapter Three

"It has the look of an unmarked police vehicle," Volker said, remaining at the window. "But let's not take any chances." He gestured at Emma to take a step back into the room, away from the glass.

Cole moved closer to her, his nerves on edge and his focus shifting from the window to the front door and back again as he prepared to move fast if he had to. Emma had already been through so much today, but sometimes the fight had to continue even when you felt like you had no strength left.

"You should get behind me," he said to her quietly, but Emma's attention was fixed on the window and then the front door and she didn't seem to hear him. The vehicle came to a halt and a man got out and walked toward the front porch.

Cole and Kris Volker had been friends since they'd played sports together as young kids. The intuition they'd developed over the years to work together came into play now as they wordlessly coordinated their movements. Kris headed for the door and Cole followed him, placing himself between Emma and potential danger.

With his hand hovering near the pistol in his holster,

Volker pulled open the front door before the visitor had a chance to knock.

Cole recognized the plainclothes law enforcement officer standing there, though he couldn't immediately recall where he knew him from. The middle-aged man had salt-and-pepper hair and was dressed in jeans, a dress shirt and a sports coat. He pulled aside the coat to display the sheriff's deputy badge clipped to his belt.

"Newman," Volker said. "What are you doing here?"

"Probably the same thing as you. Checking up on Emma Hayes. I understand she drove here from the crime scene."

Volker opened the door wider and stepped aside to let the man in, then closed the door behind him. "This is Sergeant Rob Newman. He works for the sheriff's department. He normally works out of the substation at the far western end of the county."

Cole now realized that he'd worked a shooting scene with Newman a little over a year ago. The sergeant had recently joined the department after moving up from California.

"I don't know you," Emma said, suspicion darkening her tone.

"I'm here on behalf of Cliff Martel."

Her witness security contact.

"My parents are missing. Is Martel coming to help find them?"

"Actually, he's already been here and gone. He and his team moved your parents out of here to keep them safe."

Emma raised her eyebrows. "So they're okay?"

"Yes."

Cole watched the tension immediately drop from Emma's shoulders.

"But they aren't answering when I call," she said after a moment.

"Why don't we sit down and talk?"

Cole and Volker stepped aside to let Newman farther into

the room. He walked over and stood in front of a club chair. After a moment's hesitation, Emma dropped down on the nearby sofa and then the sergeant also took a seat. Cole positioned himself on the sofa so that he was between Emma and Newman. Volker remained standing where he could keep watch out the front window. Even if they got some answers right now, that still didn't guarantee that Emma was safe.

"First of all, I heard about the kidnapping attempt. Are you all right?"

Emma shook off the question as if it were irrelevant. "Why did witness security come for my parents? Why *now*?" She took a breath and when she spoke again she sounded slightly calmer. "What happened?"

"Royce Walker was finally tracked down in northern California and he's under arrest. So of course that means the trial will be resumed."

Cole watched Emma's face blanch and her jaw went slack. "Who is Royce Walker?" Cole asked.

"He's a high-powered criminal gang leader in Los Angeles," Newman said when Emma seemed unable to speak for a moment. "Some of his gang members helped him escape custody just before his murder trial was slated to begin a year after his arrest. He's been on the run ever since. Well, until roughly twenty-four hours ago when he finally got caught."

"My dad saw the murder happen," Emma said as she turned to Cole. "He wanted to testify because he thought it was the right thing to do. I was fifteen at the time, and I remember the cops watching our house round-the-clock. We figured once Dad testified, any threat to him would be over. Then Walker escaped and the authorities reasoned my dad was even more vulnerable as a potential witness. They said there was an even greater chance that Walker's gang would come after him. Or that Walker himself might try to kill my dad to prevent his testimony. That's when we went into witness protection."

Cole was stunned. All this time he'd known Emma and

he had no idea about any of this. He turned to Newman. "So why are you here?"

"I'm on the local task force that works with federal witness security when they're in this region. I got the call to watch this house until the team could get here, though I didn't have any specifics on what was happening at the time." He turned his attention to Emma. "Martel asked me to follow up on Emma and her brother once their parents were safely out of the area. Now that the children are no longer minors, security is focused mainly on the government witness and his spouse."

"So Austin isn't with my parents?"

Newman shook his head. "He is not. Do you know where he might be?"

"I don't." A note of panic crept into her voice. "I guess he officially lives here, but he's got a couple of friends from high school who moved into their own place shortly after they all graduated last June and he stays with them a lot."

"Let these friends know that if they're protecting him, they need to step up and contact me," Newman said firmly. He pulled out a business card and extended it toward Emma.

Emma ignored the contact card Newman was trying to offer her. "What are you talking about?" she demanded, crossing her arms. "Given what's happening Austin *needs* someone to protect him."

Newman blew out a breath and set the card on the arm of his chair. "It looks as if your brother is the person who gave away your parents' location to Walker's gang. Sold them the information, possibly. He's the reason they knew your dad was here in Cedar Lodge."

Cole watched Emma's body tense. Her jawline firmed and anger seemed to come off her in waves. "That is absolutely ridiculous."

"According to Martel, Austin very much resented the move up here from Los Angeles and he held on to that resentment for a long time."

"He was *ten years old* when we moved. He had to give up his friends and his school and everything he knew. Of course he was angry."

For a moment no one spoke.

Emma checked her phone again, as if someone might have called or texted and she hadn't noticed. "I don't believe this," she muttered.

"It's not like I'm looking to arrest your brother," Newman said. "He isn't officially a criminal suspect, and I haven't been tasked to bring him back to the station. But I would like him to confirm that he's responsible for the security breach. It helps with integrity of the whole witness protection system if we can understand how security failures happen. I'd appreciate your help."

"And I *want* to help you." Emma lifted her chin. "I want you to know that Austin isn't responsible."

"Okay." Newman nodded. "In the meantime, I can take you to a safe house out of town where you won't be vulnerable to another attack like the one today."

She shook her head. "No, thank you. I'm going to stay in Cedar Lodge and I'm going to find my brother and then we can get everything cleared up. I need to make sure Austin is safe and I need to talk to my parents and make sure they're okay, too."

"What about your own safety?" Cole turned to her. "Maybe you should take him up on his offer. It looks to me like the criminals came to get your dad so he couldn't testify and when they couldn't get to him they went after you instead. Sadly, criminals the world over control their target victims by grabbing family members and threatening to harm them. The plan is likely to grab you or Austin and threaten to hurt you if your dad goes through with his plan to give his witness testimony. The kidnappers have a job to do and they're going to come after you again."

"They might already have Austin," Emma said softly. She

sighed and the starch appeared to go out of her backbone. "If my parents are in protective custody and I'm hiding in some other town, who's going to help my brother?"

"How are you going to help him if you're in danger?" Cole asked. Even with her grit and determination to fight against her attackers, Emma likely wouldn't have escaped abduction on her own.

"What kind of life would I have if I walked away from my family and only worried about myself?" she responded. "Would you ever do that?"

Cole didn't have any siblings, but he did have family members and friends he cared about. And no, he would not abandon them if they were in danger. Not even if that meant putting himself at risk.

He understood how Emma felt. Fear for her safety tied a knot in Cole's stomach. Emma was going to stay in Cedar Lodge until she found her brother, and she was going to be in danger the whole time.

Cole would not let her go through this alone.

"You didn't have to stay," Emma said to Cole in the waiting area of the urgent care clinic after she'd seen a doctor.

Not that she was surprised he had waited. She'd worked with Cole enough to know that he had a strong sense of ethics and responsibility. Even if he wasn't always personable.

Okay, maybe that was unfair. He was friendly to a point but then also politely aloof. That was why, three years after meeting him, Cole was still somewhat of a mystery. But she was nevertheless grateful for the concern he was showing her now.

Shortly after Sergeant Newman had confirmed Emma's parents were safe and then turned around and accused her younger brother of selling information about their family's location to the bad guys, the conversation at her parents' house had died down. Newman left and Volker had reminded Emma and Cole that he needed them down at the police station for official statements. After he gave them a ride back to Cole's truck at the crime scene, Cole had insisted on driving Emma to the clinic to get her collarbone x-rayed before they reported to the station.

In the waiting area Cole got to his feet. Behind him, rain splattered against the window. When storms rolled into the narrow river valley where Cedar Lodge was located, they typically rolled in *fast*. It was one of the many things that was substantially different from the desert-like Southern California town where Emma had come from.

"What did the doctor say?" Cole asked.

"No fracture, just a moderate bone bruise. Over-the-counter pain meds and try to take it easy." Her collarbone was really starting to ache, too. The adrenaline rush after the kidnapping had bottomed out and now Emma felt shaky and tired. She looked at Cole, recalling that he'd worked an overnight shift before arriving at the crash scene and then searching for her. "How long have you been awake?" she asked.

He offered her a half shrug and declined to answer.

"Why don't you go home and get some rest?" she added. "I can get a rideshare back to my car."

"I'll make sure your car gets back to your apartment," he said, deflecting her question. "Right now let me drive you to the police station. I've already gotten a text from Volker asking for an estimate of when we'll get there. I told him to calm down."

Emma knew that Cole, Kris Volker and sheriff's deputy Dylan Ruiz had been friends for a long enough time that the interaction between them tended to be more informal. The three of them were absolute professionals, but there were moments when they weren't above teasing or mildly harassing one another.

"I got a text from a coworker at the library asking what happened to me." Emma shook her head. "I can't believe I completely forgot about work. I didn't give a lot of detail in my reply. Just told her something very serious had come up and I would be in touch later."

"Good. Until things get figured out, it's probably best to give out as little information as possible."

"That's what I thought." She glanced out at the rain. "Ready to make a run for it?"

Cole pulled off his fire department jacket and offered it to her.

"That's okay. I won't melt in the rain."

"Take it. Please."

Rather than make an issue of it, she nodded. "Okay. Thanks."

He stepped around to put it on her shoulders. "Probably best if you don't move your arms around too much right now."

"No argument there." Moving her arms triggered the ache in her collarbone.

Rather than heading out the door, he hesitated for a moment, looking into her eyes.

"What?" she asked.

"I thought of something while I was sitting here. You didn't tell Sergeant Newman about the man you saw behind your parents' house."

"Oh." No, she hadn't. "With my thoughts going off in so many different directions, I didn't think of it. But I'll let him know." Newman's card was still on the arm of the chair back at the house. She'd call or text him after they were finished at the police station.

"Do you think the person you saw could have been your brother?" Cole asked.

Emma shook her head. "No. I'd know Austin if I saw him. And if he saw me, he'd come talk to me. He wouldn't run away." She started for the exit and then stopped, struggling to contain a flare of anger. "Wait, are you asking me that because you think I saw Austin and I was trying to hide that fact?"

"I had to ask," Cole said mildly.

"Well, now you have." She clamped her mouth shut and exhaled audibly through her nose.

It couldn't have been Austin, could it?

She resumed walking toward the exit, tired and annoyed and angry and sore.

And *scared*. For her parents, especially her dad, who was going to have to testify in open court against a stone-cold killer. And for her brother, who might have already been taken captive by the bad guys. If the thugs had watched and planned how to best get at Emma, why wouldn't they have done the same with Austin, too?

It was just past one o'clock in the afternoon, but the heavy clouds and rain made their surroundings appear dusky and filled with shadows. The clinic and its adjoining parking lot were near the edge of Bear Lake, and right now Emma could barely even see the surface of the water. Chilled, she flicked up the collar on Cole's jacket as she stepped in unavoidable puddles on the way to his truck.

Bang!

They were almost to the pickup when a gunshot cracked across the parking lot, immediately followed by two more shots.

Cole hollered, "Gun! Get down!"

Emma dropped to the pavement near the truck's passenger door, wincing at the pain in her collarbone caused by the sudden movement.

Cole had taken cover near the tailgate, using the SUV parked beside them as a shield. In a squatting position, while staying low and taking a look around, he grabbed his radio from his belt and keyed the mic. "Shots fired at the urgent care center on Glacier Street!"

Emma didn't hear the response. One moment she was staring down at asphalt that was covered with rainwater, and the next moment someone came up from behind and threw a blanket over her head. The assailant yanked her to her feet and started dragging her backward, and she dropped her bag with her phone in it.

Shock and panic disoriented her so that she was unable scream. She could barely even breathe. When she finally took in a breath to yell for Cole, the damp fabric covering her face was drawn into her mouth and she could only make a muffled sound.

Bang! Bang!

Gunfire started up again as Emma felt her feet scrape the asphalt and she got dragged through the mud and grass and pine needles along a downward slope toward the lake.

What was the assailant planning to do? *Drown her?*

Was Cole okay or had he been shot?

She lifted her feet, hoping that carrying her full weight would slow the attacker down. But she was a small woman and the assailant was obviously strong because the move made no difference.

As they moved closer to the water she heard an outboard motor. Was a boater passing nearby? Maybe whoever was piloting the watercraft would help her. Having learned her lesson moments ago, this time she turned her head aside before drawing in a deep breath and screaming, followed by repeated cries of "Help!"

She dropped her feet back down and kicked at her assailant's legs and tried to stomp his instep and trip up his footing. He stumbled slightly but kept dragging her along.

The sound of the outboard motor grew louder and then she suddenly found herself ankle-deep in cold lake water.

Two more gunshots fired, followed by the sound of someone running.

Emma was dragged farther out into the water, shoved against the side of a boat, and then lifted and pushed the rest of the way in.

She flailed her arms and immediately felt a blow to the side of her head, stunning her. The attacker who'd grabbed her climbed into the boat with her. It sounded like the person she'd heard running jumped in with them, too.

Cold terror shot through her. Bear Lake was a sprawling body of water lined with numerous coves and inlets where the criminals could easily hide until they could make a clean getaway.

If the thugs escaped with Emma now, Cole and the cops would never find them.

Most likely, nobody would ever find *her*.

Chapter Four

Cole desperately tried to focus in several directions at once. Emma's scream had yanked his attention toward the lake, but he still needed to know where the shooter was and he also had to listen for sounds of anyone approaching that he was not yet aware of.

The rain was falling harder, making it more difficult for him to see and hear. He didn't have a weapon and he would be going up against at least one gunman. The shooter hadn't fired off any rounds in the last couple of minutes, and it seemed a reasonable assumption the attacker had moved through the strip of trees and down to the lake where Emma's scream had originated.

Cole grabbed his phone and punched in the numbers.

"9-1-1, what is your emergency?"

He recognized the dispatcher's voice. "Lana, it's Cole. I'm under fire at the urgent care clinic parking lot on Glacier Street. I came here with Emma Hayes and now someone's grabbed her." He'd been crouched on the other side of the truck and hadn't seen it happen, but it was obvious she'd been abducted. Looking around now he could see tracks in the mud that disappeared into the band of trees between the pavement and Bear Lake. "They're headed toward the lake. I'm going after them."

Lana began to ask a follow-up question in her calm, professional way but Cole disconnected. He understood that she'd want him to stay on the line and continue with updates, but there were only so many things he could do at one time. Right now he was determined to press through the pine trees and down to the lake's edge without being spotted so he could get to Emma.

Having a gun would have made things easier.

The first couple of years after he'd returned home from his final deployment, he'd kept a pistol either on him or in his vehicle. He'd been used to carrying a sidearm, and it made him feel prepared to take whatever action was needed. But as time went by, *not* carrying a gun whenever he left home felt like he was releasing an old burden and embracing freedom.

At the moment that all seemed foolish.

He reached the last of the trees at the edge of the shoreline and saw two thugs and Emma in a boat with an outboard motor. For the sake of convenience, plenty of people left the key in the ignition of small inexpensive boats like this one, especially when they were moored to private docks.

The two kidnappers wore jackets with the hoods pulled over their heads, mostly covering their faces. Their physical builds and clothes looked similar to the attackers who had grabbed Emma earlier.

These people were relentless. Could be their own lives were in danger if they didn't complete the job their criminal boss had assigned them.

One of the attackers, apparently the shooter since he held a gun in one hand, settled at the stern by the motor ready to pilot the boat. The other kidnapper was near the bow, struggling to contain Emma as she fought with him and clawed aside a ratty-looking blanket that had covered her head.

Cole assumed the thug manhandling Emma had a gun tucked away somewhere, too.

Now that he knew her story and that her father's trial testimony would put a powerful criminal in prison for life, he was fairly certain they wouldn't immediately kill Emma but rather kidnap her and use her as a bargaining chip.

Nevertheless, he couldn't let them take her away.

He took a quick glance behind him, up the hill toward the parking lot. Even with the strip of pine trees in the way, he should still see at least flickers of red and blue emergency lights if help had arrived. He would have expected to hear sirens, even if it was just a sound blip in the distance before the cops decided to opt for a stealth approach. He didn't see or hear anything.

Cole was on his own.

Surprise was the only advantage and potential weapon Cole had to draw on. He would do what he could to make the best of it.

He untied his heavy work boots and set them aside, tossing his phone into one of them. Then he broke from the cover of the trees and ran for the water, yelling *"Stop!"* He waved his arms and did his best to look panicked and witless while hoping and praying he didn't get shot. He figured he had a fairly decent chance. Hitting a moving target, in shadowy conditions and when you were taken by surprise, wasn't easy. Not even if you spent time in target practice every day. He knew that from experience.

Both assailants looked in his direction. The jerk holding Emma, Bald Guy from the car crash attack, quickly turned his attention back to her as she struggled to break free. The kidnapper at the outboard motor pointed his gun at Cole and fired just before Cole reached the waterline. The navy veteran changed his trajectory so he was still headed into the lake but at an angle away from the boat. He wanted it to look like he was in a blind panic to get away from the bullets and danger.

Apparently, his ruse worked. The criminal didn't bother to fire any more rounds in his direction and turned his attention back to the boat motor, leaning toward it as if he needed to adjust something.

Cole quickly reached deeper water, filled his lungs with air, and then dove down. He immediately changed direction and swam back toward the stern of the boat. As soon as he reached the motor he looked up through the water at the assailant above him and then shot up out of the water and grabbed the criminal's lower arm.

The criminal, Ponytail Guy from the earlier kidnapping attempt, faltered in shocked surprise. Cole quickly took a breath of air while also pressing his foot against the side of the boat for added leverage. With his free hand he reached up and grabbed the thug's other arm, completely throwing the man off-balance, and now Cole was finally able to yank him overboard.

Ignoring the creep flailing in the water behind him, Cole dived back underwater and swam toward the bow of the boat. Looking up through the clear lake water he could see that Emma and the attacker were still struggling. Cole began to surface for a breath of air when the assailant spotted him and fired into the lake.

Cole dove back down and away, waiting for as long as he could before surfacing for another breath. When he lifted his head out of the water, he spotted the kidnapper he'd already tossed into the lake awkwardly trying to swim back to the boat. He reached the side but was unable to pull himself up and into it.

Turning his attention back to Emma, Cole was gratified to see that she was still fighting her kidnapper. Meanwhile, the assailant in the water had started yelling to his partner for help.

Emma was a small woman, and the jerk holding her was able to drag her wherever he wanted to, even though she was kicking and twisting and biting. He dragged her toward the side of the boat closest to his criminal companion.

Emma's efforts weren't having much impact in terms of physically harming the thug, but she was a huge distraction as Bald Guy tried to fish his fellow kidnapper out of the water.

Distraction was exactly what Cole needed. He pulled himself up into the boat behind Emma and her attacker, unseen as well as unheard over the shouts of Ponytail Guy still slapping at the water along with the loud growl of the diesel outboard motor.

Cole rushed forward and reached for the gun in Bald Guy's hand, but the thug somehow sensed Cole was there and jerked his hand away just as Cole reached for the weapon. Cole's hand knocked against the gun and the pistol tumbled out of the criminal's hand, ending up on the deck several feet away.

Bald Guy tried to turn toward Cole, but Emma fought against the assailant, twisting and stomping on his feet. Her flailing efforts gave Cole the opportunity he needed to throw a powerful punch directly into the center of Bald Guy's face. Cole followed it up with a left hook that sent the criminal spinning and gave Emma a chance to finally break free of the kidnapper's grasp.

Cole made a move for the gun still lying on the deck, but Bald Guy was closer and he lurched toward the weapon to grab it.

At the stern of the boat, Ponytail Guy had finally pulled himself back onto the deck.

Stand and fight was generally Cole's first instinct, but he was aware that it wasn't always the smartest option. It didn't look like the best choice right now.

Beside him, Emma breathed heavily and looked around frantically, her eyes widened with fear and what looked like the leading edge of panic.

"You know how to swim, right?" Cole asked.

She nodded.

"We need to get in the water. *Now*."

"Okay."

They rushed to the side of the boat facing the shore and jumped off.

Cole hit the water and opened his eyes before he surfaced to check on Emma. She was already swimming fast toward the shoreline. It looked like she was used to being in the water. When he lifted his head above the surface for a breath of air, he heard sirens.

Bang! Bang!

Gunshots from the boat behind them hit the water between him and Emma. Had the thugs decided they'd rather have Emma dead or was this just frustration and rage? He had no way of knowing, so he just swam closer to her, staying behind to provide the best shield he could between Emma and the shooters.

He risked a quick glance back as the boat roared away.

Back toward shore, blue lights were visible through the clusters of trees at the edge of the lake. Cops had made it to the parking lot where Cole's truck was parked. He and Emma were walking up out of the water when he spotted two officers racing toward them.

Emma was moving unsteadily and she dropped down into a sitting position on the mixture of sand and wild grass. Cole sat beside her. She leaned into him and he wrapped an arm around her shoulders while they waited for the cops to approach and question them. Cole kept his gaze focused on the lake. The kidnappers had already disappeared around a bend in the shoreline, but that didn't mean that Emma was safe. The criminals coming after her were shockingly determined, but Cole was equally determined that he would keep Emma from being their victim.

Emma sat on a wooden bench in the women's locker room at the fire station and took a moment to collect her thoughts.

The police who'd arrived at the lake had peppered her and Cole with questions before radioing for a police patrol boat and setting out to search for the attackers. After that, Cole had repeatedly asked her how she was and how her collarbone felt as they made the drive to the fire station. The answer was that she was fine but her collarbone ached.

Both she and Cole kept an extra set of clothes and pair of shoes in their lockers, which was standard practice for all the emergency responders since you never knew what might happen in the course of working a shift. She'd just now finished changing into dry clothes.

The firehouse was next to the police station, and Cole's cop friend Kris was waiting to walk the two of them over there so he could finish taking their statements.

She'd recovered her dropped phone from the parking lot and was holding it now. She looked down at the unbroken screen, grateful that her EMT job had prompted her to keep the device in a sturdy case.

She had a voicemail from her mother asking her to call back as soon as possible. It was such a relief to hear her mom's voice that Emma almost burst into tears. She also had a missed call from her brother, but he hadn't left a message. She sent him a text again asking him to call her. She was the big sister. Austin, despite the tough-guy attitude he sometimes displayed, was just an eighteen-year-old kid. At least in her mind he was a kid. She didn't know what kind of situation he was in, and she hoped her own edgy emotional state after the attacks didn't make him feel even more fearful or panicked when they finally spoke.

After a prayer for help with organizing her thoughts, Emma called her mom. She'd already decided not to tell her about the attacks. She would eventually, but right now her parents had enough on their plates.

Gina Hayes picked up after the first ring. "Honey!"

"Mom." Despite her best efforts, Emma started to cry.

"Are you all right?" Her mother sounded panicked. "Your dad is right here, let me put this on Speaker."

"Hi, sweetie." Neil Hayes's voice coming through the phone felt like a warming sip of tea. The man's ability to stay calm under the most trying of situations was amazing.

Emma cleared her throat and tried to sound happier. "I'm so glad to finally hear from you guys. I was so worried."

"Yeah, well, they hustled us out to the county airport and onto one flight and then another, and we didn't get an opportunity to call until a short while ago. I couldn't believe they wouldn't wait for us to call you and your brother so we could all leave together, but according to the witness protection people you and Austin have aged out of the program and you're on your own." Mom didn't sound happy about that.

"You're all right?" Emma asked.

"We're okay," Dad said. "Your mother and I are more worried about you and your brother. We think you two should leave town."

"You've talked to Austin?" Emma asked cautiously.

"We have," Mom said. "And your brother's got it in his head that he's responsible for our location being discovered. You need to talk him out of thinking that."

"We know he got in touch online with some friends shortly after we moved to Cedar Lodge," Dad said. "We learned about it years ago. He told us he never gave away the name of the town and we believe him."

"It's just as likely our fault as his," Mom interjected. "The truth is your dad and I stayed in touch with your grandparents and aunts and uncles even though we weren't supposed to. And Dad and I just agreed that we need to let your brother know about that."

Emma felt her eyes go wide. As kids, their parents' rule had been for no one in the family to connect with anybody from their old life. Not even relatives.

"It just felt like we were being punished for your dad

doing the right thing and agreeing to testify," Mom continued. "When this first started we thought we'd only be cut off from everybody for a year or two at most. After four years we decided that was enough and we got in touch with everybody. Maybe your dad or I accidently let slip information that we shouldn't have. Maybe a relative told somebody something and somehow the information got back to the Walker criminal gang." She sighed heavily. "I don't know. But I do know we can't let your brother take on the responsibility for our cover getting blown."

Emma rubbed her eyes. "I just messaged Austin to call me. Maybe you could encourage him to hurry up and do that. When we get together we'll call you and see what we want to do next. If we want to go down to California with you two or go somewhere else."

Emma heard a voice in the background on the other end of the call.

"We've got to go for now," Mom said. "Love you."

"Love you, too," Dad added.

"I'll find Austin," Emma promised, just before the call ended.

After taking a few moments to collect her thoughts, Emma walked out of the locker room to the adjoining crew room where she smelled a fresh pot of coffee brewing. Cole stood waiting. When he looked at Emma, she felt her stomach give a nervous twist. As if she were attracted to him.

This is Cole, she told herself. *The guy you've worked with for two years. Come on.* He was just Cole. Not some man she had a romantic interest in.

Yes, he'd been courageous and amazing, not only most recently at the lake but actually starting with him saving her from the kidnappers earlier this morning.

People have tried to kidnap me twice today. For a moment the sheer bizarreness of that reality slowed down her thoughts. Her gaze had shifted away from her part-time work partner, but now she looked at him again. That feeling of nervous, fluttery attraction was still there. It even ratcheted up a notch when his initial expression of hardened determination softened into concern as he looked at her. Then he turned and reached into a nearby cabinet to grab a mug. "I know you're not yourself without *plenty* of coffee and I need you to stay on your toes." He filled the mug. "You want your usual ridiculous amount of cream and sugar?"

It was no different from their regular banter. Just a coworker offering to get her coffee. So why did his offer to get her coffee now elicit a warm feeling that felt very *personal*?

This had to be some weird emotional aftereffect, like shock. It was a chemical response to extreme stress added to emotions that had already been pushed to their limit. That was all it was.

"Most people like their coffee to taste good," she said, continuing their usual banter, understanding that he was trying to create a moment of normalcy for the both of them and appreciating the effort. "You take your coffee so bitter I don't know why you don't just chew the grounds."

Cole laughed while adding cream and sugar to her coffee and then handed it to her.

After a couple of sips, Emma told him she'd spoken to her parents and that they were okay. "I still need to find my brother, though," she said. "When I do, we'll probably leave town."

Cole leaned his back against the counter. "Sounds like a good idea."

Kris Volker walked into the crew room from the firehouse bay where the fire trucks and ambulances were parked. "You two are certainly magnets for trouble today."

"I'd rather not be," Emma said before taking a sip of coffee.

Volker gave her a sympathetic look. "Unfortunately, we don't have either of the attackers in custody. We found the boat, but they weren't in it. The search for the criminals is our top priority right now. Let's get your official statements taken care of, do an extended interview, see if there's some detail you can recall that will give us a new lead."

Emma looked down at the last of her coffee. The surface was rippling as a result of her shaking hands. Adrenaline, fear, or maybe both. The violent criminals were still at large hunting for her and probably for her brother, too. Was Austin someplace safe? She didn't know.

Emma rinsed her mug and put it in the dishwasher. Cole did the same thing.

"Let's go," Emma said. The truth was she was terrified to step out of the safety of the fire station. But as she'd very recently learned, you couldn't hide forever. She would take whatever risks were necessary to help the cops capture the kidnappers and find her brother before it was too late.

Chapter Five

"I'm sorry all of this is happening to you," Police Chief Gerald Ellis said to Emma as she took a seat in a small conference room at the police station.

"Thank you."

Cole was there, along with Kris Volker and Detective Sam Campbell, who had been introduced to Emma in the squad room a few moments ago.

"First off, Sergeant Newman from the sheriff's department contacted me and said that he thinks your brother might somehow be involved with the criminal gang that's come after you. He believes Austin might have sold them information on your family's location here in Cedar Lodge. It's something to consider as we work to solve these crimes against you. Do you have any thoughts on that?"

"Yeah, I think it's ridiculous. If information about our location got out through any member of my family, it was by accident. I'm sure of that."

"Well, I am concerned about his safety. These thugs might try to kidnap him, too. Do you know where we could find him?"

She shook her head. "I'm trying to get in touch with him because *I'm* worried about him."

She'd moved out of her parents' house and begun supporting herself three years ago. Her relationship with Austin hadn't been especially close lately. They were five years apart and that felt like a big gap when one of you was a teenager still living at home and the other was out living an independent life. Emma looked down at her nails for a moment to collect herself before she burst into tears.

She *should* have kept an eye on her brother. Over the last few months, after he'd graduated high school and turned eighteen, she should have made more of an effort to find something in common with him. An arrow of guilt speared her heart when she remembered the few times he'd reached out to her to meet for lunch or go to a movie or something and she'd told him she didn't have time.

"He has a couple of friends he sometimes stays with for a few days at a time. I'm going to talk to them. And I think he still has a job at Burger Bonanza. I'm going to look for him there, too."

"I want to emphasize that he's not wanted by police at this time, but there may come a point when it's important for us to talk with him. And I would like to know that he's okay."

Emma nodded. "I'll let you know when I finally talk to him."

"Thank you. Meanwhile, let's talk about our investigation into the attacks on you. River Patrol just found what we believe is the boat used by the attackers." Ellis glanced at Campbell. The detective tapped the screen of the tablet in front of him and then slid it across the table toward Emma and Cole.

"That's it, that's the boat." It appeared abandoned, untethered, and drifting near the lakeshore.

Cole nodded in agreement.

Campbell pulled the tablet back toward himself. "Stolen and later ditched not far from the location of your attack."

Which indicated to Emma that the assailants were likely somewhere in town since the attack had been near Glacier Street and the downtown area.

"This would be a good time for Officer Volker to complete his reports." Chief Ellis looked at Volker and the patrol officer opened a document on his laptop.

"I've already got a lot of the basic information I need," Volker said. "What I'm looking for now is a narrative of what happened."

He started with Emma, and then it was Cole's turn. The chief and detective both listened closely to the descriptions of what exactly had happened.

"Did either of the kidnappers look familiar to you?" the detective asked after they were finished, his glance taking in both Emma and Cole.

"No," Emma said.

"Never seen them before," Cole added.

Campbell settled his focus on Emma. "In the last week or so, have you noticed anyone unusual hanging around your home? Have you felt like you were being watched? Did either of your parents mention anything odd happening to them? If so, perhaps we could track down video footage from near the location where it happened."

"I haven't had any experience like that and my parents didn't mention anything." Emma rubbed her hands over her arms. It was a chilling thought that someone might have been stalking her or her family for days and they'd had no idea.

"All right," Campbell said, tapping the screen on his notebook again. "I have one more thing to ask of you. Take a look at these mug shots and see if you recognize any of them. Most are locals who have either a history of violence or criminal connections that make us think they could be the attackers. There are some mixed in that were sent to us from detectives down in Los Angeles. These would be known associates of the criminal your dad will be testifying against in California."

Emma began swiping the photos with Cole also looking at the screen. No one looked familiar. Cole agreed.

"Now what?" Emma asked. "Do I just wait and hope they don't attack me again before you can find them?"

"We've got other avenues of investigation," Chief Ellis said. "Detective Campbell and his team will be talking to confidential informants. They'll also try to track down security video from locations near where the boat was stolen, as well as where the kidnappers stole the car they had earlier this morning and see what they can learn from that. We'll be checking local hotels and campgrounds, too, since the thugs have to stay somewhere." He glanced at Kris Volker. "Until we have identifying photos of the attackers it'll be hard to have patrol officers on the lookout for the criminals, but we can beef up patrols around your home."

Ellis tapped the keyboard of his laptop. "Looks like you live at Lakeside Terrace."

"It's a pretty secure building," Emma said. At least she'd always felt that way about the four-floor craftsman-style structure. But then she'd never had anyone trying to kidnap her before. "Keycard locks at the two main entrances and for the elevators and video cameras in the hallways."

"None of that would keep out a professional who's determined to get to you," the chief said grimly. "But that could be true of virtually any place you would stay in town. I encourage you to remain vigilant. Make sure your doors and windows are locked. Don't open the door for anyone you don't know."

"And maybe sleep in the living room so if someone does get in through the front door you'll hear them," Volker added.

Emma was scared all over again. Part of her wanted to flee to safety, to take off and hide someplace hundreds or thousands of miles away. But a stronger part of her absolutely would not abandon her brother. And she stubbornly didn't want to be forced to start a new life in a new place all over again.

Maybe the friendships she'd developed in Cedar Lodge weren't based on her telling people the *entire* truth about her past. But the relationships and emotional connections were real. And in the end, didn't everybody hold back a little bit of something of themselves from other people? Not to be deceitful but simply because they felt more comfortable that way?

"I don't know what else to advise you," Ellis added. "Going into hiding on your own would not be easy. And it would be expensive. I wish I could offer you a personal round-the-clock bodyguard but right now I just don't have the staffing or budget to do that."

"I intend to spend as much time with her as possible," Cole interjected. "If you're all right with that," he added as Emma turned to him.

She was more than all right with it. But she simply said, "Thank you." Hopefully the whole situation would be resolved quickly. For everyone's physical safety and so she and Cole could get back to their normal working relationship. Because with her life in danger, and her brother at risk, too, the last thing she needed was to be distracted by this unsettling new attraction to Cole.

Ellis got to his feet and everyone else followed suit. "We're going to get back to work," he said to Emma and Cole. "Call 9-1-1 immediately if you have any concerns. Beyond that, I suggest you both get some rest."

They filed out of the conference room, Emma walking alongside Cole. "I'm tired, but I'm also too amped to go home and sit around just yet," she said. "How about you take me to get my SUV from my parents' house? After that I can stop to get something to eat on my way home." She would have anticipated a loss of appetite after all that had happened today, but that wasn't the case.

"I'll follow you two just to make sure no one's waiting to ambush Emma," Volker said, having overheard while walking behind them.

"Good idea," Cole commented.

They stepped outside and Emma glanced at the nearby street as they walked the short distance back to the fire station where Cole's truck was parked. She needed to grab her duffel bag with her wet clothes, too, so she could take them home. Maybe something mundane like doing laundry would help settle her nerves.

In the early days after her dad had witnessed Royce Walker committing murder in a Los Angeles alleyway, Emma had been vigilant in taking note of her surroundings. Over time that compulsion had faded, but now here it was again. She wondered if her family would ever be safe. Maybe the attacks weren't ever going to stop. At least not until the criminals got what they wanted and silenced her dad by harming him or kidnapping a member of his family.

I have to start carrying a gun.

Cole glanced into his rearview mirror at Kris in his patrol car on their way to retrieve Emma's SUV. The cop wouldn't be able to keep an eye on Emma all the time, and Cole was committed now to stepping up and protecting Emma as best he could.

Cole didn't have a problem with guns, it was just that he hadn't ever imagined needing to carry one around town for the sake of keeping a companion and himself alive. When he left the military, he'd wanted to continue to use his skills as a medic. When his mother became terminally ill while he was in high school, they'd moved to his grandfather's ranch and Cole had helped take care of his mom. Hearing about some of the activities of his criminal father, there'd been times when Cole wanted to become a cop and hunt down thieving, violent, drug-dealing thugs like his old man and lock them up. Make the world a better place. But in the end, going out to rescue people who were injured or seriously ill and helping them felt more like his true calling.

At the moment, it looked as if his life needed to contain a mixture of both those types of action. Keep his job as a paramedic and be an armed bodyguard for Emma.

He glanced over at her seated beside him, taken aback at the drive he felt to care for her and protect her. Earlier in the day, he'd told himself that he was motivated to help out a co-worker and fellow member of his community. But in truth, this was something more and it had come at him unexpectedly.

Cole had been engaged once. A long-distance relationship that was probably a bad idea from the start. Both of them had been serving in the military, and they didn't have much actual time together in person until they both returned to civilian life and each got an apartment in San Diego where they could spend some quality time together while getting ready for their wedding, which would be a year away.

The relationship fizzled. It just did. There wasn't a big blow out over a specific problem, there was just the simple fact that they each had expectations about the other that didn't match reality. After it ended, Cole moved back to Cedar Lodge. It was something he'd wanted to do, anyway. He'd dated some very nice women, but nothing had *clicked*. He hadn't been able to imagine a future with any of those women.

Now, with Emma, maybe he could imagine that.

Whoa, wait. Where had *that* come from? Cole couldn't let himself think like that because Emma was eight years younger than him and they worked together and, well, it just didn't make any sense.

"I'm going to call Shari at the main city library and see if she'll come by my apartment to pick up the books I was supposed to deliver and get them out to the Meadowlark branch library," Emma said.

Cole turned to her and laughed, grateful to have his thoughts redirected.

"What?" Emma demanded.

"After everything you've been through today, you're still worried about those books?"

"People want to read them," she said emphatically. "They cared enough to *request* them. It's my job to get books into people's hands, especially people who can't get to the main library and who might not have the ability or desire to read books in a digital format."

He couldn't keep the smile from his face. "I admire your commitment." He meant it.

They reached her parents' house, and Cole pulled up into the driveway behind Emma's SUV.

The moment for humor was gone, and Cole became especially alert to their surroundings.

Emma started to open her door.

"Let's wait for Kris to have a look around first," Cole said, watching his friend pull up behind them. "He'll want to make sure the kidnappers aren't nearby."

"Doesn't seem likely they are."

"Better to check and know for certain."

Emma gave him a thoughtful look before digging into her bag for her keys and car fob and then holding them toward him. "The silver-colored key unlocks the front door."

Cole opened his door, got out and handed the keys to Kris. "Silver key for the front door. I'd go with you to search the house but I don't want to leave Emma alone."

"I can see that," Kris said in a teasing tone.

Cole glared at him. "Somebody's got to stay with her and make sure she's safe."

Kris held his hands up. "I'm not criticizing." He flashed a grin that only lasted a few seconds before his features became more serious. He drew his service weapon and went to check around Emma's SUV and then inside the house.

Cole kept his attention focused on the house while Kris was inside, listening for any sounds of trouble. Emma appeared to do the same thing, as they sat together in tense silence.

Kris finally exited the house and slid his gun back into the holster. "Doesn't look like anybody's been in there since we left," he said as he walked up to Cole's window. "I'm going to get back on patrol."

"Thank you," Emma said, finally getting out of the truck as Kris drove away.

"Do you want to go straight home while I go get you something to eat?" Cole called out to Emma through his rolled-down window.

"I'd rather just pick something up now and go home. As soon as I eat I want to climb into bed and hide there for a while. I'm hoping Austin will call soon and I can get him to come to my apartment."

"Fair enough. What do you want to eat?"

"A sandwich and some German potato salad from Dill Pickle Deli sounds good. That okay with you?"

"Sure, whatever you want."

Emma got into her SUV. Cole backed out and then had her get in front of him so he could watch her and make sure she was okay while they started toward the center of town. As he drove, he hoped and prayed they wouldn't come under attack again before he could see her safely home.

Chapter Six

"I got the chocolate coffee sugar bomb you asked for." Cole stepped into Emma's apartment the next morning carrying her double-shot mocha, his own brewed coffee with a splash of cream, and a bag with fresh bagels and small containers of whipped cream cheese.

"Thanks." The word came out scratchy, matching Emma's rough appearance.

"Looks like you didn't get much rest last night." They'd exchanged texts before Cole left the ranch this morning and he already knew that Emma hadn't yet heard from Austin.

Emma closed the door behind him and bolted it. She pulled her drink from the cardboard carrier and offered him a mocking glare. "I suppose you think *you* look fresh as a daisy."

The banter was a good sign. She was acting like her normal self, which was significant given all she'd been through in the last twenty-four hours.

"I feel rested," Cole said. "Fell into bed as soon as I got back to the ranch and was instantly asleep." He'd been awake for well over twenty-four hours at that point. The adrenaline spikes and anxiety as a result of the attacks hadn't been enough to overcome his need for solid rest.

"Yeah, well, I pictured my brother in some kind of horrible, dangerous situation every time I closed my eyes. Wasn't doing it intentionally, it just happened. When I did fall asleep, I had night-mares about him that woke me up." She took a sip of her coffee, quickly followed by two more. "Thank you. This is perfect."

"I told them to put in double the normal amount of choco-late syrup."

A slight smile broke through her scowl. "Good call." She looked inside the white bag he'd brought, then picked it up and headed toward a toaster oven on her kitchen counter.

Cole glanced around. Her apartment was on the third of four floors. Beside the dining area, a glass door opened onto a balcony and beyond that he could see sunlight sparkling on the surface of Bear Lake. "You really have a nice view." He'd been here yesterday, after seeing her home, but the curtains had been closed.

"I've been happy here," Emma said over her shoulder as she split the bagels and started them toasting.

Cole walked toward her, noticing that the place looked im-maculate and smelled faintly of lemon. When he reached the kitchen, he spotted several household cleaners on the counter. "Did you spend the night cleaning?"

"Figured I might as well do something useful since I obvi-ously wasn't going to sleep." She took the unmarked whipped cream cheese containers out of the bag and looked at them.

"One's plain and the other has pimento and chives."

"Both sound good." She grabbed small plates from a cabi-net and then butter knives from a drawer.

"Look, I know you're an EMT and you've witnessed trau-matic events and learned to cope with the aftermath," Cole said. "But what you're going through is different."

She studied him silently and took a couple sips of her mocha before the timer on the toaster oven rang. She took the bagels out, and both of them smeared on some cream cheese before going over to the dining table to sit down to eat.

Cole took a moment to offer up a quick prayer of gratitude. Emma appeared to do the same. "I just want to say that after my tours in combat zones I had a rough time," he said awkwardly, trying again to bring up what he considered to be the sensitive topic of dealing with one's emotions. "It takes a while to process things. Sometimes you need help. It's good to ask when you do."

"Wow," Emma said after chewing and swallowing a bite of bagel. "That might be the first personal thing you've ever told me."

"Yeah, well." A feeling of self-consciousness crept over him. Maybe he shouldn't have shared that about himself. But the topic was important. He ate a bite of his bagel and then changed the subject. "So what are the plans for today?"

Thanks to their earlier texts, he knew that she hadn't heard from the cops this morning, which seemed to indicate they hadn't made any headway in their search for the attackers. Meanwhile, he was at the end of his rotation for twelve-hour shifts and would be off the work schedule and available to help Emma try to find her brother for the next three days.

"My mom gave me the address for the apartment where Austin's been hanging out with his friends. It's on Marsh Avenue near 10th. She also gave me the phone number for one of the friends but I'd rather not call ahead. I don't know that Austin would leave if he was there and knew we were coming, but I don't want to take the chance."

"Makes sense to me. How's your collarbone feeling?"

"Not that bad. I've been taking the over-the-counter pain pills at regular intervals like the doctor suggested to stay ahead of the pain and so far it's been working."

Her phone chimed and her eyes widened as she reached to grab it from her purse. "Not Austin," she said to Cole after glancing at the screen. She answered the call. "Hi, Shari."

Cole listened as she told Shari that she'd be down in the

parking lot within fifteen minutes. "What's going on?" he asked after she disconnected.

"Shari's here to get the library books that are still in my SUV."

Again with the library books.

"After I hand over the books, we might as well go to that apartment and see if Austin is there." She took a sip of her mocha as concern darkened her eyes. "I like to think the kidnappers targeted me because my life is boring and predictable and I'm easy to find. An eighteen-year-old guy like Austin who's kind of untethered and all over the place would be tougher to locate and grab." She took another sip of coffee before tossing the empty cup into a trash can. "I hope I'm not wrong and they've already taken him."

"Let's not get ahead of ourselves." Cole stood and felt the weight of the holstered pistol at his hip, covered by a light jacket. The last thing he wanted to do was shoot anybody. He didn't want to fire his gun at all when he was in town. Bullets could hit something solid and ricochet. Innocent people could get hurt. He'd chosen not to be a cop and he didn't particularly want to function as if he was one. But Emma needed him to use his skills to protect her and keep her safe and alive until this situation with the Los Angeles criminals came to an end.

He drained the last of his coffee and tossed his cup. By then Emma had put on a sweater over her jeans and long sleeve T-shirt. She slung the strap of her shoulder bag over her head. "The coffee and all that sugar helped," she said. "I actually have some energy."

"Enjoy it. We both know you're going to crash in a couple of hours and probably feel worse."

"So I'll let you buy me another extra chocolaty mocha."

The corner of Cole's mouth lifted in a half smile. But then it dropped because he had a point to make and it was serious. "Hold up a minute," he said as she neared the door.

She faced him, hands on her hips. "What?"

"I want to remind you that we need to be extremely vigilant once we step outside that door. No lingering in the parking lot to chat with Shari. Constant attention to our surroundings. Limited amount of time we spend outside of a building or vehicle. We keep a close eye on anybody who comes near us."

"Okay." She dropped her hands from her hips. "I realize you don't have to do this. Thank you."

Cole nodded and then opened the door to check the hallway. Moments later they were downstairs and out in the parking lot where Emma handed over her library books. And, despite the fatigue visible in her eyes and the dark circles beneath them, she actually appeared as if she'd brightened up a little. Cole was happy for her.

Moments later, they were in his truck and on their way to the apartment on Marsh Avenue. Driving through downtown Cedar Lodge, Cole glanced at his rearview and side mirrors as often as was safe. He was gratified to see that Emma was also paying close attention to the other cars and drivers around them.

When they reached their destination, Emma spotted her brother's car. "Looks like it's got a flat, and I know he doesn't have a spare," she said. After they got out of Cole's truck they walked over for a closer view of the listing rattletrap and its deflated tire. Then they changed directions and walked up to the apartment on the ground floor of a two-story building, Cole stepped in front of Emma and knocked on the door. He shielded her body with his, letting his hand hover near his holster. It wasn't so much that he thought Austin and his buddies would be a threat, but that he was concerned the kidnappers might have already tracked Austin to this location. He didn't know how they could have done it, but he'd learned the hard lesson that it never paid to underestimate your adversaries.

A gangly young man with a shaved head and a thin goatee answered the door. A kid trying hard to look like a tough guy was Cole's first impression. Common for so many teenagers. But when the young man's gaze landed on Emma and he smiled, the effect was ruined. Now he looked like a tall, skinny puppy.

"Hey, Emma," the young man said.

"Benny?" she asked after a moment's hesitation.

"Yeah. We met a couple of times."

She nodded. "I remember you."

"So, what's up?" he asked uncertainly.

"I'm looking for Austin. Is he here?"

"Nah. He was here night before last. We stayed up super late playing a game online so he slept over. But then he went home in the morning. His car had a flat so he had to walk. Haven't seen him since."

"Have you *heard* from him?" Cole asked.

"No. I texted him a couple times but never heard back. He hasn't logged on to our favorite gaming site, either." Benny's eyes took on a worried expression. "What's going on?"

Cole was no expert, but he thought the kid's concern and confusion looked genuine.

"I'm worried about my brother," Emma answered. "Someone dangerous came by our parents' house yesterday morning. They've attacked me twice. I think they might be after Austin."

"What?" After staring at her dumbfounded for a few seconds, Benny stepped back inside the apartment and waved them in.

Cole went in first, hand still lingering near his gun in case his reading of Benny was incorrect and this was somehow a trap. Once inside, things appeared fine and Emma followed him in. There were fast-food wrappers and empty soda cups everywhere and the blare from the sounds of an online battle coming from another room.

Benny closed the front door and yelled, "Shawn!"

When there was no response, Benny stalked into the other room and Cole followed him just to be safe. Emma stayed close behind him.

A chubby guy about Benny's age sat in a gaming chair. He gaped at Cole and Emma, then paused the game and took off his headset. "Hey, Emma, what's up?"

Emma might not have remembered much about these guys but they sure remembered her. And honestly, Cole wasn't surprised. She was a striking-looking young woman with dark hair and coffee-colored eyes who typically wore a thoughtful expression on her face, something that Cole had, admittedly, always found appealing.

Benny quickly summarized the situation, and a short conversation made it clear that Shawn hadn't heard from Austin, either. Now both of the roommates looked concerned.

"Where do you think he might be?" Emma asked. "If you had to take a guess."

Benny shrugged and Shawn copied him. "I'm not really sure who he hangs out with besides us these days," Benny added. "He's serious about his job at Burger Bonanza. He's taken on a lot of hours lately. Have you tried there? Otherwise, maybe he's skateboarding at Skate Trek over by Lodgepole Park."

"We saw his car with the flat tire out in the parking lot. How do you think he's getting around town?"

Benny offered another shrug. "His bike or maybe his skateboard? When he left here he said he was going to walk to your parents' house."

Emma's disappointment was obvious by the expression on her face followed by the tone in her voice when she said, "If you see him or hear from him, please tell him to contact me. In fact, I'd like *you* to contact me, too. Give me your phones so I can make sure you have my contact information, and I'll need your numbers, as well."

Cole was impressed by her obvious command of the situation when both guys unlocked their phones and then handed them over so she could add herself to their contacts and then add both of them to her own contact list.

"Let's go," she said to Cole as soon as she was finished and had thanked the young men.

"Sorry you didn't learn anything," Cole said on their way out to his truck. "I know you're disappointed."

"Not just disappointed," she responded in a grim tone. "*Terrified.* If his closest friends haven't heard from him, I can't help wondering if he's in a horrible situation or if he's even still alive. Who knows what could have happened if the kidnappers went after him and he put up a fight. Maybe they'd rather kill him than let him escape."

Cole simply nodded to acknowledge he'd heard her. Offering reassurances that Austin was likely fine would be dishonest. He walked with his head on a swivel, looking around and staying vigilant. If Austin had already been grabbed, Cole wanted to make sure that Emma wasn't taken next.

"So do you want to try Burger Bonanza next and see if Austin showed up for work yesterday or even today?"

They were seated in Cole's truck, still in the small lot at the apartment complex. Late-morning sunlight shone bright in the blue sky, making the mid-spring day look warmer than it actually was. "Yes." She cleared her throat, tamping down the worry for Austin that was threatening to choke her. *Do not cry.* She wasn't concerned with Cole seeing her break down. He'd seen that already. But she was wary of the possibility that once she started crying, she wouldn't be able to stop for a long time.

"It's getting close to lunchtime," she added. "Maybe he'll have shown up to work a shift." She could hope.

"Let's go." He started up the truck and she turned to him, her attention settling on his strong profile. She used to think of that strong chin and set jaw as hints of politely controlled arrogance. Now it seemed more like confidence and focus. Two qualities she really appreciated. If he wasn't by her side helping her, where would she be now? Even if she'd survived the attacks, she would likely be huddled at home worrying about Austin or dashing around town searching for her brother without much practical knowledge of how to keep herself safe from professional criminals.

Cole started to pull out of the parking slot just as Emma's phone chimed.

"It's Austin!" she called out to Cole, tapping the speaker symbol so he'd be able to hear the conversation. Given the danger to himself he was risking by helping her, it didn't seem right to withhold any information from him. He hit the brakes and put the truck back into Park.

"Where are you?" she demanded as soon as the call connected.

"Hey, sis." Austin's voice came through the phone, sounding amused. "Good to hear your voice, too."

Emma was not in the mood for joking around. "Are you okay?" She glanced toward the apartment building they'd just come from. "Did Benny or Shawn just call you?" Had they been lying to her? Were they actually in contact with Austin? Maybe she and Cole should have checked the closets and under the bed. Maybe he'd actually been hiding in there.

"*Both* of them texted me." Austin sounded more serious now. "They'd messaged and called and stuff yesterday and earlier today and I haven't replied because I've had other things on my mind."

"Is that why you haven't returned my calls?" Emma snapped.

"Kind of. Yeah. Look, I've been staying with a friend and hiking in the woods, thinking, trying to come up with a plan to help clean up this mess I've created and I finally have one."

"This isn't your responsibility." Despite Sergeant Newman's insinuations, Emma was certain her brother hadn't intentionally given away their family's location. And of course he hadn't *sold* the information. It had been her first instinct not to believe he'd done it, and as far as she was concerned the fact that he hadn't disappeared with a large bundle of payoff money never to be heard from again bolstered that opinion. And now here he was trying to come up with a way to solve things.

"Even if you somehow gave away our location back when you were a kid, it still isn't your fault," she continued. "You were a *kid*. Beyond that, were you aware that Mom and Dad were in contact with our grandparents? It's entirely possible that somebody accidentally gave out some information that ultimately led to Walker's thugs finding us." She didn't know exactly how that could have worked. Maybe she had a distant cousin who sold the information. There was no telling. At some point it became impossible to figure out everything.

"I didn't know Mom and Dad broke the rules and stayed connected with the rest of the family," Austin said quietly. "But that doesn't change the fact that I might have messed things up."

"Where exactly have you been staying? Where are you?" Emma demanded for the second time.

"I know the thugs came after you," Austin said, calmly ignoring her question. "I don't want that to happen again. I want to help, so I'm going to draw them out and make it easier for the cops to find them."

Emma's stomach dropped. "No!"

"Watch my social media posts. I'm sure the criminals are looking at my social media as well as yours to try and track us."

Emma was grateful that she didn't spend much time posting on social media, and even then she kept her accounts private. She knew that her brother used the more open public settings because he was young and social and wanted his friends and acquaintances to be able to find him.

"Maybe you could talk to somebody at the police department and let them know to be on the lookout for what I post. I know you have friends there, since cops and the fire department work together so much."

Emma turned to Cole, who was watching her carefully.

"Let's go to the police department," she said to him quietly. Fortunately, it wasn't far away.

Cole nodded, drove his truck out of the parking lot and headed in that direction.

"This social media posting is a terrible idea," Emma said to her brother, who was still on the phone.

"No, it's a good idea. I've thought it through and I'll be careful. I'm not a kid anymore, Emma."

Except *he was a kid*. Okay, *legally* he was an adult. He'd graduated high school last June. But he was still her little brother, and a wallop of guilt for not having spent more time with him over the last couple of years hit her hard. "Let's get together and talk about this."

"I'm fine and as I mentioned I have a place to stay," Austin said patiently. "Now, talk to your police friends for me and let them know what's going on. My first post is about to go up. Bye, Emma. Don't worry."

"Wait!"

It was too late, he'd already disconnected. She tried to call him back but he didn't answer.

She looked at the social media site where she knew he tended to be most active. The current post was four days old, well before Royce Walker's criminals had showed up. It was a selfie of her tall, blond-haired brother—who took after their dad—in a shop for outdoor sporting equipment in town, and he was standing beside a display of brightly colored kayaks. Austin did look somewhat grown up, she had to admit. And he was about to put himself in serious danger. She adjusted the settings on her account and her phone so that when Austin made a post she'd get an audible notification.

Meanwhile, Cole had called his cop friend on the truck's hands-free device.

"What's up?" Kris Volker answered.

Cole gave a quick recap of Emma's conversation with her brother.

"Actually, I'm at the station right now. I'll see if the chief and Campbell are available and we can let them know about this."

A short time later, Cole pulled up at the police station and he and Emma hurried inside.

"Thanks for your help," Emma said to Kris as soon as they arrived, trying to keep her cool when her thoughts were frantic.

"Anytime," the cop responded. "The chief is here but Detective Campbell is out of the office. Follow me. The chief is expecting you."

Inside Ellis's office, after a quick greeting, the chief introduced Emma and Cole to the department's public relations and communications officer, Alice Donegal, who was in charge of monitoring the department's social media. She'd already been tapping on her tablet, and she stopped just long enough to offer Cole and Emma a polite greeting and then ask Emma for her brother's name so she could add him to the department's contact list and make sure they received notifications through the department's account.

They'd barely finished their conversation when both Emma's phone and Officer Donegal's tablet chimed with a notification. Emma tapped her screen and saw a selfie of her brother taken in Lodgepole Park. Water from a tributary of the Meadowlark River was diverted to the park to create a small, decorative stream that flowed through the park with a wooden footbridge over it. Austin had taken the picture of himself on the footbridge, with the lighted signboard on the side of the parks and recreation office visible showing the current date, time and temperature. There was no mistaking that the picture had been taken just moments ago.

Underneath the photo Austin had written, "Got another forty minutes before I have to be back to work at Burger Bonanza. A little cool out here but I don't care. Warm weather will be here soon!"

He'd just told the assailants exactly where to find him.

"I'll head over there now," Volker said.

"I'll have Sanchez and Foster meet up with you." Ellis grabbed a cell phone and called the two additional officers, instructing them on the situation and telling them to meet up with Volker.

"I just forwarded the image to all three officers' phones," Donegal said after the chief disconnected.

Emma stood and turned to Cole. "I want to go to the park, too. If he's still there I want to talk to him."

"Not a good idea," Cole said calmly. "If the kidnappers show up at the park, it could go sideways pretty quickly. They might even change direction and come after you again if they spot you."

"Those creeps might not even be near town right now," Emma argued. Of course she was frightened by the thought of those violent criminals having her in their sights again. But she was more scared that they would get to her brother. "This could be my one chance to get to Austin before something terrible happens to him. Meanwhile, the thugs might not even see the stupid post."

"Then again, they might."

Frustration had her shaking her head. "But it's such an obvious trap."

"Obvious to you because you know about it. Plenty of people are careless on social media. And since your brother is young, they might assume he's not too bright," Cole argued.

"Don't assume every criminal is some kind of mastermind," the chief interjected. "Plenty of them are far from it."

Emma realized her emotions had gotten the better of her, and she took a deep breath to help center her thoughts.

"Go home," Ellis said. "I'll call you with an update."

"Can't I wait here until you learn something? *Please.*"

He sighed. "All right. Help yourselves to coffee in the breakroom and then wait in the lobby. I'll let you know what happens."

Forgoing the coffee, Emma walked with Cole to the lobby where they sat and waited. She prayed while she was there, and repeatedly checked Austin's social media site. Time slowed to a crawl, and she got up to pace and look out the windows numerous times.

Finally, an officer beckoned them from the lobby and escorted them to the chief's office.

"The officers didn't see Austin at the park," Ellis told them. "They took a good look around but he wasn't there. Volker and Sanchez then went to Burger Bonanza at the time he indicated he would return to work and they didn't see him there, either." Emma felt relieved but also disappointed. She'd dared to hope the cops might find Austin and bring him back to the station.

"I have two pieces of information for you from the Burger Bonanza visit," Ellis continued. "His supervisor said he called in this morning to ask for the day off but said he might be in tomorrow."

"What's the other thing?"

"Volker said that when they were inside Burger Bonanza, they noticed a car parked across the street with a couple of guys inside watching the restaurant pretty intently. They appeared to match the description of your kidnappers, so he went outside to get a better look. When the men saw him, the car sped away. Volker got a partial license plate, but I'm sure they've already ditched the vehicle. It was probably stolen."

"So that tells you the thugs were probably there watching for Austin and they're following his posts like he wants them to?"

"I would say so. Which would also tell me that they're still hanging around town looking for you, too. You should go home, make sure your doors and windows are securely locked and get some rest. You look tired, Emma. For good reason. You've been through a lot."

"We can get some food on the way there so you don't have to worry about cooking, unless you want to," Cole added.

They exchanged goodbyes with the chief and headed for the

exit. Emma didn't have even the hint of an appetite. She was suddenly so tired she could barely move. She probably should go home and try to get some sleep. It was starting to feel as if she couldn't quite remember what her life had been like back when things were normal. It was starting to look like they might not be normal again for a long time. Maybe not ever.

Chapter Seven

A piercing shriek yanked Emma from the depths of deep sleep.

For the first few seconds she was disoriented, her heart racing in her chest. The shriek happened again. And then again shortly after that.

By now Emma was sitting up, getting her bearings and she remembered that she'd decided to lay down on the couch in her living room for just a few moments after Cole left. A quick glance toward the dark balcony window, where she'd left the curtains pushed aside, confirmed that she'd slept a lot longer than she'd planned. Instead of just an hour's nap in the afternoon, she'd slept well into the evening.

The shriek sounded again. This time she realized it was coming from the hallway outside her apartment door and that it blared at regular intervals. An alarm. Fire?

She stumbled toward the balcony slider door, threw it open, and was greeted by swirls of smoke and the glow of flames at the ground floor of the building. The structure was designed in craftsman style with lots of exposed wood, and even with everything up to code, a fire could still move quickly.

An eerie-sounding electronic voice recording started playing in the hallway between the shrieks of the siren. "A fire alarm has been activated. Exit the building immediately. Do not use the elevators."

Emma heard the neighbors' doors opening and closing followed by the sound of footsteps and people talking. A sudden loud pounding on her door made her jump, though given all the other noise it seemed like it shouldn't have. Her nerves on edge, she started toward the door, reaching to unlock and open it, when she remembered to look through the peephole first.

Outside her door she saw the bristly bearded face of her neighbor Gary and his wife, Diana, behind him.

She shook her head. Had she really for a moment thought that the kidnappers had set the building on fire so they could get to her? She needed to find the balance between being vigilant and being paranoid.

"Emma!" Gary shouted just before she unbolted and pulled open the door. "Hey, just wanted to make sure you were okay and heard the alarm. Come on, we need to go!"

"Thanks, yeah, I heard it."

Several other neighbors were in the slightly smoky hallway, some wrapped in blankets or wearing jackets over pajamas as they headed for the stairwell. One of them had stopped to knock on another neighbor's door.

"Right behind you," she said, popping back inside to jam her feet into a pair of boots, shrug on a jacket, pick up her shoulder bag and grab her charging phone.

She followed her neighbors down the stairwell, the smoke getting thicker as they approached the lower floors. By the time she got to the second floor she felt a draft of air and at the ground floor she saw the emergency exit doors propped open. Fire sprinklers had kicked on in the ground floor hallway, as well.

Tenants streamed out the doors and most of them headed toward the building's park-like surroundings. Children were crying, and Emma didn't blame them. It was a scary situation and it was chilly. She pulled her jacket tighter around her body. She heard a fire engine rumbling in the distance, blaring its horn as it drew nearer. Moments later she saw red-and-white flashing lights from several fire trucks heading toward her building. Her friends and coworkers were coming to help.

Emma kept moving away from the building. The last thing she wanted to do was get in the way of firefighters as they hooked hoses to the fire hydrants. She didn't want to get splashed by water, either. Several of her neighbors appeared to have the same idea. She walked across the heavy grass as far as the first cluster of pine trees, which seemed like a reasonable distance.

Facing the building, she watched the emergency response. Her neighbors had drifted in different directions, some of them clustered in small groups, talking and gesturing. Other fellow apartment-dwellers, particularly the ones with children, it appeared, went to sit in their vehicles in the parking lot. Probably so they could start the engine and turn on the heater.

Emma considered getting into her SUV. Standing there cold and alone was not pleasant. At least in her car she could get warm.

"Don't turn around."

Emma felt the tip of a gun pressed against the back of her head. She recognized the voice. It was Bald Guy, the assailant she'd wrestled with on the boat, and he sounded coldly furious.

Despair and regret came over her like a heavy weight, seeming to pull her body downward. Her shoulders slumped instead of tensing in fear. Maybe she'd experienced all the fear she could handle for a while. Perhaps she'd reached the point where it was all too much.

I should have been more careful. I should have spent more time with Austin. I should have known that the bad guys would come after my family one day. I should have been better prepared.

Without moving her head she looked around as best she

could, hoping one of her neighbors had seen what had just happened. But that didn't appear to be the case. She and the gunman were in the shadows beneath the thick branches of the group of trees and the exterior lights of the apartment building didn't reach this far.

"Start backing up," Bald Guy demanded.

Emma didn't move. Seemingly all of her neighbors were watching the fire. How ironic it was that her own friends and coworkers were right there fighting that fire. But what did it matter? They didn't know she was in trouble so they couldn't do anything to help her. And Emma had no doubt that letting herself be taken away by the criminals would have horrible consequences.

"I *will* shoot you," the Bald Guy said in an angry tone, his words clipped. Would he actually fire the gun while it was pressed to her skull and kill her right there? He and his partner had the opportunity to kill her before and they hadn't taken it.

Did he figure on shooting to injure her if she didn't cooperate so he could force her away from this spot? And then later he could use the threat of killing her to stop her dad from giving testimony at his boss's trial. If the thugs captured Austin, the power of their threats would be doubled.

"Move, *now*!" The attacker grabbed a handful of the back of her jacket and pulled her toward him and farther into the darkness.

She took a couple of backward steps and then stumbled over an exposed tree root. Despite her uneven movements, the creep kept a tight hold on her jacket. He pulled her backward again, toward the section of parking lot a few yards away on the other side of the trees. Emma took several more steps and then stumbled again, this time on purpose. She threw her body toward the ground and her shoulder bag slid down her arm. The attacker still held a fistful of her jacket, but he cursed and tilted over and Emma could tell he'd partially lost his footing.

Desperately hoping he wouldn't shoot her, she grabbed the

strap of her bag and swung it as hard as she could at the criminal, aiming to knock the gun from his hand. Her plan didn't work. Bald Guy's hand and the threatening gun moved slightly away from her under the force of the impact, but he managed to keep a grip on the weapon. Her bag was still in her grasp. Screaming as loudly as she could, she swung it again and managed to clip him on the side of the face.

He still had a grip on her jacket, though, and she desperately fought to claw her way out of the thing. While struggling to escape the attacker, she caught glimpses of a car with its headlights off idling at the edge of the parking beyond the trees. Ponytail Guy, most likely. And it felt like he was frighteningly close. Once Bald Guy got a good hold on her, it wouldn't take much effort for him to drag her to the getaway car.

The thug was heavier and stronger than she was, but Emma was more limber and could move faster. Twisting at her waist and then arching her back, she didn't make it easy for him to control her. Overwhelmed with frustration and painfully aware that her energy was waning, she screamed again. Though it didn't seem likely that anyone would hear her with all of the sounds from the fire trucks and the firefighters battling the blaze.

In the next moment a bright rectangular light shone in her face. It was followed by a couple more lights and the voice of her neighbor, Gary, yelling, "Get off her!"

The thug cursed and yelled in response, "Back off or I'll kill her!"

Emma couldn't see what was happening; the lights shining in her face were blinding. Apparently, they were blinding to the attacker, too. *Finally*, she felt him let go of her jacket. From the corner of her eye, she could see him holding a hand up to his face as if to block the bright lights shining at him.

"Get a cop over here!" Gary yelled to someone.

Emma hadn't seen a cop car, but she knew it was standard procedure for at least one police unit to respond to a fire call just in case traffic control was needed. An ambulance would be staged nearby, too.

Emma took advantage of the chaos and Bald Guy's disorientation to get to her feet and sprint away in the darkness. She felt the skin crawl on her back as she anticipated a gunshot.

She'd only taken a few steps when Bald Guy actually did fire at her and she dove to the ground. Turning back, she saw that Gary and whoever was with him had doused their cellphone lights so they wouldn't be easy targets.

Emma's eyes adjusted enough to the darkness that she could see the shadowy form of the attacker racing toward the waiting car. He turned and fired two more shots, effectively stopping anyone from pursuing him. Then he hopped in the vehicle and it sped away.

She'd survived, again. *Thank You, Lord.*

Moments later, as she tried to catch her breath and calm her pounding heart, Emma heard the wail of a siren start up. She watched a cop car shoot across the expansive parking lot headed in her direction. Tears of frustration formed in the corners of her eyes as she realized she had nothing new to tell the officer that would help to find the kidnappers. She didn't know what kind of car they'd been driving. She hadn't seen even a small bit of the license plate.

How many times were these thugs going to come after her? As many times as it took to get the job done, apparently. A dark, disquieting thought tugged at the corner of her mind. If she continued to fight back and make herself hard to catch, would the kidnappers respond by putting more effort into finding her brother?

Forty minutes later, Cole knocked impatiently on Emma's apartment door and a cop opened it. Cole looked past the officer at Emma. When he saw the sadness in her eyes and the pine needles in her hair and dirt smudges on her face from her struggle with the criminal loser who'd attacked her, he was overwhelmed with a rush of protectiveness.

He wanted nothing more than to take her in his arms, comfort her and keep her safe. But they were coworkers. If he lost his head and gave in to the rush of emotion, he'd regret his actions eventually. No doubt Emma would feel awkward in the aftermath, too. So what he did instead was step into the apartment, offer a quick nod of acknowledgment to the cop, and then walk calmly toward Emma as the officer closed and bolted the door behind him.

"Hey," Cole said softly, doing his best to maintain the reasonable boundaries of a coworker. *Too late for that*, a quiet internal voice chided him.

"Hey, yourself." Her voice quivered. After a slight hesitation she stepped forward and wrapped her arms around him. Cole blew out a deep breath, one he felt like he'd been holding since his phone rang shortly before 10:00 p.m. and he saw her name on the screen. She told him she'd been attacked again.

The drive from the ranch to her apartment had felt like it took forever as he'd come close to surpassing the legal speed limit on his way there. Outside the apartment building, he'd spotted coworkers from the fire department raking through burned debris on the ground floor to make certain no smoldering ashes remained that could potentially reignite. He'd spoken with one of the firefighters long enough to learn that the fire had been set by piling up a few wooden pallets against the building in the small unenclosed yard of a ground-floor apartment and then setting them on fire. Along with reaching into the walls of the building, the flames had quickly leapt upward to the wooden balcony overhead and that had given the fire fuel to expand.

As Cole raced up the stairs to Emma's apartment, he'd smelled the lingering scent of smoke. His gut had clenched at the realization that the criminals targeting Emma had been willing to set the building on fire in their attempt to get to her.

"I know Rhonda was on shift and covering this part of town tonight," Cole said after their lingering embrace ended and he held her at arm's length to give her a once-over and make certain she was okay. "I didn't see her or the ambulance outside. I'm assuming she determined you were all right and then left?"

"I told her I was fine."

Emma didn't look like she was fine. Cole could see tears at the corners of her eyes marking a path through the dust on her face. His heart ached at the sight. He was also angry. These thugs *had* to be stopped. He loved being a paramedic, but right now he itched to be a cop so he could help hunt down these criminals.

"What about your collarbone?" Cole asked. "Do you think the injury might have gotten worse after you fought with that loser?"

Emma reached up to touch the injured area. "It doesn't hurt any worse than it did before. I just need to take some more acetaminophen. The pain isn't that bad. I'm just…um…" Her voice broke and she dissolved into tears. "I'm just so *tired* of all of this."

Watching her, Cole felt like he could be on the verge of tears, too. Emma was normally an energetic, confident woman. A great conversationalist who always wanted to talk about something she'd just read. She was solid and reliable and good to have by his side in intense medical emergency situations. Of course she'd been freaked out by the two prior attacks on her. Who wouldn't be? Plus, there was the worry about her parents, specifically her dad, since they could be targets of Royce Walker's criminal gang while they were down in Los Angeles preparing her for dad to testify. And then there was the dangerous behavior of her probably well-intentioned but nevertheless unwise little brother.

And now she'd been awakened by a fire only to be attacked yet again in the nearby park.

She was starting to crumble under the weight of it all, and

he knew the feeling only too well. Losing his mom when he was a teenager was a heavy burden that he still carried. Just a few years after that he'd found himself in combat. Seeing his military comrades get gravely or mortally wounded and not being able to do nearly as much as he'd wanted to help them was horrible. Pulling his life together as a young man in the aftermath of that was rough.

Throwing caution aside, Cole let himself give in to impulse and pulled Emma close again. She wrapped her arms around his waist and held on tight, seeming to collect herself as the tears stopped and she took several deep breaths.

Dear Lord, please comfort and strengthen Emma. He knew she was a woman of faith and hoped that she'd been praying and pressing into that faith. Clearly, this was a moment in her life when she truly needed to lean on it.

After they broke off the embrace, the cop who'd been standing by the door walked toward them. "Hi, Cole," he said quietly. "How are you?"

"Kind of have my hands full, Joel." Cole offered the cop, who he knew only slightly, a half smile. "How are you?"

The officer nodded his head toward Emma. "On top of all that's happened, I'm afraid I have to deliver some additional bad news."

"What is it?" Cole asked.

"Royce Walker escaped police custody down in Los Angeles."

For a moment Cole just stared at him, stunned. "How could that happen?"

"Apparently some of his gang members staged an accident on the highway while he was being transported from one facility to another."

"Chief found out shortly before the alarm went out about the fire here," Joel added.

Cole took a deep breath, pushing back against this new added fear for Emma's safety. One thing at a time, if possible, was his rule of thumb whenever he was working in the midst of a chaotic scene. It felt like the last couple of days had been one long chaotic scene. "Back to what happened tonight. Was anybody able to track the criminals who started the fire and grabbed Emma?"

"Not yet." The officer rested his thumbs on his gun belt. "We got a general description of the vehicle from Emma and a decent photo of the attacker taken by Emma's neighbor when he heard her scream and hurried over to help her."

"The guy helped by *taking a picture*?" Cole asked angrily.

"He and some other neighbors turned on their flashlight apps to see what was happening," Emma interjected. "I think that's when he got the picture. But then the shooting started and so they doused their lights, and shortly after that is when I got away from the thug. So ultimately my neighbor did help save my life and I'm grateful."

"I wish the neighbor had tackled the jerk. I suppose having a photo might help identify the kidnapper, but it won't exactly help capture him."

"Maybe not," Joel replied. "But it will help prove he assaulted and attempted to kidnap Emma, which can bring further charges and additional time to his prison sentence after we finally do catch him."

"Obviously these creeps know where you live," Cole said to Emma. "You can't stay here any longer."

"I know," Emma said. She visibly tensed her body for a moment, as if centering herself, and then dropped her shoulders. "It's not your job to look after me, and I'm sure you're already sick of all of this. I know I am." She smiled feebly and brushed aside her dark bangs from in front of her eyes. "I'm going to get a hotel room over in Johnson City. I'll rent a car so the thugs won't recognize me when I drive back and forth between here and there." A tear escaped from the corner of her eye and she wiped it away. "I *have* to find my brother. I'm scared, but I'm still not going to curl up and hide. Not while

Austin is still in town foolishly putting himself in danger because he blames himself for all this trouble."

"Don't be ridiculous." Cole shook his head. "You don't need to go to a town forty miles away. You can stay at the ranch with me and my grandfather. My cousin and her husband live there, too. There's plenty of room."

"I'm not asking you to find me a place to stay."

"I didn't think you were. But I'm offering, nevertheless. I've already mentioned the idea to Grandpa and he's fine with it." Cole cleared his throat. "I was raised by my mom and my grandfather. My dad was not a good person. When my mother left him and moved back to the ranch, my dad showed up armed and belligerent more than once. Grandpa had to deal with him. He's a tough old guy, and the risk of a bit of trouble is not particularly intimidating for him."

Emma stared at him for a moment while biting her bottom lip. "I hate dragging your family into this," she finally said.

Cole offered her a half smile that he hoped was reassuring. "Well, I'm already in it. And given what happened tonight with the fire, I'd say your neighbors have gotten dragged into it as well. *Not by you.* But by the criminals." He shook his head. "Let us help you. We all need to pull together."

"Nobody asked me," Officer Joel said after a few moments passed without Emma responding, "but I think staying with Cole and his family is a good idea and you should take him up on his offer. If the criminals spot you in a rental car and follow you out of town, you'll be a sitting duck on a long, empty stretch of highway."

Emma nodded and then turned to Cole. "Okay, thank you for your generous offer. I accept."

"Good. I'll wait while you pack some clothes."

While Emma got her things together, Joel hung around and chatted with Cole until the transmission came over his radio that the fire and crime scenes were cleared and all responders were returning to their respective stations. The cop left just before Emma came out of her bedroom pulling a suitcase behind her.

"Maybe this will be over soon," she said to Cole as they exited her apartment.

"Yep," Cole said agreeably, hoping that the criminals would be captured without any further violence or danger to Emma. But that didn't seem likely.

Chapter Eight

"You really do live a long way out of town." Emma looked
through the truck window at the dark forest on one side of the
road and the moonlit waters of Bear Lake on the other. They
were on the back side of the lake, heading up into the mountains. They'd been driving for half an hour.

"It's not exactly convenient," Cole told her. "But it feels like
a refuge from the stress of the job and all the people who've
moved here over the last few years. It's worth the drive."

Emma glanced over and saw him checking the rearview
mirror for probably the tenth time since they'd left town. She
checked her side mirror, also on the lookout for anyone who
might be following them. So far, all the headlights she'd seen
behind them had turned off onto smaller roads leading to residential properties. Still, she couldn't relax. Her clothes smelled
of smoke and her collarbone throbbed a little more than she'd
let on. She hadn't mentioned it because she didn't want Cole
pushing her to get X-rays again. She was sure nothing was
broken. It was just the strain of having wrestled with the man
who'd pressed a gun to the back of her head.

The memory of that moment flashed into her mind with an
emotional wallop that made her stomach queasy, and she rolled

down the window for a gulp of cool, fresh air. *You're okay. Right this minute, everything is fine.* Since the initial attack, she'd had to repeatedly remind herself to stay in the present and not relive the terrifying moments when her life had been threatened. It was either that or curl up into a ball and hide somewhere. She was determined not to do that.

"I think there's a good chance we got out of town without any of the thugs seeing us," Cole said in a reassuring tone as if he understood the anxiety Emma was feeling. "We'll be at the ranch soon."

"You have a lot of crime out here?"

"Nah." He shook his head. "Mainly we just have to watch out for animal predators coming after the livestock."

"What kind of predators?"

"Foxes and coyotes, mostly. Sometimes wolves. Bears now and then. Of course we get hawks coming after our chickens fairly often. We've got to stay vigilant, change up how we respond. Keep guns handy so we can fire warning shots when necessary. Set up traps sometimes."

It really was wilderness out here.

They continued until the lake disappeared from sight and there was only thick forest on either side of the two-lane highway. The topography was more jagged here at the base of a sharp mountain ridge, with the road rising up and then dropping down at regular intervals. Finally Cole slowed almost to a stop and made a sharp turn past a mailbox onto a narrow dirt road.

"We're here," he said.

The driveway up to the house was long. They bumped atop it for several moments, pine branches sometimes brushing against the sides of the truck in the darkness, until they finally crested a small ridge. There, they reached a clearing and Emma could see a sprawling single-story ranch house with warm light shining through a set of big windows at the front of it. They drove closer and she was able to see a wraparound porch. It looked as if this had once been a simple homestead and rooms had been added over the years. The different sections didn't exactly match, but the house looked solid and roomy and homey.

In the moonlight she could see the outlines of a barn and stable with a nearby corral. There were sheds and storage buildings and some other sort of animal enclosures farther away, but she couldn't see them clearly in the dim light. A couple of large pickup trucks were parked in the gravel turnaround driveway, and more vehicles and a horse trailer were parked in a nearby pole shed.

"Looks like everybody's up even though it's the middle of the night," Cole said. "I know they're looking forward to meeting you."

"'Everybody' being your grandpa and your cousin?"

Cole nodded. "My cousin Lauren and her husband, Brent, live here. Grandpa has boarded and trained horses here at the ranch for as long as I can remember, and we all help him with that. Lauren's really into crafts and after Grandpa mentioned that our great-grandparents raised sheep out here when he was a boy, she suggested we start raising sheep for the wool. She has people dye it and spin it into yarn. Turns out there's a market for artisanal craft supplies, and the yarn's been bringing in some pretty good money, so we'll probably expand the operation."

Cole parked the truck and Emma took one more look at her side mirror just to make certain they hadn't been followed before climbing out.

The front door of the house opened, spilling light onto the floorboards of the wraparound porch. Emma saw the silhouette of a tall, slender and slightly stoop-shouldered man.

"My grandpa," Cole said. "John Webb."

"So this is your paternal grandfather?"

Cole shook his head. "No, he's my mom's dad. My parents got divorced when I was very young. Mom got her original surname back. She had my surname changed to Webb, as well. Apparently my father was willing to go along with the change in return for my mother not pursuing any financial help in raising me."

Emma didn't know what to say. But here was a reminder that having a challenging family life wasn't unique to her. Yeah, they had to go into a witness protection program, but there were worse things that could happen.

Cole grabbed Emma's suitcase and they headed for the house.

"Come on in," the older man urged as they drew closer. "It's chilly out there."

Emma walked past Cole's grandpa, who appeared to be in his mid-or late-seventies. The older gentleman still retained chiseled facial features similar to his grandson, but he had brown eyes instead of blue and a head of thick silver hair.

"Welcome," he said after he closed the door. "I'm John, but feel free to call me Grandpa. Everyone does."

Emma smiled and shook his outstretched hand. "Pleased to meet you."

A couple of large dogs made their way to the shallow foyer. "This here's Liza," Grandpa said, patting a mellow black lab with a graying muzzle. "And that's Misty," he added, indicating a younger-looking German shepherd with a furiously wagging tail.

"We live here, too," a young dark-haired woman in sweatpants and a long-sleeve T-shirt said with a laugh. "Hi, I'm Lauren, Cole's cousin." She took hold of the hand of the man standing beside her, a stocky guy with a round face and wavy dark-blond hair. "This is my husband, Brent."

"Nice to meet you," Brent said with a smile.

Emma nodded. "Good to meet you, too," she added while scratching the head of the black lab.

Both Lauren and Brent had errant locks of hair sticking out at odd angles, and Brent had a button obviously fastened through the wrong buttonhole on his shirt. Emma was painfully aware that she'd gotten these people out of bed late at night when they likely were used to getting up very early in the morning. Feeling suddenly awkward and burdensome, Emma leaned to pet the German shepherd as it chomped on a chew toy.

"Thank you all so much for letting me stay here," Emma said after straightening. "I don't plan to be here long."

"You stay as long as you need to," Grandpa said in a warm growl. "Decent people shouldn't have to seek refuge from danger, but the world is what it is. It's a blessing for us to do what we can to help." He pulled out a drawer from a small table beside an easy chair and gestured at the handgun that was inside. "Given all that's happened to you lately, I'm determined to stay prepared for trouble."

Touched by the man's gruff kindness, Emma blinked back tears and glanced around the front room. There was a large fireplace, with no fire burning at the moment, understandably. The floor was made of wooden planks, with colorful thick rugs thrown atop it. The sofa and chairs were sturdy and upholstered in leather, with knitted throws folded and lying along the backs of them. She figured the beautiful yarn used to make them was a product of the family business.

Ahead of her and to the right, hallways led to other rooms. To the left, she could see a large, heavy wooden dining table and part of a kitchen.

"Let me get you something to eat," Grandpa said. "Or I can put on a pot of coffee."

Emma quickly shook her head. "Oh, no. Thank you." These people were already doing so much for her.

"I made a couple of apple pies day before yesterday," Brent said. "Surprisingly, there's still some left." He shot Cole a meaningful look.

"I'd think you would take it as a compliment when you bake things and people want to eat them," Cole said unapologetically.

Lauren stepped forward and reached for the handle on Emma's luggage. "Would you like to go to your room and get some rest?"

"I'd love to."

"The dogs will bark if anyone comes around the house," Cole said quietly.

Emma gave him a grateful nod. "Thank you, for everything." The words seemed so small in relation to all the man had done for her. But she didn't know what else to say. "Good night," she said to Grandpa and Brent. Lauren had already started down the hallway, rolling Emma's suitcase behind her.

They walked past an office, a bathroom and a den with more thickly padded furniture and knitted throws and a big TV on the wall.

"Did you knit the throw blankets?" Emma asked.

"Yes," Lauren said over her shoulder. "I knit in the winter when things slow down a little and I have the time. I do a little spinning, too, though most of that I contract out. There are a lot of people around here learning or trying to preserve some of the old ways of doing things. It's work, but it's also rewarding. And there are people who are willing to pay for good-quality hand-spun yarn, which obviously helps. We aren't a big ranch, but we're doing our best to keep things going and trying to expand little by little."

Emma appreciated the friendly chatter as they walked. On the drive over she'd started to feel as if her life was contracting into a pinpoint of intense anxiety and fear. She needed a reminder of what it was like to have her thoughts dwell on things other than the security of her family and her own battle to stay safe.

"Here's the guest room," Lauren said, flicking on a light switch. There was a large window on one wall, and Emma immediately stepped toward it to pull the curtains closed so that she wouldn't be an easy target for someone outside. So much for trying to get her thoughts away from danger.

"Sorry," Lauren said quietly. "I should have thought of that."

Emma offered her a smile and then said, "It's a beautiful room." A handmade quilt covered the double bed. A rocking chair sat in one corner with a tabby cat curled up on the cushion.

"Louie, come on." Lauren started toward the rocking chair. The cat lifted his head, opened his eyes and then slowly blinked a couple of times.

"Don't take him out of here on my account," Emma said. "I love cats and I'd like the company. I'll leave the door open when I go to bed so he can go out if he wants to."

"You'd better be sure. There's a good chance he'll climb in bed with you. Louie is a cuddler."

"I'm sure."

Lauren scratched the cat under the chin. "You be good." Then she gestured toward a narrow, partially open door inside the bedroom. "This room has its own bath with a shower. Towels are in the cabinet. There's body wash and shampoo in there."

The hospitality being offered was beyond anything Emma had expected, and it was a bit overwhelming.

"I'll go so you can get some rest," Lauren said, walking toward the hallway. "If you need anything, let us know. Good night."

"Good night." Emma sat down on the bed as Lauren closed the door behind her.

Louie got up and stretched and then jumped on the bed. Emma needed to go to sleep soon. Morning was not far away and she had to resume her attempts to find Austin. His decision to taunt the criminals and draw them out so the cops could capture them was such a terrible, misguided idea. One that could get him killed.

She should have kept a closer eye on him over the last couple of years. If she had, she would have known him better and it might have been easier to predict his behavior and find him.

Emma lay on the bed, fully clothed, resting her head on the pillow and staring up at the ceiling. Changing into pajamas and getting under the covers would make her feel too vulnerable. She needed to be ready to run at a moment's notice because anything could happen at any time. The most she could bring herself to do was kick off her shoes so they wouldn't damage the quilt.

Louie curled up beside her.

Emma had done her best to appear pulled together and calm in front of Cole and his family. But the truth was, she was still emotionally processing all of the events of the night. How many attacks could she survive? As many as she had to was the only reasonable answer. And it wasn't enough for her just to survive. She needed to take whatever risks were necessary to protect her family.

"You want to keep repairing that gate or should we just build a new one?" Cole walked up to his grandfather the next morning where John was working on strengthening a few sections of fencing at the corral. Cole carried his own cup of coffee plus one for the older man. He knew his grandpa would need a little extra caffeine after having his sleep interrupted last night.

John straightened and stretched his back before reaching for the mug. "I got the gate fixed so that it will hold for a while, but we should probably go ahead and build a new one." He took a long, lingering sip of coffee.

Cole glanced up at the clear blue sky overhead. It was still dusky-looking on the horizon and still early for most people, but not particularly early for ranch life. Even though Cole had his paramedic job with its own hours, he still found it hard to sleep in on workdays when he wasn't on the schedule at the fire station. The rhythm of getting up and getting things done as soon as there was daylight had settled into his blood at an early age and wouldn't let go.

"Is Emma awake yet?" Grandpa asked.

"Apparently she wasn't as of a few minutes ago. I didn't see her in the kitchen, and I know if she smelled coffee she'd come and get some." Nobody in his family drank the flavored coffee creamers that Emma was so fond of. The best he'd been able to do was put a bag of sugar on the counter alongside a bottle of chocolate syrup. She had to know there was milk and cream in the fridge, and a determined woman like her was bound to figure out a way to make it all work to her liking.

"So, these men that are after her, you think they might target you now, too?" Grandpa asked. "At this point they must have figured out you're helping her."

Cole shrugged. Grandpa obviously knew the answer by the way he framed the question. "I'll be careful," he said.

"See that you are."

A clanging sound came from the stables, and moments later Lauren walked out carrying a metal bucket in each hand. She grabbed a hose, rinsed the buckets and filled them with fresh water and then took them back inside. Brent led a trio of horses out of the stables and into a nearby fenced meadow.

"It's looking good out here," Cole said. When he'd returned to Cedar Lodge from his stint in the Navy, the ranch had fallen into disrepair. The horses his grandfather boarded were well taken care of, but other buildings on the property were close to tumbling down. Grandpa had been out here by himself, doing the best he could, but it had looked like the family ranch might end with him. Cole hadn't been willing to let that happen. He was grateful that Lauren and Brent had likewise seen the value of their heritage, and they'd moved to the ranch to help out. It had been slow going and expensive getting things back on track, but the investment of time and money was paying off.

Atop a nearby grassy hill, a couple of sheep bleated. Liza and Misty trotted among them, keeping an eye on things. While not trained to herd sheep, both dogs had a natural protective instinct and strong territorial drive that meant they'd bark a warning and even launch an attack if they smelled or saw animal predators nearby.

Grandpa took another sip of coffee. "You know, when I mentioned that I was looking forward to you bringing a girl home, I didn't mean like this. A woman with criminals chasing after her." The older man laughed quietly at his own edgy joke and then turned to his grandson. "But I should have known this was how it would be." His expression became more thoughtful. "You've always wanted to help people or heal them, like your mom. It's a good instinct to have."

"Emma doesn't need me to help or heal her." Cole glanced at the dogs and then back at his grandfather. "I mean, she needs our help to give her a place to stay where the thugs can't find her. But she, personally, is a strong woman who doesn't need me to fix her in any way."

It was true. And the realization struck Cole that this was something different for him. He'd dated four very nice women over the last few years, but in each case they'd been facing a tough situation in their personal life and they'd needed him to lean on until things got better. And then they'd broken up because that kind of connection by itself just wasn't enough to build a long-term relationship.

It was just now dawning on Cole that he'd chosen those kinds of situations, even if unconsciously. And now with Emma, well, things were different. And confusing. Because the more he was around her, the more he realized he just flatout liked her. Those countless conversations they'd had while working together had formed a foundation. She was smart and funny and strong. A woman he felt he could lean on if he had to. Even after finding out she wasn't exactly who she said she was. And that was a situation he'd been wary of since he was an adolescent and his mother had started telling him the truth about his father. How he had been a con man who exuded charm and trustworthiness that just wasn't real.

Cole understood why Emma hadn't been forthcoming about

her true identity. He'd been put off at first, and suspicious. But after learning her family was in a witness protection program, he realized how reasonable it had been to do that.

"Emma seems like a nice woman." John took another sip of coffee.

"She's a coworker," Cole said, mostly to remind himself. Because this new understanding of whatever relationship they had made him realize things were in danger of getting out of control between the two of them and he couldn't allow that. Cedar Lodge was a small town. They both worked for the fire department. If their relationship turned romantic, that could potentially put both their livelihoods in danger if things didn't work out. Or even if things did work out, it could be a problem working together.

"I brought her here because she needed a safe place to stay," Cole emphasized again. "That's the only reason."

His grandfather made a scoffing sound. "The both of you work in the fire department right next to the police department where you have lots of friends. I'm glad she's here, don't get me wrong, but you can't convince me there wasn't anybody else who would have helped her out if you hadn't."

Cole turned to his grandfather and lifted an eyebrow. "You taking up a new career giving romantic advice this late in life?"

John drew himself up. "I won over your grandmother. The kindest, smartest, most beautiful woman in the state of Montana agreed to marry me. So yeah, I'd say I am indeed qualified to give romantic advice."

"You make a good point."

The kitchen door of the house opened and Emma walked out. Glancing toward the corral, she spotted Cole and his grandfather. She started in their direction, coffee mug in one hand and phone in the other.

She exchanged greetings with both men before gesturing to Cole with her phone. "I've been looking for a new post from Austin, but I haven't seen one yet."

"Maybe he thought about it and realized his plan wasn't so smart." Cole quickly summarized Austin's recent activities to his grandfather, who shook his head in response.

Emma sighed heavily. "I'd like to believe my brother had a sudden burst of good sense, but I can't count on it."

Cole noted the dark circles still under her eyes. "How'd you sleep?"

She shrugged. "I was awake for a while, thinking, but I finally drifted off. Right now I've got some energy, but I don't know how long it will last. So we need to get moving."

"Okay," Cole said cautiously. "Where do you want to go?"

"Burger Bonanza. They serve breakfast sandwiches so they'll be open. I want to see if Austin is reckless enough to show up for work even after mentioning it in his social media post. He's got to need money so he might risk it. If not, well, maybe we can learn something useful from one of the other employees."

"All right." His first choice would have been to keep her at the ranch and away from danger, but it wasn't his decision to make. The kidnappers were determined to get to her. Cole would do his best to stand in their way.

Chapter Nine

"It's not only your brother who could put himself in danger by coming here," Cole said to Emma as he pulled into a parking space at Burger Bonanza. "If the kidnappers are watching this place in hopes of finding your brother, they'll obviously see and recognize you, too." He made sure to keep his tone mild because it wasn't his intention to imply she didn't know better. What he was hoping for was that she'd change her mind and let him drive her back to the ranch.

"If you have a better idea on how to find Austin, I'm listening." She turned to him.

Cole's gaze settled on her face for a moment. Her coffee-colored eyes held an expression of trust that made his heart feel like it was expanding. His breath tightened a little bit and he felt a pleasant fluttering his stomach. *Butterflies? Seriously?*

He really was falling for his work partner, and he was determined not to allow those emotions free rein for so many reasons. Not least of which was, at the moment, he needed to keep a sharp eye on their surroundings. He forced himself to break his gaze away and have a look around.

Turning back to her, he cleared his throat. "The only thing I can think of to do is go back to the apartment and talk to his buddies again. Get names and contact info for some of the other people in Austin's social circle. Maybe we can figure out which friend is helping him. While we're at it, we could look to see if Austin's car is still out front. If not, it would suggest he came by to fix the flat tire. Seems likely that before he drove away he'd take a minute to visit with Benny and Shawn."

Emma lifted her eyebrows, pursing her lips as she offered an approving nod. "I knew you'd find a way to make yourself useful."

Cole smiled in return. He really had enjoyed working with her the last couple of years. Too bad he hadn't truly appreciated that until now.

They got out of the truck and headed for the restaurant. Like so many establishments in Cedar Lodge, Burger Bonanza had started out small and expanded more recently. The original walk-up window with nearby picnic tables was available in warm weather; otherwise, there was a drive-through and an enclosed dining area.

"Let me do the talking," Emma said as they stepped inside and headed toward the order counter. "For one thing, no one's likely to find me intimidating."

Cole flashed her a half smile. "They would if they knew you." But he realized what she meant. She was a petite woman and not physically imposing.

She drew herself up, a grin playing across her lips. "Thanks for the compliment."

By the time they approached the counter, her expression had sobered. The momentary lightheartedness was gone. Once again, she appeared to have the weight of the world on her shoulders. And right now Cole wanted nothing more than to ease that burden for her.

There were a handful of customers in the dining area but it wasn't especially busy. Emma walked directly up to a young woman who looked to be in her early twenties behind the counter. She wore a denim shirt with the name Leanne embroidered on it.

"Hi, Leanne," Emma said. "My brother Austin works here and I need to speak with him for a minute."

"Austin?" Leanne glanced over her shoulder toward a pass-through into the kitchen area. "I haven't seen him. Are you sure he's working today?"

"Actually, I'm not. Has he been at work for the last few days?"

"I don't know. I generally work store opening, breakfast service and lunch prep, so I just see him now and then when he comes in early to help cover for the lunch rush."

"Is there a manager on duty I could talk to?"

"Sure."

Leanne stepped out of sight and moments later returned with a woman who appeared maybe a decade older than her following behind. She also wore a denim shirt with the name Wendy, Assistant Manager, embroidered. "How can I help you?" Wendy asked politely.

Leanne explained that Emma was here to ask about her brother.

"Austin is such a good worker and a nice young man," Wendy said. "He shows up on time and does a good job. Please don't tell me he's in some kind of trouble."

"He's not in trouble." Emma shook her head. And then she appeared to reconsider her words. "Not in trouble in the sense that he did something wrong. But some dangerous people have a grudge against him."

The front door opened and both Emma and Cole quickly turned. A couple of moms each with a small child. Not the kidnappers. Cole let out the breath he hadn't even realized he was holding. He and Emma turned back to the counter as the women and children came up behind them.

Wendy nodded toward a door at the end of the counter and then walked down and opened it, stepping into the lobby to speak more privately. "Austin called out for the day yesterday. Didn't claim he was sick, just said he couldn't come in. He did the same thing last night, only he sent a message instead of actually calling, saying he wouldn't be in to work today, either."

"Maybe some of his other coworkers know where he's been the last couple of days?" Emma said hopefully. "Perhaps we could ask them if they know anything."

Wendy looked at her for a moment. "Wait here." She went back through the door into the work and kitchen area.

"Maybe we'll get a good lead," Emma said.

Uncertain whether it would be kinder to encourage that hope or to downplay it, Cole ultimately said nothing. Seeing the spark of happy anticipation in her eyes made his heart feel like it was balancing on the edge of a precipice. If she ended up painfully disappointed, he would feel her hurt, too.

Wendy returned to the lobby. "A couple of people said they see him in Lodgepole Park now and then. And sometimes riding his skateboard nearby at Skate Trek."

Cole watched Emma's shoulders sag with disappointment and he shared the feeling.

"If I leave you my contact info, can you ask your other employees if they know anything about Austin's whereabouts when they show up for work?"

After a moment's consideration Wendy shook her head. "I don't know exactly what's going on and I don't think I should involve myself or our employees. If you want to come back just to see if he's here, that's fine. But when it comes to asking all the other employees about Austin, well, I need to ask my manager what he thinks before I do that. I don't want to step over some HR privacy boundary."

"I understand." Eyes downcast, Emma nodded. "Thank you."

Wendy went back to work and Emma stood for a moment before turning to Cole. The combination of toughness and vulnerability he saw in her eyes drew him to her. But right now she seemed so focused on what she was doing, so determined to get the job done, that reaching out with a comforting touch or hug didn't seem like the right thing to do. So instead, he asked her if she wanted a coffee while they were there. Burger Bonanza might emphasize their chili dogs and onion rings, but like any self-respecting food and beverage business in northern Montana, they offered an array of hot and cold coffee drinks.

"Yes, please," she said in response to his offer. "Double mocha with a marshmallow syrup."

Cole cringed and didn't hide it. "That's a lot of sugar."

"I know," Emma said. "That's the point. Right now I need all the caffeine and sugar-fueled energy I can get."

"You're going to sugar crash hard this afternoon."

"Not if I drink another one."

Cole sighed.

Emma glanced over her shoulder at the booths. "I'm going to go sit down."

"Probably be better if we stay together."

"Oh, right."

The windows were lightly tinted, and each of them had at least one cardboard sign attached to it advertising an item or food combo on special so it probably wouldn't be easy for anyone outside to spot them. If the kidnappers were watching the restaurant, they'd already know that Cole and Emma were there. An attack would more likely come when they walked outside. Still, staying close together struck Cole as a good idea.

They ordered their coffees and the drinks were ready just as Emma's phone chimed.

She looked at the screen. "It's Sergeant Newman, the federal witness protection liaison. I wonder what he wants."

Cole picked up both coffees so Emma could take the call. He carried them toward a corner booth away from the windows where there were no other customers seated nearby.

Emma put the call on Speaker. "Hello."

"Hey, Emma," the familiar voice came through. "Thought I'd call to see how you're holding up."

Emma looked at Cole before answering, a guarded expression on her face. "I'm doing okay," she said cautiously. "How are you?"

"Keeping busy. So, I was wondering, have you seen your brother? I'm concerned about him."

"Why exactly are you concerned about him?"

"To be blunt, I'm worried that the criminals from Royce Walker's gang who've been coming after you will come after him, too." He cleared his throat, "Look, if Austin sold them information on how to find your dad, but your dad was whisked away before the thugs could get to him, they're going to be angry. At the least, they'll want any money they paid out to him returned. Worst-case scenario, they might hurt him."

Cole watched an expression of horror cross Emma's face. He reached across the table to lightly grasp her forearm. Just to let her know he was there with her. To remind her that he had her back. Maybe to somehow give her added strength because she was going through so much.

"Are you there?" Newman asked after Emma didn't respond right away.

"Yes." Emma appeared to struggle to speak as she looked down at her phone. "I'm here."

Cole loosened his grip on her forearm and reached up to rest his hand on her shoulder. He didn't have any siblings, but he had three friends who were like brothers. He had cousins like Lauren that he was close with. He had at least an inkling of what Emma was feeling right now and it was awful.

Emma lifted her gaze to look at Cole. There were tears in the corners of her eyes and her face was red. To Cole's surprise, instead of looking scared or hopeless now, she looked angry. "Thank you for the warning about the danger my brother is facing." She directed the words, in a roughened voice, toward her phone.

"Emma, you haven't answered my question," Newman responded with a hint of reprimand. "Have you seen Austin? Do you know where he is?"

Cole wasn't wild about the deputy's tone. It was tempting to say as much, but this was Emma's battle and she was handling it just fine without Cole butting in.

"The answer to both of your questions is 'no,'" Emma said to Newman. "I haven't seen Austin, I don't know where he is, and I will tell you right now that he *did not* betray our parents. If anybody in my family said or posted something that helped the vicious criminal gang find us here in Cedar Lodge, it was done by accident. Stop trying to pin the blame for all of the horrible things that are happening on my brother."

After wiping the angry tears from her eyes, she added, "I have to go. Goodbye." Then she disconnected the call.

Cole took his hand from her shoulder, sat back and took a sip of his coffee. If she wanted to talk, she would. If she wanted to sit together in silence while she collected her thoughts, he was fine with that, too. He glanced out the windows to check the parking lot, but he didn't see anything out of the ordinary. Emma took several sips of her sugary coffee. A handful of customers had come into the restaurant while they were on the call with Sergeant Newman. None of them looked suspicious to Cole.

Emma sniffed loudly. She dug a tissue out of her purse to wipe her eyes and then her nose. "At first there was a tiny little part of me that suspected Austin might have intentionally done something impulsive and stupid to give away our family's location." She shook her head. "Now I feel so bad for having doubted him." New tears started to fall. "I feel so bad for not having made more of an effort to hang out with him the last couple of years."

She'd mentioned that same regret before, and Cole was saddened to see that it still had such a tight hold on her.

Her phone chimed. "Now, what?" she grumbled, tapping the screen.

Cole looked down and saw a notification from the social media platform where Austin had previously posted his location to try to draw out the bad guys.

"Austin's put up a new post," Emma said, her voice barely more than a whisper. "It's a picture of him at Lodgepole Park. Looks like it's on the edge of the park near the woods."

Cole was looking at the picture upside down. Austin had a bag of chips and a silver can of soda in his free hand while he snapped a selfie with the other.

"Beautiful spot to enjoy the morning near Cub Inlet before I have to go to work in an hour," Emma said, reading the post. "So fortunate to live in Cedar Lodge."

"Let's head to the police station," Cole said. Maybe the cops would find Austin before it was too late.

They got up and left the restaurant, with Cole cautiously scanning the parking lot for signs of danger before they headed for his truck. Sergeant Newman's call and Austin's post were both fresh reminders of the danger that surrounded Emma. And Cole, too, if he got caught in the crossfire.

Once again, the wait at the police station was excruciating. Chief Ellis had promised an update after his officers went to Lodgepole Park to search for Austin. Emma sat in the lobby beside Cole, her hands clasped tightly together, feeling like her stomach was being clamped in a vise. "I should have gone to the park," she finally said. "Maybe if Austin could see me, he'd talk with me and I could convince him how foolish this is." She'd phoned him many times since their last conversation, but he never picked up the call.

"I don't want to be harsh," Cole said, "but you intentionally putting yourself where the kidnappers might show up is not a great idea, either."

"I know," Emma muttered. She wasn't offended by his comment, and she knew he was right. "It just feels crummy waiting around and not doing anything."

"I get it. We both work as first responders, and we both have the drive to do something to help. It's frustrating when the most beneficial thing you can do is stay out of the way."

Terrible images popped into Emma's mind of things that could be happening at this moment. Like the thugs violently attacking Austin. Killing him, even. She couldn't seem to stop the horrifying thoughts no matter how badly she wanted to. She rubbed her fingertips against her temples, trying to ease the pounding tension headache that had a tight hold on her. She'd forgotten to take the acetaminophen tablets this morning and now her collarbone was throbbing. Probably because her whole body was pulled tight with nerves.

"Kris is a good cop," Cole said. "If there's something that needs to be done, he and his team will take care of it."

"I know."

When Emma and Cole arrived at the police department shortly after leaving Burger Bonanza, they'd learned Kris Volker was on duty. Officer Donegal had already alerted the Chief to Austin's post, and Kris had been called into Ellis's office. Kris, along with three other officers, had been directed to change into civilian clothes so they would blend in and then head to the park to search for Austin while keeping an eye out for the thugs.

Now, an hour later, Emma checked her phone yet again, thinking maybe her brother would put up something new on his social media account. Maybe he'd even call or text her to let her know the cops had shown up and the assailants had been captured.

But there was no new communication from him.

Dear Lord, please protect Austin.

She took a sip of the marshmallow mocha she'd brought with her from Burger Bonanza. It had gone cold, but it was still sugary and full of caffeine and that's what she needed.

Finally, the door to the lobby from the patrol room opened and Kris Volker, dressed in jeans and a flannel shirt instead of his usual police uniform, stuck his head out. "Come on back."

"Is he with you?" Emma asked, bounding to her feet and following him through the door. "Did you find Austin?"

Kris stopped and looked at her. "No, I'm sorry but we didn't." He turned and briskly led the way past rows of desks and toward the chief's glass-walled office.

Emma stood for a moment, doing her best to collect her colliding emotions of disappointment and despair, and then she began to follow the cop at a slower pace. Her footsteps felt heavy and her heart sank in her chest.

"Have a seat," Ellis said to Cole and Emma when they reached his office. Then he turned to Kris. "Go ahead and tell them what you told me."

Kris cleared his throat. "When the other officers and I got to the park, we fanned out and individually headed for the spot Austin indicated in his post."

"Was he there?" Emma interjected impatiently. "Did you at least see him?"

"A flash of movement a few yards away caught my eye. I thought maybe it was a reflection off the can your brother was holding in the picture, so I headed in that direction. By that time one of the other officers had caught up with me. The person I spotted, or *think* I spotted, vanished in the forest and we couldn't catch up with them." Kris shrugged. "Might have been Austin. Might have been one or both of the kidnappers. Or it might have been someone completely different."

"Maybe it was an animal," Cole said quietly. "Light filtering down through tree branches to the forest floor can play tricks with your eyes."

"That's right," Chief Ellis agreed. "Clearly Austin had the simplistic idea that the bad guys would brazenly show up to the spot that he'd posted about and it would be easy for us to grab them. Apparently theses crooks are more sophisticated than that." Ellis cleared his throat. "Detective Campbell has a team of investigators working hard to find the thugs who've targeted you. They're very busy interviewing witnesses, visiting locations to look for security video and then actually watching that video. That takes a lot of time. I don't have the staff available right now to keep responding to your brother's posts. In fact, I believe responding to your brother's postings might encourage him to keep going with that plan and that's not what we want to do."

"So you're no longer going to look for him and make sure he's okay when he posts those selfies and announces where he is and how long he's going to be there?" Emma demanded, panic clawing up her throat. "He's doing that to try and help you catch the criminals." What would she do now? Head for the locations herself if Austin kept posting them?

"Call Austin, and if he doesn't answer leave him a message summarizing what I just said," the chief responded calmly. "Let him know we tried to work with his plan and it's failed both times. Despite what you might think, as his older sister you probably have more sway over what he decides to do than you realize. Tell him it's time to knock this off. We don't have the resources to waste on something that's not going to work. We need to find these thugs before they kill somebody." He gave Emma a lingering look, as if to emphasize the danger that had been stalking her. "Tell him he's not in trouble, but we'd like to talk with him. At the very least, he should talk with you."

"Maybe he'd listen to your parents if you got them to relay the message," Cole suggested.

Emma shook her head. "I don't know how much I want to tell them about this." She'd spoken to them earlier this morning, but she'd kept her communication with them about the dangers she and Austin faced at a minimum. Her mom and dad already had enough to worry about. As a result of Royce Walker's escape, his murder trial was back on hold again, of course. But the US Marshals were confident they would find him quickly, so the prosecutor's office had asked Emma's parents to remain in Los Angeles for at least a week.

It felt to Emma like things kept going from bad to worse. Her parents were stuck in Royce Walker's home territory. Even with professionals protecting her mom and dad, there was always the possibility that vicious criminals could get past the guards. Beyond that was the fact that their lives had been completely disrupted and there was no telling how long that would last. Both of her parents worked from home, but that didn't mean they could walk away from work obligations without eventually facing financial repercussions. It was all a big mess, and as much as she wanted to fix it, she couldn't.

Cole reached for her hand and squeezed it. "We'll get through this."

She nodded. "Yes, we will." Faith and prayer had held her together so far. But Cole and his caring demeanor had helped, too. Very much.

Emma took a deep breath and got to her feet. Cole stood alongside her. "I'll try again to get Austin to stop what he's doing with these posts," she said to the chief.

"Might be best if you just hung out at the Webb family ranch where you'll be safe," Ellis replied. "Maybe you could stay out of town and let us find your brother and the kidnappers."

Emma simply nodded in response. While she didn't want to cause problems for the police, she also didn't want to give assurances she didn't intend to keep. She and Cole exchanged their goodbyes with Kris and the chief, and then they headed for the exit.

Emma understood the chief's frustration with her brother. She was frustrated and annoyed, too. But that didn't mean she would stop trying to find him before it was too late and he got himself killed.

Chapter Ten

"I don't want you to miss any more work because of me," Emma said to Cole. They'd just left the police station and were now approaching the fire station a short distance down the road. "In fact, I should apologize for dragging you into all of this," she continued. "It isn't fair that your whole life is being disrupted by my problems."

In the wake of the initial attack on Emma, both the police chief and her boss at the library had agreed to an open-ended leave of absence until her situation could be resolved. Just now, Cole had said he wanted to talk to the chief about taking more time off. As it stood, Cole was scheduled to report back to work tomorrow.

"If I didn't want to get involved, I wouldn't," Cole said as they walked through an open roll-up door into one of the cavernous fire engine bays. "Besides, if something happened to you, I could end up with a work partner who never cracked a book and had nothing interesting to talk about on slow nights."

Emma let a smile play across her lips. His teasing tone lightened her mood a little despite the dangerous threats swirling around her.

"I'll sit in the crew room while you talk to the chief," Emma said. Cole nodded and walked toward the administrative offices while Emma threaded her way between an engine and ladder truck parked in the bay and headed for the breakroom. A team of firefighters inventorying the ladder truck greeted her, and they spoke for a few minutes. Through the open doors at the back of the station, she could see another team rolling up a recently used fire hose and readying it to be packed back onto an engine.

When she reached the breakroom, she dropped down onto a couch and took out her phone to call her parents. She tapped the screen for her mom's number and the call rolled to voicemail. She left a message: "I hope you and Dad are being well-protected. Please call Austin and tell him the cops want him to stay completely off social media. Also, tell him to contact me. Thanks. Love you."

Her next call was to Austin. "Call me. *Now.* The social media posts obviously haven't worked and the cops are not going to respond to them by showing up at the location you post anymore. Placing me in the position of having to go look for you is exposing me to added danger and I don't appreciate that." She exhaled a small sigh. "Look, I'm not mad at you," she said in a softer tone. "I just want you to be okay. And I genuinely want to see you and talk to you. So call me. Bye."

What if the thugs had already gotten to him? What if that flash of movement Kris had thought he'd seen was real and it was the kidnappers taking her brother away? They could be dragging him down to their home turf in California by now. And what if they offered to set Austin free if their dad traded himself in return for the freedom of his son? It would be just like Dad to do that.

Lord, I know our times are in Your hands. I pray for Your protection and comfort for all of us. I pray for guidance and wisdom. I pray for strengthened faith.

The prayer helped to ground her. She was still afraid, still uncertain and still frustrated with her brother's foolish behavior.

But in spite of that, she now felt a sense of being upheld. She remembered that she was not on her own in all of this. Her concerns remained, but the spiraling, frantic energy of her thoughts began to settle down.

The door to the crew room opened and Cole walked in. "You didn't brew a fresh pot of coffee while you were here? *Seriously?* How are you going to get that follow-up dose of caffeine and sugar to keep you going?"

Emma turned to him and rolled her eyes. "Funny." But then she smiled and added, "So what's your work schedule?"

Cole walked around and sat beside her on the couch. "Rhonda is happy to pick up extra shifts since her daughter is a high school senior this year, and we know how expensive that can be. County Fire and Rescue is willing to stage a paramedic and EMT crew at our station house if it's needed. This is with the understanding that if your situation drags on for more than another three or four days, it will all have to be renegotiated. Maybe you'd be willing to spend more time hanging around at the ranch while I work, if need be. And then I could take time off of work to come to town with you when you have a specific lead to follow. Something along those lines."

"I don't know about just *hanging around* at the ranch," Emma said. "I can help out. I'm sure I could wrangle chickens or take the goats for a walk or something."

Cole laughed. "That would be helpful. Maybe you could frolic with the sheep, too. Keep them company. Put bows on them so they look cute."

Unaccountably, she found herself tearing up at the generousness of his offer, as well as the willingness of others to go along with it. Maybe she'd begun to indulge in a little too much self-pity. Despite everything, there was a significant blessing here to be appreciated. She had the support of her work communities here at the fire station and at the library. People employed by the county emergency services were willing to adjust where they based their services to help her while still keeping the people of Cedar Lodge covered. That was something to be thankful for.

"Do you want to get lunch?" Cole asked with a glance at Emma. "I could use something substantial to eat and I think you could, too."

She nodded. "Good idea. I am hungry." It looked like the task of locating her brother and ensuring his cooperation would be more of a marathon than the quick sprint she'd initially hoped for. Adequate meals were definitely in order to keep up her energy. She knew the police were hard at work following up on all the investigative angles related to the attacks on her. At this particular moment, she wasn't sure what *she* should be doing. But it was apparent she needed to be ready for anything.

Emma looked at the food basket in front of her holding an empty paper sandwich wrapper alongside an empty paper cup that had previously held German potato salad. Cole's suggestion that they visit her favorite deli was much appreciated. The world and her situation in it was no safer, but at least she felt a little bit stronger.

Dill Pickle Deli sat in a quiet location three blocks over from Glacier Street and the downtown area of Cedar Lodge. There was minimal foot traffic through the area, so the chance of the bad guys happening by and seeing Emma didn't seem too great. She and Cole were seated at the very back away from the windows. Nevertheless, Cole consistently watched the windows and the front door. Somehow he managed to remain vigilant while helping Emma feel relatively safe and relaxed.

"Is there anything you need to grab from your apartment before we head out of town and back to the ranch?" Cole asked.

Emma shook her head. She didn't need a particularly varied wardrobe while she was tromping around the Webb property and she could do laundry while she was there.

They left the table and Cole took their trash to a receptacle in the corner. Emma walked over to look at the desserts in a display case by the cash register, figuring the least she could do to show the Webb family her appreciation for their generous hospitality was to bring back a luscious-looking Black Forest cake.

She was waiting for Cole to come over and let her know if he thought his grandpa would prefer an apple strudel when she decided to check her phone for any notifications she might have missed over the buzz of conversation in the busy deli.

She had no missed calls or texts from Austin. The drop of disappointment gave her a hollowed-out feeling despite her recent meal. Compelled by the need to do something, she tapped the icon for the social media account where her brother had been posting. Both of the posts he'd intended to use as bait to draw out the kidnappers had some clicks of approval from Austin's friends who clearly had no idea what was really going on, along with a few vague comments such as "Enjoy the sunshine," and "Wish I had a long enough break from work to go to the park." But then Emma saw a new comment and she stared at it until Cole came up alongside her.

"Listen to what somebody commented to Austin," she said. "'Bro, while you were goofing off again I got your tire fixed. Heard you were looking to hire somebody to take care of it. Called and texted but no response and I need to get paid. Need gas money, you know? Waiting here at the Super Mart where you told me to drop it off for a little bit if you want your key back right now. Otherwise, can get it to you later.'"

Attached to the comment was a photo of Austin's car, which Emma had last seen parked outside his friends' apartment with a flat tire, now in the market parking lot with the front driver's side tire repaired.

"Looks like this was posted about fifteen minutes ago," Emma said. "The commenter's name is Lucas Rowe."

"That name sound familiar?" Cole asked.

"No. But I'm out of the loop when it comes to knowing most of Austin's friends." Lucas Rowe's account photo showed a young man about Austin's age. Emma clicked for basic biographical information on the guy. "His security settings are keeping me from seeing very much," she said. "But the account is four years old. It looks legit to me."

Cole gave her a thoughtful look. "Do you want to stay here while I go check things out and see if the car's still there? Or if Austin shows up? Maybe I can talk to Lucas and find out if he has any idea where Austin has been for the last couple of days."

Emma shook her head. "I don't want to stay here without you. I wouldn't feel safe. And if Austin's at the market and he sees me, he won't run away. He'll at least talk to me. I'm sure of it. But he doesn't know you. He's never met you. So if you approach him, there's no telling how he'll respond. I doubt he'd hang around to talk to a stranger, given the circumstances."

"Yeah, but the kidnappers might have seen this post. They could be waiting there."

"I know. And in spite of what Chief Ellis said, I'm sure Officer Donegal is at least monitoring the situation. Maybe the department will send somebody and maybe they won't." She shook her head. "I can't just wait and hope something good happens. I don't want to be foolish and walk into a potential trap of some sort, either. Maybe we could just watch the car from a distance and see if Austin shows up."

"Okay," Cole said. "Let's go."

They stepped outside and took a good look around to make certain it was safe before walking to his truck. It was a short drive to Super Mart, which was in a mixed commercial and residential section of town. It had been a small local grocery store back in the day but was now more of a snack shop with a few common household items and a well-known hot food service counter in the back where you could get everything from take-out plates of meat loaf and potatoes to deep-dish pizza.

Since it was still around lunchtime, the store was doing a brisk business and the narrow parking lot was full when Cole drove by. "I don't want to park in the lot," Cole said.

"If the thugs are waiting for us to show up, we'd be easy to spot. Plus, if things go sideways and we need to get away in a hurry, there's a greater possibility we could get blocked in by other vehicles."

"I see Austin's car!" Emma called out, her heart nearly leaping out of her chest when she spotted the vehicle. She twisted in her seat trying to get a better look and hoping to spot her brother as they continued on in the flow of traffic, but ultimately she didn't.

Cole drove around the block and came back. There weren't any openings where they could park across the street from the store. Half a block farther down the road, on the same side of the street as the store, there was a moderate-size condominium development. The store faced its own parking lot, rather than the street. That meant coming from the direction of the condos they'd be approaching the store from the backside, which seemed safer to Emma.

Cole pulled into the condo parking lot. "If we keep a low profile and approach on foot from this direction, we should be able to get close enough to Austin's car to see what's going on without being noticed." Cole grabbed a weathered hoodie from the back seat of the truck's cab and handed it to Emma. "Let's disguise you a little. Put this on. Pull the hood down to hide your face as much as you can while still being able to see enough to walk."

She slipped on the hoodie, zipped it up and pulled the top down over part of her face. The thing was so oversized on her that it felt like a dress. Cole checked the pistol he'd taken to carrying and then tucked it beneath his waistband at the small of his back beneath his shirt.

Outside of the truck, Emma took a fortifying deep breath. She'd faced danger several times over the last few days, but she had in no way gotten used to it. Nerves tingled uncomfortably across the surface of her skin and her stomach twisted with anxiety and fear. She was scared for herself, scared for her brother and scared for Cole. Had it been wrong of her to allow Cole to put himself in danger on her behalf? She mentally shoved aside the question. It was too late to change anything now.

They walked from the asphalt to the sidewalk and then headed toward the store.

Emma nervously glanced at a couple of people on the sidewalk heading in her direction, both of them carrying Super Mart take-out packages, but they passed by uneventfully. Then the sudden growl of a car engine caught her attention and her body tensed as she got ready to run for cover. But when she looked over at the street, the driver of the car looked unfamiliar and he didn't seem to be paying any attention to her as he tried to maneuver his vehicle into a parking spot that had just opened up alongside the curb.

She took a deep breath, moved her shoulders a little to loosen them and tried to calm down. If Austin were here she would find him, they would leave together with Cole, and at least one worrisome aspect of her life would finally be over.

She turned her attention to the sidewalk in front of her again. The only person approaching her was a young woman with long dark hair pushing a stroller with one hand and holding an ice cream cone with the other. Hardly a threat.

There was a parklike stretch of grass and shrubs and a few trees at the end of the condominium property where it abutted the Super Mart property. As the woman drew near, Emma stepped off the sidewalk onto the grass to let her and her child pass by. In an instant the woman flung aside the stroller and her ice cream and grabbed Emma by the arms, dragging her backward. The man Emma had noticed parking at the curb a few moments ago was out of his car in a flash and launching himself at Cole before Cole could draw his weapon.

Forced to take multiple steps backward, Emma got tangled in the stroller lying on its side, which she could now see held only empty blankets, and she fell. By the time she righted herself the woman had let go of one of Emma's arms and drawn a gun, pressing it now at the back of Emma's neck. "Stand right here," the woman ground out her words. "If you fight with me I'll kill you."

A car barreled down the street toward them before braking with a loud squeal. For a few seconds Emma hoped it might bring help, but her heart sank when she saw Ponytail Guy sitting behind the wheel and Bald Guy in the passenger seat. They must be working with the criminals who'd just taken Cole and Emma by surprise.

Heart thundering in her chest, Emma shifted her gaze to Cole. He was fiercely punching the creep who'd jumped him, although the assailant appeared to be giving as good as he got in return. Trembling with fear, Emma knew that once Ponytail Guy and Bald Guy jumped out of their car and joined the fight, it would be all over for Emma and Cole. She would be taken hostage and for all she knew Cole might be killed. No way would she let that happen.

Angry determination fueled a shot of energy that surged through her body. She twisted and jabbed her fist at the woman holding on to her, obviously taking the attacker by surprise as she didn't throw up any kind of defensive move before Emma's punch connected with her jaw. Moving on instinct, barely thinking before taking desperate action, Emma grabbed a fistful of the woman's hair and yanked it downward while at the same time grabbing the attacker's gun and twisting her hand and wrist in a desperate attempt to force the woman to drop the weapon.

In return for her efforts, Emma got kicked hard at the side of her knee, causing her to lose her balance and fall again, but this time the attacker fell with her. Looking beside her she saw the woman's gun on the ground, but before Emma could crawl to it the assailant pinned her face-down so she couldn't move. Emma heard gunshots fired in the direction she'd last seen Cole. Terrified that he'd been struck, she turned to look in his direction. At the same time she felt the attacker who was holding her down shift her weight as if she were reaching for her gun in the grass. Emma quickly took advantage of the situation to shove the woman off her, roll aside and then scramble to her feet. Her head was swimming. In the blur of movement and color, she recognized Cole with his gun drawn. She also saw people coming from the direction of the store. She heard a sound that might have been a siren but she wasn't sure.

Unsteady on her feet, she hesitated in the moment of confusion and disorientation and felt two hands grasp her ankles and yank hard until she fell forward and was on the ground again. In the next instant she was being dragged across the grass, toward the street and the car waiting with the thugs to grab her and drive her away. Emma screamed and kicked and tried to twist around so she no longer had her face in the grass. The dragging stopped and something hard, like maybe a gun, struck her on the side of the head. Stunned, she fought to stay conscious.

She heard gunshots again, this time coming from Cole's direction instead of toward it. The woman who'd been dragging her seemed to give up on the job. The sound she'd heard in the distance was definitely sirens and they were growing louder. She heard running footsteps on the sidewalk and slamming car doors and then the roar of a single car engine as it sounded like the two attackers had gotten into the vehicle with Ponytail Guy and Bald Guy before it sped away.

"Hey," Cole said softly. He was now kneeling in the grass by her head.

"Don't worry, I'm all right," Emma said, though her voice was shaky and weak and she didn't think she sounded at all convincing. She began shoving herself to a sitting position.

"Don't move," Cole cautioned.

"We're not at work, so you're not my boss."

She heard him laugh quietly. When she turned to get a look

at him, she was relieved to see that he appeared to be okay. "You didn't get shot."

"No," he said. "The baldheaded attacker aimed at me, but he missed."

"Hey, are you two all right?" A stranger came up to them, but after taking a moment to focus her eyes, Emma could see that he was wearing a policeman's badge on a thick lanyard, even though he wasn't dressed in a uniform. Probably an undercover cop. She didn't recognize him.

"I'm okay," Emma said, getting to her feet. "I'll just have a headache for a while."

Two cop cars pulled up to the curb and silenced their sirens. Kris Volker and another officer hurried over to them. The undercover cop gave the patrol officers the specifics on the vehicle the four attackers had escaped in, as well as descriptions of the assailants. The other vehicle used by the assailants had been left behind. Volker relayed the information over his radio and then he and the other patrol officer left to try to chase down the criminals' car.

"Officer Donegal saw the comment on your brother's post and she thought it seemed suspicious," the undercover cop said to Emma. "There wasn't time to prep anything elaborate or put together any kind of surveillance team, but Chief Ellis had me come over to Super Mart and watch for a little while in case something significant happened."

Emma smiled faintly. It looked as if the police chief had changed his mind about reacting to Austin's posts. Or at least about reacting to the comment on the most recent one.

"Apparently somebody saw your altercation out here and called it in. I didn't actually see it. I was watching the front of the store and keeping an eye on your brother's car to see who might be inside it or who might approach it."

"Did you see anybody?" Emma asked.

The cop shook his head. "No. The chief is sympathetic to what's going on with your brother. But the only reason he had me respond to this comment today was because I happened to be in the station and available." The cop gestured toward the street where the latest criminal's car remained. "So, looks like there are at least four thugs determined to come after you now."

"It does." Emma nodded her aching head in agreement.

This had obviously been a setup. Whether the commenter Lucas Rowe was legitimate and the thugs had just happened to see his comment, or if the comment itself was fabricated by Royce Walker's criminal gang, she didn't know. Perhaps it had been a ruse with the intention of drawing out Austin, herself, or possibly the both of them.

Just when she thought things couldn't get worse, they did. Every time. She wanted out of the nightmare her life had become. She was furious with her brother for making things so much worse despite his good intentions. Even so, there was no way she'd leave Cedar Lodge to escape the danger without him. She glanced at Cole, who was talking with the undercover officer. When she did find Austin, and the time came for them to leave town for a safe location, it would break her heart when she had to say goodbye to Cole.

Chapter Eleven

"I have to do *something*," Emma insisted. "And going back to the apartment to talk to Austin's friends again is the only thing I can think of."

"Don't you want to go back to the ranch and lay low for a while?" Cole didn't want to sound pushy, but that was precisely what he wanted her to do in the aftermath of the attack outside Super Mart. Ultimately, however, what she would do next was her decision to make.

"I want to go back to the ranch and rest, believe me. But not just yet."

The two of them were sitting in Cole's truck still parked at the condominium parking lot. The undercover cop had taken their statements so at least they didn't have to worry about going back to the police station to follow up on that. It was beyond unnerving to know that there were now at least four thugs trying to grab Emma. The fact that they hadn't been able to gain complete control over her and spirit her away was due in large part to Emma's determination to fight back with all that she had when they came after her.

The criminals' getaway car had been found abandoned roughly twenty-five minutes after the attack. Of course it had been reported stolen, but maybe there would be finger-prints inside that could be used to identify the attackers and perhaps that could somehow help the cops locate them. Cole was willing to lean into hope because right now that was about all they had.

"Austin's car had been parked right outside the apartment building," Emma said, interrupting his thoughts. "Benny and Shawn must have seen something. Maybe they saw Austin and talked to him. Maybe they saw Lucas and talked to him when he showed up to repair the tire. Assuming he's a real person."

They still had no clear answer regarding Lucas and whether he was actually a friend of Austin's or he was just a false on-line identity the Walker gang used when they needed one.

"All right, let's go talk to Benny and Shawn again." Cole started up the engine and drove onto the street. They arrived at the apartment building a few minutes later.

"Maybe I should wait at the back door in case Austin's in there and he tries to run away," Emma said as they parked.

"I think not." Cole took a look around. "It would be better if we stayed together."

"Okay, you're probably right."

He glanced over and Emma was rubbing the area around her collarbone. "If you keep getting jumped, that bone bruise is never going to heal."

"It's more annoying than painful." She gave him a half smile. "It will be one more thing to yell at my brother about when I finally catch up with him. Would be nice if that hap-pened within the next few minutes."

"Hopefully at least one of the guys will be home. I wouldn't count on Austin being here."

"I don't see any security cameras," Emma said as they ap-proached the apartments. She glanced at the building and then over at the spot in the parking lot where Austin's car had pre-viously been parked.

"Excuse me." Cole stepped in front of Emma as they approached the door and then he knocked on it. If someone came out swinging, or shooting, he wanted to be a layer of protection between the assailant and Emma.

Feeling edgy and impatient after getting assaulted outside the Super Mart, he waited just a few seconds before knocking on the door again, a little more forcefully this time.

"I'm coming," a voice called out and then the door was yanked open. Benny stood there with headphones on, but he'd slid the earpiece away from one of his ears so he could hear better. "You guys are back," he said in a friendly tone. "What's up?"

"Is my brother here?" Emma demanded, pushing past Cole and inviting herself into the apartment without waiting for an answer.

There wasn't much Cole could do other than follow her in and stay close by her side.

Emma barreled through the small living room to a narrow door beside the kitchen that led to a tiny unfenced back patio. She shoved the door open and stepped outside, looking around. By now Cole was right beside her. A narrow strip of grass stretched across the ground behind the apartments. Cole and Emma looked in both directions.

"I don't see anyone," Cole said, assuming they were looking for Emma's brother. He looked down. "Doesn't appear that the grass has recently been stomped on."

Emma nodded that she'd heard him, and then hurried down the stretch of lawn toward the street for a look anyway. Cole went with her. He understood the compulsion to see things for yourself when you were worried. After they stood for a moment and she looked up and down the street a couple of times, she turned to him. "Guess you're right. He wasn't here."

Cole nodded. "Let's go back and talk to Benny."

They returned to the apartment's back door where Benny stood waiting, his headphones removed, a quizzical expression on his face. "Why would you think I'd hide Austin?"

he asked as Cole and Emma stepped back inside and Benny closed and then locked the door behind them. "After you came by last time, I started keeping a closer eye on the local news. I know you've been attacked. I *really* get it that Austin must be in serious danger."

"Have you gotten any ideas of where he might be staying?" Cole asked.

Benny shook his head. "No. I've talked with a few friends and nobody's seen him."

"Where's Shawn?" Emma asked, looking around.

"Working. Help desk at Montana Computer Source."

"Have you been here all day?"

Benny nodded. "I work from home. Medical billing. Not always exciting, but the pay is good and I don't have to deal with irate customers like Shawn does."

"Did you see who came and got Austin's car?"

"Somebody got his car?" Benny raised his eyebrows. "That's news to me."

"So you didn't see anybody?" Cole jumped in. "Nobody knocked on the door, maybe asked for a key to the car?"

Benny frowned and shook his head.

"Do you know someone named Lucas Rowe?" Emma asked. "He posted something on Austin's social media account today about coming by to repair Austin's flat tire for him. Do you know anything about that?"

"I don't have any friends named Lucas. I don't know if Austin does."

"Being tech guys I'm surprised you two don't have security cameras," Cole said, not certain if he trusted the guy. Maybe he was just good at acting friendly and helpful.

Benny pointed at a couple of small cameras on shelves in the living room. "We turn these on when nobody's home. We might buy outside ones eventually, but there haven't been any break-ins around here since we moved in. Both of us are trying to save money for some better furniture and maybe a trip to Hawaii." He shrugged. "Neighbors might have cameras."

Emma sighed heavily. "Thanks, Benny."

"Look, if you want to check in the closets and under the bed to see if Austin's here you can. He's not, but if it'll make you feel better, be my guest."

Emma shook her head. "That's all right. I believe you."

"Well, I'm worried about him, too, you know. I've called and texted him a few more times but got nothing in response. I'm sure you saw the social media stuff he supposedly posted. I didn't respond to it because it seemed weird and out of character for him. I kind of thought his account had been hacked."

Emma didn't explain the situation with Austin's social media so Cole didn't talk any further about it, either.

After they left the apartment, Cole turned to Emma. "Do you want to knock on the neighbors' doors and see if they have some security video?"

She shook her head. "I think I'll send a text to Kris Volker and see if he wants to come by and talk to the neighbors. I doubt they'd want to cooperate with us very much. I'd be suspicious if some stranger showed up at my door asking for video footage, so I wouldn't blame them. But maybe they'd talk to the police. Right now I'm starting to feel pretty tired and I'd like to go back to the ranch. Seems like everything's catching up with me."

"Sorry you didn't get to yell at your brother in person," Cole teased her as they got into the truck.

She smiled weakly in return. "I can call him and yell at him over the phone even if I'm just leaving a recording. That will probably be therapeutic enough."

"Okay."

"I'd like to go by my apartment to get my SUV and take it out to the ranch since it looks like I'll be staying there for a little longer."

"All right."

Cole couldn't help noticing how sad and exhausted she looked. It was a miserable feeling not being able to make things better for her. And it was a frightening and unsettling feeling knowing another attempt at kidnapping Emma was inevitable, and the attackers—all *four* of them now—were still at large.

"Let me make dinner tomorrow night," Emma said after the evening meal at the ranch. *Assuming I'm here and not out pursuing a lead on finding my brother.*

Lauren and Brent, who had made tonight's dinner, both uttered mild exclamations of protest. "You don't have to do that," Brent said. "Lauren and I both enjoy cooking."

"And I enjoy eating." Grandpa laughed at his own joke and slapped his hand down on the kitchen table. "Those stuffed bell peppers were delicious."

They were all in the cozy dining room beside the kitchen, seated at the sturdy, aged oak table. There were family photos plus decorative objects on the walls, along with oil lamps and candles on the shelves that gave Emma the impression the power probably went out fairly often in rough weather. Even with a backup generator, smaller sources of light could come in handy while going through the steps to get the generator going.

There were also plenty of books jammed onto shelves in the dining room, as well as most other rooms in the house. The Webb family like to read. Emma had already been approached about offering suggestions on good books, and she'd been happy to help.

"I'll probably be around all or most of the day tomorrow," Emma pressed on with her topic. "Planning a nice dinner will give me something to do. It will also offer me at least one small way to repay your kindness."

The family again started up with their polite protests.

"Please don't tell me you're going to make station-house chili," Cole said in a joking tone of complaint. "I've had enough of that to hold me for a while."

Emma indulged in an affronted lift of her chin. "I'll make something fascinating and you'll love it."

"You've seen the storehouse of food we keep around here," Grandpa said. "Feel free to make use of any of it."

Emma grinned at him. "Thank you."

On their arrival back at the ranch, Cole had brought up the idea of Emma taking a day off to rest and recover from all she'd been through while he worked an eight-hour shift. She'd rebuffed the idea at first, saying that it made her feel as if she were giving up on finding Austin. But in the end, she admitted she didn't actually have any specific new plan for how to find him and staying at the ranch to rest and recover might be a good idea after all.

Everyone started to get up from the table, and Emma quickly set about helping to clear the plates.

"I can take care of this," Cole told her when they ended up together in the kitchen. "It's my turn to do them. I just need to hand-wash a couple of pans and put the rest in the dishwasher."

"All right," Emma said, grabbing a dish towel. "You wash the pans and I'll dry."

When they'd returned from town, Cole had gone out to help his grandpa repair a gate. Brent and Lauren had spent a couple of hours filling online orders and packaging their beautifully dyed wool yarn to ship out the next morning. Emma knew there was more work to get done after dinner while there was still daylight, most of it having to do with tending the livestock. The Webb family worked hard all day, and while Emma hadn't quite known how to help earlier, she figured tomorrow she could feed and water the animals if someone told her exactly what to do.

Cole scraped the plates clean and set them in the washer, then rolled up his sleeves and filled the sink with hot, soapy water. It felt good for Emma to have something physical and practical to do to help take her mind off her brother. And her parents. The last she'd heard from them, the authorities had told her mom and dad they believed they were close to finding Royce Walker. Maybe it was fact and maybe it was wishful thinking. They were still being afforded round-the-clock protection, so the possibility that Walker or one of his thugs would come after her dad seemed remote, but it was not completely out of the realm of possibility.

Cole washed a pan and handed it to Emma to dry. It was warm to the touch, as were Cole's fingertips as they brushed against hers. Her heart began to beat faster. Cole looked at her, she caught his gaze, and he didn't turn away for several lingering moments that had Emma holding her breath.

The paramedic had been impressive from the very first time she'd seen him working. She'd been a volunteer EMT back then, and she'd been added to his ambulance to assist on the response to a collision out on the state highway involving a semi and multiple passenger vehicles.

It had been bad. She'd seen Cole in action, watched him saving lives and making critical decisions under incredible pressure. Intense and focused, but also calm and relatively cool at the same time. She'd admired him then, and later when she'd gone from volunteer to part-time paid fire department employee, she'd enjoyed working with him. But he'd always been professional to the point of being aloof at times, which was fine. He was eight years older than her. Was a combat veteran. It wasn't like they'd had anything in common beyond working together. She hadn't been romantically attracted to him. But now, things had changed.

Working beside him and doing something as mundane as washing dishes had her thinking about how she'd gotten used to being around him, not as distracted coworkers, but as two people who were connected on a deeper level. People who really were connecting with each other and becoming a team, though the word *team* seemed too tepid and emotionless.

For the longest time Emma had been afraid to develop a true, deep romantic relationship. Her identity had been fake.

She'd been living a lie in a way, and how could she keep that from someone she truly cared about? When and if they learned the truth, how could they not feel betrayed and wonder what else she'd kept hidden from them?

But now, well, there was no denying that it was horrible how her family had been thrown into danger and disarray with their new identities and location being uncovered. But it also meant she wouldn't have that burden of holding back a big secret from Cole. Maybe she could dare to want a personal relationship with him. And there was so much about his recent behavior that made her think he felt that way about her.

"It's strange to realize that I've known you for years, worked countless shifts with you, but I didn't really know you until now," Emma ventured. It wasn't like they'd had much opportunity to talk about themselves on a personal level over the last few days. They'd been busy keeping themselves alive while trying to track down her brother. And it was clear that Cole was in danger now, too. The bad guys had to see him as a threat. Never mind an obstacle to them easily grabbing Emma and dragging her off to a situation she didn't want to think about.

Cole glanced at her over his shoulder, his hands still in the soapy water washing another pan. "My work life is separate from my personal life. I like to keep it that way."

"Well, that has certainly changed," Emma countered, making sure to add a lighthearted, teasing tone to her comment. While at the same time realizing that she didn't feel at all lighthearted about the topic at hand. That topic being the possibility of the two of them continuing on as friends after this horrible situation with Royce Walker's thug employees was resolved. Hopefully with Walker recovered by the US Marshals service and the criminal and his gang members all locked up in prison where they belonged.

"You're in danger," Cole said, still not looking directly at her. "I'm going to do everything I can to make sure nothing happens to you. I'd do that for anybody."

The hope that had started to well up in her heart began to deflate a little. But then she thought of the moments they'd shared. The gazes that had lasted longer than they would have if either of them were not particularly important to the other. The embraces that had likewise lingered to the extent that Emma had been sure they'd meant something. They'd absolutely meant something to her.

The feeling of closeness right now as they washed dishes together was something new and different. Something that seemed to be strengthening a connection between her and Cole. She'd stood with Cole washing dishes countless times in the breakroom at the fire station when crew members working a shift through dinner had come together to make and share a meal. They'd talked and joked and she was certain her fingers must have brushed his at some point and it had meant nothing.

But now there was *something* between them. She was sure of it.

For a moment she considered dropping the subject for now. Maybe pressing Cole for an acknowledgment that he felt something too would ruin things.

No.

Emma Burke, who'd been forced to take on the surname of Hayes to protect herself and her family, was tired of hiding and holding back. She'd done that since she was fifteen and was relocated in Cedar Lodge. She had friends to hang around with growing up but she hadn't really had the *close* friendships she'd craved because she had such a big secret in her life. That secret had been a roadblock to romantic relationships because she just couldn't see herself building a long-term relationship on a lie. She hadn't been able to stop herself from worrying about what would happen if she were to keep the lie and marry someone and later they learned the truth.

What would happen to the trust that had existed between them? Would it be forever broken?

Enough with hiding. Enough with worrying about what someone would think. Despite all the horribleness going on with these terrifying attacks, at least she was free to be herself now. Free to speak without having to second-guess everything.

"Why are you so afraid to get close to anybody?" Emma boldly asked. Admittedly, and rather selfishly, she wanted to know why he didn't want to admit that he'd gotten emotionally close to *her*. Because she was sure that he had. But now she found herself thinking about how he was at the fire station. He'd been friendly enough with her, at times. But then other times he would seem to withdraw. She'd just figured it was a personality quirk. Hadn't thought all that much about it. Until now.

"You already know the reason why I've stayed out of serious relationships," she said. "Having a secret identity will do that. What's your reason?"

Cole stilled, leaving his hands in the soapy water. He looked out the window over the sink and didn't say anything for a while.

Emma's heart sank. She'd obviously struck a nerve. She'd hurt this man who'd only tried to help her. She'd been so caught up in herself and what she wanted that she hadn't bothered to consider that an obviously strong man would still have feelings. And a right to privacy.

"I'm sorry," she said, her emotions now a whir of pain and regret. She'd pushed too hard. At this point she wasn't certain which was more painful, realizing that she'd misread the situation and he wasn't interested in her romantically, or knowing that she'd hurt and possibly embarrassed a very kind man. A person had the right to keep their own confidence. She should know that better than anybody.

"I'm talking too much," she added lamely.

"What else is new?" Cole responded.

Emma let out a breath, relieved to hear the familiar teasing tone in his voice, though it sounded a bit forced.

He handed her the last pan and then dried his hands. "We work together, Emma. When we're on the ambulance, I'm your supervisor. That's a problem when things get too personal. I don't have a great romantic track record, and I don't know that I have it in me to try again. I like my life the way it is and I'm not looking for anybody. I'm sorry."

Emma wanted to argue every point, but she bit her tongue. Apparently she had misinterpreted his actions. She'd read too much into them. She'd only *thought* those moments were meaningful. They hadn't actually been. Well, they'd only been meaningful for *her*.

Cole walked to the door leading outside from the kitchen, grabbed a cowboy hat off a hook on the wall, and then put the hat on his head. "I'm going to go help Lauren and Brent and Grandpa get the animals settled down for the night. Why don't you kick back in the living room and rest for a while."

His tone was different now. Distant, and somewhat like he sounded when they were at work. Which made the whole situation more painful because it proved to her that they had reached a point where they were closer and more open with each other and now that was gone.

Hugging her stomach, Emma headed toward the living room. Already, she felt a severing of the connection between them. How would it feel to be around him now that things had changed? And how was she supposed to let go of the hope that they'd continue to spend as much time together as possible after she found Austin, and the thugs were captured?

She blinked back tears and wiped at her eyes, determined to clear away every trace of her sadness before anyone returned to the house. She was getting ahead of herself worrying about her future with Cole, anyway. She might not even have a future, period. She and Austin were still in danger. Another attack could come at any time. It was foolish of her to assume that none of the attacks against her could be successful. Or fatal if she got caught in the crossfire. Turning her attention away from danger and toward imagining a future with Cole wasn't something she could afford to do, anyway. It was time to pull herself back together and carry on.

Chapter Twelve

Cole sat at a desk at the fire station the next day and tapped the send button for the medical supply reorder he'd just completed. It was early afternoon and after a busy morning things had slowed down enough that he had time to take care of some administrative work.

As soon as his restock was digitally on its way, however, his thoughts turned back to Emma. He'd been thinking about her since he left the ranch early this morning. In fact, he'd been thinking about her pretty much all the time since he'd stumbled upon her abandoned car beside the lake three days ago.

Their conversation in the kitchen yesterday evening had been unsettling and it still weighed on his mind.

Up to that point he'd managed to convince himself that he wasn't *really* romantically interested in her and that she wasn't seriously interested in him. The two of them were simply caught up in a highly emotional situation with her life in danger and him doing his best to protect her, and that kind of situation was bound to stir up emotions. But those emotions would be fleeting.

Maybe that was true. But then again, maybe it wasn't.

Maybe the feelings of attraction and connection she'd awakened in him had more substance than he'd wanted to admit.

It had been hard to fall asleep last night as he'd found himself questioning what he personally wanted out of life for the first time in ages. At some point he must have stopped imagining a future with a wife and children. Emma had proven to be the strong kind of woman a man could rely on. There was no escaping that she was attractive. She had a faith life that was similar to his own.

So what was holding him back? The work situation, with him being her supervisor, was a significant problem. But what else? He didn't want to make the same mistake his mother had and marry someone who faked a depth of character and trustworthiness they didn't truly possess. But did he really want to use that as an excuse to never take the chance of falling in love again? Was that really something he wanted, or was he just continuing with it because it had become habit and it was easier to keep his distance?

He glanced at his phone on the desk, thinking about calling her just to make sure everything was all right. But she or Grandpa would call if there was a problem, and he needed to get his focus back on work. It would probably be better to wait until he could talk to her in person after the end of his shift, though he had no idea what he would say. He figured he'd know when he saw her. Maybe by then he'd be clearer on what he wanted.

He'd been updating the departmental calendar with the next round of free basic first aid courses to be offered to the community when his phone rang. It was Emma.

He tapped the screen. "Everything okay?"

"Better than okay!" she replied happily. "I heard from Austin! He finally called me. And that's why I'm calling you. I'd like to invite him here to your ranch if that's okay. I know technically it's your grandfather's place, but I wanted to talk to you about it first."

Cole felt a stirring of unease in the back of his mind. "Why is Austin reaching out to you now when he didn't do it before? What's prompting this?"

"He just found out about the assault outside Super Mart and that I was in the middle of it all. He says he's done with those stupid social media posts. He doesn't know anybody named Lucas Rowe and he didn't make any arrangement to get his tire repaired. So it turns out that actually was a setup to draw *me* out so they could try to grab me. The police impounded his car while they check for fingerprints or any other useful evidence that might have been left behind."

So the criminals who'd been hunting Emma were not just relentless, they were clever and technically sophisticated, too. That didn't bode well.

"How is it that Austin just now found out about the Super Mart attack?" Cole asked. "I thought he was following his own social media posts and he was on top of things."

"He's been staying with a friend in their family's fishing cabin and that friend drove him into town to take the photos and make the social media posts. Phone reception where he's been staying is almost nonexistent."

That was believable. Lack of phone connectivity around Cedar Lodge was a topic almost as common as the constantly changing weather.

"Why does he need to come to the ranch? Why can't he remain at the cabin where he's been staying?"

"Because I want to see him," Emma said, sounding confused or maybe even offended by his question. "And I want us to spend time together while we figure out what to do next. Where we should go."

She might leave. Cole's stomach knotted.

"You're safe at the ranch," he said. "I don't want to take any chances on having that change."

"What do you mean?" she demanded. "Do you not trust him? Do you think Sergeant Newman was right from the start?

Do you really believe Austin sold out my family and he'll sell me out to the kidnappers as well?"

Cole wasn't sure what he thought. He only knew he didn't want to take any risks with Emma's safety. "What if the thugs have gotten to Austin and they're using him to get to you?" Cole asked. "What if they had a gun pointed at him while he made the call to you just now? I think we need to slow down with this. Take smaller steps."

There was silence on the other end of the phone. "Talk to me, Emma," Cole finally said.

"I'm thinking." She sounded tense, but no longer angry. "I want to see him as soon as I can, but you're right and we need to be cautious. Maybe I could meet up with him someplace in town. Like a coffee shop. If I got there first, I could see if he showed up alone or not. If things seem okay, we can head out to the ranch from there. Or he and I could find someplace else to stay. I will not leave him on his own."

"I still think that sounds dangerous." Cole rubbed his forehead while he thought for a moment. "How about I meet Austin here at the fire station. It's a public place with other people around, which is a good start. I can talk to him and if everything seems okay, I'll drive him to the ranch. I can watch for anyone tailing us along the way."

"Works for me. I'll call him to set it up."

"And I'll call Grandpa to make sure he's okay with your brother staying at the ranch. I'm pretty sure he will be."

"Thank you," Emma said.

"Right," Cole said, not wanting to accept her gratitude because he wasn't certain that bringing Austin to the ranch was a good idea. But in the end, what Emma did was completely her choice. At least if there was trouble at the ranch, Cole would be fighting to protect Emma in familiar territory. He just hoped this reconciliation with Austin was not a dangerous setup that would lead the criminal gang members directly to Emma.

* * *

"I'm so happy to see you and know that you're okay!" Emma hugged her brother while continuing to ignore his tearful apologies.

"I'm so sorry, Emma," Austin sobbed into her shoulder. "I thought putting up the posts was a good idea, but it was stupid. I never meant for you to get hurt."

"I'm all right. I got tackled in that little park behind Super Mart, something I *never* imagined would happen to me, but I'm okay," she said in a teasing tone, hoping to lighten her brother's misery and regret.

In the midst of his crying, she heard a little bit of a laugh and it eased the ache in her own heart. She'd been so frustrated with Austin, but she hadn't blamed him. Not for anything. At the end of the day, the fault for all of the terrible things that had been happening lay with the murderous criminal Royce Walker. He committed the horrible crime that set all of these recent attacks in motion.

Austin released her and stepped back. Emma took another good look at him. They were in the living room at the Webb family ranch where he and Cole had just arrived. Of course her brother didn't look hugely different from the last time she'd seen him a couple of weeks ago, but even in the soft light of the ranch house she noticed the worry and exhaustion in his face. And she noticed when hugging him that he felt thinner, like he'd lost weight.

"Welcome to our home." Cole's grandfather stepped up to introduce himself and shake hands with Austin before moving on to introduce Lauren and Brent.

Austin offered up a nervous, self-conscious smile. "Hi."

"So, who exactly is this friend you've been staying with for the last three days?" Emma asked, leading the way to a sofa and gesturing at Austin to sit down beside her.

"You remember my friend Dave?" he asked hopefully.

Sadly, she did not. Maybe Dave had been at her parents' house with Austin at some point and they'd been introduced and she hadn't really paid much attention. "I'm afraid I don't."

His hopeful expression dimmed.

Emma had paid attention to her own interests and ignored his, using the five-year age difference between herself and Austin to rationalize her detachment. *Dear Lord, please forgive me.* She was determined to change her attitude and never let herself behave that way again.

"You were staying with Dave?" she prompted.

"Yeah. His family has a cabin up on Sawtooth Ridge. He told his parents he wanted to go up and do some hiking and fishing and they were cool with that and let him have the key. He didn't tell them about me, though."

Emma nodded. "Tell me, were you at Mom and Dad's house when I was there? The day they had to leave? I saw somebody in the backyard and later I thought it might have been you."

Austin raised his eyebrows. "It might have been me. Man, if you were there, I wish I'd known." He shook his head. "I'd been crashing with Benny and Shawn for a couple of days and got tired of it. My car had a flat tire so I walked to the house. When I got there, I could see the front door had been kicked open." His voice had become shaky with emotion and he cleared his throat. "I called out for Mom and Dad. Nobody answered and I went inside. The house was empty and I was sure that Royce Walker's people had finally located them after all these years. I went out in the backyard, just frantic and wanting to believe I was wrong and I'd find them outside pulling weeds or something.

"When I heard somebody in the house I was scared that the Walker gang members had returned for some reason after already grabbing Mom and Dad. I took off running and didn't look back." Austin drew a deep breath and ran his fingers through his hair. "I kept calling Mom and Dad and finally I got through to Mom. While I was calling and neither of them was answering, I kept praying they were all right and thinking about how this was probably my fault. Sorry I took so long to return your calls, but after I got your first message and knew you were okay I was more focused on our parents. And on figuring out what I should do next."

Emma thought back to Newman's accusations that Austin had sold out their parents. The deputy had made it sound as if he and his witness protection task force associates had a fleshed-out theory regarding Austin betraying their parents and that they had some kind of actual evidence. But she'd never seen that evidence. Never heard it described specifically or in detail. In her heart she'd trusted Austin, but seeing and hearing him now, how could anyone doubt his sincerity? She certainly didn't.

"Why do you blame yourself?" she pressed. "Is there some specific post that haunts you or was it just the random messages or comments you posted?"

Austin twisted his hands in his lap. "When we first moved here when I was ten, I was just so mad. I was supposed to cut myself off from all my friends. I was supposed to get used to being in cowboy country when I was just starting to skateboard." He looked at Cole and his family. "No offense. I've got nothing against cowboys now. But I didn't fit into all of the cowboy lifestyle as a kid."

"No offense taken," Cole said. Like the rest of his family, he was seated in the living room, listening to the conversation while a fragrant pot of coffee finished brewing in the kitchen.

Austin turned back to his sister. "I broke the rules. I contacted my friends down in California. I chatted with them while we played online games and I made snarky comments about where we live. But I never mentioned the actual name of Cedar Lodge. Eventually I outgrew all that, but as I got older it stuck in the back of my mind. When I got a little smarter I felt really bad. It was stupid of me. When I saw our front door kicked in and Mom and Dad were missing, all that old regret and guilt came flooding back. I assumed it was all my fault and that somehow I'd put our lives in danger so it was my responsibility to fix things."

Emma leaned back into the couch and wrapped an arm around his shoulder. Which felt awkward, since he was quite a bit taller than her. "Even after I told you that Mom and Dad had been in contact with our relatives, you still blamed yourself?"

Austin turned to her. "Yes. I know what I did, and it just seems more likely that I'm the one who messed up and said something that I shouldn't have, rather than our grandparents."

"Turns out creating a new identity and cutting yourself off completely from everybody in your past isn't easy for anybody," Emma said. "Not even for adults and not even when you know it could help save your life. Who knows if what you posted caused all this trouble or whether it's happened because one of our grandparents mentioned something to somebody and that's how the Walker people found us? However it happened, I know Mom and Dad don't want you to blame yourself." She squeezed her arm around his shoulder. "We need to call them tonight."

"Okay." He turned to her. "What happens next?"

"So, Royce Walker escaped custody."

Austin's eyes grew round. "Which means we're right back to where we were before. We've got to go back into hiding and get new identities all over again."

"Well, we are going to have to do *something*. We can't just go back to the lives we had four days ago. We'd be sitting ducks. Dad is still the key to putting Royce away for murder. You and I are vulnerable to being kidnapped and used as bargaining chips so Dad doesn't testify." Emma looked at Cole, who'd been listening with apparent interest. "We'll be out of your hair as soon as we can figure out the best place for us to go." She shifted her gaze to the floor because looking at Cole right now hurt too much. He'd told her they didn't have a future together, and she accepted that. But the feelings she had for him hadn't gone away despite her best efforts to dismiss them. She would miss Cole after she left town. She'd miss him terribly.

She looked up and his grandpa had his gaze settled on Cole before finally turning it to Emma. "You and your brother are welcome to stay here at the ranch for as long as you like. In fact, it might be wise to take your time before you make a move."

"Thank you."

"I'm going to get a cup of coffee," Lauren said after no one spoke for a moment. "Anybody else wants some, follow me into the kitchen." She stood up and started heading in that direction.

"This is actually a pretty cool place," Austin said to Emma as he glanced around the interior of the ranch house. He looked out the window at the surrounding pastures and forest. "What kind of animals do they have out here?"

"We have horses and sheep and goats and some chickens," Brent answered. "You want to go have a look around? I could use some help gathering eggs."

Austin grinned. "Sure."

Cole got to his feet. "I'll go out to the stables and get everything settled down for the night." He headed for the door without even a glance at Emma.

Emma was drawn to the scent of fresh coffee, but at the last minute she decided to follow Cole out to the stables. She had no idea what was going to happen next in her life, or how quickly she and Austin would leave the ranch. She wanted to take advantage of what might be her last opportunity for a private conversation with Cole.

Regret that she'd spent so much time around the man without realizing what a good person he was still gnawed at her. She'd spent a good part of last night and pretty much all of today plagued with "what-ifs" as she thought about him. What if she'd taken a closer look at him sooner? What if it hadn't taken threats to her life for her to realize that she really had grown to care for him? The fact that they worked together didn't seem insurmountable. What if they just worked different shifts? Or if one of them took a job with the county fire and rescue department?

None of that mattered now, and her heart ached thinking about the fact that she'd leave soon and never see him again. And as much as it hurt to admit it, he hadn't exactly jumped at the opportunity for a relationship with her when she'd brought it up. In fact, his reaction had been the opposite. And thinking about that reaction last night and today was what brought her to this point of following him up toward the stables.

"Hey, slow down," she called out as he reached the corral fence beside the stables.

Cole stopped and turned, a guarded expression on his face.

"All that time we worked together and you never could slow down so I didn't have to jog to keep up. You and those long legs."

He leaned against the corral railing. "Really? You came out here to fuss at me about how I walk?" He leaned down for a moment to scratch the dogs, who'd ambled out from the stables to greet him.

Emma planted both feet in front of him and brushed her hair out of her eyes. Dark clouds were rolling in and the breeze had gotten brisk, blowing tendrils of hair across her face.

"Actually, I came out here to apologize."

"For what?"

Embarrassed, she cleared her throat. "I'm sorry for what I said to you while we were washing dishes last night. I shouldn't have pushed you. I had no right. I don't know anything about your life's history and it isn't my business anyway." Realizing that she'd started to flail her hands as she spoke, she now crossed her arms over her chest. "Look, I just really appreciate all you've done for me, and seeing this other side of you, experiencing some of your personality that you keep hidden, well, I just really liked that."

Cole tilted his head slightly and a warm smile spread across his lips. It appeared he was about to say something when he straightened his head and his entire body stiffened. He stared at something behind Emma and then grabbed the collars of both dogs. "Take Liza and Misty and shut them up in the tack room in the stable so they don't get shot. You stay there, too."

Emma took control of the dogs.

Cole reached for the gun tucked in his waistband.

Emma turned. Four figures who'd just emerged from the tree line on the other side of the property were rapidly moving toward the ranch house.

Her stomach dropped. "They've found us."

Chapter Thirteen

"I'll take care of the dogs, but I'm not going to stay here and hide." Emma turned and hurried toward the stables with the animals.

Certain she meant it, Cole caught up with her and they rushed to get the dogs secured before racing toward the house.

Lord! Protect my family!

Slowing down to call someone in the house made no sense when Cole was this close and he was armed and he'd actually be able to *do* something as soon as he got there. Emma was hot on his heels, so he called out to her, "Phone 9-1-1!"

He veered toward the back of the house. Had the thugs spotted him and Emma by the corral? He didn't think so. If they had, they probably would have started shooting.

The criminals were close to the front door. If Cole went in through the back he could approach them from inside the house and take them by surprise. Racing into the house and yelling for Grandpa and Lauren to grab their guns might be the exact thing to instigate a shootout with the assailants that would get them all killed. He needed a smart strategy if he wanted this to end well.

He reached the back of the house and pressed his ear against the door to listen.

Emma caught up with him, still on the line with the emergency dispatcher.

Cole held his fingers up to his lips to indicate that she should be quiet and then gestured for her to move back. Instead of walking away, she ended her call and mouthed the words "they're on their way."

Even so, their response would take a while. The Webb family ranch was on the backside of the lake in a sparsely populated area with very little crime. Police and sheriff's deputies didn't spend much time patrolling out there. They would likely be responding from town. For now, Cole and his family plus Emma and Austin were on their own.

He heard raised voices inside the house. The bad guys were already inside. Cole couldn't tell how many thugs were in there, so he gestured at Emma to keep an eye on their surroundings in case one of the kidnappers had broken away from the group and snuck up behind them.

Cole eased the back door open, the loud voices apparently covering the squeaking sound. Then he moved forward down the hallway on the old wooden plank floor.

"Get out of our house!" Lauren shouted, followed by the sound of someone, presumably her, getting smacked.

"Shut up!" A different woman's voice. The female thug with the baby stroller who initiated the attack outside Super Mart.

"Please don't hurt us," Grandpa said in a broken, frail voice.

Cole smiled grimly. Grandpa was putting on a show. Trying to appear weak so he could take the criminals by surprise when he grabbed the gun he kept handy.

Cole took another couple of steps forward, trying not to let his attention get diverted by the threats one of the male attackers was making toward Grandpa and Lauren in between demanding to know Emma and Cole's whereabouts.

One more step and Cole was able to peer into the front room from the edge of the hallway. He saw Female Thug and

Bald Guy. Where were the other two kidnappers? Where were Brent and Austin?

Grandpa sat in his favorite chair. The older man had one of Lauren's knitted throws in his lap with his hands tucked underneath it. The drawer in the table beside him had been pulled out and it was empty. Very likely, Grandpa was holding his handgun beneath that throw blanket. Faced with multiple armed attackers, it was wise for the older man to wait for the right moment to take action.

Cole's assumption was confirmed when Grandpa caught sight of him hiding in the hallway. While continuing to cower and plead with Bald Guy not to hurt him and his granddaughter, the older guy gave Cole a quick wink.

The female accomplice was on the other side of the room, focused on keeping Lauren under control. Cole still didn't see the other two kidnappers.

Emma made a soft sound before coming up behind Cole so he wasn't startled. Turning slightly, he whispered, "Stay here and run out the back door if things go sideways. *Please*."

Emma nodded.

Cole's muscles tensed as he focused his gaze back on Grandpa. The weathered old rancher looked him in the eye and slowly raised his chin before suddenly dropping it down. In that moment he pushed aside the throw blanket and revealed the pistol he'd hidden underneath. Cole darted forward as Bald Guy and Grandpa fired at each other at the same time, the sound deafening in the normally cozy room.

Fear that his grandfather had been shot energized Cole as he leapt onto Bald Guy's back, taking him by surprise and knocking him to the ground.

Female Thug fired a shot at Cole that missed him and struck a wall in the dining area. There was nothing Cole could do about her right now as he grappled on the floor with Bald Guy and furiously tried to wrest the gun from the criminal's grasp.

Bald Guy threw a hard punch that connected with Cole's

jaw, shoving his face aside and forcing him to look in the direction of the Female Thug, who was now fighting back an
attack from Lauren. Cole was grateful to see that his cousin
could hold her own. His greater concern at the moment, however, was trying not to get shot by Bald Guy, who was still
fighting with him. Cole gripped the wrist on the attacker's
gun hand, twisting it to force the kidnapper to loosen his grip,
but the criminal was strong and kept control of his weapon.

Finally Cole was able to shift his weight to an angle where
he could jab his elbow into his assailant's midsection and
knock the air out of the guy. Cole then gave another hard turn
on the man's wrist and Bald Guy's grip loosened. Another
twist and the gun finally dropped to the floor.

Grandpa was already on his feet and he kicked the weapon
out of the Bald Guy's reach on his way to help Lauren as she
still struggled with the armed woman.

Cole grabbed Bald Guy's shirt collar, pulled him partway
up from the floor and then threw a jab that connected with the
criminal's chin, knocking him out cold. He let the thug fall
to the floor and then sprang to his feet, ready to help Lauren.

Lauren didn't need his help. Together, she and her grandfather had disarmed the attacker she'd been fighting, and Female Thug was now face-down on the floor with her hands
behind her back. Grandpa kept an eye on the criminal, his gun
at the ready, while Lauren scrambled for a ball of yarn from
a nearby basket to tie the woman's hands. When she was finished with that, she quickly moved to tie the bald assailant's
hands before the creep regained consciousness.

Grandpa gave Cole a tired smile. "I think we got these two
idiots under control."

Breathing hard after his fight, Cole nodded. "Yeah. But
there are two more of them lurking around here somewhere."
He grabbed the guns belonging to both attackers to make sure
they couldn't recover them and then looked toward the hallway. "Emma!"

She darted into the room and grabbed him in a hug, her face buried in his shoulder.

"I'm all right," he said. "We're all okay."

"You won't be okay for long," the female criminal taunted with her face still pressed to the floor. "Our organization is big. Emma and her family know that only too well. You lock any of us up, they'll just send replacements. This is never going to end, Emma. Your family will never be safe."

"That's enough out of you," Grandpa growled.

The woman ignored him and kept talking. "Be a smart girl and work with us, Emma. Get your dad to shut up and refuse to testify at the trial. Get him to tell the court he made a mistake and identified the wrong man as the killer. Do that, and you'll see your little brother again."

"Austin!" Emma cried out in a horrified voice, pulling away from Cole. "Where's Austin?"

"Long gone by now," the assailant said with a harsh laugh. "Taken somewhere you'll never find him."

Emma's jaw went slack and tears immediately formed in her eyes.

"Ignore her," Cole said, letting disgust saturate his tone. In his overseas experience, combatants spoke all kinds of lies to try to dishearten and demoralize their opponents. He turned to his grandfather. "But we do need to find Austin. I know Brent was going to show him around and take him to the chicken coop to gather eggs. Do you know which way they went first?"

"Brent wanted to go to the chicken coop last so they could gather eggs and bring them directly to the house," Lauren interjected. "I think they were going the other direction to look at the goats, first."

Cole stepped over to a front window. Careful to move the curtain only slightly so as not to draw attention to himself, he took a look outside but didn't see anyone. He moved through the ranch house, looking out several other windows, but didn't see anyone and returned to the living room. "I don't know if

Austin and Brent are nearby and just happen to be out of sight or if they're up at the stables or in the barn or somewhere else." *Or if they've been dragged away into the forest.*

While he was looking out the windows, Lauren had grabbed her phone and called 9-1-1. "Cops are almost here," she said to Cole with the phone up to her ear. "Maybe you should just wait inside."

"All of you should wait inside," Emma said in a steely tone, wiping the tears from her eyes. "But I *can't* wait. I've got to look for my brother. Maybe he's still on the property. I might be able to keep him from being taken away." She turned to Cole and held out her hand. "Give me your gun. I'm a decent shot," she added when he hesitated to respond. "My parents made me take a gun safety class and learn to shoot when we first moved here. I get out to the range every once in a while and practice with my dad's pistols. I know what I'm doing."

Cole handed over his gun, then grabbed the gun he'd taken away from Bald Guy and checked that it was loaded. "Let's slip out the door on the side of the house. It's possible the other two thugs haven't found Brent and your brother yet. We want to stay as quiet as we can and keep a low profile while we look around."

"Got it."

Cole nodded. "Let's go." He led the way to a small laundry room and looked out through a window in the door, but didn't see anyone. He took a breath and glanced at Emma before he slowly twisted the knob and took a cautious look outside.

"Emma Burke!" a voice called out from around the corner of the rambling house. "If you want to see your brother one last time, step outside now. Otherwise, you're never going to see him again."

Cole stilled. The voice sounded like it came from Ponytail Guy. He and the other assailant must have heard the shots fired inside the house. Since they hadn't heard from their partners, they could guess their fellow criminals had met with trouble.

Beyond that, even if Emma hadn't been the one who'd opened the door, they knew their threatening message would be relayed to her.

Cole ducked back inside the house and turned to Emma. "Can you talk to them and distract them while I run through the house, go out another door and sneak up behind them?" he whispered.

She nodded. "Yes."

The mixture of fear and courage in her eyes touched his heart. Cole leaned forward, quickly pressed his lips against hers, then dashed into the house and headed for the door by the kitchen. It was possible that the two thugs outside had split up and he was walking into some kind of trap, but Emma had been right. They couldn't just wait inside the house for the cops to arrive. They had to do something to help Austin and Brent before it was too late.

Gun at the ready, Cole crept around the house, listening to the ongoing tense conversation between Emma and Ponytail Guy. Finally, he rounded a corner and found himself closely behind the guy who'd driven the getaway car outside of Super Mart. This creep was pointing a gun at Brent. Figuring there was no point in hesitation, Cole threw an arm across the criminal's neck and pressed hard against it, cutting off Getaway Guy's air supply while pressing his gun into the man's back. "Drop your weapon."

The attacker didn't comply at first, but then the pressure on his throat began to work and after fighting for breath, he finally dropped his gun. Cole kicked it away. Though there was no longer a gun pointed at him, Brent stood frozen to the spot, staring wide-eyed at Cole as if he were uncertain what to do.

Ponytail Guy, while still talking to Emma, kept his gun pointed at Austin. He took a quick glance at Cole. "Sent your boyfriend out here, huh, Emma?" He let go a barking laugh. "How about that. Here I was trying in good faith to negotiate with you, give you a chance to see your brother again, and this is what you do. You have your *sweetheart* sneak up on me."

"Let Austin go!" Emma yelled.

The criminal laughed harshly. "Not a chance. Grabbing him is what I get paid for. Come with us, Emma. You'll be fine. You and your brother can be together. We just don't want your dad to testify. That's it. The only thing it will take for your dad to save your lives is to shut up. How easy is that? And after the case falls apart and the trial is over, we'll let you and Austin go."

"Don't believe him, Emma!" Cole yelled. He knew under normal circumstances she'd be smart enough to see the lie. But her emotions had to be off the charts. And she'd been under so much stress the last few days.

"Listen to Cole," Austin added. "Ignore this creep."

Approaching sirens wailed in the distance. Ponytail Guy began backing up toward the tree line, dragging Austin with him. The criminals must have left a vehicle on the highway and hiked onto the property through the woods so they could sneak up on the house.

Cole was limited in what he could do. He was still holding on to Getaway Guy and needed to keep track of him. Brent, still standing there, would be an easy target if Ponytail Guy decided to take a shot at him to scare off any attempt at pursuit as the thug dragged Austin away. It felt like a stalemate where any action could get someone killed.

"Wait!" Emma called out.

Cole could hear the side door of the house slam behind her. She'd come outside.

"Let go of my brother!" Emma demanded. She held her gun, but it was pointed at the ground instead of at Ponytail Guy. The man was holding Austin as a shield, so if Emma tried to shoot him, she could accidentally hit her brother instead. She continued walking toward the retreating criminal.

Cole felt his heart rise up in his throat, terrified she was about to get shot.

Austin might have had the same fear as he suddenly twisted and attempted to fight off his captor. Afraid things were about to get deadly, Cole shoved Getaway Guy toward Brent, shouting, "Don't let him escape!"

Brent darted toward the criminal, receiving one hard slug to the jaw before knocking the criminal to the ground. Meanwhile, Cole raced toward Austin. Ponytail Guy was a much better fighter than Austin, and Emma's brother was getting pummeled. Before Cole could get to them, Emma leaped onto the back of the attacker fighting her brother.

Bang!

Cole reached the flurry of fighting and yelling just as a gun fired.

"Emma!" Cole grabbed for Ponytail Guy and the kidnapper collapsed under Cole's assault. Cole dropped down and pressed his knee against the man's back to keep him from getting away while also taking the man's gun. It was then that he realized the thug's leg was bleeding. He must have accidently shot himself.

Cole looked over at Emma as she squeezed her brother tightly. Austin appeared to hug her back with equal intensity.

"Everybody okay?" Cole called out, wanting to make certain no one else had been struck by a bullet.

"I'm fine," Emma replied.

"I'm all right, too," her brother said as the two of them finally stepped apart.

"Got everything under control here," Brent added.

Red-and-blue flashing lights appeared along the driveway coming through the forest. Police had finally arrived. Cole took a deep breath, trying to get his racing heart under control. The fights had been a challenge, but the fear that Emma had been hurt had nearly overwhelmed him.

Cole got to his feet beside the kidnapper. The man was

crumpled in pain with a gunshot to his thigh, though the bleeding wasn't profuse. It didn't appear likely that Ponytail Guy could get away before the approaching cops took custody of him.

Cole turned to Emma and her gaze locked with his. She smiled tiredly, and then burst into tears. "Thank you," she said, laughing, though he didn't know why. Maybe she was laughing at the absurdity of the situation. Her reaction could also be the result of a sudden drop of adrenaline. Exhaustion was a likely possibility, too. As usual, Cole's paramedic brain wanted to figure out the cause of her upset and try to fix it.

"Thank you," Emma repeated, trudging toward him and then dropping a kiss on his lips like the one he'd given her a few minutes ago. Only this one lingered a bit longer.

"You don't need to thank me," Cole said. "You're the one who went after this guy—" he indicated Ponytail Guy "—and you brought an end to everything. I don't know how you did it."

"It's all that sugar I put in my coffee," she joked. "Gives me extra energy." Her smile softened. "Really, thank you for everything you've done for me. From the very start."

Cole looked into her eyes. Truth was he'd do pretty much anything she asked, anytime. There was no denying that now.

"Hey, you two trying to do my job?" Deputy Dylan Ruiz called out to them as he approached. His patrol car was parked nearby and three more cop cars were coming up the drive.

"Nope," Cole said. He nodded toward Emma. "*She*'s the one who had to do your job for you."

Cole looked at Emma, thinking about his own job with her at the fire department. About the two years they'd spent working together when he'd had no idea what an amazing, strong, compassionate woman she was. But that past was behind them. How would things be in the future? Would she and her brother be forced to change their identities again and go into hiding in some other town?

Right now, he didn't know. Just the thought of it made his heart feel hollowed out. He missed her already.

Storm clouds reached the ranch and began to pour down rain as the criminals were cuffed and put in separate patrol cars. There were plenty of law enforcement officers on scene now. It looked like half the cops in the county must have responded to the emergency call, including Cole's friends Deputy Dylan Ruiz and Officer Kris Volker.

To Emma's surprise, Sergeant Newman showed up, too.

"I thought you were assigned to the station on the other end of the county," she said when she found herself standing next to him on the front porch of the ranch house as they tried to get out of the rain. The inside of the house was packed with people and the temperature outside was refreshing after all the heated fighting and anxiety Emma had just been through. "How'd you get here to the ranch so quickly?"

"I happened to be at the main office in downtown Cedar Lodge working with some colleagues when the call came through," Newman told her. "Obviously, I was going to respond."

Made sense. He'd been in on this case since the original attack.

"Well, I guess now you know Austin didn't sell out our family." Emma couldn't keep the residual annoyance out of her voice. She glanced over at Austin, who was talking to Cole and Kris, and the two siblings shared a smile. The truth was she was grateful and relieved that things had turned out all right. The grudge she'd been holding against the witness protection task force member was something she needed to let go of. "Where did the idea that Austin had intentionally given away our family's location even start?"

Newman met her gaze. "It came from someone way above my paygrade who has access to your family's official records."

"Huh. Well, at some point I'd like to talk to that person

about that. It was a dangerous idea to suggest. But they must have had some specific reason they thought it was a legitimate concern. I'd like to know what that was."

"How about we focus on something that will help wrap up your concerns over this entirely?" he suggested with an enigmatic smile. "Austin," he called out. "Could you come over and join us for a couple of minutes?"

Austin hustled in their direction. "What's up?"

"I want to let the both of you know that your concerns over your dad and the Royce Walker trial are at an end. Shortly before the initial call came out regarding the attack out here, Chief Ellis and I received notification that Royce Walker was shot and killed by rival gang members late this afternoon down in California. The trial is over before it even started, and I'm sure the criminal gang will leave you and your parents alone. They no longer have any reason to go after your dad or to try to kidnap you and your sister. They have a much bigger concern with the turf war that just got started. The dynamic of the gang will change. You and your family will be the least of the new leadership's concerns."

Cole had drifted over by this point. He stood behind Emma and squeezed her shoulders lightly after Newman made his announcement.

Cole's nearness and his touch set her heart racing in ways it hadn't until a couple of days ago. How would things be as their lives went forward? How much had the kisses they'd exchanged meant something that could lead to a shared future, and how much of it was just due to the strong emotion of the moment?

The kisses meant something to her, but what about Cole? She'd misread his reactions before. If she had to go back to working alongside him as if nothing had changed between them, could she take it? Or would the daily reminder of how much she'd grown to care for him and how much his nearness to her affected her bring her too much heartache and grief?

"Hey, do our mom and dad know about this?" Austin asked Newman. He grabbed his phone from his pocket.

"Surely they would have called us." Emma reached for her phone, too. "Oh," she said immediately after unlocking the screen. "I've got some missed calls from both of them. And some texts."

"Me, too." Austin tapped his phone, as did Emma, to look to read the messages.

The next hour was a flurry of activity as Emma and Austin talked to their parents. Mom and Dad wanted Emma and Austin to come down to California so they could all be together and visit old friends. Austin was all for it, but Emma needed to get back to work. Both for the money and for the return to routine and normalcy that she'd been craving. Benny and Shawn were willing to come out to the ranch to get Austin and have him stay at their apartment until they took him to the airport tomorrow.

"Well, I suppose I should get going, too," Emma said to Cole an hour later after Austin left with his friends. All the cops were gone and everything seemed wrapped up for the moment. She'd been sitting at the dining table with the Webb family as they sipped hot chocolate, ate homemade banana bread and tried to wind down.

"Why don't you stay one more night?" Cole said. He sat beside her at the table, and while the rest of them had rehashed the day's events, he'd been fairly quiet. "It'll be raining hard on and off through the night." He gestured at a nearby window where rainwater splashed against the glass. "It's dark and sections of the road will likely be flooded. You're tired. How many calls have we gone on where someone rolled their vehicle or crashed because of that combination of conditions?"

"If you stay tonight, I'll make waffles in the morning," Lauren said with a tired smile.

Emma didn't actually want to leave. She liked staying there with the Webb family. Most especially, she'd liked spending so much time with Cole. She felt a tension between them, but this time *he* would have to be the one to bring up the topic.

But then again, maybe what she felt was *her* problem. It was possible that Cole had gotten as emotionally close to her as he cared to. The wise decision would be to get back to her apartment and her normal life as soon as possible. Get used to spending a lot of time alone again.

But she didn't want to be rude. "You know, I'll stay for more waffles," she said to Lauren, forcing a smile on her face.

Tomorrow Emma would make the break. Leave the ranch. And she and Cole would return to the professional relationship they maintained before all of this started.

Chapter Fourteen

"Shari just replied to my message and let me know they could use me at the library today," Emma told Cole the next morning before sliding her phone back into her pocket. The delicious breakfast Lauren had made was over, and now it was just Emma and Cole in the kitchen washing dishes again. "So add that to the chief agreeing to put me back on the EMT schedule and things have just about returned to normal."

"Good," Cole said, though he didn't feel at all good about her moving out. While the imminent danger over the last few days had been something he would never want to repeat, being around Emma virtually all day every day during that time was something he'd gotten used to. And he liked it. A lot. But how exactly did he tell her that? Especially when the vision he had for his future still wasn't clear.

Except when he'd tried to imagine his future, Emma showed clearly in it every time. Should he tell her that? Maybe it was too much and it would scare her off. Especially after she'd put her heart on the line trying to have an open, honest conversation with him and he'd balked like a stubborn mule.

Beyond that, what if they took a chance on developing a relationship and it fell apart? What about their work relationship going forward?

Wanting to know things ahead of time, imagining scenarios and planning what he would do next, and considering all the variables was something he'd learned to do while in a war zone and had continued to do as a paramedic back home. But when it came to personal relationships and figuring out how he wanted things to go forward with Emma, that sort of thinking just wouldn't work. People and relationships weren't predictable.

He handed an oversized mixing bowl to Emma for her to dry, the last of the dishes that needed to be washed. Then he glanced at the old clock beside the refrigerator. "I've got to go. I'm going to be late for work."

"All right," Emma said without looking at him as she dried the bowl. "I'll be leaving soon, too. Thank you again for everything, and I'll see you later."

Was she mad at him? Or had she changed her mind regarding her feelings about him? Maybe all of this was just a case of over-the-top emotions coming to the surface during an intense situation.

"Emma…" He glanced at the clock again. He really had to get going. "I'll give you a call later today," he finally said, though he wanted to say a whole lot more. But this just wasn't the time.

"All right," she said brightly, her attention still on the bowl.

He walked out of the kitchen. Grandpa and Lauren and Brent were all outside taking care of their morning chores. Cole grabbed the daypack he usually brought to work with him and headed out the door.

The driveway was muddy after last night's rain, which made for slow going, but soon enough he was on the two-lane highway and headed toward downtown Cedar Lodge. After a few minutes of driving, a call came through from his grandpa. "What's up?" Cole asked over his truck's hands-free device.

"Do you know where Emma is?"

"Probably heading for work."

"Not without her vehicle."

Cole's blood chilled. "What are you talking about?" He slowed and looked for a place to pull off the road.

"Her SUV is still here, but she's nowhere to be found. I tried calling her a couple times because I was concerned, but she didn't answer. Just now Lauren and Brent went up to the stables and animal pens to have a look around in case she went over there."

Cole had found a spot where he was able to turn. "I'm on my way back. Call me if you hear from her. I'll be there in a few minutes."

He floored it back to the ranch and up the muddy drive to the house, hoping that he'd see Emma standing on the porch and find out that Grandpa's concern had all been a misunderstanding. But that wasn't the case. Instead, Grandpa and Lauren and Brent were all standing on the wide porch, looking worried.

"Do you think we should call 9-1-1?" Lauren asked as he got out of the truck and ran up the steps.

"I think you'd better," Cole replied, hurrying past her and into the ranch house to get his gun. He'd thought danger had passed and so he'd stopped carrying it. "Let's take a look around and see what kind of tracks we can find," he said as he returned to the living room where his family were all waiting and Lauren was on the phone with an emergency operator.

"I'm going to head in the direction the attackers came from yesterday," Cole said. "Kris told me the cops found the kidnappers' car on that old logging road. They'd left it there and hiked in. If somebody's taken Emma, they might have tried doing the same thing.

"I'm going to take a horse," Cole added as he tucked his gun beneath his waistband. "I don't want to take an ATV and risk giving away my location if I'm coming up on a thug who might have grabbed Emma."

He strode out to the porch and the others followed him.

"How can we help?" Lauren asked.

The last thing Cole wanted to do was put his family in danger. They were good at surviving in the wilderness and at tracking, but none of them had been trained for a criminal encounter or combat. Last night's battle when they fought off the criminals was their first, and he hoped last, experience with that.

"You should probably arm yourselves," he said.

Grandpa pulled aside the front of his corduroy jacket so Cole could see the pistol at his waist. Cole nodded. "Good. You all stay here at the house."

"I'm not going to do that," his grandfather said.

Cole wasn't surprised. "Look, I can check the perimeter faster than any of you. As soon as I find relevant tracks, I'll let you know. If you stay here and I have to call for help, you could all gather together faster if you're in the house than if you're spread out all over the property." He took a steadying breath and blew it out. "And if Emma's just been out hiking around on the property outside of cell range and she comes back to the house, you can let me know right away."

Without waiting for their response, Cole ran to the stables. He saddled up his favorite mare, Suzie, as quickly as he could and then rode off. The edge of the drive looked like the best place to start and from there he rode along the tree line where forest met the grassy clearing surrounding the house. He set a moderate pace where he could cover a reasonable amount of ground while at the same time looking for broken twigs or branches or footsteps or recently disturbed mounds of pine needles on the forest floor.

His muscles tensed with stress as his focus narrowed on searching for signs of which way Emma might have gone. He trotted along for a hundred yards or so before he spotted a freshly snapped twig and reined in Suzie to a stop. She snorted impatiently, obviously warmed up and ready for a good gallop. Cole dismounted, patted his horse on the neck to hopefully quiet her a little, and then took several steps into the forest. The freshly disturbed ground confirmed someone had come this way very recently. Looked like it was at least two people.

After taking several more steps, holding onto the reins so Suzie didn't wander off, an uneasy mixture of dread and relief settled in his stomach. There, caught in a bundle of thick green pine needles, were several strands of sable-colored hair, just the color of Emma's. It was good to know which way she'd gone. It was terrifying to know some criminal must have finally gotten hold of her. For what reason someone would take her at this point, he had no idea. Didn't matter. He had to find her.

Cole placed a quick call to his grandfather to let him know what he'd found and where. "Let the cops know," he said before disconnecting. Then he stepped onto a stirrup and swung up into the saddle on Suzie's back. He drew his gun before giving the horse a gentle kick to get her moving. All the while he kept an eye out in case he was being watched.

Once again Emma had a gun pointed at her head, only this time it was held by a cop.

"Keep moving," Sergeant Newman growled after Emma caught her toe on an exposed tree root and had to flail her arms to keep her balance.

Emma's heart had pounded in fear the moment the sheriff's deputy grabbed her as she'd gone out to get into her SUV, and it hadn't stopped racing since.

The deputy was dressed in a coat with the hood pulled down and the collar flipped up, presumably so he'd be unidentifiable if anyone saw him from a distance. But Emma had recognized his voice when he'd approached her from behind, and none of the things that had happened afterward made any sense.

"Where are we going?" she asked for the third or fourth time.

As before, he didn't answer. He just shoved her and forced her to keep moving faster.

"*Why* are you doing this?"

"Don't tell me you haven't figured it out by now."

"What are you talking about?" she shot back. It probably would have been smarter to keep her tone placating so he wouldn't get mad and shoot her on the spot, but she was at the point where her fear was turning to anger.

"You asked me last night why I focused the blame on Austin for your family's location being disclosed and where that information came from. You said you were going to start an investigation into that."

"Yeah, so?" Her mind raced over what he'd just told her. Why would any of that matter? Did he think he'd get in trouble for blaming the wrong person? But it was somebody else with witness protection who'd come up with the idea that Austin was responsible. Why would Newman get the blame?

He'd been lying when he said that. An idea formed in her mind that seemed unbelievable, and yet it fit. Fit the situation right now. Fit with everything. "Did *you* give the Walker gang my family's location?"

He didn't answer. She wanted him to. She wanted him talking because if anyone was looking for them maybe they'd hear his voice. Or hear her voice if she kept talking. Then again, maybe no one was looking for her. Maybe none of the Webb family had gone back to the house yet and they didn't realize her car was there but she was missing. Maybe she was on her own.

No, not on her own. *Lord, please help me. Please be with me and guide me.*

"Did you sell them the information about us?" she pressed.

"See, I knew you'd figure it out."

"But I hadn't."

"Well, now you know for sure and you won't be able to do anything about it."

She didn't know for certain what that meant, but she had a

pretty good idea. And if he planned to execute her out here in the woods, she wasn't going to make it easy for him.

They reached a creek, swollen with water from the recent rains and natural dams created by deposits of forest debris. Emma paused at the edge, looking in both directions and desperately trying to see how she could escape or where she could hide. Newman pushed her and her feet sank into the mixture of mud and pine needles. He pushed her again and this time she fell, landing in the cold, briskly moving water and unavoidably taking in a mouthful. She pushed herself partway up, coughing and spitting out the water and trying to catch her breath.

Sirens sounded in the distance.

Newman crossed the creek and turned to face her. "This is as good a place as any to do this." He pulled out a second gun from beneath his jacket and pointed it at her.

"What are you doing?!" Panic clawed at Emma's chest.

"I got this pistol off one of the idiots who got himself captured last night," Newman said, gesturing with the second gun. "I'm going to shoot you. The cops will find the round inside your body and possibly the gun if I drop it nearby. Hopefully the police will then connect all the evidence I'm leaving behind to the Walker gang. Detectives will focus their murder investigation on those lowlifes and I'll be off the hook."

Murder investigation. He meant to kill her right here, right now.

Figuring at this point she had nothing to lose, Emma pushed off her hands and knees and scrambled up the creek bank. Running as fast as she could, she heard a gunshot fired in her direction. It was followed by another, and before she got very far she was compelled to dive to the ground behind a large tree so she didn't get hit. Seconds later she heard more gunshots, only these came from a different direction and they didn't sound like they were aimed at her. They were accompanied by the sounds of breaking tree branches and unnaturally heavy footsteps.

Emma peered around the tree and saw Cole. He was on horseback, with his gun pointed toward Newman. "Drop your weapon!"

The disgraced deputy, who had both his hands held up, let the pistol he was still holding drop to the ground.

"Emma?" Cole called out.

"I'm here!" She stepped out from behind the tree. On shaky legs, she headed toward Cole as he dismounted his horse.

Cole moved forward. Emma headed in his direction, and as she got closer to Newman she saw the deputy make a sudden move. In a flash, she realized he'd reached for his other gun, and without questioning her decision Emma flung herself at him.

Newman staggered under the weight of her surprise attack, giving Cole enough time to rush toward him and throw a flurry of hard punches that quickly had the criminal cop off-balance and ultimately knocked unconscious. Newman dropped to the ground.

Cole quickly secured the deputy's guns as Emma got to her feet.

"You found me!" Emma said breathlessly. Exhausted by physical strain and the aftereffects of so much fear coursing through her body, she staggered toward Cole and he swept her up in his arms. Pressed up against him, she could feel his heart pounding in his chest.

"Of course I found you," he said. "I wouldn't have stopped looking until I did."

It was all too much, and Emma burst into tears. Cole hugged her even tighter. At some point she would have to let him go. She knew that. But she also knew that she wasn't ready to do that yet.

Chapter Fifteen

Two hours later Sergeant Newman had been arrested and taken away and all the necessary police statements had been given.

Emma had showered and changed into clothes not covered with mud and creek water and forest floor debris. Now she stood in the doorway of her room at the Webb family ranch, making sure she hadn't left anything behind. "It's over," she said to herself softly.

She was thinking of the threats to her family as well as herself. Of course, she'd thought it was over once before, after the four thugs had been arrested. Then Sergeant Newman had shown up out of the blue to kidnap her with the intention of murdering her and hiding her body in the forest.

But she had survived. *Thank You, Lord.* In some regard there were always risks and potential dangers in life. Emma wasn't flippant about that realization. Her nerves were still stretched tight after the attack in the forest. Her hands still trembled a little. Her mind wanted to snap her back to some of the most frightening moments and push her to relive them again. But she knew that it was all part of processing trauma. Something she'd first become aware of eight years ago after her dad witnessed Royce Walker committing murder and the whole family had their lives changed.

Emma's stay with the Webb family was at an end. She would miss waking up at the ranch in the morning with its surrounding forest and gorgeous view of the nearby jagged mountain peaks. She'd miss the warm hospitality of Cole's grandpa and Lauren and Brent. She'd miss the animals, especially the dogs, Liza and Misty, and the good, strong coffee that was always available and the substantial made-from-scratch breakfasts.

Most of all, she would miss Cole and the closeness they'd shared.

Thank You, Lord, she prayed again, trying to focus on gratitude for what she had experienced with getting to know Cole rather than the heartache she felt now that it had all come to an end. It might be difficult to work alongside him in the future knowing that he didn't love her the way she loved him, but she would get used to it.

What she felt truly was *love*, after all. She knew that now. It wasn't just a desire to somehow possess him because he was handsome and courageous and compassionate. She genuinely wanted the best for him. Whatever made him happy. Whatever gave him peace. And if that meant forcing herself to take a step back from him emotionally, she would do exactly that. Or at least give the appearance that she had. For his sake.

She turned from the bedroom, packed bag in hand, and headed out to the living room.

Emma had said her goodbyes to everyone before she'd gone to her room to pack up. Grandpa, Lauren and Brent all had work to do around the ranch this morning and Sergeant Newman's kidnapping of Emma had already gotten in the way of them accomplishing their tasks.

Cole had been scheduled for a twelve-hour shift before he'd been forced to turn around and return to the ranch after learning that Emma was missing. He could still get in at least eight hours on the ambulance, and Emma didn't want to be responsible for him losing any more work hours and income. Besides that, a quick parting of ways was easier on her and undoubtedly more convenient for Cole.

She was surprised, then, to see him when she walked into the living room.

"Hey," he called out. He looked nervous, which was unusual for him. He shoved his hands into his jeans pockets and leaned back on his heels.

"Hey, yourself," Emma said cautiously. She set down her bag.

"I made some coffee," he added after a moment. There were two mugs on the table close to him. He picked up one and handed it to her.

Emma glanced down at the contents. The brew looked more like hot chocolate. She took a sip. It was chocolaty and very sweet, just as she liked it. "Thanks," she said cautiously. Was he buttering her up for some reason? Did he want something from her? All he had to do was ask. She owed him big-time and she knew it.

The way he looked at her started to make her feel jittery and nervous. But not in a bad way. In a way that drew her in, almost physically, as she found herself wanting to move closer to him. Her heartbeat sped up a little, compelling her to find out exactly what was on his mind. "Don't you need to get to work?" she asked, before taking another sip of the mocha coffee.

She offered him an encouraging smile, and the expression on his face slowly changed. He stopped fidgeting. He squared his shoulders and solidified his stance, and now he looked like the confident man she'd always known him to be. The calm and collected paramedic. The self-assured military veteran.

"What I need is to have you by my side." A soft smile crept across his lips.

Now Emma was the nervous one. She thought she might know where this was going. But she was afraid she might be wrong. "You'll have me by your side soon enough. You know I'm already back on the work schedule."

"That's not what I mean." Cole reached for her coffee mug and slid it from her fingers. He set it on the table, and then reached for her hands. "I had no idea what I was missing out on, but now I do."

She blinked at him, still afraid to get her hopes up.

"I thought my life would be better if I played it safe," Cole said. "Well, my *personal* life, I should say. I thought it would be wiser not to take too much of a risk in trusting a person. I was afraid to truly fall in love with a woman because what if things didn't turn out the way I hoped? What if it was a mistake?"

"I don't know how many guarantees there are in life, really," Emma said quietly. "Every day is a blessing, and we forget that sometimes. I know I did. But I've sure been reminded of that lately."

"Me, too." He stepped forward, took her in his arms and kissed her.

All Emma could do was blink after the warm, lingering kiss was over. The combination of happiness and security she felt had her wanting to simply soak up the moment. Cole had talked about the risk of expecting something in a relationship and potentially not getting it. Well, Cole Webb had turned out to be something she *hadn't* expected. And she was a little bit afraid of the hope building in her heart, because right now it felt out of control and impossible to restrain.

Cole wasn't the only one who was nervous.

"I know you, Emma," Cole said. "I've spent time with you, I've seen you take action and express concern and caring. You're smart and funny and you make me laugh."

"This is quite a change from just a couple of nights ago," she said gently. The last thing she wanted to do was derail where this conversation was going. But she wanted their relationships to be solid, so she needed to understand. "What changed your mind?"

"Thinking about it. Knowing you were worth the risk. Realizing that whenever I pictured myself with a happy future, you were there."

Emma laughed. She couldn't help it. His analytical paramedic's brain doing a risk assessment on falling in love with her was so spot on for him. But it was all right, because these last few days had proven to her that behind his practical nature Cole Webb did have a very warm and loving heart.

"Just so you know, I'm taking a risk with you, too," she teased.

"I know." Cole wrapped his arms around the small of her back and pulled her closer. "What do you say we take a chance and do our best to work things out together?"

"After all we've been through, I'm pretty sure we already know we can do that."

Cole leaned in for another kiss, this one lingering even longer than the first. Emma's knees went weak, but it wasn't from nerves; it was from sheer joy. By the time the kiss was over and Cole began nuzzling the side of her neck, she was actually beginning to feel lightheaded. Good thing she had a paramedic on hand.

One year later

Cole swept Emma up in his arms and carried her over the threshold and into the front room at the Webb family ranch house.

"Welcome home!" Lauren and Brent called out in unison.

Austin and Grandpa, both smiling mischievously, each brought a hand from behind their backs and flung bright confetti at the newlyweds, who'd just returned from their honeymoon in the Bahamas.

"About time you two got back," Grandpa said in a mock-complaining tone. "There's work to be done around here."

"That's right!" Austin teased in a tone that sounded remarkably like the older man. "You've been goofing off long enough!"

Laughing and smiling, Emma reached up to brush the confetti from her hair. Austin and Grandpa had hit it off and spent a lot of time working together at the ranch over the last year. Austin, especially, had benefited from the friendship and had become much more confident as he'd learned new skills and developed the beginnings of a real rancher's work ethic.

Cole still hadn't put Emma down. She turned to him and he planted a quick kiss on her lips, followed by several more, until he finally set her on her feet. "Welcome home," he said.

Home.

It hadn't taken long for Emma and Cole to decide they wanted to get married. The wedding had taken place at the church Emma's family had been attending since they'd moved to Cedar Lodge, and her mom and dad had insisted on paying for the reception at Elk Ridge Resort. They'd had a nice dinner in the resort's steakhouse located near the edge of a mountain ridge with a beautiful view of the lights of the town of Cedar Lodge sparkling down below.

Grandpa had told them he'd be delighted if they lived at the ranch. Making it their home was an easy decision. Emma loved being there, and she and Cole both thought it would be a great place to raise children.

"I'll go get our bags," Cole said, before planting a kiss on Emma's cheek and then going back out for their luggage.

"Lauren and Brent are teaching me how to make a cherry pie from scratch," Austin told his sister with a wide grin. He walked over to give her a hug. "We should probably get back at it if we want to have the pie for dessert tonight." Lauren and Brent each gave Emma a welcome-home hug before the baking trio wandered off to the kitchen.

Grandpa gave her a hug as well, and then headed for the

dining room table with a crossword puzzle book and a couple of mechanical pencils in his hand.

The household was settling into their early-evening routines and that was just how Emma loved it. Life was back to normal in some ways and completely different in others. Emma and Cole both continued to work for the Cedar Lodge Fire Department, but the chief made certain they were assigned to different crews, which seemed to Cole and Emma like a wise idea.

Cole came back into the house with their luggage, took it to their bedroom, then returned to embrace Emma in yet another hug. He never seemed to get tired of wrapping his arms around her, and Emma had no complaints about that.

"Those years we worked together I had no idea you were so cuddly," she said, smiling.

"It took the right woman to bring out the best in me," Cole said, hugging her again.

"And the right man to bring out the best in me," Emma said into his shoulder.

Both of them had needed the love and support of someone else to learn how to face life's challenges with grace and acceptance and forgiveness. They'd also needed faith strong enough to push through the tough times. Faith had brought them this far, and ultimately faith would bring them all the way home.

* * * * *

A Lethal Truth

Alexis Morgan

MILLS & BOON

Books by Alexis Morgan

Love Inspired Suspense

A Lethal Truth

Love Inspired The Protectors

The Reluctant Guardian

Harlequin Heartwarming

Heroes of Dunbar Mountain

The Lawman's Promise
To Trust a Hero

Visit the Author Profile page at LoveInspired.com for more titles.

Be strong and of a good courage, fear not, nor be afraid of them: for the Lord thy God, he it is that doth go with thee; he will not fail thee, nor forsake thee.
—*Deuteronomy* 31:6

To my wonderful agent Michelle Grajkowski—
thank you so much for always encouraging me to try
something new. And to my friend Janice Kay Johnson—
thanks for always being there when I need to
bring a new story to life.

Chapter One

As far as Aubrey Sims was concerned, it was pretty much a toss-up who was more excited about the fact that there were only two weeks left in the school year—the kids or their teachers. While she dearly loved her third grade students, keeping them focused on their classwork pretty much burned up every ounce of energy she had. Right now, all she wanted to do was go home, fix a snack and put her feet up for a while.

Unfortunately, she had a couple of errands to run before any of that could happen. So far, she'd gotten gas and picked up enough groceries to last until the weekend. That left just one more stop—her weekly visit to the post office to pick up her mail. It wasn't exactly convenient, but she preferred to have it delivered somewhere other than directly to her house. After all, a single woman could never be too careful.

Inside the post office lobby, Aubrey unlocked her box and dropped all of the mail into the canvas bag she'd brought in from the car. There was also a key for one of the larger boxes the post office used for oversize items. When she unlocked it, inside was a padded envelope addressed to her.

Aubrey studied the envelope and frowned. She gave it a gentle squeeze and thought maybe it held a small box. She hadn't ordered anything recently, but maybe her mother had wanted to surprise her with something. On second thought, that didn't seem likely. Her birthday was still months away, and there weren't any upcoming holidays that warranted a gift. That was a puzzle to solve later. For now, Aubrey dropped the envelope into her bag, more than ready to be done for the day.

On the drive home, she found herself glancing at her canvas bag and wondering about the unexpected envelope. What on earth could it be? As much as she wanted to learn the answer to that question, other things had to take priority. Once she was parked in her driveway, she concentrated on carrying in the groceries as well as the stuff she'd brought home from school to work on that evening.

Once everything was inside, Aubrey carefully engaged the two locks on the front door, fastened the security chain, and finally turned the dead bolt. The security system showed no alerts, but still she did a quick inspection of every room. She hated being so paranoid, but when something unexpected happened—however innocent—it sometimes triggered a powerful compulsion to check inside the closets and even under the beds.

Satisfied that she was safe, Aubrey dumped all of her mail out on the dining room table to sort. Junk mail went into the recycling bin while the bills joined the stack next to her computer. That left the mystery envelope. To postpone opening it a little longer, she fixed herself a glass of ice water before sitting down at the table. There, she picked up the mysterious envelope and studied it. Her name and address was written with a felt tip pen, the handwriting sloppy and not very professional-looking. The more she studied it, the more uncomfortable she became, and her curiosity morphed into something closer to dread.

It was tempting to get up and walk away, but delaying would accomplish nothing. After taking a deep breath, she gently tugged on the tear strip that would open the envelope. It took her two tries to rip it off completely. Peeking inside, she saw that she'd been right about the small box. It was the size and style that might hold earrings or possibly a necklace. Tipping the padded envelope over, she let the box and a pink envelope slide out onto the table.

Which should she open first? Not that it really mattered. She really hated that her hand was shaking when she gently lifted off the lid off the box. Nestled in a layer of padding was a rare coin, a type Aubrey recognized on sight. She'd only seen one other like it in her lifetime, but the image had been burned into her memory forever.

Chills ran up and down her spine as she quickly shoved the lid back onto the box. The truth was that even out of sight the coin had the ability to terrify her. That was because other than the police, there was only one person who understood the significance of a buffalo nickel in Aubrey's life. And if the coin was scary, the accompanying note would likely be far worse.

The pink envelope was the size that normally held greeting cards or maybe fancy stationery. Even without opening it, she sensed her life going off the rails again, but ignoring the threat wouldn't help. Experience had taught her that the only way to deal with life-altering disasters was to keep moving forward one step at a time. She forced herself to pick up the envelope to see what she could learn from it.

The sender had tucked the flap inside the envelope rather than sealing it shut. That made sense. He—and she was sure it was a "he"—probably hadn't wanted to risk giving the authorities his DNA by licking the envelope. Her name had been written in the same messy handwriting, but this time with a ballpoint pen.

Having learned all she could from the envelope, she reluctantly moved onto the note inside. Taking great care not to damage it, she unfolded the paper and set it back down on the table. Before reading it, she stopped to sip some water, hoping to ease the huge lump in her throat. It didn't work. Rather than try again, she turned her focus to the message on the paper. At first, she couldn't make sense of what it said even though the writing was legible and the words correctly spelled.

No, the problem was that her brain wasn't functioning properly and couldn't string the individual words together into any kind of coherent message. Maybe reading them aloud would help. It took a second try before anything began to make sense. Horrible, terrible, terrifying sense. She found herself being plunged back into the middle of a nightmare that had begun twelve years before and changed her life forever.

There were differences this time. Back then the words had been spoken to her face, not written in an anonymous note. She read through it again, hoping against hope that she'd only imagined the similarity, but no such luck. Even if the message wasn't verbatim, its meaning was the same.

Hi, Aubrey. Have you missed me? Well, I have good news— I finally have time for you. I promise we'll have fun—or at least I will. See you soon.

The words continued to play like a drumbeat in her head to the point she wanted to scream. She finally gripped the edge of the table hard enough to make her hands ache. It was the best way to stop herself from sliding down onto the floor to curl up in a ball of pure misery. Using every bit of determination she could muster, she pushed past the acid-burn of fear to formulate a plan.

When she could finally draw a full breath, Aubrey carefully refolded the note and stuffed it back into the pink envelope. Then she shoved both it and the box into the padded envelope. Hoping to find a moment of peace, she closed her eyes and offered up a prayer asking God for strength and guidance. As always, putting her trust in Him helped her feel centered and back in control. Finally, she braced her hands on the table and stood, moving slowly to make sure her legs would support her. Proud of her success, she put the padded envelope back in her canvas bag, picked up her purse and headed for the door.

It might have been smarter to call the police, but she didn't want them swarming all over her home. It was her sanctuary, and she was careful whom she let come inside. No, she would go to them and share the news. Finally, after twelve years, her cold case had just turned hot.

Detective Jonah Kelly nodded in response to greetings from several of his coworkers as he made his way through the cluster of desks that formed the heart and soul of the small police department in Elkton, Washington. Under other circumstances, he might have stopped to chat with a few people, but right now it was all he could do to keep moving forward. He'd spent the late morning and early afternoon at the doctor's office followed by one of his twice weekly physical therapy appointments. Translation: he was now in a world of hurt.

The therapist had warned him that he'd pushed too hard and done too much, but Jonah disagreed. He'd do whatever it took to get both his life and his career back on track. To work out in the field, he needed to regain a lot more mobility in his right leg. Progress was being made, but there was a long way to go. Even a single bullet did a lot of damage to a knee joint.

When he finally made it into the minuscule office they'd assigned him, Jonah closed the door and quit pretending that he could walk without limping. Gritting his teeth, he slowly lowered himself into the desk chair and stretched out his right leg, trying to find a position that didn't hurt. When that didn't pan out, he gave up and settled for one that ached a little less.

Choosing a file at random, Jonah began reading, forcing himself to go slow and not just skim over the information previous investigators had recorded in their reports. He jotted down a few notes, but nothing of consequence. From what he could tell, that seemed to be the nature of working cold case files. Every so often someone would review the file in case a fresh pair of eyes would spot something no one else had seen. It wasn't that the police didn't care about cold cases, but sometimes the evidence simply didn't lead anywhere no matter how much they hoped it would.

An hour later, he got up to get a cup of coffee. It was really more of an excuse to stretch his legs and ensure the right one didn't lock up completely from being in one position too long. After adding two sugars and a heaping spoonful of creamer, he started the slow trek back toward his desk. If he were at home, he could've used heat and then ice to ease the pain. He might have also taken one of the prescription pain pills he allowed himself only on the worst days.

Here at work, the most Jonah could do was a few slow stretches and then try to get lost in the next file in the huge pile of reports left to him by his predecessor. Detective George Swahn had worked the department's cold cases for over two decades. He'd been ready to retire for a while now, but he'd been waiting for the right guy to come along and take his place. When that didn't happen, he'd given up and settled for Jonah. They both knew this wasn't the kind of work Jonah wanted to be doing, but right now he didn't have much choice but to accept a position that was pretty much a desk job.

At least working alone eliminated the possibility of watching another officer bleed out in the street. On the night he'd been shot, Jonah had screamed himself hoarse as he crawled to his dying partner's side. He'd gotten there too late to do anything except pray that God would watch over Gino's widow and their three kids.

That had been two months ago, but the memory of watching Gino die was never far from Jonah's thoughts. At night, he often lay awake for hours trying to find answers to the questions that plagued him from the beginning. How had a simple interview with a witness gone so wrong? And if someone had to die in that alley, why had it been Gino, loving husband and father, instead of Jonah? That was something he'd been asking himself, his therapist, and even God over and over again.

Sadly, he was no closer to understanding the why of it all than he'd been when he'd regained consciousness in the hospital.

Heavy footsteps approached, stopping a few feet away. "Hey, Jonah, the desk sergeant is looking for you. Evidently there's an Aubrey Sims downstairs in the lobby, and she's insisting on speaking to you. Something about a weird envelope."

With some effort Jonah shut down his prior train of thought and turned to face Sergeant Tim Decker. The standing joke was that Decker had been part of the original equipment when the precinct was first built. Jonah had never had the courage to ask the man how long he'd been on the job. But based on his wiry gray hair and the deep wrinkles framing his eyes and mouth, the sergeant had a lot of long, hard miles on him.

That said, Decker's mind remained razor sharp, and Jonah wasn't the only detective who consulted him when they needed advice on a case. There wasn't much he hadn't seen or done when it came to law enforcement.

"Did they say what was weird about the envelope?"

"Nope, other than she insisted it was definitely something you needed to see. Seems she made it pretty clear that there was no way she'd leave it with anyone else."

When Decker didn't immediately walk away after delivering the message, Jonah figured the sergeant's own curiosity had kicked in. "It must be one of Detective Swahn's old cases. I'll hunt up the file, and then we'll go see what's up."

It didn't take Jonah long to pull the file. Rather than keep the woman waiting any longer, he decided he could wait to review the details when he found out more about what had brought her to the station today. He and Sergeant Decker left his office and turned in the direction of the elevator in the far corner. The staircase was closer, but everyone knew steps weren't exactly Jonah's best friends these days. Decker quietly adjusted his stride to match Jonah's as they crossed the room. When he pushed the button to summon the elevator, he quietly asked, "You're probably tired of being asked a lot of questions, but are you doing okay?"

It was wrong to react to genuine concern with anger, and the older man certainly deserved better than for Jonah to growl at him. Instead, he waited to answer until they were inside the elevator with the door closed. "It varies. I had physical therapy today, so right now my knee is barking at me."

They both knew Decker wasn't only asking about the state of Jonah's knee, but at least he didn't press the issue. "It'll get better. Those docs work miracles these days. I had a knee replacement last year, and it's amazing how much more I can do these days."

The slow-moving elevator settled on the first floor, one level down from where Jonah's office was located. They started toward the lobby at the front of the building. The desk sergeant looked relieved to see them coming.

"Thanks for coming down, Detective Kelly."

"Anytime, Sergeant. Decker here says an Aubrey Sims asked to see me."

"Yeah, she did." He dropped his voice to a low whisper as he glanced down at the clipboard in front of him. "Just so you know, I recognized her from her previous visits. She used to ask for Detective Swahn, but I guess maybe she'd heard he'd retired. I put her in the first conference room."

Sergeant Decker followed Jonah down the hall. They stopped by the window into the conference room long enough to check out the woman inside. At the moment, her attention was focused on a canvas bag lying on the table, which afforded them an opportunity to study her for a few seconds.

"Do you recognize her?"

Jonah started to shake his head, but then an image popped into his head that changed his mind. He'd worked alongside Detective Swahn the last week before the other man had officially retired. About the third day, they'd spent the morning reviewing cases Swahn thought deserved special attention.

They were on their way to lunch when Swahn spotted some-one standing on the far side of the lobby.

He'd drawn a sharp breath, his shoulders sagging slightly. In a low voice, he explained his reaction. "No matter how hard we all try, there are cases that won't ever have a satisfactory ending, which means some folks will never find closure. For those of us who work cold cases, that percentage is even higher. My advice is to learn how to let go of the frustration and take satisfaction from the cases you do manage to close."

The older detective gave the young woman a pointed look. "Having said that, there are always going to be some that stick with you and always will. Aubrey Sims over there comes in every few months to see if there's been any progress on her case. I hate—really, really *hate*—having to tell her that noth-ing's changed. I'm not going to miss this part of the job."

With that depressing memory in mind, Jonah finally answered Decker's question. "Sadly, I'm pretty sure I do."

Then he entered the conference room alone and closed the door.

Chapter Two

Aubrey was already regretting her decision to leave the safety of her house to drive down to the police station. It had seemed like a good plan right up until she found herself waiting alone in a room with a door without a lock. Worse yet, it had a large window right beside the door, which meant anyone out in the hallway could see her. Granted, the vast majority of the people passing by probably worked there, but she still felt exposed, her nerves raw. The tension had her pacing the length of the room rather than sitting down at the table.

She supposed she could simply leave if it all became too much to handle. After all, the desk sergeant had offered to personally deliver the envelope to the new cold case detective. It was tempting to take the man at his word and scurry back to the security of her own home. Unfortunately, the new detective was bound to have a lot of questions about the envelope and its contents, ones that only she could answer. The bottom line was that she could either do that here at the station or wait until after he inevitably showed up at her house.

Preferring to get back home before dark, she decided to wait no more than another five minutes. After that, maybe she would leave and try again tomorrow. The decision was made for her when footsteps came to a stop right outside the room followed by the muffled sound of two men talking. A few seconds later, the door opened just a crack, but no one entered immediately. However, there was an older uniformed officer watching her through the window. When he realized he'd been spotted, he offered her a smile she thought was meant to be reassuring before disappearing from sight.

It seemed a bit odd, but she was more concerned about the man who finally stepped inside the room. After shutting the door, he stopped to close the blinds on the window. Maybe she wasn't the only one who preferred some privacy.

"Ms. Sims?"

"Yes."

His smile was a little less practiced than the other officer's, but it seemed more sincere as a result. "I'm Detective Jonah Kelly. I took over your case from Detective Swahn when he retired. I asked Sergeant Decker to get us some bottled water. I don't know about you, but I always find talking to be thirsty work."

As he spoke, he stepped closer and offered his hand. After she shook it, he retreated to the other side of the table. "He should be back soon, and then we can get started."

She sat across from him and folded her hands in her lap while he set down the file folder he'd brought with him and then took out a small notebook and a pen. The door opened a second later, and the sergeant stepped inside to set two bottles of water on the table. "Is there anything else you need?"

He directed the question at the detective, but he kept his gaze on Aubrey as he spoke. She shook her head at the same time Detective Kelly answered, "Not right now."

"You've got my number if that changes."

Then he left, quietly closing the door on his way out. As soon as the sergeant was gone, Detective Kelly opened his water and took a quick drink. Aubrey did the same while she struggled to get her chaotic thoughts to settle into some semblance of order.

"So, Ms. Sims, I understand that you wanted to show me something."

Swallowing hard, she pulled the envelope out of the canvas bag and set it on her side of the table. Pointing at his bare hands, she said, "You should wear gloves before you touch it. I wish I had thought to do that myself. Unfortunately by the time I realized what was inside, it was already too late."

At least he didn't question her suggestion. Instead, he pulled a pair of gloves out of his suitcoat pocket and slipped them on. Before surrendering the envelope, she asked, "How familiar are you with my case?"

He looked a bit chagrined as he shot a guilty look at the file on the table. "To be honest, I only recently took over the cold case files from Detective Swahn, so I'm still going through everything. I thought about reviewing your file before coming downstairs, but I didn't want to keep you waiting any longer than necessary."

She hated having to start over from scratch, but maybe it wasn't a bad thing. At least he would be looking at everything with fresh eyes. "Actually, there's not much to tell. Twelve years ago, my friend and I were kidnapped at gunpoint in a parking lot after we got out of a late class. He drugged both of us, so I don't remember anything from then until we woke up chained together in a cabin somewhere in the woods. After he decided to only keep one of us, I was found on the side of the road a day later. My friend hasn't been seen since."

By the end of her quick spiel, Detective Kelly definitely had his cop face on. "I'm sorry."

Her answering smile had nothing to do with happiness. "Me, too."

She finally shoved the envelope across the table. If he noticed how badly her hands were shaking, he was kind enough not to comment. "I have my mail delivered to a post office box and usually only pick it up once a week. I have no idea when that envelope actually arrived."

Detective Kelly had started taking notes, so she waited for him to catch up before continuing. "I waited until I got home to open the envelope. That's when I noticed there was no return address. Maybe that should have set off alarms, but it didn't. I'm sorry if I've contaminated the evidence."

"Have you ever gotten anything like this before?"

When she shook her head, he said, "Then there's nothing to apologize for. How were you supposed to know something was wrong?"

She appreciated his effort to reassure her even if it didn't really help. "Regardless, something about it made me uncomfortable."

"Besides the lack of a return address?"

"Yes. At first, I thought maybe my mom or a friend might have ordered a surprise present to be sent directly to me, but it's not my birthday or anything. Besides, a commercial shipment would normally have a printed label."

By that point, she couldn't bear to look at the envelope. Instead, she kept her gaze focused on the man across from her. "There's a small box with a buffalo head nickel inside along with a note addressed to me."

"Does that specific coin hold a special significance?"

She managed a small nod. "It looks like the one they found hidden in my shoe when I was rescued. I figure he put it there because I didn't have any pockets. The note also echoes something my abductor said twelve years ago. Back then, he said he didn't have time to enjoy both of us. He flipped that coin to choose between us. After that, they found me tied to a tree on the side of a road. We've never found out what happened to Marta."

She swallowed hard, her fear a huge wave that threatened to overwhelm her. "Basically, this note says he finally has time for me."

Detective Kelly's hand slammed down hard on the table, his anger clear. He immediately apologized. "Sorry for losing my temper, Ms. Sims. You've been through enough for one day and don't need any more drama. My temper wasn't directed at you but at whoever mailed that envelope."

"It's all right, Detective. I'm pretty upset about this situation myself. So what do we do next? And how long will it take? I'd like to get back home before dark."

He frowned. "Do you have friends or family you can stay with?"

That was the last thing she wanted to do. "I'd rather go home."

"Okay, then." He studied the envelope for several seconds before finally meeting her gaze again. "Right now, I'm trying to decide whether I should open the envelope myself or have the forensics team take over now."

A second later, he nodded. "Yeah, the forensics people should have first crack at it. I'll ask them to give it priority, but I can't make any promises. I'll come to your house when I know what they find."

He checked the time. "I'm guessing that won't be until tomorrow sometime. Is that all right with you?"

She knew that last part was his attempt to let her think she had some control over the situation. While she appreciated his consideration, they both knew he would show up whether she wanted him to or not. Besides, she needed his help.

"I'm a school teacher. I normally get home around four thirty. Any time after that should be fine."

All too ready to be done and out of there, Aubrey picked up her purse and her canvas bag, leaving the envelope on the table. With keys in hand, she rose to her feet. "I'll be going. Thank you for meeting with me on such short notice, Detective Kelly. I appreciate it."

"Any time, but give me a minute before you leave. I'd feel better if Sergeant Decker makes sure you get back home safely."

He pulled out his cell phone and made a quick call. "Sarge, I need you to escort Ms. Sims back to her house. She might appreciate it if you make sure everything is secure when you get there."

When Detective Kelly ended the call, she offered him a small smile. "I'd like to say that's not necessary, but the truth is I'll sleep better if he really has time, that is."

"He's on his way. I'd walk you out to your car myself, but I have to stay with the evidence." Then he held out a business card. "That's my number. Call any time, day or night. Otherwise, I'll see you tomorrow."

"I'll be waiting."

Sergeant Decker walked in a minute later. "You ready to go, Ms. Sims? I hope it's okay, but I'm going to ride with you while one of our patrol officers follows behind. I'll do a perimeter check as well as check the inside of the house while she stays outside with you. Afterward, she'll bring me back to the station."

Detective Kelly looked happier. "Good thinking, Sergeant. I'll also ask the officers who patrol that area to drive by the house more often until we figure out what's going on."

Aubrey followed Sergeant Decker out to her car. While they waited for the other officer to join them, she couldn't decide if their efforts to provide safe escort back to her house were reassuring or only scared her more knowing they thought it was necessary.

Despite his decision to have the forensics people take charge of the evidence, Jonah was seriously tempted to rip the envelope open right then and there. He knew better: procedures were meant to be followed for good reason. It was important to protect the evidence to ensure the case would hold up if and when it ever came to trial. The last thing anyone wanted to happen was to have the case thrown out of court because someone got careless.

With that in mind, he pulled out his phone and made a quick call. "I need someone from Forensics in the conference room off the lobby ASAP."

While he waited, he skimmed through the case file to familiarize himself with the basic facts. Even the little he read was the stuff of nightmares. No wonder the coin and the note had left Aubrey Sims pale and shaking. He'd only gotten through the initial report when the forensics tech arrived. After she did her thing, Jonah followed her down to the lab.

For the next hour, he hovered as close as he could to the two technicians who were processing the envelope and its contents. He snapped pictures at each step of the way even though the forensics team handled the official documentation of the evidence. At least this way he would have his own photos to use until they finished processing everything.

They finally opened the envelope and gently slid its contents onto the counter. Just as Aubrey had told him, there was a small box about two inches square and a pink envelope, which held a single piece of white paper folded in thirds. The technician carefully removed the lid from the box to reveal a coin nestled on top of a thin layer of cotton. After photographing that much, she unfolded the note and laid it flat next to the box.

Then she stood back to allow Jonah a closer look. The coin didn't tell him much, but his breath caught in his chest as soon as he read the words scrawled across the paper. No wonder Aubrey had been so badly shaken by the contents of the envelope.

The tech gave him a curious look. "From your reaction, I'm guessing there's good reason to be concerned about the young woman who brought this in."

"Yeah, there is." Although Jonah wished he was wrong about that. Sadly, the threat was all too clear, especially after what he'd read in Aubrey's case file.

Leaving the techs to finish their work, Jonah hustled out of the lab as fast as his aching leg would let him. He didn't even try to hide his need to limp as he headed back to his office.

When he sat down at his desk, he did his best to ignore the jagged shards of pain shooting up his leg. His knee clearly wasn't very happy about all the walking and standing Jonah had done over the past couple of hours.

Too bad. Right now he had more important things to worry about, like doing a much deeper dive into the case file to learn everything he could. He started with the investigating officer's report along with all the notes Detective Swahn had added over the years. On his second pass through the jumble of information, Jonah started taking notes, adding his own observations of the potential new evidence.

The details on the case sent chills up Jonah's spine. One thing Aubrey hadn't mentioned was that their captor had used a device to distort his voice. He'd also dressed from head to toe in black, including a mask that hid his face and hair. Those things accounted for why Aubrey couldn't give any useful description of the man who had abducted the two women.

The few things she did remember clearly were the stuff of nightmares. Like how the kidnapper had sounded almost gleeful when he informed the two women that he wouldn't have time to enjoy both of them. No doubt he got off on their terror. Worse yet, they had to watch as he flipped a coin to determine which one would stay and who would get a reprieve. Marta had never been heard from again, but the next day Aubrey had been found beside a rural highway near the Cascades. She'd been groggy but otherwise unharmed, at least physically. The only real evidence they'd found was the coin—a buffalo head nickel.

Jonah studied the picture of the coin in the file and compared it to his photo of the one down in the forensics lab. They were identical in style; the only significant difference was the year they'd been minted. According to the file, the description of the coin had never been released to the public. Unless Aubrey or possibly someone close to her had let it slip, only the kidnapper would've known what kind of coin he'd used.

Finally, Jonah reviewed Aubrey's original description of what her captor had said in the cabin and compared it to the note that had accompanied the coin. There was no doubt that he'd be coming for Aubrey, and soon.

Jonah picked up his phone and dialed his boss's number. "Captain, we've got a problem."

Chapter Three

The next afternoon, it was a relief to walk through the front door and kick off her shoes. The day had been a rough one, and Aubrey was tired. As promised, Sergeant Decker had checked out her house inside and out yesterday. Aubrey had appreciated his efforts, but she hadn't been able to relax enough to actually sleep well. It had been all she could do to drag herself out of bed and get to work on time.

At least there, she'd been able to put her worries on the back burner and focus on her students. No matter what was going on in her own life, she would do whatever it took to prepare them to move on to fourth grade in the fall. After they boarded the buses for home, she'd rushed through getting organized for the next day and then headed back home.

It was tempting to kick back and relax, but unfortunately her day was far from over. Detective Kelly had texted to remind her he'd be stopping by. Rather than sit and stare at the door while waiting for him to arrive, she fixed herself a glass of iced tea and sat down at the dining room table to pay a few bills. Once those were taken care of, she decided to review the current balances in her three bank accounts. Even after paying the bills, there was plenty in her checking account to cover her expenses for the two next months. Her regular savings account was slightly below her comfort zone. But barring unforeseen circumstances, it should be back up to normal after her next paycheck.

That left her secret account, the one she never mentioned to anyone, especially her parents. After studying the bottom line, she did a few calculations. Sadly, it would take her at least two months to accrue enough money to hire another private investigator. The police had never been able to find out what had happened to Marta, but Aubrey had kept hoping another trained professional could. Of course, with the arrival of the coin and the note, maybe all of that would change.

Scary as it all was, she hoped so.

Over the past twelve years, she'd paid out a lot of money in the hope that someone would miraculously discover something that would blow the case wide open. That had yet to happen, so she had kept all knowledge of the investigations to herself and for good reason. For starters, Detective Swahn had expressed considerable doubt that a private investigator would be able to ferret out any information that the police had missed. She truly believed that wasn't his ego talking, that he was giving her what he thought was good advice. Regardless, she'd never forgive herself if she didn't make every possible effort to find answers. At least he'd never once questioned her determination to make sure the police kept looking for Marta.

The biggest reason for the secrecy regarding her efforts to keep the investigation moving forward had more to do with opinions expressed by Aubrey's parents and most of her friends. They stood united behind the idea that it was well past time for Aubrey to put the kidnapping behind her and get on with her life. Even the ones who'd known Marta personally believed whatever had happened to her was tragic but hardly Aubrey's fault.

Her parents had insisted Aubrey see a therapist when she couldn't simply let it all go. In his opinion, she was developing an unhealthy fixation. She'd quickly quit going to him when it became obvious he never really listened to her. Instead, he simply parroted everything her parents had already told her—that nothing good would come from her insistence on wanting answers.

They were wrong, and so was he.

To this day, she was as puzzled by their attitudes as they were by hers. Just how was she supposed to forget the two days she been held captive? After all, those forty-eight hours and everything that had occurred afterward had changed her life on a fundamental level. With a flip of a coin, the person Aubrey had been when she and Marta walked out of class that night had ceased to exist. She understood why her parents wanted that girl back, but that was never going to happen.

Besides, did they have no sympathy for Marta's family? Mr. and Mrs. Pyne would give anything, do anything, to find out what had happened to their daughter. She prayed that Detective Kelly would somehow make that happen.

Speaking of him, she had a phone call to make before he actually arrived. He might not appreciate her reaching out to his predecessor, but that wasn't going to stop her. After finding Detective Swahn in her contacts, she dialed his home phone number. He'd given it to her the last time they'd spoken at the police station, just in case. He wasn't clear in case of what exactly, but she'd appreciated the gesture. When he didn't immediately answer, she debated whether to stay on the line long enough to leave a message or if she should simply hang up. The decision was made for her when his voice finally came on the line.

"Ms. Sims, sorry to keep you waiting. I'm mowing the lawn and didn't hear it ringing at first. What can I do for you?"

She managed a small laugh. "No need to start being formal now that you're retired. You've always called me Aubrey, Detective Swahn."

"Fine, Aubrey. How can I help?"

That was the question, wasn't it? "I apologize for bothering you, and maybe I shouldn't be asking this, but I was wondering what you could tell me about Detective Kelly."

She tried to sound calm, as if she were asking the question more out of curiosity than real concern. However, something in her voice must have alerted Detective Swahn that something was going on. "What's happened, Aubrey?"

She gave him the basics. "I received an anonymous envelope with a buffalo head nickel and a note inside. I'm pretty sure it's from the kidnapper. I turned it over to Detective Kelly yesterday, and he's stopping by this evening to give me an update on what the forensics people found."

After a heavy silence, the detective sighed. "I'm so sorry, Aubrey. You must be scared, but you did the right thing by taking it directly to Jonah. He's a good detective, and you can trust him. I wish there was something I could do to help."

"You already have just by vouching for him." She forced a cheerier note into her voice. "Now I should let you get back to your chores. That grass won't mow itself."

"So true. But one more thing before I go, Aubrey. Tell Jonah to call me if I can do anything to help."

She pointed out the obvious. "You're retired."

"I know, but tell him anyway."

"I will."

She hung up and put her bank statements back in the file cabinet and then started working on her lesson plans for the remaining days of school. She was just finishing up when the doorbell rang. She closed the file on her laptop and then got up to peek out the front window. There was an unfamiliar black sedan parked in the driveway. Next, she checked the security feed on her phone app to verify it was Detective Kelly standing on her porch. He was dressed much as he had been yesterday although his suit looked a bit rumpled, and he'd removed his tie at some point. Evidently she wasn't the only one who'd put in a lot of long hours already, and the day wasn't over yet.

Aubrey took a deep breath and forced herself to unlock the door. When she finally swung it open, Detective Kelly had retreated to the far edge of the porch, probably trying not to crowd her. "I hope I didn't catch you in the middle of dinner."

"Not at all. I was just finishing up my lesson plans for tomorrow."

"Well, hopefully I won't take up too much of your time." He studied her and then asked, "Would you feel more comfortable if we talk out here on your porch?"

She looked up and down the street and was relieved to see that several of her neighbors were out and about. Feeling slightly more in control of the situation, she stepped outside. At the same time, Detective Kelly sat in one of the two Adirondack chairs that flanked a small wicker table. The roomy porch was one of her favorite features on her small bungalow. She liked to relax out there and watch the bees buzz around the riot of flowers in her front yard. Right now, though, she doubted anything would soothe her nerves.

The detective sat quietly, as if he'd give her all the time she needed to get settled. When she finally got herself situated, he picked up a file he'd left lying on the table and briefly studied it before speaking. "I've reviewed the details of your case. I wanted to make sure I was up-to-date on everything that has happened since the beginning. I know it probably doesn't help, but it's clear that your case has always been important to Detective Swahn. He was really frustrated that he could never find answers for you."

She bit her lower lip and tried to decide if she should mention she had just spoken with the other detective. Considering there was likely a good chance that Detective Kelly might consult with his predecessor at some point, it was probably better to come clean from the get-go. "I should probably confess that I just got off the phone with him a little while ago. He gave me his number the last time we spoke. He wanted me to have it in case I ever I had questions."

Detective Kelly surprised her by grinning. "So you were checking up on me?"

At least he wasn't angry. "Yeah, pretty much. He said good things about you and that you could call him about my case if there's anything he could do to help."

"I will probably reach out to George at some point. He knows more about not only your case, but all of the others I inherited from him. He went over as many of them with me as we had time for before he left. I really appreciated all the good advice he gave me."

"He's always been very kind to me. I was truly sorry to hear he was retiring, which probably sounds pretty selfish of me. I hope he has some fun adventures planned."

"From what he told me, George plans to do a lot of fishing." He grinned a little. "At least after he gets caught up on the long list of chores his wife had lined up for him. He also grumbled something about an Alaskan cruise she booked for later this summer."

She could picture the dour detective being grumpy about that, but she'd always suspected he was a marshmallow inside. "I bet he'll have a great time despite himself."

"I hope so. After being on the force for so long, the man deserves to have a little fun. So does his wife."

Evidently the pleasantries were now over, because he turned to face her more directly. From the way his brows were riding low over those bright blue eyes, whatever he was about to say wasn't going to be easy to hear.

"So, let's go over what we know so far."

He handed her a piece of paper with an enlarged picture of the front and back of the coin that had been in the envelope. After she studied the photo closely, he handed her a second one. "That first one is the coin you received yesterday. I got the second picture from your case file. Presumably, it's the coin the kidnapper used to decide which of you he would release."

She shuddered at the memory of that moment. "So we're

dealing with two different coins. I admit I was wondering if the police had lost track of the original one somehow. Not that I think they're normally careless about such things, but it has been twelve years. No offense, but sometimes things happen."

He waved off her apology. "Don't worry about it. To be honest I wondered about that myself. Earlier today, I personally verified the original coin is still in our evidence lockup. The two coins do look a lot alike, but they were minted in different years. The original one from twelve years ago was minted in 1925, while the one you got yesterday is from 1932."

She handed back the photos. "I'll take your word for it. I haven't seen that coin in twelve years. It was taken into evidence along with all of my clothes at the hospital."

The truth was, though, the memory of that coin still haunted her dreams.

Next, the detective handed her a photocopy of the note. "I've reviewed your statements from twelve years ago. I wish I could tell you that your memory was faulty and that the wording in the note isn't remarkably similar to what you reported at the time, but I can't. I've gone over everything with my captain and one of the original investigating officers. It's our opinion that whoever sent you that note clearly had insider knowledge. He's either the actual kidnapper or he was there."

He wasn't telling her anything she hadn't already suspected. But there was a big difference between mere suspicion and hearing a trained professional state it as fact. Aubrey wanted to deny the reality of the situation, but she couldn't tear her eyes away from the words on the page. At first glance, they were clear, but then they seemed to melt and swirl on the paper. Black spots danced in her eyes as she struggled to deny the meaning of what she'd read. She kept blinking, hoping to clear her vision.

When that didn't work, she tried to give the paper back, to put some distance between herself and the terror that threatened to overwhelm her. Why would this be happening after all these years? Granted, she'd always hoped to find out the truth about what had happened to Marta, but she'd never expected to get sucked back into the nightmare herself.

Why did he finally have time for Aubrey? There was no way to know. As the truth of the situation slowly sank in, she rose to her feet and struggled to speak to the detective. To tell him to leave and take the threat with him. When she couldn't manage even that much, going into full retreat was her only option. But before she could find the way back inside the house, a wave of pure darkness washed over her and sent Aubrey plunging toward the ground.

Chapter Four

Jonah lunged forward to catch Aubrey before she hit the ground. His knee protested the additional weight he put on it as he lifted her back up to the chair. She was already coming around, which was a good thing. He remained next to her, his hand resting on her shoulder with enough pressure to make sure she kept her head down between her knees. She'd already been skittish around him. The last thing he wanted to do was crowd her so much that she'd panic again.

In a matter of seconds, she waved him off. "I'm fine."

No, she wasn't; not really. Rather than argue the point, he asked, "Will you be all right here while I get you some water to drink? I promise I will go in and come right back out." He took a small step back and held up his phone. "Unless you'd rather I call the EMTs so they can check you over."

She immediately shook her head. "There's no need. I'll be fine, but water would be nice. The glasses are in the cabinet above and to the left of the sink. The fridge has a built-in ice and water dispenser on the door. Fix yourself some, too, if you'd like."

Still he hesitated but finally decided a quick trip inside

would be okay if she was thinking clearly enough to play hostess. "I'll be right back."

Hustling as fast as he could, he ducked inside and headed for the galley-style kitchen beyond the dining area to his right. A cozy living room was on his left with another doorway on the far end that probably led to the bedrooms. Once in the kitchen, he filled two glasses halfway with ice and topped them off with water. He also grabbed some cookies from a glass jar on the counter. A bit of sugar would probably do her some good.

Aubrey's coloring had improved by the time he returned with their drinks. He set his drink and the cookies on the table. Then he wrapped his hand around hers to support her glass until he was sure she had a solid grip on it. "Drink a little of that and then eat a cookie."

She took several sips and then offered him a tenuous smile. "Thank you. That helps."

"I'm not sure you should be thanking me for anything since it's my fault you almost took a header." Jonah was pretty sure his smile was nearly as shaky as hers. He returned to his seat and took out his spiral notebook to take notes. "I'm sorry about that. I should've found a better way to let you know what we're thinking."

"No apologies necessary, Detective Kelly, although I'll admit all of this has hit me hard." She reached for one of the cookies before continuing. "I've always hoped something would break loose on the case. Twelve years is a long time to wait for answers."

As far as he could tell, they didn't actually have any answers, only more questions. Jonah considered his next words carefully. "Like I said, I'm operating under the assumption that whoever wrote that note is the same man who abducted you and Ms. Pyne twelve years ago. At the very least, it would have to be him or else someone who had firsthand knowledge of the original case."

Jonah paused to give her a chance to process that much before continuing. When she nodded, he picked up where he'd left off. "I wish I could say I've uncovered something everyone else missed in the initial investigation, but I haven't. I have started searching our database for other incidents with similar details in the intervening years. Basically, cases involving young women, a remote cabin, black clothing, a coin, etc."

He stared off into the distance and ran his fingers through his hair in frustration. "So far, I haven't found any in our general area that meet those criteria, but I'll widen the search as I have time. Considering the almost total lack of forensic evidence from the original incident and the fact your friend has never been found, it seems unlikely your abduction was the first time the guy did something like this. He made sure there was nothing that would lead us back to him, which speaks of practice."

Aubrey sighed. "I've always hoped he'd spontaneously stopped."

"Sadly, that's highly unlikely. This kind of compulsion usually builds over time to the point it picks up speed. If he did stop for a time, there could have been some outside force at play. For example, he might have served time for an unrelated crime. Recuperating from a severe injury or even an illness might also be possibilities. Regardless, it appears he's back now, even if the note and the coin don't give us much of a starting point."

Aubrey studied him a few seconds and bit her lower lip, probably trying to decide whether she should tell him something. He decided to wait her out rather than trying to force the issue. Finally, she drew a sharp breath and spoke in a rush. "I have other files that you can review."

That comment had him sitting upright again. "What kind of files?"

"Detective Swahn told me what I wanted to do was a bad idea. He knew about the first time, but not the others. For

sure my parents would have a fit if they found out, but I had
to do something."

"I'm sorry, but I'm not following."

Her chin took on a stubborn tilt as if she was feeling a bit
defensive. "Over the years, I've hired various private investigators to look into the case. Most did a cursory review and
told me there wasn't any reason to continue. I think they felt
guilty taking more of my money when they didn't turn up any
promising leads."

Some detectives didn't much appreciate having civilians
poking their noses into police business, but Jonah couldn't
blame Aubrey for resorting to extreme measures to find answers. His trip into the house had been brief, but he hadn't
missed seeing the multiple locks on the front door or the baseball bat sitting within easy reach. There was also a container
of pepper spray on the lamp table next to the sofa. She might
have survived the abduction, but it had profoundly changed
the trajectory of her life.

"Did these investigators learn anything useful at all?"

She sighed. "If they had, I would've immediately taken the
information to Detective Swahn. I'll understand if you don't
want to bother looking through the reports, but I thought you
should know about them."

He wasn't about to ignore another source of information.
"Is it all right if I copy them and return the originals?"

"There's no need. You can take my hard copies with you.
I have it all backed up on both my laptop and a flash drive."

"Great. I'll take the files with me when I leave. I'll read
through them as soon as I can and let you know if I find something useful."

"I would appreciate that. I've read them all, of course, but
a trained eye might see something I missed."

It was time to ask some difficult questions. Hopefully, they
wouldn't send her into another tailspin. "I have to be honest
with you, Ms. Sims. This guy made a pretty bold first move

sending you the note and the coin. He has to suspect you would call us. Our involvement would only complicate any plans he might have."

Just that quickly, she latched on to the arms of her chair as she looked up and down the street with wide, panicky eyes. "Maybe it wasn't the first thing he did."

Jonah sat up straighter and scanned the surrounding neighborhood. "Why would you say that?"

"I know this might sound strange, but recently I've had the strangest feeling that I'm being watched. Not all the time, but enough that I've noticed."

She closed her eyes and then opened them again as she turned to meet Jonah's gaze. "I haven't seen anyone, you understand. It's more like a weird feeling that someone is watching the house or staring at me as I load the bags into my car at the grocery store."

"Why didn't you call Detective Swahn or me to let us know?"

"Because in the absence of any kind of proof, it would sound like I'm just being paranoid." She shifted her eyes away from him, "And I might know who it was. If I'm right, they would never hurt me. I believe that."

By that point, Jonah was beyond frustrated with her half answers. "What exactly are we talking about here, Ms. Sims? Because from where I'm sitting, it sure sounds as if someone has been stalking you. If there's any chance it's same the person who sent the note, then his behavior has escalated big-time."

Her dark eyes filled with tears that trickled down her cheek. "Marta became engaged shortly before we were abducted, and her fiancé took her disappearance understandably hard. I'm sure Ross doesn't blame me for what happened, not really. Regardless, I'm not sure he's ever forgiven me for being the one who was set free."

Seriously? Did the jerk not realize that Aubrey was as much a victim as Marta had been, even if they'd suffered very different fates? The burden of guilt Aubrey carried for just being alive took its toll over time and was enough to break some people. Jonah knew that for a fact. After all, he'd learned the hard way exactly what it was like to live with the crippling guilt that came from surviving when your best friend didn't.

He fought the unexpected urge to wrap his arms around Aubrey's slender shoulders and offer whatever comfort she would accept from him. It would be unprofessional on his part, and he needed to maintain an emotional distance for his own sake. That wasn't going to be easy when something about her brought out every protective instinct he had. He flipped through his notebook until he found the guy's name. "To be clear, are we talking about Ross Easton?"

She nodded as she swiped the tears away with the back of her hand. "Yes, but I can't believe that he sent that note. Ross would never torment me like that. Besides, he wouldn't have known about the coin. The police insisted I not share that particular information with anyone. That was especially true after Marta's parents offered a reward for any information that resulted in the return of their daughter. The investigating officers said it was very important that only the kidnapper, the police and I knew what kind of coin he'd used. Keeping it secret would help them sort through any calls that came in on the tip line."

"So, no one outside of you and the investigating officers knew it was a buffalo head nickel?"

"I can't swear to that, but I never even told my parents."

"What about the person who spotted you tied to that tree and called the police?"

Aubrey shook her head. "No, I don't think he would've seen it. The coin was still stuck under the insole in my tennis shoe when the police turned all of my clothes over to your forensics people. They were the ones who found it."

Jonah made a mental note to check the evidence logs to see if anyone had shown any unusual interest in the evidence related to Aubrey's case. The problem was that after twelve years, there were any number of people who had worked on the case. It had started with the patrol officers who had responded to the 911 call when Aubrey had been found, then there was the detective who handled the initial investigation, and so on, until it had eventually been turned over to George Swahn. It was always possible someone had slipped up and mentioned the coin to the wrong person and might not even remember doing it.

"Let's get back to this sensation of someone watching you. Is there anyone else other than this Ross Easton guy who might do something like that?"

She fidgeted in her seat and delayed responding to the question until after she ate another cookie. Finally, Aubrey spoke in a soft whisper. "I don't want to cause any problems for them."

This time he couldn't control his temper. How was he supposed to help the woman if she held back crucial information? No longer able to sit still, he stood and leaned against the porch railing far enough away to avoid hovering over her. "Aubrey, don't play games with me. I need names."

She slapped her hand over her mouth and looked horrified. "Did I actually say that aloud?"

"Yes, you did, so that cat is out of the bag. Tell me what you're thinking."

"Fine, but I meant what I said. I would really prefer you not bother them with this. They've been through too much already."

"Who has been through too much?"

Although Jonah figured he already knew. Crimes like this one often affected a surprising number of people, just like a stone dropped into still water caused an ever widening series of ripples. Logically speaking, Marta's parents would have been right near the epicenter of the event.

Aubrey's next words confirmed his suspicions. "Mr. and Mrs. Pyne are good people, but they resented that I was the one who got to come home. Marta's disappearance obviously tore a huge hole in their hearts. I understand that, and I continue to pray that they somehow can find some peace in their lives."

That was admirable of her, but he still needed to know what he was dealing with here. "So I take it they've caused you problems in the past."

"Nothing I couldn't handle."

His gut reaction told him that was an out-and-out lie. Whatever they'd done had hurt this woman deeply. She might have found a way to cope with their antics, but she hadn't escaped unscathed.

"I need details."

Aubrey crossed her arms over her chest and shook her head. "No. Besides, I haven't spoken to them in ages. Leave them alone."

Jonah wasn't in the habit of taking orders from civilians and wouldn't start now. Still, the change in her demeanor was interesting to see. A few minutes ago, she'd looked like a stiff breeze would send her tumbling across the yard, but her sympathy for the Pynes had her ready to do battle.

He tried again, this time with a softer approach. "I appreciate your concern for them, but I can't let you tie my hands like this. Tell me what they did. If it's all in the past, then there may be no need for me to ask them about it."

After letting her digest that much, he leaned forward. "But you should know that I will be speaking with everyone who was connected to the case twelve years ago."

When she started to protest, he held up his hand to ward off her next argument. "Yes, I've already reviewed the original statements. That's not the same as hearing it firsthand. I'll be talking to your parents tomorrow."

Her dark eyes flashed hot with anger. "Thanks for the warning. You should know that they will likely refuse to talk to you. I'm sure in your line of work you learn pretty quickly that people handle these situations in vastly different ways.

My mom and dad did everything they could to shield me from anything having to do with my case. They didn't want me talking about it to the press, the police, or even them. My mom's attitude was that if we simply quit focusing on what happened, the sooner everything would get back to normal."

She stared into the distance and softly added, "As if it could ever be that easy."

Once again looking haunted by her memories, Aubrey glanced at Jonah before turning her attention to the huge flower bed in her small front yard. "But back to Mr. and Mrs. Pyne—they couldn't handle seeing me patch the pieces of my life back together. It was as if they thought we should all put everything on hold until Marta finally got to come home."

Jonah wasn't surprised. "Time probably has remained frozen for them. In my experience, families have a hard time doing anything beyond watching and waiting for their loved one to walk through the front door again. Nothing else matters and giving up isn't an option."

"I know." She fell silent again for several seconds. "Anyway, I took a semester off from college to recuperate, but then I went back to finish my teaching degree. I couldn't simply sit around and do nothing forever, especially with my parents doing their best to pretend nothing had ever happened at all. At first, I stopped by periodically to check on the Pynes, but it got harder to face them as time went on. Mr. Pyne did his best to be polite, but it was more difficult for his wife to be around me. Finally, he quietly asked me not to come around anymore. To be honest, that was a huge relief."

He jotted down a few notes as he spoke. "I'm guessing that was probably true for them, as well. While your intentions were good, it was a constant reminder of all that they lost. Regardless, you shouldn't feel guilty about no longer visiting them."

She stood and stepped down off the porch. Trying not to crowd her, he followed along as she began systematically dead-heading the flowering bushes next to the sidewalk. After a bit, he prodded her into finishing the story. "What happened next?"

"Eventually, I got a job teaching. That's when I bought this house using some money my grandmother left me. I love my parents, but by that point I really needed my own space. While they never liked to talk about what happened, somewhere along the line they turned into... I think the term is 'helicopter parents.' Seriously, if I was five minutes late getting home from work, you would've thought I'd committed a major crime. For sure, they didn't want me to leave the house except to work."

She tossed the dead flowers in a pile and went back to work. "When I moved here, I could finally breathe again, like life had taken a big step back toward normal. A short time later, I met a nice guy at church, and we started dating. I don't know how the Pynes found out, but Mrs. Pyne showed up on my doorstep and demanded to know why I got to have a life when Marta didn't. It would've been one thing if she had limited it to me, but she went after the guy as well. Needless to say, that relationship was over before it even really got started."

"Have they ever done anything like that again?"

Her cheeks flushed a bit pink. "Once. After that, I pretty much gave up dating."

Jonah had to forcibly unclench his fists. He understood the Pynes had been hurting. Probably still were, but that didn't mean their behavior was any kind of okay. Aubrey added her latest collection of dead flowers to the pile and dusted off her hands. "Is there anything else you need to know?"

Her tone made it clear that she thought he'd already poked around in her past enough for one day. "Not right now. If you notice a bigger than normal police presence in your neighborhood, I've asked the patrol officers in this area to do more frequent drives past your home. I've also told my captain that we really need someone detailed to watch your back twenty-four seven. He agreed to make the request but said the budget is tight, so it's unlikely to be okayed unless the threat becomes more specific."

She looked resigned, if not particularly happy about that possibility. "I don't want you to think I'm not appreciative, but is that kind of surveillance really necessary?"

"That we'd even consider the possibility is a sign that we're taking this threat seriously. I would suggest you do the same. Use extra care when you go anywhere. Park near lights if you have to go out at night. Call 911 if anything happens or doesn't look right. Better yet, go stay with your parents so you're not alone."

"That's not going to happen. I fought too long to regain my independence." Then she shivered even standing in the direct sun. "That said, I don't like living scared and jumping at shadows."

"No one does." He handed her another of his business cards. "This is my direct line. Call any time, day or night."

"Thank you." Aubrey studied it for several seconds and stuck it in her pocket. "Before we forget, I'll go get those files for you."

He watched her walk away, sensing that she wouldn't appreciate him following her inside. She was back surprisingly fast, which sadly meant she kept the files close by at all times. As she handed them over, Aubrey mustered up a small smile. "Don't think I'm not grateful for your concern, Detective Kelly. It's just this has stirred up a lot of bad memories."

"It's all right. I know this is difficult. I'll be in touch." He took a step back and added, "And I meant what I said. Call if anything comes up."

"I will."

As he set the box of files in the trunk of his car, he couldn't help but notice how quickly she'd hustled to get back inside. The door was already closed, and no doubt all the locks firmly back in place. All in all, it didn't sound as if those memories she'd mentioned had ever been laid to rest, which was too bad. In a perfect world, a woman like Aubrey Sims deserved a happy life, maybe with that nice guy she mentioned earlier, along with a couple of kids. But instead, the shadows of the past had forced her to take shelter in that tiny house behind locked doors and drawn shades.

He supposed it could be worse. After all, she did get out to run errands and held down a good job. She'd also mentioned church, so maybe she found strength and solace there. He hoped so, because the ghost from her past had raised its ugly head again. Feeling frustrated, he slammed the trunk lid closed with more force than necessary. After one more look up and down the street, he headed back to the office to update the captain on what he'd learned and maybe review the files Aubrey had given him. Tomorrow morning he'd start interviewing the other people connected to the case.

Meanwhile, he offered up a silent prayer that he wouldn't fail Aubrey Sims like he had Gino. Hopefully, this time God would be listening.

Chapter Five

Aubrey checked her appearance in the mirror before picking up her purse and keys to leave. She didn't have to be at work for another hour, but she preferred to get there a little earlier than usual this time of year. As she stepped out onto the porch, her phone rang. It was tempting to simply ignore it, especially when she saw her mother's name on the screen. It didn't take a genius to know why she was calling.

"Mom, I'm just leaving for work, so I can't really talk now. I'll call you when I get home this afternoon."

She was almost breathless from trying to bulldoze over whatever her mother was saying even though she knew resistance was futile. Her mother was nothing if not stubborn. Surrendering to the inevitable, Aubrey sat down in the closest chair and prepared to listen to the tirade that was coming. "Sorry, Mom, I didn't hear what you were saying."

"That's because you were trying to talk over me, which is nothing short of rude."

"Sorry." Though she really wasn't. "What's up?"

"There is a detective on my front porch demanding to talk to us. What have you done now?"

Aubrey pinched the bridge of her nose and closed her eyes.

"I haven't done anything, Mom. And I'm sure Detective Kelly will happily explain the situation if you would simply talk to him."

Her mother's voice jumped up an octave. "Have you been pestering the police again about things we all know are better left in the past?"

"No, but something has happened regarding the case. I did ask Detective Kelly not to bother you and Dad, but he recently took over Detective Swahn's workload. Since the case is new to him, he plans to talk to everyone concerned. Now, I really need to leave for work."

"This fixation is not healthy for you, Aubrey. Perhaps it's time for you to see Dr. Wilcox again."

She tried to head her mother off at the pass. "I've already made it clear that's never going to happen. I can't stop you from talking to Dr. Wilcox about your own issues, but leave me out of it. I have to hang up now. Go talk to Detective Kelly. I'm sure it won't take long."

Then she made good on her threat and disconnected the call with her mother still babbling on the other end of the line. At least the good detective couldn't say he hadn't been warned about how her parents would react to him showing up on their doorstep. No doubt she'd be hearing from one or both of her parents later after she got home from work.

Most likely she'd hear from the detective as well. For some reason that thought wasn't nearly as upsetting as the idea of being lectured by her folks for the umpteenth time on how she should simply forget the past. Detective Kelly might have not appreciated her efforts to shield the Pynes and her folks from the current situation, but at least he'd never once questioned why she still needed answers after all this time.

Under other circumstances, she might've even found him attractive, but those intelligent blue eyes saw way too much. There was a watchfulness about Jonah Kelly, as if he could see right through to the heart of her fears and insecurities.

She worked hard to present a facade to the world that she was strong and whole, not the patched-together mess that she could be at times. The last thing she wanted was a man who saw her as weak or needy.

At least the drive to work was uneventful. Once there, she did her best to shake off her problems and focus on her job. She refused to carry that darkness into the school building with her. The children under her care deserved better.

"You're here bright and early."

She didn't quite contain a squeak of fear at the sound of a man's voice coming from right behind her. It was a huge relief that she recognized who it was before she did something foolish like taking off running for the front door of the building. Pasting on a bright smile, she turned to face her boss. Lyle Peale had taken over as principal of the elementary school the previous school year. He was well liked by the staff as well as the students and their families. Her pulse began to slow down as she greeted him. "Sorry, I didn't see you. Good morning."

He smiled at her. "I didn't mean to startle you. I was just saying that you're here bright and early this morning."

She fell into step with him as they made their way toward the building. "There are a few things I want to get done before the munchkins arrive. You know how it is this time of year. The last few days of school fly by so fast that it's almost impossible to get everything finished before we wave goodbye to the kids for the summer."

"So true. Sadly, my to-do list seems to get longer every day." He reached around her to open the door to the building. "Do you have big plans for the summer?"

"Nothing special. I have some projects lined up to do around my house. A couple of rooms need to be painted, and I love working out in the yard."

"Well, I hope you take time to relax a little. Personally, I'm planning to get away for a while, maybe driving along the Oregon coast without any particular itinerary."

"Sounds like fun. It's been a long time since I've been down there, but I remember how beautiful it was."

In fact, she'd barely left town in the past twelve years, but he didn't need to know about that. It would only bring up questions she didn't want to answer.

Lyle headed toward the main office where the school secretary immediately stood up with a handful of phone messages in her hand. "Well, looks like I'm needed. Have a great day, Aubrey."

"You, too."

Her classroom was at the far end of the building. Other staff members called out greetings on her way down the hall. She smiled and waved back, stopping to confer with the other third grade teacher about the end-of-the-year activities they had planned. By the time she reached her classroom, her mood was much improved, as if she'd left her worries back out in the parking lot. They'd be waiting for her when she left work, but for now she had happier things to think about.

Hours later Aubrey left the building with a couple of friends, which saved her from having to walk out to the parking lot by herself. Detective Kelly would be so proud of her for taking the precautions he'd suggested. Little did he know that she almost always made sure she wasn't alone when she left work. After all, she and Marta had been grabbed as they headed to the parking lot after class. A person didn't forget something like that.

Once in her car, she gave in and did something that she'd been dreading all day. She checked her phone. Just as she'd expected, both her mother and father had left voice mails demanding she return their calls immediately, even though they knew she was at work. When that had failed, they'd resorted to long angry text messages. She groaned after skimming their content.

Not only did they want to talk about what was going on,

they were coming to her house to do so in person. Great, just what she needed. Worse yet, if she didn't get a move on, they would already be there waiting for her. It would be nice if they would at least give her a chance to unwind and maybe even eat a little dinner before they started in on her. Not that she'd be able to actually relax knowing they were on their way, but it was the principle of the thing.

Surrendering to the inevitable, she drove the short distance to her house. It was a relief that her parents' car was nowhere in sight. Instead, there was a certain black sedan parked on the street in front of her house, and its owner had made himself comfortable on her front porch. She wondered how long Detective Kelly been waiting and why he was there at all.

He stood as soon as she pulled into the driveway and then hustled to help her carry in the pile of papers and other stuff she'd brought home to work on that evening. As he followed her back toward the porch, she said, "Detective, I thought you were going to call."

"I was in the neighborhood and thought I'd stop by to see how you were doing." He looked past her toward the car slowing to pull into her driveway. "I also wanted to warn you how things went when I talked to your folks this morning. I know your mother called you to demand answers before she'd even let me inside the house."

Aubrey actually laughed at that. "Yeah, she wasn't happy, especially when I hung up on her because I had to get to work. If she took her anger out on you, I'm sorry."

He managed a small smile. "I've been in tougher situations and survived."

As they talked, she unlocked the door and led the way inside. "Can I fix you a glass of iced tea or a can of pop? I think I have cola and root beer."

"Iced tea sounds good. Should I let your parents in?"

She pretended to think it over as she poured four glasses of tea and tossed a few cookies on a plate and set them all on the dining room table. That was going to be pretty much her limit on playing hostess, especially since none of her guests had actually been invited. "I suppose there's no getting around it. If I don't open the door, they'll start banging on it."

Jonah followed her to the door, standing slightly behind her as if providing backup in case it was needed. She took a deep breath before turning the doorknob. "Brace yourself, Detective."

Just as Aubrey had expected, her mother had her fist raised to start pounding on the door. It was hard not to laugh when she almost fell across the threshold as Aubrey opened the door. "Mom, Dad, what a pleasant surprise."

Her companion made an odd noise like he was trying to cover up a laugh with a fake cough. At least someone was amused by the current situation. Her mother sailed into the room as if she owned the place, while her father shot her an apologetic look on his way past.

"Why don't we all have a seat at the table?"

Rather than follow the simple directive, her mom stopped to glare at Detective Kelly. "What are you doing here? I told you to stay away from our daughter."

He shrugged. "That's not your decision to make. I have a job to do, and I will see it done."

Jonah sauntered over to the table and politely pulled out a chair for Aubrey before settling into the one next to her. Maybe he assumed her father would do the same for his wife, or else he'd decided that her mother's behavior didn't deserve his best manners. After a second, her mother huffed and pointed toward the door. "Detective, we're here to have a discussion with Aubrey, a *private* discussion. And in case you didn't get the hint, you're not welcome here."

Aubrey sincerely hoped that Detective Kelly never aimed that kind of smile in her direction. He calmly met her mother's gaze as he reached for a cookie. "I'm here for the same reason,

Mrs. Sims. I'm not leaving until I have a chance to review a few things with your daughter."

His voice remained calm even as his expression turned harsh. "And as I explained this morning, my investigation into the events of the past couple of days, as well as what happened twelve years ago, will continue—with or without your approval or cooperation."

Her father joined the conversation. "Why can't you understand that we don't want the case reopened?"

Aubrey wasn't going to sit on the sidelines and let the other three people in the room debate the issue. "Mom, Dad, stop this right now. The case isn't being reopened. It was never closed in the first place."

She turned to face Jonah. "Correct me if I'm wrong, Detective Kelly, but my understanding is that the file will never be closed until whoever kidnapped me and Marta that night has been brought to justice."

Detective Kelly backed her play. "That's correct, Ms. Sims. Cold cases may go inactive. However, they are all reviewed periodically to see if perhaps new forensic techniques are available or if some new evidence has come to light."

Her parents exchanged unhappy looks before her father spoke. "Twelve years ago, we were told that there was little or no forensic evidence. They also never found the actual crime scene. If that was true, then there's nothing for your forensics people to work with."

"That's true, but everything will be reviewed anyway. As I told you this morning, the case has gone active again because some new information has come to light."

"The nature of which you refused to share with us, so forgive us if we don't believe you."

Aubrey stared at her mother in shock. That was a pretty outrageous statement from a woman who preached tolerance and good manners at all times. Meanwhile, her mother plowed right on ahead.

"My husband and I discussed the situation after you left this morning. Our obligation is to make the best decision for our daughter, which is to shut down this farce before it goes any farther. Her therapist is really concerned about how she continues to be fixated on that incident from twelve years ago. I spoke to him today, and he says this could exacerbate the situation."

Her mother's callous words ripped opened deep wounds that had never really healed. Her parents meant well, but Aubrey could never find the right words to convince them that they were wrong. It was also humiliating to have them sit there and talk about her in front of Jonah Kelly as if she was incapable of making decisions for herself. This was her life they were talking about, and she was the one who was in charge of it.

When Jonah opened his mouth to respond to her mother, Aubrey shot him a hard look and shook her head. After a slight hesitation, he nodded and leaned back in his chair. She didn't doubt for one minute that he would charge right back into the fray if he thought the situation called for it.

She liked that about him.

Aubrey rose to her feet to stare down at her parents. It was tempting to scream at them, but that would only reinforce their belief that they knew what was best for her. "Mom, I'm sorry but you and Dad need to leave right now. Detective Kelly is a guest in my home, and I won't let you be rude to him. That's the first thing. Second, you've somehow forgotten that I'm an adult and have been for a long time. You may think you're protecting me, but what you're really doing is diminishing me. Third, Dr. Wilcox may be your therapist, but he definitely isn't mine. I fired him ten years ago and haven't spoken to the man since. I don't appreciate him rendering baseless opinions about me. If it continues, I will file an official complaint about his unprofessional behavior with the proper authorities."

Then she gestured toward Jonah. "As far as I'm concerned,

right now Detective Kelly is the only person in this room who actually has my best interests at heart."

When her parents made no move to leave, she walked over to the door and opened it. "That wasn't a suggestion, folks. It was an order. Go home before you permanently damage our relationship, because right now it's on pretty shaky ground."

Her mother's face was ashen, and her father wasn't looking much better when he spoke for both of them. "Aubrey, we're just trying to do what's best for you."

"And failing miserably at the moment. I'm sorry if that's hurtful, but it would be nice if for once you talked with me instead of *at* me."

When they finally did as she asked, she stood by the door. As they passed by, she gave in to a strong urge to hug each of them. "I've never doubted that you love me and that you wish none of this had ever happened. So do I, but it did. I sincerely believe that the only chance I have to ever put all of this to rest is to learn the truth. I pray to our Lord every night that someday that will happen."

Her mother drew a ragged breath. "Then that's what I'll pray for, too. We'll go now."

Aubrey suspected she wasn't the only one who was seeing through a sheen of tears right now. It was tempting to slam the door shut and turn the locks. Instead, she patiently waited until they were backing out of the driveway to wave at them one last time.

Finally finding the courage to tell her parents exactly how she felt was surprisingly cathartic but also exhausting. She closed the door and leaned against it, needing its solid strength at her back while she reined in her emotions. Even with her eyes closed, she was acutely aware of the silent man watching her every move. Finally, she returned to the table.

He waited until she sat and had a sip of her tea to speak. "I'm sorry for riling them up like that."

"It's not your fault, Detective. All the blame rests squarely on the shoulders of the monster who started all of this twelve years ago. Like I told my folks, the only way to end this threat is to find the truth."

Despite the roller-coaster ride of emotions she'd been on since her current companion had showed up on her doorstep yesterday, she was determined to keep moving forward. "I don't know about you, Detective Kelly, but I've worked up quite an appetite. What do you say we order a pizza and then figure out where we go from here?"

"I say call me Jonah, and the pizza will be my treat."

Chapter Six

Jonah parked his car a few houses down the street from his target's home. Before making his final approach, he decided to sit back and observe for a short time. He hadn't set out to spy on Ross Easton, but just by happenstance the man was outside working out in his front yard when Jonah turned down his street.

All in all, Easton's home was picture-perfect, which was a little surprising. He'd gotten the impression from Aubrey that Ross Easton had never recovered from the loss of his fiancée in the intervening twelve years. Jonah had expected the man's home to reflect some of that dysfunction. Maybe Ross had finally moved on with his life.

Jonah hoped so.

There was only one way to find out. He drove forward to park directly in front of Easton's house. The man had just finished putting away his lawnmower. He shut the garage door and started toward his front porch, but paused when he noticed Jonah climbing out of his car.

"Can I help you?"

Jonah stopped at the curb to take out his identification before stepping on Easton's property. He held it up to show his badge and picture. "Mr. Easton, I'm Detective Jonah Kelly. I would like to talk for a few minutes if you have time."

Easton's expression instantly morphed from friendly curiosity to disgust. "Like it's ever made any difference if I said I was busy whenever one of you shows up without even bothering to call first."

He probably wasn't wrong about that. "This shouldn't take long."

Still not looking any happier, Easton nodded. "Fine, come on in. Just know that I have to leave for work in an hour and need to get cleaned up before I go."

Jonah followed him inside and up the stairs to the main level of the house. He stopped at the top of the steps to see where his unwilling host wanted him to go. Pointing to the right, Easton said, "Might as well do this in the kitchen. I don't know about you, but I could use a drink."

He shot Jonah a hard look. "I'm talking a glass of water or iced tea, nothing alcoholic. I finally got my act together and gave that stuff up about five years back."

Interesting.

"Either would be fine."

Easton motioned toward the small kitchen table. "Make yourself comfortable. I'm going to wash my hands first, and then I'll fix the drinks."

Jonah took advantage of the delay to quietly look around the kitchen and the limited amount of the living room that he could see from where he was sitting. Nothing looked new or fancy, but it looked...cozy. That was the best description he could come up with. It was the kind of place that his mother would likely say had benefited from a woman's touch. It was difficult to decide if Easton actually had someone special in his life, though. There was only a single plate and cup in the dish drainer next to the sink, and the three pairs of shoes lined up next to the back door were all men's.

His unwilling host set two glasses of iced tea on the table

and sat down. While he got settled, Jonah took a long drink. "Thanks. That hit the spot."

Easton ignored his own drink as he crossed his arms over his chest and leaned back in his chair. "Now that the pleasantries are over with, what's going on? Why are you here instead of that other guy who used to hassle me on a regular basis?"

Jonah took out his notebook and a pen. "I'm new on the case. I took over Detective Swahn's workload after he retired."

"And you decided to ruin my day by stopping by just to introduce yourself? If so, you can leave now that you've done that."

"Not exactly." He met Easton's gaze head-on. "I'm reinterviewing everyone connected to the kidnapping."

Easton reached for his iced tea and held it in a white-knuckled grip as if debating whether or not to toss it in Jonah's face. "Why can't you people simply leave the past in the past?"

There was no easy way to break the news, so Jonah launched his opening salvo. "Someone sent an anonymous note that presents a very clear and present threat to Aubrey Sims. I'm here to see if you know anything about that."

Easton's shock seemed clear-cut as he leaned forward, his elbows on the table. "Me? Why would you think that?"

"Because you used to stalk Aubrey, Mr. Easton," Jonah declared bluntly. "She has good reason to think you never forgave her for being the one who came home."

The other man's expression turned grim. "I'm not proud of it, but she isn't wrong about that. Like a lot of fools, I tried to numb my pain with alcohol. When that didn't work, I looked for a handy target for my anger. For sure, Aubrey deserved better from me. I pretty much hit bottom, but I thank God every day that my pastor convinced me to get help. It hasn't been easy, but I haven't touched a drop of alcohol for nearly six years now."

He stared at the tabletop for several seconds as he visibly struggled to regain control. When he finally looked back up at Jonah, his eyes were full of regret. "I also haven't gone near Aubrey since I first got sober, even though I should've apologized to her. The two of us used to be friends, but I figure I burned that bridge a long time ago."

He lapsed into silence for several seconds, no doubt lost in the pain of his memories. When he finally spoke again, his words were laced with cold, hard anger. "Seriously, some joker is threatening Aubrey? Who would do that and why now?"

"I can't reveal the exact content of the note, but I assure you that the threat was very clear. As of right now, we don't know who sent the note or why they picked this particular moment in time."

"Is she okay? The poor thing has got to be scared out of her wits."

Easton's concern felt genuine, as if it really upset him that Aubrey might be in danger. Perhaps he was putting on a good act, but it was too soon to tell.

"So, Mr. Easton, when was the last time you spoke to or saw Aubrey?"

The other man stared out the window next to the table as he mulled over the question. "Look, this probably won't be the only time we'll be talking. Could you please just call me Ross? Mr. Easton feels a little too much like I'm being interrogated."

That wasn't too far off the truth. But if using his first name made the man feel more comfortable, Jonah wouldn't argue the point. "Fine, Ross it is. So, to be clear, when did you last interact with Aubrey?"

"Five years ago at least, right before I did a stint in rehab. Afterward, I started going to meetings to help stay sober. That's when I realized what I was doing wasn't right. For sure it wasn't helping either of us deal with what had happened."

"And what exactly had you been doing?"

Ross's face flushed red. "Watching over her. Following her whenever she went out. I told myself I was keeping an eye on her to make sure nothing happened to her, but that wasn't it at all. Like you said, I was stalking Aubrey, plain and simple. I count myself lucky that she didn't have me arrested for it."

He was right about that. If she'd told Jonah's predecessor what was going on, Swahn would have tossed Ross behind bars in a heartbeat. "Why were you doing that?"

"Back then, I spent a lot of time with Marta's parents. Too much time, to be honest. After a while, instead of comforting each other, we somehow revved each other up instead. It was so frustrating that the cops couldn't find the guy that did this, and we wanted...no, we *needed* someone to blame. That was especially true for Marta's mom. I don't know why, but Aubrey became the main target for Dina's anger. She was always asking why had Aubrey gotten to come home and not Marta. She went so far as to wonder what Aubrey had done to convince that kidnapper to let her go instead of Marta. That sort of thing."

Jonah fought down a surge of anger and prayed for patience. How could they not realize that Aubrey had been a victim, too? None of what happened had been her fault. But judging from the deep lines bracketing Ross's mouth and eyes, he'd suffered enough. He didn't need Jonah to read him the riot act for his past bad behavior. It was time to get back on topic.

"Do you still remember many details about what happened twelve years ago?"

Ross shivered. "Yeah, despite all the alcohol I consumed, it did nothing to dull those memories. Marta and Aubrey had a late afternoon class. They were supposed to meet up with some friends at a coffee shop afterward to review for a test they were having the next day. When neither of them showed, their friends tried calling them. After leaving several messages, they finally drove back to the college to look for Marta and Aubrey. They found Aubrey's car in the parking lot with both of its back tires slashed. The campus cops took their statements and then called the regular police. I pretty much stayed with Marta's parents around the clock for days while we waited for word."

He stopped to drink some more tea. "At first, we were all thrilled to learn Aubrey had been found and kept waiting for someone to find Marta."

His voice dropped to a rough whisper. "Twelve years later, we're still waiting."

Ross looked around the room, his eyes dull with pain. "I bought this place right after Marta and I got engaged. The only reason I could afford it was that the house was in foreclosure, and the previous owner had let it get really run-down."

He smiled just a little. "Unlike me, Marta was always super organized, so naturally she started a notebook of everything we needed to do to fix it up. Lists of paint colors, flooring, even the style of furniture she wanted. Over the years, I've checked off nearly every item on her to-do lists. There isn't a day that goes by that I don't wish she were here to see it all. Marta would've loved seeing how close I've come to making her dreams come true."

That was probably true, but Jonah thought maybe Ross would be better off if he never looked at that notebook again. Not that he'd tell him that. He understood all too well how one tragic moment in time became the center of someone's universe. The gaping hole that Gino's death had left in Jonah's own life remained a steady ache every minute of every day. His entire life was now seen through the filter of knowing he had lived but his friend hadn't.

For now, the best Jonah could do for Ross was stay busy jotting down a few more notes to give him time to regain his composure. Finally, he picked up the interview where they'd left off. "Looking back, is there anything else you can tell me? Especially anything significant that might have happened before that evening?"

Ross closed his eyes for several seconds. "I've spent years wondering if there was something I missed...something that might've clued us in that Marta and Aubrey were in danger, but there's nothing. No near misses. No weird encounters with a stranger. No sign of anyone sneaking around or watching them. At the time, the police did their best to reconstruct Marta's movements for the week prior to her disappearance. I assume they did the same for Aubrey."

Jonah looked up from his notebook. "I know they were roommates at the college. Do you know if they had more than that one class together?"

"After all this time, I'm not sure. They were both education majors, but Aubrey was aiming for elementary school, and Marta wanted to work with older kids." Then Ross frowned. "Aubrey worked a few hours a week in the admissions office as part of her financial aid package. Marta had a part-time job in the library that she was going to quit at the end of the semester. She was leaving right after Christmas to study abroad."

"So both of them worked in positions where they might have met a wide variety of students and faculty?"

Ross gave him a curious look. "Is that important?"

"Right now I don't know what's important and what isn't. But I didn't see anything about their jobs in the file. I'll have to talk to Aubrey about it when I see her again. Is there anything else you think I should know?"

"Not that I can think of." Ross glanced at the clock on the nearby microwave. "Look, I need to get a move on if I'm going to get to work on time."

After sticking his notebook and pen back into his pocket, Jonah pulled out his business card and laid it on the table. "Call me if you think of anything. I'm sorry that I've stirred up a bunch of painful memories for you, but my priority right now has to be keeping Aubrey Sims safe."

Both men rose to their feet. To Jonah's surprise, Ross held out his hand. "Actually, it was nice being able to talk about Marta with someone who understands why I still miss her after all this time. If she'd died in an accident or something *normal*...although I'm not sure that's the right word exactly, but you get the idea...maybe I would've been able to move on. But it's the not knowing that lingers on, so there's never been any real closure for those of us who loved her. I'm guessing that's true for Aubrey, too."

He wasn't wrong about that. "Listen, I can't swear I'll succeed in finding you the answers you need, but I can promise that I'll try my best. For now, I'll let myself out so you can get ready for work."

As he walked away, Ross called after him, "Tell Aubrey I'm sorry."

"I will."

Jonah stepped out on the small porch and pulled the door closed behind him. He stopped long enough to breathe in the scent of fresh-cut grass and the scattering of flowers in bloom around the yard. It took two more breaths to clear out the miasma of misery that had permeated the very walls inside Ross's home.

Closing his eyes and lifting his face to the warmth of the sun, Jonah considered what he should do next. Finally, he silently offered up a small prayer. *Father, guide my steps so I can help You bring peace to Ross and the others connected to this case. Amen.*

He realized how good it felt to be talking to God again. And having done all he could for Ross Easton, it was time to move on to the next stop on his agenda. After that, he'd check in with Aubrey before calling it a day.

Aubrey made another round through the house to look out each and every window. It was the third time she's done so since she'd gotten home from work two hours ago. She wasn't sure exactly what she was hoping to see—or maybe not see—but she couldn't seem to resist the compulsion to keep peeking outside. It would be dark soon, so there wasn't much point in maintaining the vigil much longer.

This small house was her sanctuary, the place she always felt safe. The one thing she rarely experienced while inside its four walls was loneliness. She was comfortable in her own skin, content to spend her evening hours preparing for the next day's lessons at school or reading a good book.

That anonymous note had changed everything, leaving her wondering if she was really safe anywhere. Rather than focus on that thought, she reminded herself of all the security features she already had in place, starting with strong doors with more locks than any rational person would deem necessary. All of her windows were covered with sheets of the top-rated security film inside and out. She had also invested in a top-of-the-line alarm system that she upgraded every time a better one came on the market. None of that had come cheap, but it was all necessary as far as she was concerned.

The only question was if there was anything else she could do to ensure the person behind the note couldn't breach her home. Maybe she'd ask Jonah the next time they spoke, not that she knew when that would be. Yeah, he'd told her to call any time, but that didn't mean she should bother him unnecessarily.

Looking around for any kind of distraction, she settled on something she'd already put off longer than she should have. She settled into her favorite chair in the living room and dialed her parents' number. While she hadn't quite forgiven them for their bad behavior, at least the source of their concern was understandable. They were her parents and worrying about their only child came with the job description. The least she could do was reassure them that she was all right.

Her father picked up on the second ring. "Hi, Dad. Before I start on the stack of work I brought home from school, I thought I'd call to see what you two are up to."

"The usual. I washed the car. Your mom did the grocery shopping. We're going to watch the ball game here in a little while."

From the time Aubrey was a young girl, she and her father

had spent many hours watching sports together. It was one of the few things she'd missed after she'd moved out. "I'll probably turn it on myself while I grade papers."

"Don't work too hard, sweetheart. You should be out with your friends doing something fun."

It wasn't the first time he'd made that suggestion. "It's almost the end of the school year, so I've got to get everything finished up. Two weeks from now I'll be free to kick back and relax."

Hopefully. If Jonah and his associates managed to track down the note writer by then. Until that happened, doing something fun or relaxing would was out of the question.

"Oops, kiddo, Mom is yelling that dinner's ready. I'd better go."

"Okay, Dad. Tell her hi for me. Love you both."

There was a brief silence before he spoke again. "I know it might not seem like it sometimes, but we do know you're an adult and capable of making your own decisions. We can't help but worry, though. The compulsion is an unavoidable part of the whole being-a-parent package."

She laughed, mainly because it would make him feel better. Her too, for that matter. "Enjoy the game, Dad."

As soon as she hung up, the doorbell rang. Just that quickly her good mood disappeared. Once again, she wasn't expecting anyone. Well, unless Jonah had decided to stop by without calling first. She checked the camera feed from the front door to see a young woman standing there holding a bouquet of flowers in her hand. A peek out the front window revealed a small SUV with the name of a local florist emblazoned on its exterior.

Everything seemed to be on the up-and-up, but who would be sending her flowers? There was only one way to find out. She unlocked the door and opened it just enough to be able to look out. "Hello, can I help you?"

"I have flowers for Aubrey Sims."

"I'm Aubrey."

She opened the door wider. As soon as she did, the delivery woman thrust the flower arrangement at her, leaving her no choice but to take it. "Do you know who they're from?"

"There's a card."

The woman stepped off the porch and kept going while Aubrey remained frozen in place, not sure what to do next. She was probably being foolish, but there was no way she was going to take the flowers inside her house. Not until she knew who had sent them. She loved fresh flowers as much as the next person, and the bouquet of a dozen roses in a variety of colors was gorgeous—and a seriously romantic gesture. There was a problem—she couldn't remember the last time she'd even been on a date. So there was no significant other, no boyfriend, not even a casual friend who would have forked over big bucks to buy her flowers.

That didn't mean she could just keep standing there holding the bouquet. Eventually she was going to have to take action of some kind. It was tempting to throw the flowers in her yard waste bin, but that wouldn't provide any answers. While she stood there dithering, it finally occurred to her that whoever had sent the flowers could be watching to see how she reacted. That possibility finally stirred her into action.

Rather than take the flowers inside, she gently set them on the table right there on the porch. Then, trying to act as if she was actually thrilled about the surprise bouquet, Aubrey leaned down to breathe in their perfume. Normally, she liked roses, but she found the scent of this bunch to be too strong and cloying. It was probably only her imagination working overtime, but she couldn't wait to put some distance between herself and the flowers.

After one more look around, she headed back inside the house to summon help. It was time to call Detective Kelly.

Chapter Seven

Jonah hung back and watched as the forensics team once again did their thing. The techs had finished taking photographs and then planned to dust everything for fingerprints. He doubted they'd learn much of anything from the flower arrangement itself, but it was important to do everything by the book. The most likely scenario was that only the employees at the florist shop had actually touched the flowers, the vase and the cardboard box that came with them.

While he dealt with the situation at Aubrey's house, Jonah had sent a patrol officer to stop by the florist shop to take preliminary statements from the owner and her employees to see what they could remember about the person who had ordered the roses. Predictably, it wasn't much. It had been a man, probably around six feet tall, with brownish hair that had been mostly covered up with a baseball cap. He'd worn sunglasses and was dressed as if on his way to play softball, right down to the batting gloves.

The bottom line was that nothing about him set off any alarms—just a regular guy sending last-minute flowers for a special occasion. He'd paid for the flowers in cash rather than with a debit or credit card. While not all that common these days, it still happened from time to time.

Even the card that had accompanied the flowers proved to be useless as evidence. The man had left the shop without filling one out. Instead, he'd called half an hour later using a burner phone to say he'd forgotten that one little detail. The florist had offered to print the card for him, something she routinely did on orders that were phoned in. The message had been short and sweet: *I'll always be grateful for the gift of sharing time with you.*

It might have all sounded innocent enough to the florist, but Jonah knew better. It was another threat aimed right at Aubrey Sims. Another message intended to terrorize her while heightening the kidnapper's own pleasure.

"Is that everything?"

The tech finished bagging the note. "As much as we can accomplish here. We'll let you know if we manage to find anything useful."

"Thanks for responding so fast."

He left them to finish up. It was time to check in with Aubrey. She'd had no interest in watching the techs deal with the flowers, which was fine with him. There was always the chance that whoever sent the bouquet was close by as the drama played out. With that in mind, Jonah had quietly monitored the small crowd of curious neighbors across the street. According to the first officer on the scene, they'd started gathering not long after he had arrived to watch over Aubrey until Jonah could get there himself. He'd been on the other side of town at his physical therapy appointment when she'd called, and he hadn't wanted her to have to wait by herself.

He snapped a few more pictures of the small crowd to show Aubrey in case she recognized anyone who shouldn't be there. After one more look up and down the street, he knocked on the front door. "Aubrey, it's Jonah. Can you let me in?"

She must have been hovering near the door, because he could hear her turning the locks almost immediately. He slipped inside as quickly as possible, figuring she wouldn't feel safe until the door was closed and secured again. Her relief was palpable as she turned the dead bolt and fastened the chain.

He held out his phone. "I'd like you to look at these pictures I took of the people watching from across the street. They're most likely your neighbors, but I'd like to verify that if at all possible."

She glanced at the phone and then shook her head. "I will in a minute. I just made a fresh pot of tea and thought you might like some. I also thawed some banana bread I had in the freezer."

While he'd prefer to get right down to business, it was obvious that she needed the little bit of normalcy playing hostess would give her before she could deal with the current situation. "Tea actually sounds good. I usually take it with two sugars, no milk."

"Have a seat, and I'll be right back."

Half of the dining room table was covered in rows of folders made out of large sheets of brightly colored construction paper. There was a single name written at the top of each one, no doubt the members of her class. He had to admire Aubrey's determination to keep up with the needs of her students despite what was going on in her own life.

Which meant she wasn't going to appreciate what he was about to suggest. Whoever was behind the note and the flowers was definitely amping up his game. After twelve years of total silence, all of a sudden the kidnapper had reached out to Aubrey twice in less than a week. That didn't bode well for the coming days when they currently had no idea who the guy was, where he was located, or what his personal timeline looked like. To make matters worse, the man also knew both where Aubrey received her mail and her actual street address.

All of that made it much more likely that Aubrey had been right about someone following her recently. Jonah didn't know about her, but he knew he'd sleep better at night knowing that she was tucked away somewhere safe and sound.

As promised, she returned with their refreshments. After setting the tray down, she gathered up the files into a neat pile and set them out of the way on the far corner of the table. "Pardon the mess. I always send a folder of my students' best work home with them on the last day of school. They get to decorate the folders as an art project."

"I'm sure their parents love that."

At least his own parents had liked stuff like that. Meanwhile, Aubrey set his tea in front of him along with a plate with two thick slices of banana bread. "I didn't know if you liked the bread with anything on it, but I brought both butter and cream cheese."

"Plain would have been fine, but cream cheese sounds good."

As he spread a thick layer on the bread, Aubrey did the same with the butter. When she set her knife down, she gave him a tentative look. "Are they gone?"

It wasn't clear if she was talking about the forensics team or the flowers themselves. He decided to cover all the bases. "The techs were packing up to leave when I knocked on your door. They took everything with them—the flowers, the vase, the packing materials and the card."

Her relief was obvious. She took a small bite of the banana bread and then washed it down with a sip of tea. After setting her mug back down on the table, she visibly braced herself and asked, "Were you able to learn anything from the card?"

"Unfortunately, no. The guy didn't write it himself, so we can't compare the handwriting to the previous note. He paid cash, gave them your address and then left. The florist printed the note for him and stuck it in the envelope."

"What was the message?"

Jonah really didn't want to tell her. It wasn't just the message; it was the type of card he'd requested. "Something about being grateful for your time together."

Aubrey flinched as if the words actually caused her physical pain. He figured that was likely true. She picked up her mug and wrapped both hands around it, maybe needing that touch of warmth. A second later, she made eye contact with him and set the mug back down hard enough to splash some over the rim. After shaking the hot tea off her skin, she frowned at him. "There's more, isn't there? About the card, I mean. Something worse."

It was tempting to lie, but he needed her to trust him. "Yeah. It was a sympathy card, the kind that normally accompanies flowers sent to a funeral home."

Jonah gave her time to absorb that little bombshell and regroup before they continued. To his surprise, she simply nodded and then pointed toward his phone, which he'd laid on the table. "You wanted me to look at some pictures?"

He brought up the first one and handed her the phone. "I took them at different times, trying to capture the faces of everyone who stopped to watch. Even if you don't know them by name, it will help me narrow down anyone we need to check into."

She quickly flipped through the pictures one after the other without saying anything, and then went back to the first one. After setting the phone on the table, she scooted her chair a little closer to his so they could both see the screen. "All three people in this first one live on this block. The additional guy in the second one lives on the next street over. He walks his dog down our block almost every day about this time."

"That's helpful to know."

She was probably relieved to recognize everyone he'd photographed. Personally, he was disappointed but not surprised. It was too much to hope that there would have been a guy in a ball cap and gloves carrying a sign saying he'd sent the flowers. Time to move on.

After returning his phone to his jacket pocket, he brought up the next subject on his list. "So, I met with Ross Easton at his house."

That actually caused Aubrey to perk up a bit. "How is he?"

Leave it to her to care more about how her former stalker was doing than if he was any kind of threat to her. "From what I could tell, he's doing okay. More or less, anyway. I'm no psychologist, but I think that it means something that he's taking good care of his house and yard. He's holding down a job, too. I checked with his boss earlier today, and he says Ross is a hard worker and reliable."

"That's good news. He bought that house for him and Marta to live in after they got married. I kind of wondered if he'd sold it. Too many memories, you know."

Jonah decided not to tell her about Marta's notebook and how Ross had spent years creating the home she had wanted but that they would never share. Instead, he focused on the good news, such as it was. "He said his pastor helped him get into a rehab program five or six years ago. He claims he hasn't had a drink since."

He paused to take a sip of his tea. "He also said that once he got sober, he'd considered reaching out to apologize to you. In the end, he figured by that point you wouldn't want to hear from him. Regardless, he was upset that someone was threatening you now and was adamant it wasn't him."

"And you believed him?"

Jonah had given that particular question a lot of serious thought after leaving Ross's house. "Yeah, I did. He wasn't happy when I first showed up, but he definitely switched gears once I explained someone had threatened you. He didn't deny what happened before, but immediately swore he wasn't involved this time. I believe he was genuinely upset by what's been going on."

Aubrey sat in silence as she drank more of her tea and nibbled on a small bite of banana bread. Finally, she said, "If you talk to Ross again, please tell him that his apology is accepted. I guess we all handle grief in different ways. He had his life with Marta planned out. They were so happy together, and someone stole that away from him. It must have felt as if he'd lost half of himself."

Her description of what Ross had experienced hit a little too close to home for Jonah. Yeah, he'd lost his partner, but Gino's family had lost so much more—father, husband, son. All those relationships destroyed because one man got scared and decided to start shooting. Jonah was long overdue to stop by and check on Gino's wife and kids. They always seemed happy to see him, but he often wondered how long that would last. He wanted them to know that he'd come running whenever they needed him, but he feared that eventually he would become a painful reminder of what all they'd lost.

An unexpected movement near his face startled him, causing him to jerk his head back and almost go diving for cover. A second later, he realized that it was Aubrey waving her hand in front of his eyes as she tried to get his attention. He snapped, "What?"

Before she could explain, he immediately apologized. "Sorry, I didn't mean to snarl. I got lost in thought there for a second, and you surprised me."

Her expression turned sympathetic as she sat back in her chair and out of his reach. "It was more than a second, Jonah. You stopped talking and then just sat there staring off into space. I don't know where you went in your head, but I'm guessing it wasn't a good place."

Aubrey had enough problems on her plate without having to hear about his. "I'm okay. It was nothing."

Her skepticism was clear as she scoffed, "You might tell yourself that, but I don't believe it for a second. It wasn't nothing, Jonah. I've seen that same look in my own eyes too many times to believe that. What's going on?"

He found it interesting how she could look fragile one second and so fierce the next. He'd first seen it happen when she defended him against her parents. He found her inner core of strength fascinating. Meanwhile, she arched an eyebrow, still waiting for him to explain. He only realized that he was rubbing his knee when she gave it a pointed look. "Does it have something to do with how you hurt your leg?"

Despite his determination to keep his history private, the words slipped out. "I took a bullet in my knee when a case went sideways."

No sooner did he speak than he somehow found himself holding Aubrey's hand. Not at all sure how that had happened, he forced himself to release it and tried to rebuild the emotional barrier he lived behind these days. She didn't try to stop him, but that didn't mean she was letting the matter drop. "I think I heard about that on the news."

Then she gasped. "You weren't the only one who was shot that night, were you?"

"No, I wasn't. My partner was killed." He stared down at the half-eaten banana bread on his plate as if it were the most fascinating thing he'd ever seen. "Gino left behind a wife and kids. I can't help but keep wondering why him and not me. They needed him, while I didn't have anyone waiting at home for me."

"You can't think that way, Jonah. You didn't pull the trigger. That's all on the other guy. You know your friend wouldn't have blamed you. He knew the dangers that come along with being a cop, but he chose to serve anyway. You should honor his service and his memory, but don't let it keep you from getting on with your own life."

That was rich coming from her. He knew she meant well, but did she really think she had been successful at that? Yeah, she held down a steady job. She took good care of her house, but so did her old friend Ross. All of that was superficial, keeping up appearances in an effort to fool the world—and themselves—that everything was okay. But in so many ways, the two of them had stopped living life to the fullest twelve years ago. A glance at Aubrey's front door was proof of that. How many people had a security chain, a dead bolt, and two other heavy-duty locks on their front door?

When she noticed where he was looking, she literally shrank in on herself. Her shoulders slumped and her arms wrapped around her waist as if to ease her pain. "I guess I don't have any room to talk. In fact, forget I said anything at all. Rather than offering advice, I should stick to asking if you'd like some ibuprofen."

Then she picked up her plate and mug and disappeared into the kitchen.

Chapter Eight

Aubrey dumped the rest of her tea down the drain and stuck the mug in the dishwasher. She followed it with her plate after brushing the last crumbs of her banana bread into the trash. With that done, she looked around for something else to give her shaky hands something productive to do. She settled for getting the ibuprofen out of the cabinet and filling a juice glass with water just as Jonah stepped into the small confines of the kitchen.

"I'm sorry, Aubrey."

"For what exactly, Detective Kelly? Like I said, I'm the last one who should try telling someone how to deal with tragedy."

She pointed toward the glass of water and the pills on the counter. "Help yourself, and then you should leave. I still have a lot of work to do tonight. Thank you for coming when I called."

"It's my job."

Why didn't that make her feel better about the whole situation? "I'm guessing it's well past your normal quitting time. You can see yourself out."

Meanwhile, Jonah took two ibuprofen and washed them down with the water. After setting the empty glass down, he paused to study her, his eyebrows riding low over his eyes. "Look, Aubrey, I didn't mean—"

She cut him off. "It's been a long day for both of us, so just go. I'll call you if anything else comes up that I think you need to know about."

"There is one more thing we need to talk about before I go."

What now? Ordering him to leave again wasn't going to work, not until he had his say. She leaned against the kitchen counter and crossed her arms over her chest. "I'm listening."

"I think we should look into moving you someplace safer. You should also take a leave of absence from your job."

That so wasn't happening. She needed the routine of work, and this house was her sanctuary, the one place where she could breathe. She couldn't imagine staying anywhere else, so she focused on his second suggestion. "My students depend on me. You can't really think I would abandon them so close to the end of the year."

Although she hadn't phrased it as a question, he treated it as one. "Yes, that's exactly what I mean. You're in danger, Aubrey. I know it, and you do, too. We have no idea who is after you, but it's only a matter of time before he makes his next move. Right now, he appears to be having fun toying with you, but he's also busying finalizing his plans. If this is really the same guy, don't forget how he managed to snatch you and Marta from a busy college campus with no one being the wiser. How hard do you think it will be for him to do something similar this time? Especially if you insist on hiding your head in the sand."

It might be a losing battle, but she wasn't going to surrender easily. "But I have responsibilities. I'll stick close to home for now. You know, have my groceries delivered and stuff like that. I'll only drive from here to school and back."

Jonah took a half step closer to her. "I can't force you to do anything, Ms. Sims. You might not care about your own safety, but think about the effect of having you disappear again will have on your mom and dad. They might be helicopter parents, but what they really are is terrified that what happened to Marta will happen to you."

For the space of a heartbeat, his expression softened. "For the record, so am I."

Without giving her a chance to respond to that shocking statement, he walked away. "Don't forget to lock the door after I go."

Yeah, like that would ever happen. She trailed after him, glad he was leaving even if a part of her wished he wouldn't. After stepping out onto the porch, Jonah started to walk away but turned back one last time. "Call me if anything happens, no matter how small, or even if you simply need to talk."

Somehow, that sounded more like an apology than him issuing another order.

"I will. Thank you for coming today. I know you must have other cases that require your attention, and I appreciate how much time you've spent working on mine."

Not wanting to hear another reminder that it was his job, she quietly closed the door and starting turning the locks.

By the time Aubrey got to work the next morning, her nerves were stretched to the breaking point. The fact that she'd barely been able to sleep at all was beside the point. Over the past twelve years, she'd developed a few techniques for dealing with sleeplessness: gulping down some warm milk, listening to soothing music, drinking chamomile tea, getting up and going through her bedtime routine all over again. All of those things usually worked with some degree of success, but not last night.

On the way to school, she had decided she deserved a little treat and made a quick stop at the drive-through of her favorite coffee shop to buy a latte and a peach scone. One sip of the coffee brightened her mood considerably, even if her conscience twinged a little over taking the short detour. After all, she'd promised Jonah that she would drive straight to and from school without stopping. At least there hadn't been anyone in line ahead of her, so the delay was minimal. She pulled back out into traffic and drove the last distance to the school.

When she reached the parking lot, Jonah's car was parked in the front row. What was he doing there? She pulled into the spot next to his and got out. He did the same.

She gathered up everything she needed to take inside with her. It took some juggling on her part to manage her canvas tote, her purse, the latte and the bag containing her scone. Once she had everything situated, she walked around to the back of her car where Jonah stood. As he waited, he quietly scanned the surrounding area. Was he expecting trouble? She did a quick survey herself and then frowned at him. "Did we have an appointment that I forgot about?"

"I wanted to make sure you got to work all right."

She stated the obvious. "Obviously I did."

He finally looked down at her. "So it would appear. Do you need help schlepping all of that stuff inside?"

Ever the gentleman. "No, I do this all the time. Thanks for checking on me."

"Anything to report?"

"I didn't sleep all that well, but that happens from time to time." Noting the dark circles under Jonah's eyes, she added, "I suppose you have your own experience with nights like that."

He shrugged. "Comes with the job. I'll walk you to the door."

Stubborn man. "I can get there on my own."

His mouth twitched in a hint of a grin. "I know that. It's the fact that your hands are full that makes me question your ability to actually open the door."

Okay, he wasn't exactly wrong about that. "Fine, it's this way."

"I'd also like to get a look at your classroom since I'm already here. Stuff like where it's located and the layout of it. It won't take long."

So he wasn't just being polite or helpful. She surrendered her keys to her classroom. "Fine, but you'll have to stop in the office to sign in. They keep track of outsiders coming in and out of the building."

"I'd rather not tell them I'm a cop. Is it okay if I tell them I'm just a friend?"

No doubt she'd get grilled by her coworkers after he left about this unexpected man in her life, but there wasn't much she could do about that. "It's fine."

Viola, the school secretary, had Jonah sign his name on the clipboard she kept on the counter for visitors to sign on their way in and out of the building and then gave him a temporary badge. When he turned his back to her, she waggled her eyebrows and gave Aubrey a thumbs-up. Over the years they'd worked together at the school, Viola had often questioned why an attractive young woman like Aubrey didn't have a man in her life. No doubt she'd corner her at the first opportunity to complain about her keeping secrets. Great. Either Aubrey would have to lie to her friend, or she'd have to tell her the truth and have another person worry about every move she made. The trouble with that was that Aubrey had never told anyone she worked with about the kidnapping.

"My classroom is this way."

The two of them drew a lot of attention as they made their way down the hallway. Several of her friends had looked a bit wide-eyed as they passed by, causing to Jonah lean in closer to ask, "Do you always create such a stir like this?"

"It's not me they're curious about, it's you. They're not used to seeing me with a man, especially a handsome one."

Her blunt assessment of his appearance had Jonah looking a bit uncomfortable, which she found amusing. The man had to own a mirror and know what he looked like. At the moment, he was sharply dressed in a dark navy suit with a white shirt and red tie. The color combination played nicely with his wavy blond hair and bright blue eyes. His limp was a little more pronounced than usual, but it did nothing to make him less attractive.

"It's this next room."

When he pulled her keys out of his suit pocket, she pointed out the right key for him. "The lock is a bit temperamental. You might have to wiggle the key a little to get it to turn."

She hustled into the room as soon as he opened the door and headed for her desk to unload everything. "If I'd known you were going to be here, I would have bought you a coffee, too."

He eyed the cup in her hand. "I thought you were going to drive to and from work without stopping."

"I never got out of the car, and there was no line. Otherwise, I wouldn't have stopped."

He gave the barest of nods as he wandered through the classroom, pausing to stare out the window toward the playground. "You should lower the blinds and close them. Anyone could be out there watching you."

She joined him by the window. "This place feels like a cave when the blinds are closed."

Jonah gave her a sideways glance, his expression all serious cop. "Better a cave than dead."

"He wouldn't shoot me." That much she was sure of.

"I never said he'd be aiming at you. In the ensuing chaos, he might even have a fair chance to grab you before anyone noticed."

His words, delivered in a chilling monotone, brought her up short. Was she endangering her students and colleagues just by showing up at work? "Do you really think that's true?"

"I don't think we can afford to discount anything at this point. It's not as if we have any clue how this guy operates these days. Kidnapping you and Marta on a busy college campus shows that he's willing to take chances."

She wasn't sure if it was her coffee or his words that left such a bitter taste in her mouth. "You said you were searching the records for similar cases. Did you find any?"

"Not so far, but that doesn't necessarily mean anything. Chances are that his pattern was still evolving back then, and he's had twelve years to hone his skills."

While she digested that grim statement, Jonah walked toward the door in the corner that opened directly onto the playground. She remained where she was while he stepped outside to study the school grounds.

By the time he returned, she had surrendered to the inevitable. "I'll talk to my principal today about taking a leave of absence for the rest of the year. It's too late for me to call for a substitute today, and I'll need a day to organize everything for whoever they hire to replace me."

"I know this is hard for you, Aubrey, but it's the smart thing to do. I'd suggest that you tell him that it's a medical or family emergency."

"I'm not disagreeing, but why do you think I should lie to my boss?"

He looked slightly more sympathetic now that she'd given in to his suggestion. "Because you never know who people talk to outside of work. The fewer people who know the truth of what is going on, the safer you'll be."

It must be hard to be so distrustful of everyone, but she supposed he'd learned that lesson the hard way. During the night when she couldn't sleep, she'd given in to the urge to learn more about when Jonah had gotten shot. Apparently, he and his partner had been meeting with an informant in regard to a case. Before that night, they'd had a long-term relationship with the guy and no reason to think he posed any threat to them. As it turned out, he'd let slip the upcoming meeting to the wrong person, an ex-con who had a real grudge against Gino from a prior case. He'd threatened the informer's wife and kids unless he turned on the two cops. The rest was history.

Jonah's phone buzzed. "I've got to take this."

Probably needing a little privacy, he stepped back outside onto the playground. Whatever the call was about had him pacing up and down in front of her windows, repeatedly clenching his free hand in a fist. It was none of her business, but she couldn't help but wonder if it was about her. When he glanced in the window and then deliberately turned his back again, she figured she had her answer.

He'd either tell her or else he wouldn't. Until Jonah made up his mind, she kept herself busy lowering the blinds and then closing them. When he came back inside, he looked at them and gave her a nod of approval. "You're right about the whole cave thing, but safety precautions outweigh classroom aesthetics."

Okay, that was funny.

"I'm going to head out. Thanks for making the right decision."

She drew a ragged breath and looked around the classroom, one of the two places that she'd felt safe. "I really hate that this is happening. I'm so tired of being afraid all of the time."

Jonah had been heading for the door, but he did an about-face and came right back to her. Instead of offering her words of comfort or issuing another lecture on how to stay safe, he enfolded her in his arms and held her close. "We'll get through this, Aubrey. I'll do whatever it takes to prevent this guy from getting his hands on you."

She believed him, but it was his warmth and strength that helped the most. It had been so very long since she'd experienced the simple comfort of another person's touch. Yeah, her parents hugged her, but it wasn't the same. Jonah was a warrior, a hero, the kind of man who would stand between her and the world if that was what it took to keep her safe. Not that she would want him to sacrifice himself like that, but it gladdened her heart to know that he actually cared that much.

He released his hold on her when she gently pushed against his chest. Stepping back, he mumbled, "That was probably unprofessional of me."

"I won't tell if you don't."

She wasn't sure which of them was more flustered about what had just happened. Judging by the way he was looking everywhere but at her and the way her pulse was racing, it was pretty much a tie. "You'd better go. You have better things to do than babysit me. I'll let you know what happens about my request to take a leave of absence. I will have to work tomorrow, but that should give them enough time to get someone in place."

He wasn't happy about the delay, but at least he didn't argue.

"Call me when you're ready to head home after school. If I can't be here to follow you back to the house, I'll ask one of the patrol cars to escort you."

She didn't have it in her to protest. "Okay. I usually get off at four o'clock, but I will probably need to stay late to get things organized."

"See you then." He hesitated. "That call was from my captain. Earlier this morning, I reached out to Mr. and Mrs. Pyne to tell them I would be stopping by to talk to them today. It won't come as a surprise that they didn't want me to come anywhere near them. I explained that they could either talk to me in the comfort of their own home, or else I would have them brought into police headquarters."

Aubrey could just imagine how well that went over with the couple, but there wasn't anything she could do about it. She'd already tried without success to convince Jonah to leave Marta's parents out of this mess. There was no reason to think she'd meet with any more success now. "What did your captain have to say about it?"

"Captain Martine backed my play, but he wanted to remind

me to go easy on them if at all possible. I'm well aware that
they're victims, too, and I feel bad that this will stir up a lot
of bad memories for them. Having said that, I have to do my
job. No one else is going to die on my watch."

Then he was gone.

Chapter Nine

Jonah pulled out of the school parking lot and turned right, the opposite direction from where he needed to go. His next stop was to meet with Mr. and Mrs. Pyne, but he had to get his head back on straight before he faced off with them. Right now, his thoughts were spiraling out of control, all of them circling around the stubborn woman he'd just left. That hug had been a huge mistake. As he'd told her, it had been unprofessional. But beyond that, it could compromise their working relationship.

Even before the shooting, Jonah had known better than to get attached to the civilians he dealt with in the course of his job. Emotions only confused things, and all too often lives depended on clear thinking. But somehow, the rules didn't seem to apply when it came to Aubrey Sims. Maybe it was the aura of solitude that surrounded her. He wasn't sure he'd ever known anyone who seemed more alone than she did.

It wasn't that she didn't have any friends. That much was clear from the way her coworkers responded to her back at the school. She must also have friends at church. Still, he wondered how well any of those people actually knew her. How much of her past had she shared with them? After all, the abduction had taken place twelve years ago while she was away at college. Old friends and relatives would know for sure, but somehow he couldn't picture her bringing up what had happened to her in the course of casual conversation. She probably worried it would change how people saw her—as a victim rather than a survivor.

It would make sense that her pastor perhaps knew at least the bare bones of her kidnapping. With luck, he'd actually been around when it all went down. If so, Jonah hoped the man had really been there for Aubrey. It helped a person to deal with the lingering effects of trauma to have someone you felt safe enough with to express your grief, your pain and, most of all, your anger. That last one was the biggie.

Jonah had been blessed to have two people who'd stepped up to help him. One was the psychologist the police department had recommended. It hadn't taken Jonah long to realize that Dr. Borrelli had plenty of experience helping officers cope with all the ugliness their jobs threw at them on a daily basis. It hadn't taken him long to convince Jonah that whatever he was feeling was okay.

The other person Jonah had turned to was Reverend Kim Waring, the assistant pastor at his church. She'd listened to everything he'd said without judgment and with endless patience when he couldn't find the words. Kim had also prayed with and for Jonah, and even understood why his friend's death had shaken his faith. Her calm demeanor had helped soothe his anger, and her advice about moving forward had gone a long way toward helping him pick up the pieces of his life.

He was pretty sure that Aubrey hadn't been that lucky. Yes, her parents had tried their best to shield her from the aftermath of the kidnapping. However, their forget-it-and-move-on philosophy, even if well-intentioned, hadn't been the right choice for Aubrey. All it did was force her to hide her true feelings from them. Knowing she'd never told her parents that she'd hired private investigators to look into her case was proof of that.

As he waited for a stoplight to turn green, he slammed his fist on the steering wheel, frustrated on so many levels. All of this was getting him nowhere. Aubrey's relationship with her parents was none of his business as long as it didn't impede his investigation. He'd do them both more good by reestablishing some professional distance between them for both their sakes. That meant getting on with his agenda for the day. He'd start by talking to the Pynes. Afterward, he was supposed to meet with his captain to give him an update on Aubrey's situation as well as a couple of other cases.

He'd also planned to call George Swahn and ask if he could meet Jonah for breakfast near the precinct in the morning. He wanted to pick George's brain to see if the man had anything in his private notes that might help Jonah get a better handle on Aubrey's case. He hoped so, because right now Jonah was chasing shadows.

His itinerary for the day set, he turned back toward the part of town where the Pynes lived.

Considering the length of time it took someone to answer when Jonah rang the doorbell, he had to wonder if the Pynes had decided to ignore him or, more likely, left home in order to avoid him altogether. He was about to ring the bell a second time when he finally heard the scuffle of footsteps inside the house. He stepped back and waited impatiently for the door to open.

The man who peeked out at him appeared to be far older than Aubrey's father. It was hard to tell if that was actually true or if it was the loss of his daughter that had left Riley Pyne stooped and fragile-looking. He squinted at Jonah as if he wasn't accustomed to bright sunshine. "What do you want?"

Jonah flashed his ID. "I'm Detective Kelly, Mr. Pyne. We spoke on the phone."

"And I told you we didn't want to talk to you."

Seriously? Were they still going to play this game? He'd promised his captain that he'd tread softly with these folks, but his patience would only last so long. "Yes, sir, I know you did. However, I wouldn't be here if it wasn't important. If you'll give me a little time to explain the situation and answer a few questions, I will do my best to not bother you again. I can't promise that the current situation won't require me to reach out again, but please understand that I won't unless I have no other options."

"Let him in, Riley."

Jonah wasn't the only one who hadn't noticed Dina Pyne had joined her husband. She was still talking. "Let's get this over with."

Turning her attention to Jonah, she studied him with angry eyes. "Nothing you have to say today will bring our daughter home after all this time. I want to hear why you want to torment us like this."

Her husband huffed a disgusted sigh, but then he stepped aside and opened the door wide enough to allow Jonah to come inside. As soon as he crossed the threshold, he wanted to go into full retreat. The inside of the house was dank and dark. It provided an interesting contrast to Ross Easton's house. He kept his polished and shiny, partly in memorial for the woman he'd loved, and maybe because on some level he hung on to some small bit of hope that life was still worth living without her in it.

Marta's parents' home reeked of their despair. After years of waiting and wondering, they'd given up on ever finding out what had become of her. The two of them existed, going through the motions only because they didn't know what else to do. Jonah prayed that somehow he could find a way to give them closure and maybe a little peace.

Before that could happen, he had to solve this threat to Aubrey.

The older couple shuffled their way down the narrow hallway to the family room. They settled into matching recliners, which left the couch for him.

After he was seated, he started in. "Let me give you a brief overview of what has been happening, which will explain why I felt it was necessary that we speak."

He stuck to the highlights to keep thing moving along at a quick pace. He ended with the delivery of the flowers, but didn't mention that Aubrey was taking a leave of absence. "And that's pretty much all of it in a nutshell. As I explained on the phone, I only recently took over the case after the previous detective retired. I'm speaking with everyone I can who was connected to the case twelve years ago."

Mr. Pyne looked slightly less angry than when Jonah first arrived. "So you think it's the same guy who took our daughter and Aubrey back then."

"Yeah, but we don't know that for sure." He leaned forward, resting his elbows on his knees. "Having said that, it seems to be highly likely. The note definitely hinted at insider knowledge."

"How is Aubrey dealing with all of this?"

Jonah was a little surprised by the concern in Mrs. Pyne's voice. "As well as can be expected. She's understandably scared."

"Poor girl. None of this has been easy for her." Mrs. Pyne's eyes glittered with a sheen of tears. "To my everlasting shame, my actions only made it worse for her. Even back then, my head knew none of it was Aubrey's fault, but my heart was broken. All that anger had to go somewhere, and I aimed it right at her."

Platitudes wouldn't change a thing, but asking for their help might. "Can you think back to right before the kidnapping took place and tell me everything you remember about that time in your daughter's life?"

Unfortunately, there wasn't much new in what they shared. Well, except one thing. Ross had indicated Marta was still working at the school library when she was kidnapped. According to her parents, Marta had already quit. She'd never actually told them much about what had happened, but they thought maybe she'd had a problem with another student. She'd assured them it was no big deal, and she would've had to quit soon anyway.

At least it was something to talk to Aubrey about. Detective Swahn, too, for that matter. Jonah stuck his pen and notebook back into his pocket and stood up. He set one of his business cards on the coffee table. "Here's my number if you think of anything else. Thank you again for talking to me today. I know this wasn't easy for you."

With some effort, Mr. Pyne pushed himself up out of his chair. "I can't say I'm happy about having all of this brought up again, Detective, but we understand why you had to do it."

He started back down the hall to open the door. As Jonah walked out, Mr. Pyne whispered, "It was nice to talk about our daughter with someone. Most folks are afraid to mention her name for fear of upsetting us, but it hurts worse when they act like she never existed at all."

There wasn't much Jonah could say to that. "I should be going."

Mr. Pyne followed him out onto the porch. "At this late date, it won't change a thing, but I sure hope you can bring the man who stole my Marta to justice."

"Me, too, Mr. Pyne. Me, too."

Aubrey was exhausted. She'd managed to meet with her principal during her lunch break. He hadn't exactly been angry that she had to leave for the rest of the year, but he wasn't happy about it either. She'd given him a list of substitutes she liked and agreed to work one more day to give him a chance to make the necessary arrangements.

A school was a small world, and it didn't take long for the news to spread about it being Aubrey's last day tomorrow. Understandably, it had generated a lot of questions. She'd fielded them as best she could while trying to avoid giving too many specifics about the nature of the emergency. She regretted that she and Jonah hadn't come up with a plausible explanation before he'd left that morning. Desperate to offer up something believable, she'd said that it was a personal family matter and left it at that.

Keeping secrets from her friends didn't sit well with her, but it was better than having to explain what was really going on. She could only imagine how they would all freak out if she were to confess a threat from her past had resurfaced, a true life-and-death situation. There was never an easy way to admit she'd been the victim of a kidnapping. The few times the subject had come up in conversation, the response from the other person had been difficult to predict. Sympathy and horror were the most common reactions, but occasionally the other person wanted to know all of the dark and twisted details of Aubrey's experience. Those were the worst times.

Eventually, she was going to have to tell her friends the truth, but that was a problem for another day. Right now, she needed to make sure she had everything she needed to take home with her. She'd already texted Jonah that she was ready to leave. He'd answered that he was on his way. After taking one last glance around the room, she picked up her stuff and left, stopping only to lock the classroom door behind her.

The hall outside was deserted. No surprise there since it was after six o'clock. Normally the only people likely to be in the building at that hour were the evening janitor and maybe the principal. Lyle often worked late, especially if there was a meeting at the district office or some event going on at the school during the evening.

She started down the hall, hating the way her footsteps rang out in the otherwise silent building. Jonah had asked if she wanted to wait for him to come to her classroom, but she'd told him that wouldn't work since the building would be locked by that point. Now she wished she'd told him to circle around the building to the door that opened to the playground. Too late now.

As she neared the school office, she spotted the janitor stepping out of a classroom a few doors down. Ruben waved at her and called, "Do you need help carrying stuff out to your car?"

"No, I've got it all."

He set down the bag of trash he was carrying and started toward her. "What's this I hear about tomorrow being your last day? You'll be back next year, won't you?"

"For sure. It's just a personal problem I have to take care of."

His smile was sympathetic. "I'm sorry to hear that, and I hope it's nothing serious."

There wasn't much she could say to that, so she changed the subject. "I should warn you that I cleaned out a bunch of stuff today, so the trash cans in my room are overflowing. I wanted to make sure everything is in good order when my substitute starts."

He waved off her concern. "Don't worry. I'll take care of it."

"Thanks, Ruben."

It was time to get going. It wouldn't be fair to keep Jonah waiting out in the parking lot any longer than necessary. Ruben had started down the hall but circled back in her direction. "I just realized how late it is. If you don't feel comfortable heading out to an empty parking lot alone, I'll walk you out to your car."

Rubin was known to offer to escort any of the women who stayed later than usual at the school. Normally she would've told him that wasn't necessary, especially when it was still light outside. Under the circumstances, though, maybe it wouldn't be a bad idea. "There's no need for you to walk me all the way out, but you can keep an eye on me from the door if you want."

He hesitated. "If you're sure."

"It will be fine. I have a friend coming to meet me. He's on his way and should be here any minute."

Ruben was near retirement age and had grandkids. She knew that because he took such delight in sharing pictures of his family members every chance he got. He also tended to treat all of the school staff, regardless of age or gender, as if they were extensions of his family. "I hope your young man is treating you right."

She went with the safest answer she could think of. "So far, so good."

Then she ducked out of the door to avoid any further discussion on the subject. There was still no sign of Jonah, but surely he'd be there any second. As she got closer to her car, she noticed there was something odd about the way it looked, as if it was listing to one side. Her steps slowed as she tried to make sense of what she was seeing, which didn't take long. Suddenly, she was flashing back to twelve years as she and Marta had walked out to her car in the college parking lot to find her tires had been slashed. This time, someone had driven a spike into her rear tire.

Her blood ran cold—her stalker had struck again.

Chapter Ten

Aubrey remained frozen in place, breathing hard and looking around in panic. Was the culprit still nearby, waiting to grab her again? Unlike the college parking lot, there were no nearby bushes or any other hiding spot close by. That didn't mean she was safe. The sound of an approaching car had her backing up several steps, ready to break and run back toward the school.

At the last second, she realized it was her boss's SUV. That was a relief. The sound of footsteps coming from behind had her glancing back over her shoulder. Just as she'd hoped, it was Ruben heading her way.

"Is something wrong, Ms. Aubrey?"

"Unfortunately, yes. Someone vandalized my tire." She pointed toward her car. "They rammed some kind of spike in it."

His usual genial expression turned grim. "Who would do something awful like that? And right out here in the open, too?"

"No idea."

Okay, that was a lie. Sort of. It was true that she didn't know the perpetrator's name or even what he looked like. By that point, Principal Peale was out of his vehicle. He stopped to study her car before joining her and Ruben on the sidewalk. "Aubrey, are you okay? Did either of you see anything?"

Ruben shook his head. "I've been working in the rooms that face the back of the building."

Aubrey did her best to sound calm. "I'm fine, but I didn't see anything, either. For sure, there was no one around when I came out of the building."

Lyle stood with his hands on his hips as he studied their surroundings. He looked pretty disgusted by the whole affair. "I can't believe someone would do something like this. We should probably call the police."

He pulled out his phone just as another car turned into the lot. Aubrey breathed a sigh of relief when she saw it was Jonah. He pulled into the spot next to hers and hustled over to where she was standing. "Aubrey, what's happened?"

Gesturing to her companions, she said, "My friend Ruben was watching from the front door to make sure that I made it to my car okay. When I saw the condition of my tire, I was going to go back inside the building to wait for you, but that's when my boss arrived. Lyle Peale is our principal, and Ruben Jacobs is the evening custodian here at the school."

The two men gave her identical expectant looks, obviously waiting for her to continue the introductions. "And this is my friend Detective Jonah Kelly."

Jonah nodded at her coworkers in turn. "Gentlemen."

None of them seemed inclined to shake hands. She wasn't sure what to make of that, considering both her boss and Ruben were normally friendly and outgoing. That said, she had to admit this didn't exactly feel like a social situation. Jonah walked around to the driver's side of her car and squatted down to study the damage. After snapping a couple of quick pictures, he rejoined her on the sidewalk. "Are you okay?"

Not really, but she figured she could hold it together until she got home. "Yeah, I was startled when I first saw the damage. Now, I'm more mad than anything."

That made him smile. "I can understand why. I'll call it in for you. After the patrol officer takes your statement, I'll change your tire."

Jonah kept his eyes on her as he made the call. As soon as he hung up, he peeled off his suit coat and draped it across Aubrey's shoulders. It was a warm evening, but she was chilled to the bone. "Thanks."

"No problem. The patrol officer should be here any minute."

Ruben didn't look convinced. "I called the police when somebody broke a window in one of the classrooms a couple of months back. It took them two hours to get here."

He'd no sooner said that than a police car turned into the parking lot, its lights flashing. Jonah looked down at Aubrey. "I'll be right back."

He walked down to meet the police officer and talked to her in a low voice. Then he led her around to look at the damage to Aubrey's car before coming back to where Aubrey waited with Ruben and Principal Peale.

The officer had a clipboard with a form on it, her pen poised to take notes. "Hi, I'm Officer Goff."

Jonah introduced Aubrey. "This is Ms. Sims. She worked later than usual and came out to find that someone had driven a spike into her tire."

The officer gave Aubrey a curious look. "I'm sorry that happened. Did you happen to see anything?"

Aubrey shook her head. "Like Detective Kelly said, I worked late. I didn't realize anything had happened until I came out to go home."

She pointed toward her two coworkers. "Ruben Jacobs works evenings here at the school, and Lyle Peale is our principal. Detective Kelly arrived right after I first discovered the damage."

She half expected the woman to ask what Jonah was doing there in the first place, but maybe he'd filled her in on the circumstances before she approached Aubrey and the others.

She'd ask him later. Right now, all she wanted to do was get this over with and go home.

Mercifully, it didn't take long to give her statement. Officer Goff also took down the contact information for both Ruben and her boss, but that was probably only a formality. When they were done, Ruben asked, "Are you sure you wouldn't like me to change your tire for you?"

Aubrey looked to Jonah for advice before answering. He smiled at the other man. "I'll take care of it, Mr. Jacobs."

Ruben gestured at Jonah's suit. "You're not exactly dressed for getting your hands dirty."

Jonah smiled at him. "That's what dry cleaners are for. Don't worry about it."

While they talked, Lyle sidled closer to her. "Are you sure you're all right?" He glanced toward Jonah. "There's no reason for him to hang around and change the tire for you. I'm sure you have some kind of roadside service coverage. Why don't you call them instead and then wait in my office?"

"Thanks, but I'll be fine. It's just been a long day."

It almost sounded as if there was a hint of snark in Lyle's voice when he mentioned Jonah, but surely not? Like her, he was probably just tired. His day must've been longer than hers, and this time of year was a marathon as everyone rushed to get everything done by the last day of school. Her needing to take a leave of absence had only complicated things for him. To hurry things along, she mustered what she hoped looked like a genuine smile. "I appreciate your concern, but you have more important things to do than babysit me. Jonah can handle the tire. It will take less time for him to do it than having to wait for a tow truck to arrive. I do appreciate you and Ruben coming to my rescue."

At least Lyle didn't argue. "I came back to pick up some papers I need for a meeting at the district office in the morning. I'll go grab them and head out since you have everything under control."

He caught Ruben's eye and jerked his head toward the building. The older man immediately broke off whatever he was saying to Jonah and Officer Goff to follow Lyle up the sidewalk and back toward the building. He stopped only long enough to speak to Aubrey one last time. "If you need anything, even if your fellow needs to wash up after changing the tire, come back into the building. I won't engage the alarm until I know you're gone."

She patted him on the arm. "Thanks, Ruben. We appreciate it."

Officer Goff waited until Ruben was out of hearing before she approached Aubrey. She held out a copy of her report as well as her business card. "I'm sorry this happened, Ms. Sims. Detective Kelly knows how to reach me if you or your insurance company have questions, but you can also call me directly."

"Thank you, and I really appreciate the fast response."

"Any time."

When she was gone, Jonah rejoined Aubrey. "Do you want to wait in my car while I work on the tire?"

"I'll stay with you if that's okay."

"It won't take long." Then his eyes flared wide. "I didn't even think to ask. Do you have a spare?"

For the first time all day, she laughed and held out her keys. "It's in the trunk."

Jonah was still assembling Aubrey's car jack when the school principal came back out. He spoke to Aubrey as he walked by, but barely glanced at Jonah before he got in his car and drove off. Aubrey seemed puzzled by her boss's behavior, but Jonah just shrugged it off. A lot of people were uncomfortable around police officers. Right now, he was more concerned about how well his knee would hold up while he changed the tire. It might end up being one of the nights he'd end up taking a pain pill before bed.

He could have avoided the wear and tear on the joint by accepting Ruben's offer to change the tire. But that might have raised a few questions he didn't want to answer, like why Jonah was taking such care in documenting the damage. As far as Ruben knew, it was just a random act of vandalism, not a serious threat against Aubrey. Jonah wore gloves to preserve any evidence that might be on the spike and the tire itself. Considering how careful Aubrey's stalker had been to date, he didn't hold out much hope. Just in case, he planned to drop everything off in the lab on his way home.

After tightening the lug nuts one last time, he pushed himself back up to his feet and peeled off his gloves. Aubrey held out his suit jacket. "Thanks for doing that for me, but I'm sorry that you've wasted a good part of your evening babysitting me again."

"No apologies necessary." He handed back her keys. "Let's get you home."

Then he checked the time. "Look, I don't know about you, but I'm not going to want to bother cooking tonight. Would you like to stop somewhere to grab a bite before we head to your place?"

"Haven't you had enough of me and my problems for one day? You've already gone above and beyond by changing my tire. You don't need to feed me, too."

She wasn't exactly saying no, but neither was she jumping at the chance to spend more time in his company. He straightened his tie as he considered what he wanted to say. It would be smarter to follow her home, check to make sure everything was as it should be, and then grab a burger on his way home. The truth was that he wanted to spend a little time with Aubrey when they weren't dealing with her case. His reasons behind the invitation were personal, not professional, and therefore it probably wasn't the smartest idea.

Too bad.

"Let's just say that I get tired of eating alone and would appreciate the company."

Aubrey's answering smile was all he could wish for. "Then I'd love to have dinner."

Two hours later, they walked out of a local seafood restaurant, one of Jonah's favorite places in the area. The decor wasn't fancy, but the service was always good and the food excellent. They'd chatted about books, movies and sports. Anything and everything except Aubrey's case and Jonah's job. He didn't know about her, but he'd really enjoyed the chance to simply chill for a while.

Seeing Aubrey so relaxed and happy had given Jonah an enticing glimpse of the woman she could've been all of the time under other circumstances. From the beginning, he'd thought she was pretty, especially with those huge brown eyes and sweet smile. But tonight, the candlelight had emphasized her warm skin and the hints of red in her dark brown hair. They weren't on a date, but it felt like one at times. It was a nice bit of normal, something he hadn't had much of since the night Gino died.

As soon as that guilty thought crossed Jonah's mind, he cringed. How could he have forgotten his friend for even that long? His good mood gone, he instantly snapped right back into cop mode.

"I'll follow you to the house and make sure you get inside safely. I can't hang around, though. I've still got some work to do tonight."

That probably came out harsher than he'd meant it to because Aubrey gave him a confused look. "If you needed to get back to the office, you should've said so sooner. I have work to do, too. I'm also perfectly capable of getting myself back home. It's only a few blocks from here. If you want to know I made it there safely, I could always text you."

"That's not what I meant…"

He realized he was talking to himself. She had already walked away, heading for her car. He thought about catching up with her long enough to apologize, but maybe it was best if he reminded them both that theirs was a business relationship, nothing more. It couldn't be. Not when he needed to concentrate on figuring out who was threatening her.

Rather than chase her down to offer his apology, he decided to wait until they reached her house. He soon got another hint that she wasn't particularly happy with him at the moment. When they approached a traffic light that had already turned yellow, Aubrey punched the gas and scooted through the intersection a hair before the light turned red. He was far enough behind her that he had no choice but to stop. By the time he caught up with her, she was already pulling into her garage.

What was she thinking? They both knew her stalker had been nearby today. If she'd forgotten, he could remind her by showing her the spike in her tire. If the guy had broken into her house while she was gone, he could've been waiting to grab her. Jonah slammed his car door and charged after her before she could close the garage.

From the shock on her face when she got out of the car, she'd been totally oblivious to his approach. "Jonah, you scared me half to death!"

"That's not my fault. You should've been able to see me, considering I walked right down the middle of your driveway and straight into the garage. I didn't hide or sneak in."

He waved his hands in the air. "What if it had been your kidnapper instead of me? If somehow he'd managed to break in, he could have been waiting inside for you. For all the attention you were paying to your surroundings, he could have subdued you in a matter of seconds."

She drew herself up to her full height and glared right back at him as she waved her phone in his face. "I have a security system with cameras in every room. I stopped on the street long enough to check all of the footage. There's no one in the house or the garage."

Not ready to surrender or even admit that he was overreacting, he moved closer, forcing her to tip her head back to look him in the eye. "Fine, I'll give you that much. The point is I came in through the open door, and you weren't watching for a threat in that direction. If he'd gotten you..."

He couldn't complete that thought, but somehow his hands had ended up on her shoulders. Aubrey responded by placing her hands on his chest. He kept his hold gentle, and she didn't push him away. Neither of them said anything for what seemed a long time. Finally, Aubrey said, "I'm sorry, Jonah. You're right. I got careless. I'm sorry for making you worry even more about me. I won't do it again."

"And I'm sorry that I lost my temper." It was time for some honesty. "You know what happened to my partner. I figure you probably understand better than most people what it means to have survivor guilt. When we came out of the restaurant, I realized that it was the first time I'd actually enjoyed myself since the night Gino died. The guilt knocked me sideways for a minute there."

"There's no need to apologize, Jonah. I mean that."

He stared down into her dark eyes as he slowly slid his hands around her, pulling Aubrey in closer, needing this connection. Tucking her head under his chin, he held her lightly, knowing he would let her go the second she wanted him to back off. All he could hope was that she needed this peaceful moment as much as he did. She didn't resist at all, but that didn't stop her from asking, "Jonah, why were we fighting?"

"Stress, probably, even though the last thing I want to do is to fight with you."

"What are we doing now?"

Deciding it was time to go big or go home, he smiled at her. "Probably something else I'll need to apologize for."

Then he kissed her.

Chapter Eleven

Wow, simply wow. It had been a long, long time since Aubrey had been kissed, but she was pretty sure she'd never experienced anything like this before. Maybe it was because Jonah held her so carefully and treated her with such care. It only lasted a few seconds, but she was pretty sure she would still be feeling the impact for a long time.

Even after she broke off the kiss, Jonah continued to hold her. With her head tucked against his chest, Aubrey sensed he was smiling as he asked, "Well, should I apologize?"

That had her laughing. "Do you hear me complaining?"

"It was unprofessional."

She was caught between him and the car, so she gave him a gentle push to give them each a little room to breathe. "Again, I won't tell if you don't."

"Fair enough, but it probably shouldn't happen again."

"Ever?"

She'd meant that as a small tease, but Jonah evidently took it seriously. "That would be a real shame, but any kind of personal involvement would muddy the waters right now. I need a clear head if I'm going to protect you. And we both know that right now, you're not safe."

The flash of grief in his eyes was a powerful reminder that he was still dealing with the loss of his friend. Logic said that neither of them was at fault for what had happened to Marta or Gino, but they both still carried a burden of guilt from their loss.

She reached up to cup Jonah's cheek. "Then we'll revisit this moment when it's safe. Until then, we should place our trust in God to see us both through this. With His help, we'll both find peace and safety."

Jonah closed his eyes as he leaned into her touch. "Amen, Aubrey. Amen."

Then he stepped back. "We should get you inside. We both have work to do."

She closed the garage door and let Jonah lead the way into the house. Once they were in the kitchen, she entered the code on the security system while Jonah did a quick scan of the kitchen, dining room and living room. "I'm sorry if it feels like I'm invading your privacy, but I should check the bedrooms, too."

Having someone else go through her house like this wasn't comfortable, but she knew she should let him do it for his peace of mind, as well as hers. "Do whatever you need to do."

He was back within a few minutes. "Everything looks good. Is there anything else you'd like me to do before I leave?"

"No, I'm good."

"What time are you leaving for work in the morning? I'll come here, then follow you."

She hated to ask him to do that but suspected she had little choice in the matter. "I have to be there by eight o'clock, so we should leave by seven thirty."

"Got it. If I can't make it for some reason, I'll text you and ask a patrol officer to do the honors instead."

Aubrey unlocked the front door for him. "I guess I'll see you in the morning."

He brushed a lock of her hair back away from her face. "Call if you need me."

"I will."

She watched and waved from the front window until he drove away.

The next morning, Jonah arrived at the diner twenty minutes late. He paused right inside the door to scan the crowd for George Swahn. As soon as he spotted him, he wended his way through the cluster of tables and chairs to a booth in the back next to the window.

"Sorry I'm late. I followed Aubrey Sims to school first, and traffic was worse than I expected."

George had been about to take a drink of his coffee, but he set the mug back down on the table with a thud. "What's happened now?"

Their server appeared before Jonah could answer. They waited to continue the conversation until after they'd given their orders. As soon as they were alone, Jonah launched into a summary of what had happened since they'd last spoken.

By the time he'd finished catching him up, George was looking pretty grim. "This guy is ramping up fast."

Jonah nodded. "Yeah. He's locked in on Aubrey as his target, but he's not ready to make his final move quite yet. It's impossible to know why that is. Maybe he gets off on having all of us running in circles or knowing that Aubrey is living in fear, never knowing when he'll strike again."

George had been taking notes, probably out of habit from when he'd been on active duty. He looked up from his notebook. "And the lab hasn't been able to pick up anything useful from the original note, the coin or the spike?"

"Not so far. They didn't get the tire until late yesterday, so I doubt they'd have had a chance to get to it as yet. I'm not holding out much hope, though."

"How is Aubrey holding up? This has to be taking a toll on her."

Jonah stared out the window, not wanting to look at the other man in case his expression would reveal more than he wanted it to. "She's stronger than she looks. It's amazing she's doing as well as she is considering how little support she's had from her family over the years."

"What makes you say that?"

"Her parents were furious when I first showed up at their house to review the facts of the original incident in light of the new threat. They actually ordered me not to reopen the case and to stay away from their daughter. I happened to be at Aubrey's house later that day when they showed up. They can't understand why she can't simply forget about what happened and move on. They won't even let themselves believe there is any reason for concern. It's like hiding their heads in the sand is the only way they can cope with any of this."

That encounter hadn't been fun for any of them, but he couldn't help but admire the way Aubrey had stood up to her parents. "Aubrey fought back and then ordered them out of her house for insulting me. Like I said, she's stronger than she looks."

Their food arrived, interrupting their conversation again. Jonah took a few bites and then set down his fork. "I also talked to Ross Easton and the Pynes. Did you know that Ross used to stalk Aubrey?"

George looked up. "Seriously? She never mentioned that to me. Could he be behind this?"

"I don't think so. He's gotten sober in the interim. He also didn't strike me as the kind of guy who would be an accomplished liar. When I told him there was a new threat to Aubrey, he seemed genuinely shocked and angry."

They stopped talking long enough to finish their meals. As they relaxed and drank their coffee, Jonah said, "It wasn't easy, but at least I've convinced Aubrey to take a leave of absence for the rest of the school year. She really wanted to finish out the last week with her students. I think she might have been having second thoughts about taking off work until she saw the tire last night. Knowing he followed her to school pretty much clinched the deal. I suggested she stay with her parents, but that was a definite no-go."

George briefly grinned. "I've always known she was stubborn. Most people would've given up looking for answers years ago."

"True enough. Did you know she hired multiple private investigators over the years to look into the case?"

"Yeah, although she never told me herself. A couple were former cops themselves and reached out to talk to me about the case. As far as I know, none of them found anything useful."

"She gave me the files, but I haven't had a chance to read through all of them yet. What I have read is pretty much what we already knew."

"I could read the rest of them for you, or anything else that might help. My wife's out of town visiting her sister for a week, so I'm free."

That was just what Jonah had been hoping for. There were only so many hours in the day, and his gut feeling was that the hours before this guy struck again were ticking down rapidly. "That would be great. I've also been doing searches for similar cases over the past twelve years. Nothing local fits, so I need to search farther afield. I talked to the captain yesterday, and he said it was okay if I brought you on board if you were interested."

"I'm in. Did you learn anything new from talking to Easton or Marta's parents?"

Jonah flipped back through his own notes. "Yeah, actually I did. It's likely nothing, but their stories don't line up on one small detail. I asked Ross what he could remember about what the girls were involved in back then, other than going to class. He mentioned that Marta had a job at the college library she would have had to quit at the end of the term because she was leaving to study abroad. But when I went over the same info with her folks, they insisted she'd already left her job before she was abducted. Evidently something happened that caused her to quit sooner than expected, but why Ross wouldn't have known or remembered that, I don't know."

George frowned. "Funny, I don't remember anyone mentioning any of that in the original reports."

"They didn't. Maybe there's nothing to it, but it makes me wonder how they missed it."

"Does Aubrey know anything about it?"

Chagrined, Jonah shrugged. "I haven't asked her. With everything that's happened, I haven't had a chance. I will when I see her later today."

Back at the station, they got started on the files Aubrey had given Jonah. For the most part, they didn't contain anything that they didn't already know. Frustrating, but not surprising.

Jonah stood up and stretched. "I need to walk around a little to stretch my leg."

George gave him a considering look. "How's the knee?"

"Actually, better than I thought it would be, especially after changing Aubrey's tire last night." He picked up his coffee mug. "I'm going to go top off my coffee. Want some?"

"Sure. One sugar, no creamer."

When Jonah returned, George was leaning back in his chair, his fingers entwined behind his head as he stared up at the ceiling. "I've been thinking about what happened in that parking lot. It could've been a random act, but I don't think so. Not when that's how the original kidnapper immobilized Aubrey's car twelve years ago."

He glanced at Jonah. "Here's the thing. The original investigators were pretty much split down the middle on whether the guy picked those two girls at random or if he'd gone after one or both of them for a specific reason. Without any proof either way, that line of investigation never went anywhere."

"But you're thinking that if the same guy has spiked Aubrey's tire again, either she or Marta was probably targeted. If so, he probably hung around last night in case he could grab Aubrey again while no one was around."

George sat up straight again. "Yeah, seems likely. The question is, how did he know that she would work later than usual yesterday? Because even if he'd somehow managed to sabotage her tire during the day without being seen, there would have been too many people around to snatch her out of the parking lot if she'd left at her regular time."

Jonah sat down and rubbed his aching leg. "What's more, he also couldn't have known that she'd have someone watching her as she left the building, or that I was coming to follow her home."

"Well, unless he was watching from somewhere close by."

"The school is on a side street, but it's only a block or so away from the main drag. Most of the staff get off work by four o'clock, and Aubrey left the building a little after six. That means the tire was most likely slashed in between those hours. I'll see if there's any traffic cameras in that area and get any video that covers that time period."

"Good idea. If you do manage to get video, let me know. That's something else I can help with."

"Not that I'm not grateful for the assistance, but didn't you retire to get away from all this?"

If anything, the other man looked even more determined. "I told you before I left that certain cases will hit you harder, especially the ones where you never get justice for the victims. This is one of them."

He paused to point at some of the other files on Jonah's desk. "If we can finally catch the guy who did this, I'm thinking it will make it easier for me to live with all those other unsolved cases. That's because it will give me hope someone, someday will find the answers for those, too. The bottom line is that I'm yours as long as you need me."

"Fair enough."

Jonah understood all too well what George was telling him. He was also thankful for the older man's advice. He'd been praying for God's guidance ever since Gino died. Maybe He had led Jonah to cross paths with both George and Aubrey, knowing having them in his life would help ease the burden of Gino's death. He liked to think so.

He checked the time. "I'll need to leave in half an hour to follow Aubrey home from work. I'm not sure how long I'll be gone."

"No sweat. If I run across anything important, I'll call you. Tell Aubrey that I said hi."

"I will."

The day had been a long one. The kids in her class had been upset when she explained that it was going to be their last day with her as their teacher. At least the sub who had been assigned to the class was familiar to them. Mrs. Denisi had come in to spend the afternoon with Aubrey and her students to help smooth the transition. Between the two of them, they'd finished the day's lessons with enough time left over for a small goodbye party. Aubrey hadn't wanted to stop at the store on the way to work, so she'd had some treats delivered to the office.

The kids and Mrs. Denisi had left for the day, leaving Aubrey alone to finish a few odds and ends before locking up. She'd already texted Jonah to say she was ready to go home.

She locked up and headed for the office to check in with the school secretary and Principal Peale, if he was available. Viola came around the counter to hug Aubrey. "When things settle down, we'll get together for coffee. I'll expect a full explanation as to how you met that good-looking guy you've been keeping secret from me."

It still hurt to lie to her friend, but there was no way she wanted to entangle anyone else in her situation. "Give me a couple of weeks. I'll even spring for some of those chocolate pastries you like so much."

"It's a deal."

Aubrey nodded toward Lyle's office. "Is he around? I wanted to check in with him on my way out."

"No, he's at the district office. You know how it is at this time of the year. Nothing but meeting after meeting. I'll let him know that you tried."

Viola stopped to glance through the window that faced the school entrance. Her expression turned a bit wicked. "Speaking of your fellow, he just walked into the building. I have to admire your taste in men. Such bright blue eyes and that blond hair...not to mention those broad shoulders. He's a real cutie. It makes me wish I was twenty years younger and single."

Aubrey snickered. "You're not wrong about him, but you've got your own guy. You'd never trade David in for another model."

"No, I wouldn't, and I'm grateful for each and every one of the thirty years we've had together. Now, you get going. Don't keep the man waiting."

"See you soon."

Aubrey joined Jonah out in the hall. "Thanks for coming inside. I have to admit that I was a bit reluctant to walk out to the parking lot alone today."

"No problem. I thought you might need help carrying all your stuff out to the car since it's your last day."

"It's already in my trunk. I got a couple of friends to help carry everything out during lunch today."

As they walked out and started toward the parking lot, he studied their surroundings, watching for any possible threats. He paused to give her a sympathetic look. "I know turning your class over to someone else is probably hard for you, but it really is the best thing for both you and your class under the circumstances."

"I know. At least it's almost summer anyway, and it helps knowing that I'll be back in the fall."

"That makes sense." He glanced at her again. "By the way, George Swahn asked me to say hi for him. He and I had breakfast this morning after I followed you to work. Then he insisted on coming into the office to go through the files you gave me."

She winced. "Is that going to get him in trouble with Mrs. Swahn?"

"I wondered the same thing, but evidently she's out of town visiting her sister."

They'd reached her car. Before letting her get near it, Jonah did a quick inspection to make sure there weren't any more unpleasant surprises. "All clear."

"Good. I'll see you at the house?"

"Yep, and I'll check inside the house for you again."

"I appreciate it," she said, allowing her gaze to linger on his face for a second too long. She mentally checked herself and got into her car before he could see the blush rapidly spreading across her cheeks.

Once they got to her place, Jonah made good on his promise to do a quick walk-through of the house. After he gave it the all clear, it took them several trips to carry everything she'd brought home from school inside. She dumped all of it on the dining room table to sort through later after Jonah left. It would give her something to do other than worry.

As soon as he drove away, she did her own inspection. It wasn't as if she didn't think he'd done a thorough job, but old habits died hard. As soon as she'd reassured herself that all was as it should be, she went online and ordered groceries. She was low on a few things, and she'd promised Jonah she'd handle her errands remotely as much as possible.

With that done, there was one more thing to take care of

before she settled in for the evening. She had a few flowerpots on the front porch and a couple on the small patio in the back that needed watering; the sprinkler system took care of the rest.

She waved at her neighbors as she watered the plants in front. Since there were several people within sight, she took advantage of the opportunity to spend a little more time outside pulling a few weeds. She had just finished when her phone rang. Seeing it was her mother, she answered it as she let herself back into the house.

"Hi, Mom. What's up?"

"Dad and I haven't seen you since…well, when we had to cut the visit short. We've missed you and were wondering if you'd like to come over for dinner one night next week after you get off work."

Heading for the bathroom to wash her hands, Aubrey considered how much, if anything, she should tell her folks about what was really going on. The truth would only upset them, but she thought it would hurt them even more to learn that she was keeping secrets from them—especially the potentially life-threatening kind.

"I'm not sure that's a good idea, Mom."

Nothing but silence.

"Mom?"

"What's happened now, Aubrey?"

She hated the fear in her mother's voice. "First of all, I'm fine, and Detective Kelly is working hard to make sure I stay that way," she said as she washed her hands in the sink, the cell phone tucked between her shoulder and her ear. "With that in mind, we decided I should take a few precautions. He suggested I stick close to home as much as possible, so I've taken a leave of absence from school. I'll be temporarily ordering my groceries online. Stuff like that."

That went over as well as she had expect it to, judging by the anger in her mother's voice. "Which means there's more going on than you've bothered to tell us."

Aubrey dried her hands and walked back into her bedroom, wishing she had easy answers for her mother that wouldn't set off another firestorm. But as she was debating what to say next, she saw something that made her heart turn over in her chest. She took a step closer the window on the far wall to make sure of what she was seeing and then went into full panic.

Someone had paid her another visit, this time armed with a can of spray paint.

"Look, Mom, something's just come up. I need to hang up, but I'll try to call you later."

Her poor mother was still sputtering in protest as Aubrey disconnected the call. Meanwhile, her knees were shaking so badly that she had to lean against the wall for support as she called Jonah, counting the seconds until he answered.

"Aubrey, what's happened?"

"He left me another message. Spray-painted it on the outside of my bedroom window. The words were written backwards, so I could read them from inside. The paint is still dripping down the glass."

"What's it say?"

"You can run, but you can't hide."

"I'm on my way."

Chapter Twelve

Jonah showed his injured knee no mercy as he charged out of his office with George Swahn hot on his heels. He'd already sent a patrol officer to stay with Aubrey until he could get there himself. That was the only reason he stopped long enough to update his boss on the current situation while George waited outside in the hall. Captain Martine was on the phone when he walked in. He took one look at Jonah's face and hung up.

"Sir, something's happened at Aubrey Sims's place again. Slashing her tire at the school where she works was bad enough. Now he's left her another threatening message written in spray paint on the outside of her bedroom window. It had to have happened after I followed her home. We need to get her into protective custody."

His boss was looking pretty grim. "I agree. This guy isn't going to be content to keep playing games for much longer. You go check on Ms. Sims while I call the county and see if we can use one of their safe houses. If one isn't available, I'll figure something out. At the very least I'll assign an officer to watch her house around the clock until we can get her moved."

"Thank you, sir."

Jonah walked out of the captain's office and leaned against

the wall. The news that they'd finally be able to put her in protective custody allowed him to draw a full breath of air for the first time since he'd answered Aubrey's call. George stood nearby without speaking, probably giving Jonah a chance to get his bearings. When Jonah finally stood up straight again, George got right back to business.

"I probably shouldn't go to Aubrey's with you since I'm not on active duty. If it's okay with you, I'll stay here and keep looking through the files. The traffic cam video should be cued up soon. I can start scanning through that if it would help. Any ideas as to who or what I should be looking for?"

"Not really."

Which was one of the biggest frustrations in this case. Regardless, they had to start somewhere. "I'm almost positive that Ross Easton isn't our guy, but watch for his vehicle. The make of his car and the plate number is already in the file. While you're at it, there's a janitor at her school named Ruben something... Ruben Jacobs, that's it. See if you can track down the info on his vehicle, as well as her principal's."

George looked surprised. "Do you have any reason to think either of them might be our guy?"

"No, but both of them had opportunity to spike her tire. We won't catch that on the film, but maybe the janitor arrived earlier than normal or something. The principal had already left the building before Aubrey did, but he came back right when she discovered the damage. Again, that doesn't really mean anything, but it could. It might also be worth checking to see if they were at the school at the time the paint was sprayed on her house."

He started walking toward the elevator. "We've got nothing concrete to go on, so I think it's too early to eliminate anyone. What really bothers me is that Aubrey doesn't seem to have many men in her life. Even most of her coworkers are women. And from what she's told me, it's been ages since she's even dated anyone. But whoever this guy is, he's watching her from somewhere close. We need answers."

George visibly shuddered. "I'll do my best to find them. We both will."

Jonah met the other man's gaze. "I know. The question is if our best will be enough."

Then he walked away, praying for all he was worth that they wouldn't run out of time before they were able to close in on the person who was doing this.

The trip from the precinct to Aubrey's house wasn't long by distance, but Jonah couldn't get there fast enough. Stopping to talk to his captain had been necessary, but it only added to the time Aubrey had to wait for Jonah to arrive. He knew the responding officer would do their best to reassure her, but it wasn't the same. That was *his* job, not just as the officer in charge but because…well, just because.

As he pulled up in front of her house, he groaned when he saw the car parked in Aubrey's driveway. What were her parents doing there? It didn't seem likely that she would have asked them to come running. As far as he knew, she hadn't been keeping them in the loop about everything that had happened, especially since they'd made it clear that neither of them wanted to know why her case had heated up again.

One of the patrol officers was just coming around the side of the garage from the backyard. He was relieved to see it was April Goff, who had also responded when Aubrey's tire was slashed at the school. She headed straight for him. "No wonder you took the tire thing at the school so seriously. That message written on the window is big-time scary."

"So I hear. I thought I'd check it out before I talk to Ms. Sims."

"By the way, Ms. Sims is inside with her parents. I swear you could cut the tension between them with a knife. I offered to stay with her until you got here, but she asked me to keep watch outside." Then Officer Goff frowned. "Did I do the right thing? Because I got the distinct impression she was protecting me rather than the other way around."

He didn't doubt that for a second. "It's fine. I've crossed paths with her parents before, and it wasn't any fun, especially for Aubrey. Like I told you at the school, she was kidnapped twelve years ago. We think whoever is behind the tire and the paint is likely the same guy. Her parents don't want to believe any of it is real, because that would mean she's in danger again."

His assessment of the situation clearly shocked his coworker. "Do they actually think denial will make the danger disappear?"

"Honestly, I'm not sure. I keep reminding myself that everyone handles stress and fear in their own way." He fisted his hands in frustration. "If they're not happy now, I can only imagine how they're going to react when we put her in protective custody and cut her off completely from any outside contact."

Officer Goff shook her head. "I'm glad dealing with all of that is above my pay grade."

There wasn't much he could say to that. "If you'll keep watch out front, I want to see the paint job before I go inside. If the forensics team shows up, send them on back."

"Will do."

He walked around to the backyard, needing to see this new threat for himself. After taking a close look at the words on Aubrey's window, Jonah slipped on a glove and touched the paint. Just as Aubrey had said, it wasn't completely dry, meaning the guy had been there right after Jonah had done his walk-through of the house. His initial reaction was pure fury and left him wishing there was something he could punch. Anything to vent some of his anger. It would help clear his head before he had to deal with Aubrey and her parents. He would need all the control he could muster to maintain some distance from her when his instincts were shouting at him to comfort her and reassure himself that she was all right. Maybe having her parents there to chaperone might not be such a bad thing.

He took a few pictures of the backwards writing. After forwarding one to George, he shoved his phone in his pocket as he took a slow walk around the perimeter of the yard. The cedar fence was six feet tall, pretty typical for the area. Along the way, he stood on his toes to look over into each of the neighbors' yards. It was impossible to tell if her stalker had entered the yard from one of the others, but maybe the forensics people would see something he'd missed.

He hoped so. They needed a break in this case in the worst way.

After he'd done everything he could, it was time to go inside. Bracing himself for what might be another ugly confrontation with Mr. and Mrs. Sims, he knocked on the door. "Aubrey, it's me."

He listened to the all-too-familiar sound of her going through the complicated process of unlocking the door. When she finally opened it, he was both relieved and disappointed that she quickly backed away to give him room to enter her house. Apparently, he wasn't the only one who realized they needed to maintain professional decorum in front of her parents.

"Detective Kelly, thank you for coming."

"Sorry it took me so long. I had to update my captain on the case before I came." He looked past her to where her parents stood glaring at him from the living room and nodded to acknowledge their presence. "Mr. and Mrs. Sims."

When her mother started to speak, he cut her off. "I need to talk to your daughter."

Without giving the woman a chance to respond, he turned back to Aubrey. "Before coming inside, I went around to the back to take pictures of the message, but I also need to take pictures of it from inside. Would you mind showing me the way?"

Aubrey raised her eyebrows, probably surprised that he was acting as if he hadn't been over every square inch of her house by this point. "Sure, come this way."

Her father planted himself in front of the hallway, blocking their path. "I'll go with you. Aubrey can stay here with her mother."

Jonah considered asking him to step aside, but the man was feeling understandably protective of his daughter. Rather than argue, he shrugged. "Okay."

When Aubrey started to protest, he shook his head. "It's fine, Aubrey. This won't take long."

Mr. Sims remained silent until they reached Aubrey's bedroom. When he raised the blinds to reveal the message, Jonah had no idea if it was the other man's first time seeing it or not. Regardless, his reaction was fierce. "What kind of sicko terrorizes a woman like this? And why haven't you put a stop to it by now?"

Jonah didn't take the man's anger personally. Besides, he was right to be concerned about the lack of progress on the case. "I promise you that we're working on it, Mr. Sims. Whoever is behind these stunts has done a good job of covering his tracks. We are pursuing every avenue of inquiry we can."

"That's not good enough."

Jonah would have protested, but he actually agreed with the man's assessment of the situation. "No, sir, it's not. I'm not making excuses, but it's like he's a ghost. He didn't make any mistakes twelve years ago, and he hasn't this time, either. At least not so far."

Aubrey's father lowered the blinds but made no move to leave the room. "I hate this for Aubrey. It's no surprise that what happened last time changed her. I can't stand the thought of her living in fear again."

Did he actually think she'd ever really stopped? Not that Jonah was going to ask him that. If Aubrey's parents hadn't figured out the significance of all those locks on the door and the expensive security system, he wasn't going to explain it to them. "I'm done in here."

Mr. Sims led the way back to the front of the house where his daughter and his wife still stood on opposite sides of the room, neither of them looking happy. Aubrey met Jonah's gaze. "What do you think?"

He wanted to tell her that it was no big deal, but he wouldn't lie to her. "That he's upped the ante again. I've already talked to my captain. He's working out the details to move you to a safe house."

"That's it!" Her mother pointed at her daughter. "Pack a bag. You're moving back home right now."

Aubrey all but rolled her eyes at her mother's attempt to bully her into meek compliance. "Sorry, Mom, but that's not going to happen."

It was clear which of her parents Aubrey had inherited her stubborn determination from as her mother puffed up in outrage. For a brief second, Jonah felt a little sympathy for her father for having to deal with two such strong personalities.

On the other hand, it was interesting that Mr. Sims remained at the entrance to the hallway rather than positioning himself next to either his wife or his daughter. Was he trying to remain neutral rather than choose sides? If so, Jonah had serious doubts that it was going to play out well for the man. Sure enough, his wife shot him an angry look. "Tell her, Joe. It's the only sensible option."

"I'm sorry, Sandy, but I can't do that. As Aubrey reminded us last time we were here, she's an adult and entitled to make her own decisions." He held up his hand when his wife started to protest. "Listen to what I'm trying to tell you. If Aubrey chooses to follow Detective Kelly's advice, it's not because she doesn't love us. It means she wants us to be safe, too. She doesn't want to bring her troubles to our doorstep."

Jonah wasn't sure who was more shocked by Joe's assessment of the situation—his daughter or his wife—but he admired the guy for understanding what his daughter was going through. Aubrey hurried to her father's side and gave him a huge hug. He patted her on the back and asked, "It's why you took the rest of the year off from school, isn't it?"

She nodded. "He knows where I work. He spiked my tire in the school parking lot. I can't be there and risk him doing something to harm the kids or my friends."

As Aubrey explained the situation to her father, Jonah watched her mother's reaction. He might not always like the way the woman talked to her daughter, he didn't doubt for a second that her intentions were good. She knew full well how close they'd come to losing Aubrey twelve years ago and lived in terror of it happening again. Everything that had happened since the note and coin appeared in Aubrey's mailbox was her parents' worst nightmare coming to life.

Jonah approached her. "Are you all right, Mrs. Sims?"

Her eyes snapped up to meet his gaze. "No, I'm not all right. Nothing about this is *all right*. I can't go through this again. None of us can."

"I will do my best to make sure your daughter is safe. That's all anyone can promise."

Then he pulled a worn card from his wallet and handed it to her. "My pastor gave this to me when I hit a rough patch a couple of months back. Whenever things get to be more than I can handle alone, I read it. I've found it helpful. Maybe you will as well."

She took the card and read it aloud. Her voice started off unsteady, but grew in strength as she reached the end of the verse. *"Be strong and courageous. Do not fear or be in dread of them, for it is the LORD your God who goes with you. He will not leave you or forsake you. Deuteronomy 31:6."*

Several tears trickled down her cheek. "Thank you, Detective Kelly."

When she started to hand the card back, he shook his head.

"Keep it for now, Mrs. Sims. You can give it back when all of this is over with."

She managed a small nod and then crossed the room to join her husband and daughter. "I apologize for ordering you around again, Aubrey. We'll support your decision no matter what you decide to do. I know you're trying to protect everyone around you, including us. Just remember, the only thing that matters to us is that you're safe."

Aubrey hugged her mother, her own eyes looking a bit shiny with tears. "We can't control whatever this crazy guy does, Mom. All we can do is make the best decisions we can under the circumstances. No matter what happens next, know that I love you as much as you love me."

While they continued to talk, Jonah went into the kitchen and fixed himself a glass of water. He was sure that Aubrey wouldn't mind, and it would give her and her parents a little privacy. There was no telling how long it would be before they saw each other again, and they deserved a chance to make peace with each other.

It wasn't long before the front door opened and closed, leaving a heavy silence in the house. Jonah set down his glass and went in search of Aubrey. He found her at the front window, peeking out through the blinds as her parents got in their car and drove away.

"It's hard not to think this might have been the last time I'll see them. I think they're worried about the same thing—that no matter how careful we are, no matter how we try, he's going to find me."

All of Jonah's resolve to maintain an emotional distance from Aubrey until she was safe from the current threat to her life went by the wayside. He tugged her back from the window as soon as her parents were out of sight and wrapped her in his arms. "We can't lose faith, Aubrey. We'll figure this out and bring him to justice. Then you and your family can finally have closure. Marta's parents and Ross, too."

She rested against his chest, her arms around his waist. "It's hard to believe that will happen, even though I've prayed it would every day for twelve years."

"There is strength in numbers, Aubrey, and you're not alone. You have so many people working to put an end to this. Right now, even though he's retired, George Swahn is at headquarters going through all the files and the video from cameras near the school looking for anything that will point us in the right direction. We're all praying for this to end."

She sniffled a bit, but then took a step back with renewed determination. "So, what are you hoping to find in my files that everyone else has missed over the years?"

Jonah didn't want to get her hopes up, but it might help her to know that they had found at least one small string to tug on. "We've already found one anomaly. It might not be anything, but it's a start."

"What kind of anomaly?"

Noticing how pale she was, he suggested, "Why don't you sit down while I fix us something to drink, and maybe grab a few cookies if there are any left?"

It said a lot that she gave in to his suggestion so easily. "Help yourself. I baked more."

When he returned a few minutes later, she was sitting at the dining room table, staring at nothing in particular. He handed her a cup of tea and set his own in front of the chair next to hers. He returned to the kitchen to get the cookies before settling in next to her. When she picked up her tea, he started talking.

"We know that Marta worked in the school library. When I talked to Ross, he said she was going to have to quit her job to study abroad."

"Yeah, that's right. She was so excited about the chance to live in England for a semester."

"But here's the thing—her parents said she'd already quit. They thought something might have happened there that she didn't like. Did she mention anything like that to you, do you remember?"

Aubrey leaned back in her chair and briefly closed her eyes. After a few seconds, she frowned and looked at him. "Yeah, maybe. She came home from work one night really mad about some guy. I guess he'd gotten handsy. I asked if she told Ross about it, but Marta said she'd taken care of the problem herself. I think maybe she was worried that Ross might go after the guy, but now that I think about it, she did quit working there not long afterward. I thought it was because she needed more time to get through finals and to make sure she had all her paperwork in order to leave the country."

Jonah set his tea aside so he could take notes. "I know it was a long time ago, but did she mention his name? Was he a student at the college, or did he happen to work at the library, too?"

"Honestly, I don't remember, but it happened three or maybe four weeks before we were kidnapped. Long enough that I doubt I would've thought to tell the police about it when they asked if anything unusual had recently happened to either one of us. You would think that if the guy had continued to be a problem, she would have said something or acted like something was bothering her. As far as I can remember, she was her usual self, all bubbly about leaving for England, but also about getting engaged to Ross."

That was probably true. If Marta had quit because of the incident, she might have thought that had put an end to the matter. The question was if the mystery guy had felt the same. Jonah planned to request a list of the library staff from the time the kidnapping took place. Of course, that would only help if he had actually worked at the library.

Still, at this point in time, any lead at all was worth pursuing.

His phone chimed to announce an incoming text. "It's my captain. He wants me to call him. Hopefully he's managed to line up a safe place for you to stay. Why don't you go pack enough clothes for a few days while I get the details?"

She set her tea back on the table and headed for her bedroom. Right before she would have disappeared from his sight, she stopped and looked back. "I hate this, Jonah. I really do."

He offered her a sympathetic smile. "It's probably no comfort, but so do I."

Chapter Thirteen

Sergeant Decker walked into the conference room without knocking. "Hey, Jonah, I think this is the fax you've been looking for. It's from the college."

Jonah held out his hand. "Thanks, Tim. It took them long enough."

"You're welcome." Decker started to leave, but stopped to ask, "Can I get you guys anything?"

George leaned back in his seat and stretched his arms. "A new set of eyes and a more comfortable chair would be nice."

Jonah huffed a small laugh. "While you're at it, how about a masseuse?"

Decker grinned and held up his hands. "Sorry, guys, but that's not happening. I might be able to swing some fresh coffee and a couple of sandwiches, though."

Jonah reached for his wallet and pulled out three twenties and a five. "Get something for yourself, too. Anything is fine, but my first choice would be a Philly cheesesteak. George?"

"That sounds good. My wife tries to limit how much red meat I eat, so I'm loading up on it while she's gone."

"I'll get right on it." Decker took the money. "By the way, the captain wants an update before you guys stop for the night."

"Will do."

Not that Jonah planned on leaving anytime soon. Besides, they didn't have much to report. George was still watching the traffic cam footage from the area around the school. They'd expanded their request to the area around Aubrey's house, as well. So far, they'd netted a whole bunch of nothing.

"I can finish looking at the traffic stuff, George. You should head home and get some rest. You didn't retire in order to end up back here working eighteen hours a day without pay."

"Hey, I'm getting a free sandwich. Saves me cooking when I get home. I'll probably leave after we eat, but I'll be back first thing in the morning."

There was no use convincing him that he'd already done enough, so Jonah didn't bother trying. Besides, he appreciated the help. Then George surprised him with his next comment. "You should go home and get some rest, too. You've been working pretty much around the clock. Keep that up, and eventually you'll crash and won't be much good for anything."

Jonah looked at the piles of paper on the table. "I want to get through this stuff plus the list the college sent over first."

Jonah made a show of studying one of the reports, but the ploy didn't work. George immediately leaned back in his chair and crossed his arms over his chest. "So, how is Aubrey holding up? I know she's only been at the safe house since yesterday evening, but I can't imagine that it's been easy for her."

Jonah picked up the fax from the university and started flipping through the pages. Seeing how many names were listed only made his head hurt. "She's doing better than expected, but she's already bored out of her mind."

"No surprise there. Are you going to stop by to check on her?"

"Hadn't planned on it. I've called her a couple of times, though. You know, just to keep in touch and to see if she needs anything."

George nodded as if that confirmed something he'd been thinking. "You like her, don't you?"

Where was George going with this? Jonah kept his focus on the papers in front of him as he answered, "She's a nice woman. But even if she wasn't, she deserves to live without having to look over her shoulder all the time."

His companion snorted in response. "That's the cop talking. I'm asking the man."

Jonah gave up all pretense of working. "What exactly are you saying?"

"This case has really gotten to you. I'm wondering why."

His temper stirred to life. "What do you expect? Am I supposed to not care so much? We both know the clock is ticking. If I don't get this figured out, Aubrey could very well die. That can't happen, not on my watch."

He drew a shuddering breath. "Not again."

"So this isn't just about Aubrey, or at least not only her." George sighed. "You have to get it through your head that you weren't at fault for Gino's death, Jonah. Don't shoulder the blame for something you didn't do and couldn't control. If you can't set all of that aside, you're in the wrong job."

"You weren't there that night, George. I was." The images of what had happened immediately played out in his head, just as they had so many times before—the pain, the blood, his best friend's death. "Gino died in my arms. How am I supposed to set that aside?"

The sympathy in the other man's eyes was almost his undoing. "By being the best cop you know how to be. That means focusing on the case in front of you, and forgetting about everything else until you solve it."

He held up his hand when Jonah would have interrupted him. "I'm not saying that it's easy, especially because Gino wasn't just another cop. You have every right to grieve for the loss of your friend, but what you can't do is let his death destroy you. He wouldn't want that to happen, and you know it."

George paused, probably to let that much sink in. "We're doing everything we can to protect Aubrey and to get this guy, but we're only human. We'll work until Decker comes back with our sandwiches. Then we'll eat, pack up and go home. After a few hours' sleep, we'll look at everything with fresh eyes."

George wasn't wrong, especially since Captain Martine had given him the same lecture earlier that afternoon. He'd pointed out that Jonah wasn't alone in handling the case. Even if George hadn't volunteered to assist, they had the forensics team reviewing both the new evidence and everything from twelve years ago. Then there was the team of uniformed officers watching the safe house. The list went on and on.

"Fine. Dinner and then home."

"Smart man."

Jonah had already talked to Aubrey twice that day, but he couldn't resist the temptation to call one more time. She answered on the second ring. "Hey, there."

"Did I call too late? I didn't mean to wake you up."

Her laughter came through loud and clear. "It's only nine o'clock. I'm a big girl. My mommy and daddy let me stay up later than that these days."

"Very funny. I've sort of lost track of time. I thought it was later than that."

After a short hesitation, Aubrey asked, "When is the last time you actually slept?"

"Actually, I'm not sure. Considering how foggy my brain is right now, I guess it's been a while."

"Tell me you're not still at the office. Because if you are, I'm going to hang up so you can drag yourself home to get some serious shut-eye."

That she was concerned about his well-being probably shouldn't make him so happy, but it did. "I am home and about to crash for the night. I wanted to make sure you're doing all right."

Her voice softened. "I'm fine. Well, mostly. You know how it is. I can voluntarily spend days at home alone with no problem. But tell me I can't go anywhere, and I instantly get claustrophobic."

"That sounds about right. Do you need more books or anything?"

"No, I have several left to read. I've also been watching some television. Mostly old sitcoms and ball games. Doesn't matter who is playing. I like the background noise while I read."

"Maybe we should take in a game together one of these days."

The invitation slipped out before he thought about the implications. All things considered, he shouldn't be asking her out on a date. "Look, forget I said that. We should probably write it off to me being too tired to think straight."

"So, are you apologizing for asking me out on a date because you don't want to see a game with me at all? Or is it because you can't date someone you're dealing with in the course of your job?"

"The second one. Definitely not the first."

"Good answer. We'll put the game on hold for the time being. Now, you'd better call it a night before you get yourself into any more trouble."

"Fair enough."

"One more thing, Jonah."

"Yeah?"

"No matter how this turns out, I'm glad I met you. I thank God every day for bringing you into my life."

"Right back at you. I'll call you tomorrow."

"I'm already counting the hours. Now get some sleep."

The line went silent, which was disappointing. Just talking to her eased his worry. However, right now they'd both be better off if he slept a few hours and got back to work. Before drifting off, he did his own fair share of praying—for Aubrey, and asking His guidance on how to end this nightmare for good.

After only two days, Aubrey had memorized every square inch of the tiny, run-down safe house. The only saving grace was that someone had been thoughtful enough to spring for more than basic cable. Considering she couldn't go outside, her only choice of entertainment was either reading or watching television.

She was about to check what time the baseball game was going to start when there was a knock at the front door. She glanced at the time on the cable box. Just as she suspected, it was time for a shift change. After checking through the peephole, she opened the door, happy to recognize Officer Goff. She was Aubrey's favorite of her rotating crew of guardians.

"Hi, Aubrey. I wanted to let you know I was here. An officer friend of mine just texted and offered to drop off dinner for me this evening. Would you like me to order something for you as well? And do you like Italian?"

Anything was better than the frozen dinners the house had come stocked with. "I'll have whatever you're having if it isn't too much trouble. I've got some cash with me, so I can pay you back."

"Don't worry about it. He said he'd make the delivery around six or so."

"That sounds great. It will be a nice change to my routine." She smiled at the other woman. "I know I can't offer you any wine, but I have soft drinks, coffee and tea."

"Sounds good. I'll knock when the food arrives."

"I'll be here."

Officer Goff frowned a little. "I know being shut up in this place has to be getting old already. Is there anything I can do to make things better?"

"No, I'm fine. I thought I'd watch the ball game when it starts."

"Well, let me know if you think of anything you need. Otherwise, I'm going to take a look around, and then I'll be out in my car. You have my number."

Aubrey closed the door before she gave up all pretense of trying to smile. This couldn't go on forever. The walls were already closing in on her. She could only get lost in a book or a movie for so long before she started pacing the floors. Jonah called a couple of times a day on the burner phone he'd gotten for her. Those calls were her one real lifeline to the outside world. They talked for a half an hour or more about everything but her case for most of that time. Then, right at the end, he'd given her a very brief summary of what was going on. It wasn't that he was simply being succinct; it was more that there was nothing new to report.

Resigning herself to another boring evening, she turned on the television for background noise and settled in to read. At least she had dinner to look forward to.

Aubrey finished the final page in the romance she'd been reading with a smile on her face. The story had held her attention right up until the happy ending. She got up and stretched to ease the huge number of kinks she had in her back and neck from sitting on the lumpy couch.

Dinner was due to arrive soon. Maybe Officer Goff would like to eat in the kitchen with her instead of juggling her food out in her car. Just in case, she would set the table for two. No sooner had she put out two plates and some mismatched flatware than the doorbell rang. Perfect timing. She hustled to the front door, looking forward to having a real human to talk to even for just a minute.

But it wasn't Officer Goff standing there. No, it was Jonah holding out a huge paper bag from a nearby restaurant. He was wearing a T-shirt and matching baseball cap that had the restaurant's logo on them. "Your order, ma'am."

She grinned at him. "Wow, that bag looks really heavy. Maybe you could carry it into the kitchen for me."

He winked at her as he came inside. "I live to serve."

After locking the door, she followed him into the kitchen. "So, is delivering meals your new side gig? Does it pay well?"

"Considering I only have one customer and paid for the food myself, I'd have to say no." He set the bag on the table. "On the other hand, it meant that I could check on you."

It didn't take long to figure out why he was being so careful. "So you can't stay long."

"No, not if I want this cover to hold up." He glanced down at his shirt. "Although I have to admit I totally rock this look."

Cute, but he wasn't wrong about that since the shirt was the exact shade of blue as his eyes. Regardless, her pulse picked up speed as she realized what he was really saying. "You think he's watching you?"

"There's no way to know for sure."

"So still no progress on the case?"

"We've eliminated one possibility for sure. Ruben was definitely at work when your house was spray-painted. Ross says he was at an AA meeting, but we're waiting for confirmation on that. They're pretty protective of their members' privacy, so I'm not sure if they will actually tell us. Mr. Pyne was at a doctor appointment."

It still bothered her that he seemed so focused on people she counted as friends, or at least used to. "You actually suspected it could be one of them?"

He shrugged. "Not particularly, but we have to consider all possibilities. This guy seems to know a lot about you—where you live, where you work, and even your schedule. I also checked up on your principal. According to the school secretary, he was supposedly at a meeting at the district office. I have someone heading over there in the morning to verify he was there."

She turned her back to him, not wanting him to see the

tears in her eyes. "I don't like having my friends and coworkers coming under suspicion. Besides, how can I look them in the face after they learn you've been poking around in their business?"

"If they really are friends, they'll understand that your safety is more important than a few bruised feelings."

His hands settled on her shoulders, and he gently turned her around to face him. "Don't cry, Aubrey. We'll get through this."

Once again, she found herself ignoring the boundaries they'd promised to observe. She stepped into his arms and rested her head against his chest right over the steady beat of his heart as she tried to fight off the tears. He didn't protest. Instead, he kept his hold on her light, letting her draw comfort from his embrace. She finally forced herself to step back. "Sorry about that. You should probably get going. I'm sure you have better things to do than listen to me whine."

He tilted her chin up and looked directly into her eyes. "All things considered, you've handled all of this really well."

"Only because of you. Detective Swahn would have done his best, too, but I doubt he would have hugged me whenever I'm on the verge of falling apart."

Jonah laughed just as she'd hoped he would. "His wife might not appreciate him hugging random women."

"Or kissing them."

The words slipped out before she could stop them. "Sorry, I know we decided we weren't going to go there again."

He sighed and rested his forehead against hers. "No apologies necessary. The same thought crossed my mind, too. I'd better go before I...before we..."

Jonah took a firm step back. "Look, I really do need to go. I probably shouldn't have come in the first place, but I needed to see for myself that you were all right. For now, Officer Goff is still on duty. I'm not sure who is on after that. If you need anything, hear anything, call them and then me."

"I will."

She trailed after him so she could lock up after he left. Well, that and to spend every second in his company that she could.

Jonah made it halfway across the living room and then spun back toward her with no warning. Before she could ask what was wrong, he enfolded her in his arms and kissed her like there was no tomorrow. The kiss didn't last long, but it packed quite a punch. When he set her back down, he grinned. "No way I'm apologizing for that one."

She liked that he was as breathless as she was. "I wouldn't even think of asking you to."

Jonah walked backward to the door. "Lock up and then go eat your dinner while it's still hot."

She offered him a mocking salute. "Yes, sir. Will do, sir."

He looked back one last time. "Stay safe, Aubrey."

"I'll do my best."

But they both knew no matter how careful she was and no matter how hard he worked, it might not be enough.

Chapter Fourteen

George set a cup of coffee and an apple fritter down in front of Jonah. "We've barely been working half an hour this morning and already you're frowning big-time. What's wrong?"

Jonah glanced up from the report he'd been reading from one of the private investigators Aubrey had hired. "Mostly frustration. It's like trying to catch a ghost. Even when I find something that might mean something, half the information is redacted."

"What are you looking at?

"One of the reports Aubrey gave us." He put a checkmark by the passage and slid the file across the table to George. "This guy did some checking into an incident that happened at a liberal arts college down in Oregon fifteen years ago. I have no idea how this PI even found out about it, but the case involved two girls being taken at the same time. He eventually decided the differences outweighed the similarities, mostly because it was part of a fraternity rush prank."

Jonah flipped to the second page. "Evidently each pledge had to 'kidnap' two girls and bring them to a party at the frat house. Most of them asked girls they knew, who came along willingly. But this one nitwit took the 'kidnapping' part seriously and grabbed two random girls right on there on campus and took off. Their friends saw what happened and called the campus cops. The local police caught up with them a few minutes later. The kid was only seventeen, and eventually the decision was made to let him off with a warning."

George read through the report next. "Might be worth making a call to the investigating patrol officer if he's still around. There's a good chance he might not remember the case, especially since it didn't end in an arrest or anything."

At this point, Jonah was ready to follow any breadcrumb. "I'll make the call."

Lunchtime had come and gone without any response to his inquiry into the case down in Oregon. The detective had been out of the office when Jonah had called. Waiting was never his strong suit, and it didn't help that they were running into nothing but dead ends.

He'd just finished reading through the last of the private investigator's reports when his phone finally rang. "Detective Kelly."

"This is Detective Jouvin. I hear you're looking for me."

"Yeah, I'm working on a cold case that's heated up. Twelve years ago two young women were kidnapped. One was never heard from again, but the second was set free. Now it looks like the same guy is coming after her again. I have questions about a case you handled fifteen years ago. It's a long shot, but we're doing our best to run down every possibility."

"Which one?"

Jonah gave him a quick summary of the investigator's report. "Sorry that I don't have more specifics. It sounds like no formal charges were filed, maybe because the kid was underage even though he was in college. I don't know how the investigator even found out about it. I tried calling him, too, but his phone is out of service, and his website is gone. I haven't had a chance to see if something happened to him or if he retired and moved. You were my next best chance to find out more about the kid."

"Give me a second to think about it."

Finally, the other detective spoke again. "I remember the case. I can't tell you much because the case never went anywhere. As I recall, the college handled it internally. As far as I know, the kid was let off with a warning, no formal prosecution of any kind. I was only a patrol officer at the time, so it wasn't my call to make. I figured his age was one factor since he was just shy of eighteen."

He sighed. "I assumed the fact that his parents had a ton of money and friends in the right places made the real difference. The college ended up accepting the kid's story that he'd misunderstood what the fraternity brothers wanted him to do. The parents pulled him out of the school right afterward and transferred him to a different college up your way."

What else could he ask that the detective would be able to answer? "And did the kid manage to convince you he was telling the truth about it just being a misunderstanding?"

Jouvin didn't immediately respond. Finally, he said, "Off the record, let's just say the kid was clocked going thirty miles an hour over the speed limit in the opposite direction of the frat house."

"Thanks, Detective Jouvin. You've been a lot of help."

"Whether he is your guy or not, I hope you find the guy you're hunting."

"Me, too."

As soon as Jonah hung up, he grabbed the file and his notes and headed for Captain Martine's office. They needed to reach out to the college in Oregon to see if they could learn anything else—like that kid's name.

Aubrey stared out into the backyard of the safe house. Since the sun had already set, there wasn't much to see. At the best of times, the view didn't have much to recommend it—grass dotted with dandelions, weed-infested flower beds, and several half-dead bushes. It was a sad state of affairs that the run-down mess was the most interesting thing she'd seen all day.

Sighing, she lowered the blinds and returned to the living room. She'd finished her last book earlier, and it would be to-morrow before anyone could bring her more. At least there was a movie on soon that would break up the monotony. It was one of her favorite space operas with great special effects and enough romance to make things interesting.

The question was what to do until then. It was a little too early for dinner, not that she was excited about tonight's menu. One frozen dinner tasted pretty much like another.

Still too restless to relax, she moved the coffee table closer to the couch and the two upholstered chairs out of the way to make enough room to go through her yoga routine. After that warmed up her muscles, she'd do the routine her self-defense instructor had taught her. She'd started taking classes not long after she'd been released. Not only did the two disciplines keep her physically fit, they gave her a sense of empowerment and some hope she'd be able to protect herself in the future.

She'd barely gotten started when a strange noise from out front caught her attention. A weird popping sound was immediately followed by the sound of breaking glass. By that point, Aubrey's heart was pounding so hard she couldn't hear anything at all. That didn't stop her from crawling the few feet to the coffee table to where she'd left the phone. She called her guard's number and held her breath as it started to ring. When someone answered, it wasn't Officer Goff.

"Well, hello, Aubrey. It's been a while since we last talked. I'm guessing you didn't miss me, but I suppose that is only understandable."

She was pretty sure it was a male voice, but the mechanical distortion made it impossible to know much more than that. "Where's Officer Goff?"

"She's bleeding all over her car, but she's still breathing. Tell her you're alive, Officer."

There was a soft moan. "Aubrey, call 911. Don't open the—"

"Do that, and your cop friend is dead for sure. Come along peacefully, and she might survive until someone finds her. Either way, you'll still end up leaving with me. It's your choice. Do you really want to be responsible for her death?"

No matter what he said, Aubrey wouldn't really be the one who killed Officer Goff. There was also no guarantee that the kidnapper wouldn't kill her even if Aubrey did cooperate. Regardless, there was only one option that she could live with. Aubrey closed her eyes and prayed hard for Officer Goff's safety. *Please, Father, hold her in Your hands until help can arrive.*

At the same time, Aubrey dialed 911 and whispered her name and begged them to send help quickly because Officer Goff had been shot. And finally she asked the operator to tell Detective Kelly that none of this was his fault. He wouldn't believe that, and she hated knowing her disappearance would cause him more pain. He was already living with the guilt of his friend's death, and she didn't want him to shoulder the blame for whatever happened to her. Aware that time was running out for Officer Goff, she shoved the phone out of sight under the sofa in case the man came inside. There was no telling what he'd do to her or Officer Goff if he checked her call history and learned that she'd defied his order not to call the authorities.

Then she pushed herself up to her feet and unlocked the door.

Jonah had the responding officer on speakerphone as he drove like a madman toward the safe house. He'd been on his way to pick up dinner when the call about Aubrey had come in. "How long has Ms. Sims been gone?"

"Near as we can figure, forty minutes tops. Her call came

in less than half an hour ago. We arrived on scene less than ten minutes after that."

"How is Officer Goff doing?"

"In pain, but alert. She refused to let them transport her to the hospital until she speaks to you. The EMTs aren't happy."

That was understandable, but he was grateful he'd get to talk to her before the ambulance whisked her away. If she needed surgery, it could be hours or maybe even tomorrow before he'd have a chance to talk to her again. "I'm almost there."

"I'll tell them."

Jonah swerved in and out of traffic with his lights flashing for the last few blocks to the safe house. Once there, he'd talk to Officer Goff first and then check out the scene to see what he could learn. If the kidnapper was as careful as he had been so far, Jonah wasn't expecting to find much. The only good news was that the nature of Officer Goff's injury wasn't life-threatening. She'd taken a bullet to the shoulder and some minor cuts from broken glass.

He reminded himself to be grateful and give thanks for that much. Hopefully, she'd be able to give them something to go on, preferably a description of her attacker or a license plate. They'd need every possible detail they could get in order to start tracking Aubrey's whereabouts. It killed him that even now she was reliving her worst nightmares. He railed against the injustice of it all. Aubrey had to be scared out of her wits, and yet she'd asked dispatch to tell him that none of this was his fault.

Yeah, he got what she meant. It was her kidnapper who had set all of this in motion. Her intentions were good, but the truth was that once again Jonah had failed to protect someone who had depended on him. He wasn't sure how he'd survive if he failed to bring Aubrey home safely. If he lost her, he wasn't sure he would even want to. That was an awful realization, but that was where his head was right now. The truth was that somehow she'd become the center of his universe in the short time he'd known her. If he didn't trust his own ability to find her, then he needed to put his trust in a higher power. *Father, I know You brought Aubrey into my life for a reason. Please watch over her until I can find her.*

A new sense of calm washed over him, letting him think clearly for the first time since the call had come in. He turned down the street where the safe house was located but had to park two blocks away. The responding officers had blocked off traffic up ahead, and the emergency vehicles took up most of the road. He locked his vehicle and took off at a slow lope.

It was tempting to rush inside the safe house and look around, but he owed it to Officer Goff to check on her first. He flashed his badge at each cop he passed and kept walking. He wasn't surprised at the number of officers swarming around the crime scene. One of their own had been shot, and a person under their protection had been taken. No one would rest until the culprit was found and brought to justice.

It was another reminder that Jonah wasn't alone in this.

A few seconds later, he approached the EMTs who were riding herd on Officer Goff. Jonah nodded at them and waited for their permission to approach their patient. "Make it quick, Detective. She's hurting and might need a transfusion."

"Will do."

He moved up to stand next to the gurney. "Officer Goff, what can you tell me?"

She looked like roadkill, her eyes dull with pain. That didn't stop her from trying to sit up to make her report even though she couldn't stifle a whimper when she moved. The EMT started forward, but Jonah waved him off. "Easy does it, April. Lie back and relax. You don't want to make the bleeding worse. I'm right here. Tell me what happened so these folks can get you the care you need."

Latching on to his arm, she tugged him down closer and spoke in fits and starts. "No idea where the guy came from... appeared out of nowhere and shot through the window. Best guess…he used a silencer since no neighbors came running out…must have parked on a side street. I did see a big sedan… older model, silver or gray…pull out of the street behind me a few minutes later. No way to know if it was him…it turned the other direction, so it didn't pass by me."

"Can you give me any kind of description of him?"

She started to nod, but winced again as if even the smallest movement hurt. "Tall. Maybe six feet, six-one. Wore all black, including a ski mask. Used something to distort his voice. Definitely male, though. Looked fit. Swimmer's build, not a body builder. He cuffed my hands to the steering wheel so I couldn't call it in. Aubrey must have heard something, because she called me. He grabbed the phone and answered. She asked if I was okay. He held the phone so I could speak. Tried to tell her to call it in. He threatened to kill me if she did. She called anyway."

Tears trickled down her face. "She's a brave woman. She let him take her to keep him from killing me." Her eyes glittered with tears. "I'm so sorry he got her, sir."

"We are all." Jonah patted her gently on her uninjured arm. "It's time you head to the hospital. I'll take over from here. You concentrate on getting better."

She let her eyes drift closed. "Get her back."

"I will do my best."

And pray that his best was good enough.

It didn't take long for Jonah to walk through the safe house. There was no sign of violence. That was the good news. The bad news was that he suspected it was true that Aubrey had surrendered to her abductor hoping to save Officer Goff's life. He would've done the same thing. That didn't mean he was happy that she'd made that decision. She had known help was on the way. If she'd stayed barricaded inside the house, she might've been able to hold out until the officers responded. They'd arrived on scene only minutes after she'd made the call.

But there was no way she could have known how fast they would get there. If the kidnapper had made a determined effort, he could have broken in through a window or even kicked in the door. Disobeying his orders would have only increased the likelihood that he would have executed Officer Goff in retaliation. Who knew what he would have done to Aubrey herself?

The front door opened. He looked to see who had arrived and wasn't surprised to see it was Captain Martine. "What's our status?"

"Officer Goff took a bullet in the shoulder. She insisted on staying here until she talked to me. If the wound was life-threatening, the EMTs would have taken her to the hospital right away."

"At least there's that much good news." Captain Martine looked around the living room before continuing. "My next stop is to speak with her parents. After that, I'll be at the hospital."

Jonah was relieved he wasn't going to have to face them, but he felt compelled to offer. "If you'd rather I talked to Mr. and Mrs. Sims..."

His captain shook his head. "No, I want you focused on the case. Keep me posted."

"I will."

A second later, his phone rang. A glance at the screen told him it was George Swahn. The older man had remained at headquarters, figuring he'd do more good there.

"What's up?"

"I think we may have something. That detective you talked to from Oregon called again. How soon will you be finished up at there?"

Jonah looked around. The techs were still processing the scene. Other officers were working their way through the neighborhood canvasing the area for witnesses. Deciding there wasn't much he could contribute to the effort, he started for the door. "I'm on my way."

Chapter Fifteen

Aubrey heard a soft moan. With considerable effort, she pried open one eye and looked around to see who had made the noise. The glaring sunlight shining in through the window across the room set off a firestorm of pain inside her head. Relieved to find no one in sight, she let her eyelid drop back down again and slept. She had no idea how much time had passed when another whimper woke her up again. At least this time, she immediately understood that she was the one making the noise.

Considering how bad she felt at that moment, she wasn't surprised. When she tried to lift her head to look around, a wave of dizziness left her queasy and shaking. The darkness still lapping at the edges of her mind proved stronger than her ability to resist it, and she slid back into unconsciousness again.

By the time she finally woke up completely, the sunlight coming through the one window in the room had dimmed considerably. That was one good bit of news. The other was that she was still alone. On the downside, apparently a whole lot of hours had passed since she'd been abducted. She wouldn't be left here alone for long.

Wherever *here* was.

How had she even gotten there? The last clear memory she had was of opening the front door of the safe house. A man dressed all in black had blindfolded her and then dragged her down the street and around the corner. There'd been the sound of a trunk lid opening right before he'd picked her up and dropped her inside. A second later, he'd stabbed her with something sharp. That was the last thing she remembered. She could only guess he'd shot her full of some knockout drug. Considering how long she'd been out, whatever had been in the syringe had packed quite a punch. Either that, or he'd given her another dose at some point.

Her brain was starting to fire on more cylinders, but there were still a lot of gaps in her memory that needed to be filled in. But before she could do that, she had more pressing matters to take care of. Moving slowly, she pushed herself up into a sitting position. When her head quit spinning, she took a slow look around. It took only a second to recognize her surroundings, because she'd been there before. From what she could tell, the small cabin hadn't changed at all over the past twelve years.

Her pulse picked up speed, which didn't help her headache. On the other hand, maybe having her blood rush through her veins faster than normal would help clear the drug out of her system. She started to swing her legs over the side of the bed, but it didn't go as planned. Her left one moved easily enough, but her right leg was weighed down with something. She tried again, only to realize the problem was the heavy metal shackle wrapped around her ankle.

It brought back another flash of memory from twelve years ago, one that had haunted her dreams all too often. Just like this time, she'd regained consciousness to find herself and her best friend chained to a metal ring sticking up out of the concrete floor. They'd desperately tried without success to break free of their chains. They'd also pounded on the walls and screamed themselves hoarse hoping that someone would hear them.

All their efforts had garnered them was bruised hands and sore throats. That wasn't going to stop her from trying again. She managed to swing both of her legs over the edge of the bed and scooted forward to plant her feet flat on the floor. Proud of her progress, she took a deep breath and tried to stand. After two more attempts to stay upright, she shuffled toward the curtain that served as the bathroom door. The facilities were as primitive as they were last time, but she used them anyway.

With that taken care of, she decided to check out the cooler and paper bag sitting next to the cabin door. Whoever the guy was who'd dragged her back here, he was a creature of habit. Just like before, the bag contained apples, potato chips and a variety of individual snacks. The cooler had a layer of ice on the bottom. Nestled into the melting mess were a dozen bottles of water and soft drinks. There was also a plastic container filled with prepackaged sandwiches, the kind that could be bought at any gas station.

Was it safe to drink the water or eat the food? The bottom line was that she had no choice. In order to face off against her captor, she'd need every ounce of strength she could muster. With grim determination, she picked a bottle of water at random and studied it for signs that it had been tampered with. The seal was unbroken, and there was no damage to the plastic or the label. The last time the food had also been safe to eat. Maybe he didn't want to risk having his captives overdose and spoil his fun.

She instantly slammed the door on that line of thinking. Right now, her focus needed to be on escaping. It was imperative to find some way out of this nightmare before he came back. Because he would return. And this time there wouldn't be any coin flipping to offer her a last-minute reprieve. She twisted the lid off the bottle and took a big drink. Grabbing an apple and a pack of peanut butter crackers, she shuffled back over to the bed and sat down.

Already, she was feeling better. The fuzziness in her head was all but gone, and her stomach had settled down. What next?

She tugged on the chain, knowing full well what to expect. It was just long enough to allow her to reach every corner of the one-room cabin, but no farther. Even if she could somehow open the door, she wouldn't be able to step outside. The same was true if she found a way to remove the bars on the only window. After glancing outside, she paced the width of the cabin half a dozen times to stretch her legs before returning to the window.

The view was nothing but huge cedars and Douglas firs for as far as she could see. She suspected that the cabin was tucked away at the far end of a dirt road somewhere in the Cascade Mountains. From what she'd seen outside the window, the road came to a stop right in front of the cabin, so no chance of a helpful stranger driving by. Instead, eventually she'd hear a car approach, and there was only one person who would be coming. She drew some strength from knowing that she'd finally learn the identity of the man who had altered the direction of her entire life.

As she stood there, she realized she was shivering. Some of it was due to her increasing fear, but it was also likely the temperature was dropping now that the sun had set. She picked out another snack and retreated to sit on the bed. The blanket was thin and worn, but it was better than nothing. After wrapping it around her shoulders, Aubrey ate a granola bar and some string cheese while she contemplated her situation.

Even if hope was in limited supply right now, there was one major difference between what happened twelve years ago and now. This time someone was out there looking for her who knew exactly what had happened. Jonah might not know who had taken her, but he wouldn't stop looking until he found the answer. Regardless of how this ended, he would also do his best to make sure her parents got closure.

She could only imagine what they were going through right now. After all, they already knew what it was like to have their only child go missing. The fact that they'd been lucky enough to get Aubrey back didn't mean they'd ever forgotten that pain—or the fear that it could happen again. She hated knowing the terror they were living with right now. Worse yet, they'd want someone to blame, and she was sure they would aim all of their anger right at Jonah. She didn't want any of them to shoulder the blame for this. They weren't the ones who shot Officer Goff or dragged Aubrey back to this cabin.

She wished she could tell them that herself. Instead, Aubrey did the only thing she could do. She prayed. *Father, I ask You for the strength to face whatever comes. Not just for me, but for my parents, my friends, and most of all, for Jonah and his coworkers. Give them comfort, and let them feel Your healing spirit. My one regret is that I didn't tell Jonah how much he means to me. He's a good man, and I hope he finds peace in Your love. Amen.*

Her energy at low ebb, she curled up on the bed and drifted off to sleep. She'd need to be rested when that car came driving up the road.

Jonah had been up all night, and it was looking as if sleep was on hold for the foreseeable future. George had indeed found a string, and they'd tugged on it as hard as possible without getting anywhere. As it turned out, while Jonah was at the safe house Detective Jouvin had called back. He'd unearthed one more tidbit of information when he'd found his spiral notebook from back then. He didn't know why, but the kid had registered at the college using his middle name and his mother's maiden name. Evidently, his legal name was actually her last name and his father's, separated with a hyphen. Anyway, Jouvin's notes had listed the kid as L. Mark Dennison.

It wasn't much, and they didn't find anyone with that name in any of the searches they'd tried. For most of the night, they'd watched traffic camera footage looking for a car that met Officer Goff's vague description. The captain had finally ordered George to go home and sleep. He'd made the same suggestion to Jonah, but didn't get far.

Meanwhile, Sergeant Decker had been keeping Jonah supplied with coffee and food while he worked. Finally, he'd pulled up a chair and sat down. After studying their notes on the white board on the wall, he said, "Tell me what you've got so far."

When Jonah shot him a dark look, Decker didn't blink. "Talking it out helps sometimes, so it's worth a try. You've looked at all this stuff until you're not really seeing it anymore. Tell me what you're thinking. I know about what happened twelve years ago. Start with what's happened recently"

Fine. For sure, he wasn't making any progress on his own. Jonah got up and walked around to stand in front of the white board. "Aubrey Sims said she'd been feeling as if someone has been watching her. The note was sent to her private mailbox, and flowers were delivered to her house. That means that guy has been watching her for some time. He also knows where she works, because that's where her tire was spiked. That's when I convinced her to take a leave of absence."

Decker looked surprised. "She told them that she had a stalker?"

Jonah shook his head. "No, she let them think that she had a personal problem that needed her immediate attention."

"Good thinking."

"I followed her home from school and made sure she got inside safely. Right after that, she discovered a message had been painted on her bedroom window. The captain made the decision to move her to a safe house, but the guy we're looking for found her there. He could have followed me or one of the other officers."

"Suspects?"

Pointing to that particular list, Jonah pointed at the top name. "Ross Easton was the fiancé of the girl who never made it home last time. Evidently, he used to stalk Aubrey, but he claims he stopped that nonsense when he got sober. For what it's worth, I believe him. Evidently he wasn't very good at stalking, because she would see him hanging around. She confirmed she hadn't seen or talked to Ross in years."

"Next up is Ruben Jacobs, the evening custodian at her school. That would explain how he knows where she works. Not sure if Ruben would have access to her records to get her address or PO box number. We verified he was at work when the window was painted. He's also in his early sixties, so he doesn't exactly fit the profile. He's pretty low on my list of suspects."

Jonah pointed at the next name. "Riley Pyne is the father of the girl who didn't make it home twelve years ago. He and his wife used to make Aubrey's life pretty miserable, but Mr. Pyne's health isn't good. I can't see him pulling off an abduction of a healthy young woman, at least not alone."

That left just one name on the list. "This guy's name is up here mainly because there's something about him I don't like. He's the principal at Aubrey's school. She's known him for a couple of years, ever since he took the job. By all reports, the guy is well liked and respected. However, we haven't been able to confirm for sure where he was at a couple of crucial times over the past week. That said, it's coming up on the end of the school year. Evidently that means he's in and out of the building for meetings at the district office."

"Is he single?"

"Yeah. Why?"

Decker hesitated but finally said, "Could that be why you don't like him? Because he could be interested in Ms. Sims on a personal level?"

Jonah growled, "What does that have to do with anything?"

"Lie to me if you want to, Detective, but don't lie to yourself. If your gut is telling you there's something off about this guy, fine. But make sure that's why he's at the top of your list."

The sergeant was right to question Jonah's motivations even if it made him want to toss the man out of the conference room. He closed his eyes and thought about everything he knew about Aubrey's boss and then summarized it. "Principal Peale was born and raised right outside of Seattle. He graduated from college with a degree in elementary education and a master's in school administration or some such thing. After that, he taught school in Florida for five years before moving back to Washington State. He's divorced, no kids."

"All of that sounds pretty normal. So what is it about him that bothers you?"

"Like I said, the kidnapper has been observing Aubrey for a while now. That would be pretty easy to do if he actually worked with her. As principal, he'd have access to her personnel file. On Aubrey's second to last day at school, she worked late. She was walking out to the parking lot where I was going to meet her and follow her home. The janitor offered to walk her out since everyone else was already gone. She suggested Ruben watch her from the door instead. Either way, Aubrey wasn't technically alone. That's when she found out her tire had been spiked. That's the same thing the kidnapper did twelve years ago."

He stopped to sip his coffee and review the next details in his head to make sure he had the order right. "Her principal just happened to come back to the school right when she spotted the spike in her tire. Something about picking up some papers for a meeting the next morning. Again, that could be true. I can tell you this much for certain—he definitely didn't like me being the one who changed the tire for Aubrey. I wanted to bring it in to the forensics lab, but I wasn't about to tell him that. He kept suggesting that she call for her emergency road service to come deal with the tire instead."

"Did he know who you were or what you do?"

He had to give that some thought. "She said I was a friend, but I'm pretty sure she introduced me as Detective Jonah Kelly."

"If Peale is your guy, knowing she has a cop hanging around had to give him pause even if you really were simply her friend. He'd have to wonder if you were actually there in your professional capacity. After all, why would she need someone to follow her home? Is there more?"

"Yeah, there is. He also wasn't at the school when the spray painting happened. One of the patrol officers checked with the district office to see if he was there. There had been a meeting, but it apparently ended early. The person the officer spoke to said she wasn't sure when he left the administration building. The trouble is that there are several exits. A couple of people remember talking to him after the meeting, though. Still, depending on when he actually left, there's a good chance he could've made it to Aubrey's and back to school without anyone noticing if he went missing for a while."

Decker nodded in approval. "Okay, so it's a lot of little things that may or may not add up to something significant."

"That's the problem. We've got nothing solid to go on. In the meantime, whoever the guy is, he has Aubrey."

Which made him physically ill.

Decker pointed to the other side of the board. "You haven't mentioned anyone by that name. Who is L. Mark Dennison?"

Jonah launched into a brief description of the private investigator's report and the small amount of information they'd gotten from Detective Jouvin. "We did some searching under that name and didn't find anything. Either he's not in the area or else he's changed his name again."

"Do you know what the *L* stands for?"

No, but come to think of it, he did know one person whose name started with that letter. How could he have not seen that before now?

Decker leaned forward, elbows on the table. "You've spotted something."

Jonah pointed at the *L* and smiled. "Principal Peale's first name is Lyle."

Chapter Sixteen

The waiting was the worst. A second night had come and gone with no sign of her captor. Not that Aubrey wanted him to return, but what if he never came back? He'd left her only a minimal amount of water and food, with no indication of how long it was supposed to last her. What happened if she ran out? Would she survive long enough for someone else to find her? So many scary questions with no answers. It wasn't the first time that panic had threatened to overwhelm her. Rather than give in to it, she'd turned to her faith and the firm belief that God would never abandon her.

Remembering that gave Aubrey the strength to make plans. To take control of the few things she could, starting with rationing her supplies. Half of a stale sandwich washed down with a few sips of water hadn't been a very satisfying breakfast, but for now it was better to err on the side of caution.

She admired the view from the window. While there wasn't much for her to be grateful for at the moment, the incredible beauty of nature was soothing. Focusing on a dense forest of enormous cedar trees was so much better for her emotional state than cowering on the bed with nothing to see but bare wooden walls. Finally, she shuffled back to the center of the room and once again went through her yoga stretches, or at least the ones she could do dragging a chain around. Once she warmed up her muscles, she flowed right into her self-defense routine.

Not that her self-defense techniques had helped her avoid being captured, but that was because someone else's life had been hanging in the balance. Going on the attack would've almost certainly ended in Officer Goff's death. That had left Aubrey with no choice but to willingly go with her captor. Jonah might not agree with her decision, but he would've done the same thing. If given the choice to give his life to save his partner's, Jonah wouldn't have hesitated. The man was a hero right down to the bone.

She wanted to tell him that in person, which meant she needed to be ready when she next confronted her captor. The chain clanked as she flowed from one position to the next, moving slower than normal. She'd gotten tangled in the chain earlier when she'd done a spinning move and gone down in an awkward heap. The ill-timed maneuver had resulted in a few new bruises, but no serious injuries. After that, she'd slowed everything down to make sure she was in fighting form when the time came.

As she finished her second round of exercise, a sound outside the cabin caught her attention. Freezing in position, she listened hard, although it was difficult to hear much of anything over her own ragged breathing and racing pulse. A second later, her worst fears were confirmed—a vehicle was headed her way.

She wished she had been able to fashion a weapon of some kind, but there wasn't anything in the cabin other than the cooler and the narrow bed. She'd hoped that she could somehow dismantle the frame, but it turned out to be nothing more than a box made out of plywood. Right now, her best option was to shake up one of the soft drinks as hard as she could. Then, when he walked into the cabin, she could pop the top and spray it in his face. The ploy might work in theory, but she might be better off just heaving the full can at his head.

A minute later, an older-model car parked in front of the cabin, at an angle that made it impossible to see the driver. Aubrey watched and waited for him to get out of the vehicle so she could finally get a look at the man who had plagued her life for so many years. When he finally stepped into sight, her mind couldn't process what she was seeing.

This was no stranger. She knew him well, or at least she'd always thought she did. Her brain struggled to connect the dots. How had her boss happened to stumble across the cabin where she was being held captive? For a single moment, hope surged that Principal Peale would break down the door and whisk her back to civilization. When he spotted her staring out of the window, he smiled and started toward the door carrying a pair of grocery sacks.

Aubrey watched in horror as he walked through the door, his familiar smile firmly in place as he set the grocery bags on the floor. "Good morning, Aubrey. I brought more ice and a few more supplies. Sorry to say that I can't stay long. School isn't out yet, and I have to maintain my usual schedule as much as possible."

"Why are you doing this?"

"I would think the answer to that would be obvious." He pointed toward the bags. "You need fresh food and water. Without proper refrigeration, this stuff won't last long. I'm replenishing your supplies so you don't get sick from eating bad food."

He dumped the new ice into the cooler and then added a few more bottles of water along with some new sandwiches. When he was done, he set a box of saltine crackers and a jar of peanut butter on top of the cooler. "I didn't think to ask. You're not allergic to peanuts, are you?"

She shook her head. "No, but I wasn't asking about the food. I was asking why you brought me here."

His usual friendly smile slid away to be replaced with one that made her skin crawl. "Don't ask questions you really don't want the answers to, Aubrey. Let's just say that we're going to have fun together. At least it will be fun for me. Unfortunately, the good times can't start until after school is out and I'm on summer vacation. I have a few meetings the day after the kids leave for the summer, but then I'll be able to devote all my attention to our time together. Until then, I'll stop by when I can to bring more supplies."

"Why now and why me, Lyle? We've been working together for almost two years."

His creepy smile was back in full force. "Anticipation is part of the game. I've loved knowing that this day would come and that you had no idea. That aside, letting you go twelve years ago always felt like a bit of unfinished business. I've entertained other guests over that time, of course, but somehow you've never been far from my mind."

He checked the time and frowned. "I really need to leave. See you soon."

This time her chills had nothing to do with the cool temperature outside of the cabin. "I will pray the Lord will heal your sickness."

He'd been about to walk out the door, but Lyle charged back across the cabin to grab Aubrey by her hair and gave it a yank. "I'm not sick, Aubrey. You might want to watch how you talk to me. I expect to be treated with respect. That was something your friend Marta learned the hard way. You really, really don't want to see me angry."

Then, just as if a switch had been flipped, he released her and backed away. "Enjoy your time here. I'll be back soon."

As he drove away, she collapsed on the bed and cried.

Jonah had gone home and crashed last night, but he didn't sleep for long. His dreams had turned dark and bloody, filled with gaunt images of Gino and Aubrey hovering just out of his reach with their hands outstretched and begging for his help. Whenever he tried to latch on to their hands, they faded out of sight, only to pop back into view in another direction. Finally realizing that trying to sleep was futile, he'd gotten dressed and driven back to the precinct.

After buying a bag of breakfast sandwiches at the closest drive-through, he'd arrived about two hours before sunrise only to find his boss was already there. Over coffee and egg sandwiches, Captain Martine listened in silence as Jonah reviewed everything they'd learned since the last time they'd spoken. "We've verified that Lyle Peale's full name is Lyle Mark Dennison-Peale. It seems that he's used different combinations of those names over the years. When he left the school in Oregon, he enrolled in his next college as Lyle Peale. We also traced his work history in Florida, where he changed schools almost every year. Not sure why."

He stopped to scan his notes again. "We did a search for similar cases to ours in the general area where he lived in Florida and found two that line up pretty closely. From what we know now, both cases are currently unsolved with no witnesses and no suspects. Forensics are pretty much nonexistent and victims were never found. I requested copies of the case files, and the investigating detectives promised to have them faxed overnight."

"Sounds promising. One bit of good news is that Officer Goff should be discharged from the hospital tomorrow or the day after. She'll need some physical therapy, but the feeling is there won't be any long-term problems with her shoulder."

Jonah had personal experience with the kind of damage a bullet could do to a major joint, so he was happy to hear her prognosis was so positive. It hit him that he'd missed two physical therapy appointments over the past few days, but too bad. Right now, his knee was the least of his concerns.

The captain's expression turned more serious. "Just so you know, I did speak to Ms. Sims's family personally. To say they're up in arms that we let this happen on our watch is putting it mildly. I assured them that we had an entire team working on finding their daughter. It was all I could do to convince them not to go running to the newspapers or posting anything on social media. I told them those actions could push her captor into rash action. I'm not sure they'll listen to me, but I can't say I really blame them."

"Me neither." Jonah could only imagine how the couple had reacted. "They've been through this before and know full well they had been lucky to get their daughter back. It has to be tearing them up having it happen all over again."

He wasn't telling his boss anything new. When the captain's phone rang, he answered it and asked the other person to hold for a second. "Jonah, just so you know, I've already reached out to the prosecutor's office to apprise him of the situation. Keep me posted of any new findings."

Jonah knew a dismissal when he heard one. "Yes, sir."

He left the captain's office and headed back to the conference room where he and his small team had holed up to work. He spent the next hour reviewing the files that had come in on the two cases from Florida. Even though there was no helpful evidence, the cases were near matches to both the kidnapping twelve years ago and the current one. It was killing him to know that Aubrey was out there somewhere and wondering if anyone would ever find her. "Have we learned anything new?"

Decker lifted his hand to catch Jonah's attention. "The vehicle Peale drives to work is a dark blue SUV, but we've found he also has an older-model sedan registered under Mark Dennison. It's listed as silver and would possibly fit the description of the vehicle Officer Goff saw pull out of the street down the block from the safe house the night of the kidnapping."

Okay, now the pieces were finally starting to fall into place. Each new fact helped convince him that they were on the right track. His greatest fear was that by focusing all of the attention on Aubrey's boss, they might miss something that might point in another direction. If that happened, the mistake could prove fatal to Aubrey. As soon as that thought crossed his mind, he silently prayed that the Lord would continue to guide their footsteps.

At that point, George Swahn joined the discussion. "Once we found out about that vehicle, I went back and screened the traffic cam footage from around the time when Aubrey's tire was spiked at the school. I couldn't find a clear enough angle to get the license plate number, but there was a brief glimpse of a silver sedan of the appropriate vintage turning into a parking lot about an hour before she actually walked out of the building. I couldn't find any footage showing it leaving again. There's no way to know for sure it was Peale's car, but my gut feeling is that it was him. It would make sense if he was going to take the risk of spiking her tire at their place of employment that he wouldn't do it driving his usual vehicle."

Jonah couldn't find fault with the man's logic. "I agree. I can personally testify that he was driving the blue SUV when he showed up later. Maybe he'd left his SUV in the same parking lot and switched back after spiking the tire. It would be worth checking to see what kind of businesses are in that area. We haven't seen the sedan near his condo, and he has to keep it somewhere. Maybe he rents a storage unit near the school."

George grinned. "Good thinking. I'll do some checking."

Jonah moved onto his next question. "Have we had any luck tracing properties listed under any of his names?"

"Not yet, but we're working on it."

"I'm thinking that will be the key to catching him. This guy is too careful not to have some place that he can control completely. He wouldn't want any nosy neighbors close by who might get curious about why he comes and goes at odd times or hear something that would have them calling the police."

Jonah circled around the end of the table to study the map they'd posted on the wall. He pointed to the red pushpins that marked where the school was located and the condo where

Peale lived. "Having said all of that, it's got to be close enough to where he lives and works that he can get there and back within a reasonable amount of time. We should restrict the title searches to a fifty-mile radius first. If we can't find anything there, we'll expand the search."

Decker asked, "What are you going to do next?"

Jonah needed to sit down and give his leg a break before it stiffened up completely. After taking his seat, he rubbed his knee, not bothering to try to hide his actions from the others. "I'm going to update the captain again. It's an outside shot with our lack of hard evidence, but maybe we can get a search warrant for his condo and his vehicles, at least the one we can find. If we can find a storage unit, I'll add it to the list. I'll also have patrol drive by Peale's condo again to see if there's any sign of the silver sedan."

Decker had installed a coffeemaker on a low cabinet in the back corner. He got up and brought the pot over to top off Jonah's cup and then did the same for everyone else. As he circled the table, he asked, "What do you think would happen if you paid a visit to Peale at the school? Maybe under the guise of checking to see if they'd had any more problems with vandalism since Ms. Sims's tire was damaged."

Jonah considered the idea, but it didn't feel right. "I'll think about it. I'm concerned that approaching him for any reason right now would only panic him. We know he's at work today, which hopefully means we still have a little time before he gets serious about his plans for Aubrey. I think he might have taken her this week because he knew his schedule would be erratic. Because he has meetings and other stuff going on, it makes it more difficult for people to notice if he disappears for short periods of time."

George looked up from whatever he'd been reading. "Grabbing her early was smart thinking. If news of her disappearance came out, he's been doing a good job of making it look like it's been business as usual for him at work."

The coffee was the consistency of tar, but right now Jonah needed that strong jolt of caffeine. "Yeah, the real problem comes when the summer break actually starts in a few days. Once that happens, he'll be free to disappear without anyone noticing. For now, we still have time to find her."

He hoped, because failure wasn't an option.

Jonah needed to get out of the office and do something active. Everyone was working as hard as they could, but they hadn't made any more progress. He picked up his jacket and slipped it on. "I'm going to go by the hospital to see Officer Goff. I have a picture of the type of sedan that Peale owns. I want to see if it looks like the one she saw leaving the area. Then I'm going to swing by to check in on the officer watching the school. On the way back, I'll pick up another round of sandwiches. Any preferences?"

Once he'd written down their orders, he left the building. Before getting into his car, he stopped to enjoy several breaths of cool, fresh air. As soon as he did, a new wave of guilt hit him hard. How could he enjoy anything at all knowing Aubrey was still being held captive? Depending on where Peale had her stashed, she could be cold, hungry, or even in pain. Not to mention scared out of her wits.

He got into the car and rested his forehead on the steering wheel as he fought to regain control of his emotions. He hated this for her, but she was an amazingly strong woman in so many ways. Resilient, too. Yes, her previous captivity had left its mark on her, but Aubrey had still managed to build a good life for herself. She'd done it once, and she'd do it again with God's help—and Jonah's, too, if she'd let him.

For now, he would go visit Officer Goff and then dive back into the investigation. As hard as everyone was working, something had to break on the case soon. *Please, God, let that be true.*

Chapter Seventeen

Aubrey bit back a cry of pain. She'd broken another nail, this one badly enough to bleed a little. Shaking her hand, she waited for the initial sting to dissipate and got right back to work. Lyle wouldn't be happy if he saw the damage she'd done to his cooler. Soon after he'd left, she given herself a stern lecture. Lying around and crying wouldn't accomplish anything. Rather than wallow in self-pity, she needed to be proactive and find some way to defend herself. With that in mind, she set about trying to fashion a rudimentary weapon out of the hardware on the cooler.

The collapsible handle was plastic, and probably wouldn't be much good as a weapon. And if she damaged the cooler getting it off, Lyle was bound to notice. That left the wheels. Actually, not the wheels themselves, but the axle that connected them. She was pretty sure it was a metal rod. If she succeeded in removing it, she could prop the wheels back in place, and turn that end against the wall where any damage might not be so obvious.

At the very least, she could use the rod to jab at Lyle's exposed flesh like his face and hands. If she could hurt him badly enough, she might buy herself enough time to make a run for it. Well, if she could manage to get the keys to unlock her shackle first. Her real hope was that she could sharpen one end of the rod enough to pick the lock herself. Lyle wouldn't expect her to be free of her chain, which would buy her another second or two to surprise him.

On her third attempt, the first wheel finally popped off. She tipped the cooler up enough to tug on the other wheel, slowly working it and the metal rod to which it was attached free from the cooler. It took a little more time to remove the second wheel from the axle, leaving her with a steel rod about twelve inches long. Short enough to hide, long enough to do some serious damage. She whipped it through the air and smiled. She wasn't a violent person by nature, but that didn't mean she wasn't going to defend herself.

She'd unloaded most of the food from the cooler to make it easier to maneuver and needed to put it all back. First, though, she turned the cooler around so the side with the wheels would be against the wall. That done, she propped the wheels back in position and collapsed the handle back down. After setting aside a sandwich and a soft drink, she returned the rest of the food to the cooler and latched the lid.

After taking a seat on the bed, she studied the cooler and decided that it was the best she could do under the circumstances. Either it would pass muster, or it wouldn't. Besides, if Lyle stopped to check it out, it might give her an opportunity to go on the attack. Next, she studied the shackle on her ankle. Unfortunately, it was all too obvious the metal rod was too thick to pick the lock. The only way she was going to get free of her chain was to get the keys from Lyle.

She washed down the last bite of stale sandwich with her diet cola and tossed the can into the corner with the rest of the trash she'd accumulated in the time she'd been there. The pile was a sad reminder of how much time had passed since she'd been taken captive. Every minute that ticked by made it that much sooner that Lyle would come back.

Her mother and father had to be going crazy by now. She really hoped that they didn't blame Jonah or the rest of the police for her predicament. Chances were that they would, though. They were a clearer target than the faceless bogeyman from twelve years ago. It made her heart ache knowing the pain they were in when there was nothing she could do to ease it.

No, that wasn't true. She walked over to the window where she closed her eyes and lifted her face to feel the warmth of the sun filtering down through the trees. "Holy Father, grant Your healing peace to my parents and those others who are hurting right now. Remind them of Your love and keep them safe. Amen."

Feeling better, she returned to the bed and stretched out with her new weapon tucked out of sight but close at hand. As she waited for sleep to overtake her, she let her mind drift back to her last happy memory—the moment Jonah had kissed her. For those precious few seconds, she hadn't been the victim of a crime that he had to solve. No, they'd been a man and a woman connecting in a whole different way. She'd felt cherished, loved, normal.

She hoped she lived long enough to feel that way again.

Jonah had sent the patrol officer watching the school off to grab some lunch and stretch his legs a bit. While he waited for his return, Jonah decided to check in with his team. They put him on speakerphone so he wouldn't have to repeat himself. "First, Officer Goff is doing great. She'll go home tomorrow. The docs say she'll have to be on light duty for a few weeks before she's cleared to return to patrol. She also says while she can't say for sure, she thinks the picture I showed her looks a lot like the car she saw. Now we just need to find it."

Decker spoke next. "There is a storage space place on that stretch of road near the school. Haven't verified if he has a spot there, though."

Even without verification, Jonah was sure another piece had just fallen into place. "Anything else?"

A knock on his window startled him. He looked up to see Lyle Peale staring down at him. "Gotta go, guys. We'll talk again soon."

He rolled the window down. "Can I help you?"

Lyle tilted his head to the side as if studying an interesting bug. "A parent who lives down the street called the school to let us know that someone has been parked here all morning, just sitting in the car. I thought I'd come out and check before I called the police."

His smile turned a bit feral. "But didn't Aubrey say you were a detective? If so, I guess the police are already here. Care to tell me why you're hanging around an elementary school? Because if there is a threat of some kind to our students, I should know about it."

"Nope, no threat. One of my colleagues called, and I pulled over to talk to him. I was almost done and was about to leave." To support that claim, he started the engine.

Lyle didn't step back. Instead, he asked, "Have you talked to Aubrey? I was wondering how she was doing. I didn't want to bother her, though, if she has a lot going on."

The man was toying with Jonah, which made him furious. "The last time I spoke to her, she was fine."

That was no less than the truth. He kept his fingers crossed that she still was. "Well, I'd better get moving. Those crimes don't solve themselves, you know?"

The other man smirked, making Jonah want to deck him. "No, they don't. I know the police do their best, but sometimes that's just not enough. It's a real shame."

He was still smiling as he walked back toward the school. Jonah drove around the block and called the patrol officer who was due back from lunch soon. "Set up in a different location. Our target just paid me a visit, so he knows we're snooping around."

Then he hung up and headed back to the office, forgoing the stop to pick up sandwiches. They'd have to order in, because he had a feeling that he'd just thrown a wrench into Lyle's plans. Jonah was pretty sure Lyle wouldn't leave work early, because he'd been so careful to keep to his normal schedule. If he took off now, he had to be concerned that they'd simply follow him back to wherever he had Aubrey stashed. He was more likely to wait until darkness fell.

Either way, time was running out.

Aubrey slept fitfully for several hours and finally gave up on the effort to get any more sleep. Dark dreams didn't make for restful sleep. Instead, she once again practiced her yoga and martial arts routine. It was surprising how much the simple repetition cleared her head and gave her some sense of control. From what Lyle had said, he would make more than one additional visit to restock her supplies before the end of the school year. It wasn't that she didn't believe him about that. No, it was his intent to wait until his schedule was clear before the two of them would have fun together that she didn't believe.

That meant she needed to be ready for him. In between her naps, it crossed her mind that she could put the remaining cans of pop to good use. If she threw one right at him as soon as he stepped through the door, his first instinct would be to duck. If she could get the drop on him, she could club him with another can and then attack with her steel rod. If she could somehow render him unconscious, maybe she could get the key to her shackle. Once free, she could steal his car and head for civilization.

None of it would probably play out the way she envisioned, but she had to do something because time was growing short. Lyle would be coming soon. She left a can of pop sitting on top of the cooler and tucked the remaining two next to her on the bed where they couldn't be seen from the window. Satisfied she was as prepared as she would ever be, she settled back on the bed and watched as the sun started its slow descent to the west.

An hour passed and then another one. At least that was Aubrey's best guess. Time had ceased to have any real meaning to her by that point. She was considering eating another sandwich when she heard a vehicle approaching. It was tempting to run to the window to look out, but there was nothing to be gained by that. There was only one person who would be heading her way.

Sure enough, a short time later she heard footsteps outside of the door. She checked her makeshift weapons and braced herself for the fight to come.

The door slammed open, and Lyle stepped into the doorway. This time there was no slick charm in his demeanor, no attempt to be the affable principal she'd worked for. Instead, his face was all hard lines, and his pale gray eyes were glacial. "Your pet cop has been poking around and asking questions about me, Aubrey. I've spotted some of his buddies parked outside of the school, and my home security cameras have picked them up cruising by my condo hourly."

He took a single step forward into the cabin. "What did you tell him that set him on my trail?"

Aubrey refused to cower in the face of her captor's anger. "I didn't tell him anything about you other than you're the principal where I work. I didn't know you were involved until you showed up with the new supplies. If Detective Kelly suspects you, it's not because of anything I said or did."

"There had to be something, Aubrey. I can't risk another cop stumbling across the same information the next time."

She shuddered at the thought of some other innocent woman joining the ranks of Lyle's victims. All the more reason to do everything she could to put an end to his reign of terror. He was still waiting for her to confess how she'd managed to betray his secrets. If it could've bought her either time or mercy, she would've made something up. But the hatred glittering in his eyes made it clear that the clock was running out on her no matter what she told him.

"Like I said, I told him you were my boss. That's all."

He crossed his arms over his chest and planted his feet, probably hoping to further intimidate her. "So why did you take a leave of absence if not to get away from me?"

"Because we were worried that whoever was after me might try something at the school, which would put the kids and my coworkers in danger. It's the same reason I didn't go to stay with my parents or friends."

"Nothing about my private life?"

She shook her head. "No. Other than a few social gatherings with the rest of the staff, I've never spent time with you outside of work."

He abruptly gave up all pretense of being in control. He lunged across the narrow space and shoved her onto the bed. Aubrey screamed and tried to kick him with both feet, determined to keep him at bay. It took him a couple of tries to capture her right foot, but he finally managed. When she kicked him as hard as she could with her left, he jerked her off the bed onto to the floor and snarled, "If you want to save yourself some pain, stop it. I'm removing your shackle."

She froze, not sure if his doing that was actually a good thing. Regardless, there was no way she'd get free of him as long as she was chained to the bed. After he fished his keys out of his pocket, it took him a couple of tries to free her ankle. He let the chain drop to the floor and then jerked her back up to her feet. Holding on to both of her arms, he stared down at her.

"I put a lot of time and energy into planning my summer vacation, but you and your cop buddy have ruined it for me. Now I'm going to have to start all over with someone else. Not only that, I have to destroy my cabin and everything in it."

He leaned in closer to her face, close enough that she could feel his hot breath on her skin. "And then you're going to learn the answer to a question that you've been asking for twelve years—exactly where Marta ended up. I dug your grave right next to hers just over the next rise."

His smile was evil personified. "Remember how I flipped that coin? You were heads, and she was tails. Well, I lied about how it landed. It came up heads. I loved knowing you would live with the knowledge that it was only a matter of luck that you survived and your best friend didn't."

"But why?"

"Because she was my real target, not you. At least not then. I asked her out when she worked in the school library. Even tried to kiss her to show her how good it would be between us. She shoved me hard enough that I fell down. Then she stuck her hand in my face to show off that pitiful excuse for an engagement ring and threatened to tell her boyfriend if I didn't leave her alone. Right after that, she quit the job thinking that would deter me. We all know how well that worked for her."

He clearly took pride in the pain and misery he'd inflicted on so many people. Aubrey stared up at him in horror, seeing nothing human in his smile. "But enough about good times in the past. I have to deal with you and then get back to town before they realize I'm gone again."

He frowned. "Although it might be too late for that. Traffic was worse than I expected, and I've already been gone longer than I meant to be."

When he released his hold on her, she stumbled backward to sit down on the bed, this time on purpose. She wrapped her fingers around one of the pop cans she'd tucked under a fold in the blanket. Then she grasped her steel rod with her other hand.

"Stay there. I need a couple of things I left just outside the door."

When he turned his back to her, she almost went on the attack, but held back. Even if her efforts worked, he would be between her and the door. She watched as Lyle took a single step outside, and she knew she'd made the right decision. He came back in with two one-gallon cans of gasoline. He set one on top of the cooler, and then unscrewed the cap on the second and began splashing the gas on the walls. "Move away from the bed unless you would rather die in a fire."

Eyeing the second container of gas, she realized it would do more damage than the pop can. Still holding the rod next to her leg and out of sight, she sidestepped around the perimeter of the room, nearly choking on the gas fumes in the confined space. While he continued what he was doing, she drew a deep breath then grabbed the second gas can and swung as hard as she could at the back of his head.

Lyle bellowed in rage even as he dropped to his knees. That didn't keep him from scrambling after her on all fours, trying to block her escape. Before she could hit him a second time, he latched on to her ankle with one hand. At the same time, he wrapped his other arm around his head to prevent her second blow from connecting with full force.

When that didn't work, she stabbed his hand with the steel rod to force him to release his hold on her. When his hand fell open, she tried without success to pull the rod back out. It probably wasn't a good idea to leave her last weapon behind, but right now she was more concerned about putting some distance between herself and Lyle. He'd never completely lost consciousness, so she had seconds at best to get away. There was no chance she'd be able to steal the keys to his car without him getting his hands on her again. Praying she was making the best decision she could, she charged out into the night and ran like her life depended on it.

Because it did.

Chapter Eighteen

Jonah paced the floor of the precinct, ready to explode. "What do you mean he's gone?"

The officer who was supposed to be watching the school had just called in to say that Lyle Peale was nowhere to be found.

"His SUV is still right where it's been all day, and the light is on in his office. A tow truck showed up about fifteen minutes ago and started loading up the car. It was the janitor who came out to give the guy the keys. I caught up with him to see where his boss was, only to learn Peale had already left. Supposedly, he'd told the janitor that his SUV wouldn't start when he tried to leave for lunch earlier in the day, and he'd made arrangements to have it taken to the dealership for repairs. He left his car keys with Jacobs to give the driver when he came."

"How long ago did Peale leave?"

"Jacobs thought the man planned to call a ride service to come pick him up, but he didn't actually see him go. Sounds like he was busy cleaning classrooms at the other end of the building from where the office is located. His best guess was that he'd last seen Peale about half an hour before the tow truck showed up. I can tell you for sure the principal didn't come out the front door. If he had, I would have seen him as well as the car that picked him up."

After a brief pause, the officer added, "I'm sorry, sir. He must have slipped out the back of the building and cut through to the road along the far end of the playground."

As angry as Jonah was, he knew the officer wasn't at fault. Peale was both smart and careful; otherwise someone would've caught him long before now. "You couldn't have known. Thanks for telling me."

He went back into the conference room to break the bad news. "Our target has flown the coop. He disappeared less than an hour ago, so he doesn't have much of a lead on us."

But they all knew how much damage a man could do to his victim in that amount of time. "We have to find him. We need a breakthrough right now."

Simply wishing for a solid clue that would lead them in the right direction wouldn't get them far. But maybe God had been listening, because Decker came running in with a map in his hand. He all but shoved it in Jonah's face. "We've found a small piece of property registered under his grandfather's name, Marcus Dennison. It's at the end of a forest service road in the foothills."

George spoke up next. "I just ran the sedan's plate number again. Seems our Mr. Peale must have been in a hurry after he left work. He got clocked going fifty in a thirty by a traffic camera. Judging from where that happened, he was headed toward the foothills, most likely via the interstate."

He walked around to study the map on the wall. "Here's where the camera picked him up."

Sergeant held his map up for comparison. "That jives with the most direct route to his property."

Maybe things were finally going their way. Jonah ordered, "Issue an alert on that vehicle with a warning to assume the driver is armed and dangerous. I'm going to update the captain and then head out."

George was already reaching for his jacket. "I'm coming, too."

Jonah didn't try to stop him. He headed for his boss's office and told him everything they'd learned. Captain Martine said he'd take care of getting help from the county and the state police. "Bring her back, Detective."

"I will, sir."

Five minutes later, he tore out of the parking lot, praying that Aubrey would hold on until he got there.

Aubrey ran past Lyle's car and kept going down the narrow road until it took a sharp bend to the left. With his longer legs, he would soon catch up with her if she continued much farther in plain sight. Picking a side at random, she plunged into the woods on the left side of the road and fought her way through the undergrowth. The sun rode low in the sky, barely providing her with enough light to see where she was going.

The smart thing would be to move as silently as possible, but she'd make better time running as fast and as far as she could. Getting lost was a huge risk, so she did her best to move parallel to the road. The only hope of survival she had was to find her way back toward civilization, or at least another road that would have more traffic on it.

"Aubrey! I will find you!"

Lyle's voice was faint, but there was no telling how sound traveled through the trees. She also had no sense of how far she'd come since she'd escaped from the cabin. Regardless, it was time to slow down and move with greater care. She needed to catch her breath as well as retain enough energy to put up a decent fight if he did catch up with her at some point.

A branch snapped back in her face, stinging and startling her into gasping. She blinked past the tears and kept moving, even as she heard Lyle calling her name from off to her right. He was still behind her, but closer now. It was time to start looking for a weapon to replace the one she'd left behind. A big stick wouldn't be much protection from a gun if he had one, but she needed something.

"Aubrey, I'm coming for you!"

By that point, Lyle's voice was less angry and more gleeful, as if this was a game that had become fun for him. She picked up a hefty branch and took cover in the center of a cluster of bushes, waiting for the battle to begin. The only question was which role she would play in their game—the cat or the mouse.

Jonah reached the turnoff to the forest service road in better time than he'd expected. Other cars on the highway had cooperated and got out of his way in response to his flashing lights and the occasional blast from his siren. A county deputy had joined their parade a short time before they'd turned off the highway. Once they'd left the highway behind, Jonah drove as fast as he deemed safe, which apparently was at a higher speed than his companion was comfortable with, considering the death grip George had on the bar over the passenger door.

"Hanging in there okay, Detective?"

The other man laughed a little. "I'll survive. Maybe, anyway."

"We should reach the turnoff to Peale's property soon. I'm guessing I'll have to slow down on it."

He was pretty sure George muttered, "I hope so."

As it turned out, Jonah had no choice but to actually stop after they turned onto the driveway that should lead them to the cabin. A short distance down the dirt road, there was a gate that spanned the entire width. It was made of heavy-duty steel pipe and fastened with a massive padlock.

Jonah stared at it as George asked, "Do you have a bolt cutter?"

"No, I'll ask the deputy."

Deputy Hicklin had one, but it wouldn't handle a lock with a shackle that thick. "I'll call for the fire department to send someone out with one of theirs."

"How long will that take?"

Hicklin didn't look optimistic. "Half an hour minimum."

"I can't wait that long. You two wait here while I go ahead on foot. Peale had a big head start, so he's already here. Ms. Sims might not have thirty minutes."

George wasn't happy about his decision. "More backup is already on the way. You shouldn't go in alone."

He was right. Jonah didn't care. "Tell them to be careful who they're targeting when they start after us. I have my phone on mute but I'll check for texts as I can, if we even get service up here."

Then he climbed the gate and took off running along the dirt road toward the cabin. His knee protested, but he ignored it and kept pounding down the road at a steady pace. Suddenly, he heard Peale calling out that he was coming for Aubrey. Jonah followed the sound off to his right, holding his gun down at his side as he changed course and started working his way through the trees.

He'd gone about a hundred feet when he heard Aubrey scream. It came from close by, and he thought he caught a glimpse of movement through the trees too far away to get a clear shot. Jonah slowed down enough to make sure he didn't alert Peale to his presence as he closed in on the enemy.

When Jonah reached a small clearing, Aubrey and Peale were circling each other. When Peale lunged for her, she swung for the bleachers with a thick branch, aiming for the man's head, but connecting with his shoulder instead. She managed to put maybe twenty feet between them, but the man was already up and lumbering after her.

"You'll die for that, Aubrey." He waved his gun in the air. "I'll bury you alive, which will give you plenty of time to reflect on your mistakes."

She continued to back away from him, still clutching her makeshift weapon. When Peale took aim at her, Jonah didn't hesitate. The shot left Lyle Peale writhing on the ground and holding his leg.

"Stay back, Aubrey," Jonah ordered as he approached the wounded man. He tossed Peale's gun out of reach. Then he holstered his own weapon and rolled Peale over on his stomach before kneeling down to handcuff him, ending the threat to Aubrey once and for all. Having secured his prisoner, Jonah removed his jacket and then his shirt. He wrapped the latter around the man's wounded leg and yanked it tight.

Pushing himself back up to his feet, he turned toward Aubrey and held out his arms. She came running straight toward him, reaching him just as his knee almost gave out on him.

He held her close. "Are you okay, Aubrey? Did he hurt you?"

"Bruises, nothing else." She stared up at him with tears glistening in her eyes. "You came for me. I prayed you would."

Then she kissed him.

He wanted to hold her forever, to kiss her until all these ugly memories faded into the past, but he had other obligations right now. He led her to a fallen log and wrapped his jacket around her shoulders. "Stay here while I call for backup and the EMTs to come deal with Peale."

She did as he asked. "George, Aubrey and I are both fine. Notify the EMTs that the target is down with a gunshot to his lower leg. Bring a blanket and the first aid kit from my car. We're off the right side of the road about a quarter mile up from where I left you. When you get close, start shouting, and I'll answer."

He went back over to keep an eye on his prisoner. As he did, he had something to say to Aubrey before the cavalry arrived. "After we get this situation handled, we need to talk about us and the future. It's going to involve words like love, marriage and forever. You okay with that?"

At first, her answering smile was a bit tremulous, but it grew in strength. "I can't wait."

Epilogue

The next twenty-four hours were a blur for Aubrey, mainly because she'd ended up in the hospital for observation. Her parents had arrived shortly after she'd been moved to a private room where they'd had an emotional reunion. An hour later, the nurses finally told her folks that visiting hours were over for the night.

Before they left, all three of them had shared prayers of thanksgiving that the ordeal was now over and that Aubrey was finally safe. To her surprise, Jonah's name had played a significant role in her mother's message to God, thanking Him for bringing Detective Kelly into their lives right when they'd needed him the most.

That was good, because if it was up to Aubrey, he'd be sticking around a lot longer—preferably permanently. Not that she'd seen him since the ambulance had whisked her away from the crime scene. That didn't surprise her. He had a job to do, an important one. He'd told her he had to stick around to deal with the crime scene, starting with the cabin. At least Lyle hadn't had a chance to set it on fire once she took off running.

Once the initial hubbub slowed down a bit, she remembered to tell him what Lyle had said about having dug a grave for Aubrey right next to Marta's. From what she understood, the authorities would wait until morning to start the search. Since Lyle had mentioned to Aubrey that he'd entertained other guests, they would also look for other unmarked graves.

It was sad and sick, but it was over. At least the Pynes and Ross Easton would finally have the closure they so badly needed. That was something else she'd thanked God for.

She'd already signed her discharge papers and was waiting for her parents to come pick her up. But when the door opened, it was Jonah standing there. He looked exhausted, but that didn't stop him from sweeping her up in his arms and holding her so tightly she could barely breathe. That was okay—they both needed the reassurance that they'd made it through the ordeal alive and whole.

When he finally set her back down, she had to ask one question. "Did you find her?"

He nodded. "Right where you said she'd be. We've already reached out to her parents and Ross even though it won't be official until we get the DNA tests back."

"I'm happy for them. They've waited a long time for closure."

"George Swahn asked to be the one who delivered the news. He was thrilled to close one of his files."

"I can understand why. He's worked so hard to bring answers to the people who need them the most."

Jonah hesitated as if he was reluctant to tell her something. Finally, he said, "About that—working the cold cases was supposed to be a temporary job for me. You know, just until my knee improves. I've already told Captain Martine I want the assignment long-term. I hope that's okay with you."

Now she was confused. "Why would what I think matter?"

His blue eyes twinkled with a hint of mischief. "Because I figure my future wife should have a say in my plans. Not that I'm exactly proposing. I figure we should go on a few dates first."

He looked stricken when she couldn't stop the tears from coming. He brushed them away with the pad of his thumb. "Honey, I didn't mean to rush you. We can take things as slow as you need to."

Silly man. "I'm not upset, Jonah. I'm really happy! This is the first time I've had a chance to plan for the future instead of being mired in my past. I can't wait to see where you take me on our first date."

"Maybe church on Sunday? And then out to a late breakfast with your folks? Of course, my parents will want equal time the next weekend."

"That sounds perfect!"

Then she kissed him to seal the deal.

* * * * *

Subscribe and fall in love with a Mills & Boon series today!

You'll be among the first to read stories delivered to your door monthly and enjoy great savings.

WE SIMPLY LOVE ROMANCE